THE OLD GRAY HOMESTEAD

and

THE CAREER OF DAVID NOBLE

ONE VOLUME EDITION

The Old Gray Homestead

and

The Career of David Noble

Two
Full-length
Novels
by

FRANCES PARKINSON KEYES

LIVERIGHT PUBLISHING CORPORATION
NEW YORK

PREFACE

I HAVE OFTEN heard writers speak with disparagement of
their earliest efforts and even say they heartily wished
that such and such a book had never been published. I
sincerely hope that my later novels reveal a greater mas-
tery of technique than those I wrote as a novice and also,
a greater knowledge of human nature; I should feel just
as sorry if I had failed to develop in my profession as I
should if my character had undergone no development, if
my own outlook had not widened, and if I had not become more generally experienced and more generally tol-
erant than I was as a girl. At the same time, I do not feel
I have any more reason to be ashamed of the writing I did
in my twenties than I have of anything else I did and was
then; it all represented the best of what I was then capable. In fact, I have always felt a certain nostalgic affection for my first two novels, *The Old Gray Homestead*
and *The Career of David Noble*, perhaps because the setting of both is a village similar to the two in which I spent
a great part of my early life and with which my inherited
affiliation goes back nearly two hundred years. It is because of my deep-rooted affection for the substance and
spirit of farm life in the Upper Connecticut Valley that I
sought to interpret it. Mrs. Gray, Mrs. Weston and Mrs.
Noble, Tom Gray and Susan Noble and, indeed, all the
other characters in these books are typical of men and

women I have known, and it has always given me the greatest delight to hear from readers that they, too, recognised and cherished these prototypes.

During the last year or two, I have frequently heard from other readers who voiced disappointment that they could not obtain the earlier stories. Therefore my pleasure in introducing this new volume is very great, and I am indeed happy over the opportunity this gives me to make the novels it contains available once again. The tradition and the heritage of New England are surely ones in which all of us, no matter what our places of birth, can partake; and it is my earnest hope that, through these two novels and in some slight way, I have succeeded in interpreting this heritage and this tradition, not only to New Englanders themselves, but to the rest of the country as well.

FRANCES PARKINSON KEYES

JULY 1951

THE OLD GRAY HOMESTEAD

To the farmers, and their mothers, wives, and daughters, who have been my nearest neighbors and my best friends for the last fifteen years, and who have taught me to love the country and the people in it, this quiet story of a farm is affectionately and gratefully dedicated

CHAPTER I

"For Heaven's sake, Sally, don't say, 'Isn't it hot?' or, 'Did you ever know such weather for April?' or, 'Doesn't it seem as if the mud was just as bad as it used to be before we had the State Road?' again. It *is* hot. I never did see such weather. The mud is *worse* if anything. I've said all this several times, and if you can't think of anything more interesting to talk about, I wish you'd keep still."

Sally Gray pushed back the lock of crinkly brown hair that was always getting in her eyes, puckered her lips a little, and glanced at her brother Austin without replying, but with a slight ripple of concern disturbing her usual calm. She was plain and plump and placid, as sweet and wholesome as clover, and as nerveless as a cow, and she secretly envied her brother's lean, dark handsomeness; but she was conscious of a little pang of regret that the young, eager face beside her was already becoming furrowed with lines of discontent and bitterness, and that the expression of the fine mouth was rapidly growing more and more hard and sullen. Austin had been all the way from Hamstead to White Water that day, stopping on his way back at Wallacetown, to bring Sally, who taught school there, home for over Sunday; his little old

1

horse, never either strong or swift, was tired and hot and muddy, and hung its unkempt head dejectedly, apparently having lost all willingness to drag the dilapidated top-buggy and its two occupants another step. Austin's manner, Sally reflected, was not much more cheerful than that of his horse; while his clothes were certainly as dirty, as shabby, and as out-of-date as the rest of his equipage.

"It's a shame," she thought, "that Austin takes everything so hard. The rest of us don't mind half so much. If he could only have a little bit of encouragement and help—something that would make him really happy! If he could earn some money—or find out that, after all, money isn't everything—or fall in love with some nice girl—" She checked herself, blushing and sighing. The blush was occasioned by her own quiet happiness in that direction; but the sigh was because Austin, though he was well known to have been "rather wild," never paid any "nice girl" the slightest attention, and jeered cynically at the mere suggestion that he should do so.

"How lovely the valley is!" she said aloud at last; "I don't believe there's a prettier stretch of road in the whole world than this between Wallacetown and Hamstead, especially in the spring, when the river is so high, and everything is looking so fresh and green."

"Fortunate it is pretty; probably it's the only thing we'll have to look at as long as we live—and certainly it's about all we've seen so far! If there'd been only you and I, Sally, we could have gone off to school, and maybe to college, too, but with eight of us to feed and clothe, it's no wonder that father is dead sunk in debt! Certainly I shan't travel much," he added, laughing bitterly, "when

2

he thinks we can't have even one hired man in the future —and certainly you won't either, if you're fool enough to marry Fred, and go straight from the frying-pan of one poverty-stricken home to the fire of another!"

"Oh, Austin, it's wrong of you to talk so! I'm going to be ever so happy!"

"Wrong! How else do you expect me to talk?—if I talk at all! Doesn't it mean anything to you that the farm's mortgaged to the very last cent, and that it doesn't begin to produce what it ought to because we can't beg, borrow, or steal the money that ought to be put into it? Can you just shut your eyes to the fact that the house— the finest in the county when Grandfather Gray built it —is falling to pieces for want of necessary repairs? And look at our barns and sheds—or don't look at them if you can help it! Doesn't it gall you to dress as you do, because you have to turn over most of what you can earn teaching to the family—of course, you never can earn much, because you haven't had a good enough education yourself to get a first-class position—so that the younger girls can go to school at all, instead of going out as hired help? Can't you feel the injustice of being poor, and dirty, and ignorant, when thousands of other people are just *rotten* with money?"

"I've heard of such people, but I've never met any of them around here," returned his sister quietly. "We're no worse off than lots of people, better off than some. I think we've got a good deal to be thankful for, living where we can see green things growing, and being well, and having a mother like ours. I wish you could come to feel that way. Perhaps you will some day."

"Why don't you marry Fred's cousin, instead of Fred?"

3

asked her brother, changing the subject abruptly. "You could get him just as easy as not—I could see that when he was here last summer. Then you could go to Boston to live, get something out of life yourself, and help your family, too."

"No one in the family but you would want help from me—at that price," returned Sally, still speaking quietly, but betraying by the slight unevenness of her voice that her quiet spirit was at last disturbed more than she cared to show. "Why, Austin, you know how I lo—care for Fred, and that I gave him my word more than two years ago! Besides, I heard you say yourself, before you knew he fancied me, that Hugh Elliott drank—and did all sorts of other dreadful things—he wouldn't be considered respectable in Hamstead."

Austin laughed again. "All right. I won't bring up the subject again. Ten years from now you may be sorry you wouldn't put up with an occasional spree, and sacrifice a silly little love-affair, for the sake of everything else you'd get. But suit yourself. Cook and wash and iron and scrub, lose your color and your figure and your disposition, and bring half-a-dozen children into the world with no better heritage than that, if it's your idea of bliss—and it seems to be!"

"I didn't mean to be cross, Sally," he said, after they had driven along in heavy silence for some minutes. "I've been trying to do a little business for father in White Water to-day, and met with my usual run of luck—none at all. Here comes one of the livery-stable teams ploughing towards us through the mud. Who's in it, do you suppose? Doesn't look familiar, some way."

As the livery-stable in Hamstead boasted only four

turn-outs, it was not strange that Austin recognized one of them at sight, and as strangers were few and far between, they were objects of considerable interest.

Sally leaned forward.

"No, she doesn't. She's all in black—and my! isn't she pretty? She seems to be stopping and looking around—why don't you ask her if you could be of any help?"

Austin nodded, and pulled in his reins. "I wonder if I could—" he began, but stopped abruptly, realizing that the lady in the buggy coming towards them had also stopped, and spoken the very same words. Inevitably they all smiled, and the stranger began again.

"I wonder if you could tell me how to get to Mr. Howard Gray's house," she said. "I was told at the hotel to drive along this road as far as a large white house—the first one I came to—and then turn to the right. But I don't see any road."

"There isn't any, at this time of year," said Sally, laughing,—"nothing but mud. You have to wallow through that field, and go up a hill, and down a hill, and along a little farther, and then you come to the house. Just follow us—we're going there. I'm Howard Gray's eldest daughter Sally, and this is my brother Austin."

"Oh! then perhaps you can tell me—before I intrude—if it would be any use—whether you think that possibly—whether under any circumstances—well, if your mother would be good enough to let me come and live at her house a little while?"

By this time Sally and Austin had both realized two things: first, that the person with whom they were talking belonged to quite a different world from their own—the fact was written large in her clothing, in her manner,

5

in the very tones of her vocie; and, second, that in spite of her pale face and widow's veil, she was even younger than they were, a girl hardly out of her teens.

"I'm not very well," she went on rapidly, before they could answer, "and my doctor told me to go away to some quiet place in the country until I could get—get rested a little. I spent a summer here with my mother when I was a little girl, and I remembered how lovely it was, and so I came back. But the hotel has run down so that I don't think I can possibly stay there; and yet I can't bear to go away from this beautiful, peaceful river-valley —it's just what I've been longing to find. I happened to overhear some one talking about Mrs. Gray, and saying that she might consider taking me in. So I hired this buggy and started out to find her and ask. Oh, don't you think she would?"

Sally and Austin exchanged glances. "Mother never has taken any boarders, she's always been too busy," began the former; then, seeing the swift look of disappointment on the sad little face, "but she might. It wouldn't do any harm to ask, anyway. We'll drive ahead, and show you how to get there."

The Gray family had been one of local prominence ever since Colonial days, and James Gray, who built the dignified, spacious homestead now occupied by his grandson's family, had been a man of some education and wealth. His son Thomas inherited the house, but only a fourth of the fortune, as he had three sisters. Thomas had but one child, Howard, whose prospects for prosperity seemed excellent; but he grew up a dreamy, irresolute, studious chap, a striking contrast to the sturdy yeoman type from which he had sprung—one

of those freaks of heredity that are hard to explain. He
went to Dartmouth College, travelled a little, showed a
disposition to read—and even to write—verses. As a
teacher he probably would have been successful; but
his father was determined that he should become a
farmer, and Howard had neither the energy nor the disposition to oppose him; he proved a complete failure.
He married young, and, it was generally considered,
beneath him; for Mary Austin, with a heart of gold and
a disposition like sunshine, had little wealth or breeding
and less education to commend her; and she was herself
too easy-going and contented to prove the prod that
Howard sadly needed in his wife. Children came thick
and fast; the eldest, James, had now gone South; the
second daughter, Ruth, was already married to a struggling storekeeper living in White Water; Sally taught
school; but the others were all still at home, and all,
except Austin, too young to be self-supporting—Thomas,
Molly, Katherine, and Edith. They had all caught their
father's facility for correct speech, rare in northern New
England; most of them his love of books, his formless
and unfulfilled ambitions; more than one the shiftlessness
and incompetence that come partly from natural bent
and partly from hopelessness; while Sally and Thomas
alone possessed the sunny disposition and the ability to
see the bright side of everything and the good in everybody which was their mother's legacy to them.

The old house, set well back from the main road and
near the river, with elms and maples and clumps of lilac
bushes about it, was almost bare of the cheerful white
paint that had once adorned it, and the green blinds were
faded and broken; the barns never had been painted,

and were huddled close to the house, hiding its fine
Colonial lines, black, ungainly, and half fallen to pieces;
all kinds of farm implements, rusty from age and neglect,
were scattered about, and two dogs and several cats lay
on the kitchen porch amidst the general litter of milk-
pails, half-broken chairs, and rush mats. There was no
one in sight as the two muddy buggies pulled up at the
little-used front door. Howard Gray and Thomas were
milking, both somewhat out-of-sorts because of the non-
appearance of Austin, for there were too many cows for
them to manage alone—a long row of dirty, lean animals
of uncertain age and breed. Molly was helping her
mother to "get supper," and the red tablecloth and heavy
white china, never removed from the kitchen table except to be washed, were beginning to be heaped with
pickles, doughnuts, pie, and cake, and there were pota-
toes and pork frying on the stove. Katherine was studying, and Edith had gone to hastily "spread up" the beds
that had not been made that morning.

On the whole, however, the inside of the house was
more tidy than the outside, and the girl in black was
aware of the homely comfort and good cheer of the
living-room into which she was ushered (since there was
no time to open up the cold "parlor") more than she was
of its shabbiness.

"Come right in an' set down," said Mrs. Gray cheerfully, leading the way; "awful tryin' weather we're havin',
ain't it? An' the mud—my, it's somethin' fierce! The men-
folks track it in so, there's no keepin' it swept up, an'
there's so many of us here! But there's nothin' like a large
family for keepin' things hummin' just the same, now,
is there?" Mrs. Gray had had scant time to prepare her

mind either for her unexpected visitor or the object of her visit; but her mother-wit was ready, for all that; one glance at the slight, black-robed little figure, and the thin white face, with its tired, dark-ringed eyes, was enough for her. Here was need of help; and therefore help of some sort she must certainly give. "Now, then," she went on quickly, "you look just plum tuckered out; set down an' rest a spell, an' tell me what I can do for you."

"My name is Sylvia Cary—Mrs. Mortimer Cary, I mean." She shivered, paused, and went on. "I live in New York—that is, I always have—I'm never going to any more, if I can help it. My husband died two months ago, my baby—just before that. I've felt so—so—tired ever since, I just had to get away somewhere—away from the noise, and the hurry, and the crowds of people I know. I was in Hamstead once, ten years ago, and I remembered it, and came back. I want most dreadfully to stay —could you possibly make room for me here?"

"Oh, you poor lamb! I'd do anything I could for you —but this ain't the sort of home you've been used to—" began Mrs. Gray; but she was interrupted.

"No, no, of course it isn't! Don't you understand—I can't bear what I've been used to another minute! And I'll honestly try not to be a bit of trouble if you'll only let me stay!"

Mrs. Gray twisted in her chair, fingering her apron. "Well, now, I don't know! You've come so sudden-like— if I'd only had a little notice! There's no place fit for a lady like you; but there are two rooms we never use— the northeast parlor and the parlor-chamber off it. You could have one of them—after I got it cleaned up a mite— an' try it here for a while."

9

"Couldn't I have them both? I'd like a sitting-room as well as a bedroom."

"Land! You ain't even seen 'em yet! maybe they won't suit you at all! But, come, I'll show 'em to you an' if you want to stay, you shan't go back to that filthy hotel. I'll get the bedroom so's you can sleep in it to-night—just a lick an' a promise; an' to-morrow I'll house-clean 'em both thorough, if 'tis the Sabbath—the 'better the day, the better the deed,' I've heard some say, an' I believe that's true, don't you, Mrs. Cary?" She bustled ahead, pulling up the shades, and flinging open the windows in the unused rooms. "My, but the dust is thick! Don't you touch a thing—just see if you think they'll do."

Sylvia Cary glanced quickly about the two great square rooms, with their white wainscoting, and shutters, their large, stopped-up fireplaces, dingy wall-paper, and beautiful, neglected furniture. "Indeed they will!" she exclaimed; "they'll be lovely when we get them fixed. And may I truly say—right now? I brought my hand-bag with me, you see, hoping that I might, and my trunks are still at the station—wait, I'll give you the checks, and perhaps your son will get them after supper."

She put the bag on a chair, and began to open it, hurriedly, as if unwilling to wait a minute longer before making sure of remaining. Mrs. Gray, who was standing near her, drew back with a gasp of surprise. The bag was lined with heavy purple silk, and elaborately fitted with toilet articles of shining gold. Mrs. Cary plunged her hands in and tossed out an embroidered white satin negligee, a pair of white satin bed-slippers, and a nightgown that was a mere wisp of sheer silk and lace; then drew forth three trunk-checks, and a bundle an inch thick of crisp, new bank-notes, and pulled one out, blushing and hesitating.

"I don't know how to thank you for taking me in to-night," she said; "some day I'll tell you all about myself, and why it means so much to me to have a—a refuge like this; but I'm afraid I can't until—I've got rested a little. Soon we must talk about arrangements and terms and all that—oh, I'm awfully business-like! But just let me give you this to-night, to show you how grateful I am, and pay for the first two weeks or so."

And she folded the bill into a tiny square, and crushed it into Mrs. Gray's reluctant hand.

Fifteen minutes later, when Howard Gray and Thomas came into the kitchen for their supper, bringing the last full milk-pails with them, they found the pork and pota-toes burnt to a frazzle, the girls all talking at once, and Austin bending over his mother, who sat in the big rocker with the tears rolling down her cheeks, and a hundred-dollar bill spread out on her lap.

CHAPTER II

For several weeks the Grays did not see much of Mrs. Cary. She appeared at dinner and supper, eating little and saying less. She rose very late, having a cup of coffee in bed about ten; the afternoons she spent rambling through the fields and along the river-bank, but never going near the highroad on her long walks. She generally read until nearly midnight, and the book-hungry Grays pounced like tigers on the newspapers and magazines with which she heaped her scrap-baskets, and longed for the time to come when she would offer to lend them some of the books piled high all around her rooms.

Some years before, when vacationists demanded less in the way of amusement, Hamstead had flourished in a mild way as a summer-resort; but its brief day of prosperity in this respect had passed, and the advent of a wealthy and mysterious stranger, whose mail was larger than that of all the rest of the population put together, but who never appeared in public, or even spoke, apparently, in private, threw the entire village into a ferment of excitement. Fred Elliott, who, in his rôle of prospective son-in-law, might be expected to know much that was going on at the Grays', was "pumped" in vain; he was obliged to confess his entire ignorance concerning the history, occupations, and future intentions of the young widow. Mrs. Gray had to "house-clean" her parlor a month earlier than she had intended, because she had so many callers who came hoping to catch a glimpse of Mrs. Cary, and hear all about her, besides; but they did not see her at all, and Mrs. Gray could tell them but little.

"She ain't a mite of trouble," the good woman declared to every one, "an' the simplest, gentlest creature I ever see in my life. The girls are all just crazy over her. No, she ain't told me yet anything about herself, an' I don't like to press her none. Poor lamb, with her heart buried in the grave, at her age! No, I don't know how long she means to stay, neither, but 'twould be a good while, if I had my way."

To Mrs. Elliott, her best friend and Fred's mother, she was slightly more communicative, though she disclosed no vital statistics.

"Edith helped her unpack an' she said she never even imagined anything equal to what come out of them three great trunks; she said it made her just long to be a widow. The dresses was all black, of course, but they had an awful expensive look, some way, just the same. An' underclothes! Edith said there was at least a dozen of everything, an' two dozen of most, lace an' handwork an' silk, from one end of 'em to the other. She has a leather box most as big as a suitcase heaped with jewelry —it was open one morning when I went in with her breakfast, an' I give you my word, Eliza, that just the little glimpse I got of it was worth walkin' miles to see! An' yet she never wears so much as the simplest ring or pin. She has enough flowers for an elegant funeral sent to her three times a week by express, an' throws 'em away before they're half-faded—says she likes the little wild ones that are beginnin' to come up around here better, anyway. Yes, I don't deny she has some real queer notions—for instance, she puts all them flowers in plain green glass vases, an' wouldn't so much as look at the elegant cut-glass ones they keep up to Wallacetown. She don't eat a particle of breakfast, an' she streaks off for a long walk every day, rain or shine, an' wants the old tin tub carried in so's she can have a hot bath every single night, besides takin' what she calls a 'cold sponge' when she gets up in the mornin'—which ain't till nearly noon."

"Well, now, ain't all that strange! An' wouldn't I admire to see all them elegant things! What board did you say she paid?"

"Twenty-five dollars a week for board an' washin' an' mendin'—just think of it, Eliza! I feel like a robber, but she wouldn't hear of a cent less. Howard wants I should save every penny, so's at least one of the younger children can have more of an education than James an' Sally an' Austin an' Ruth. I don't look at it that way—seems to me it ain't fair to give one child more than another. I want to spruce up this place a little, an' lay by to raise the mortgage if we can."

"Which way've you decided?"

"We've kinder compromised. The house is goin' to be painted outside, an' the kitchen done over. I've had the piano tuned for Molly already—the poor child is plum crazy over music, but it's a long time since I've seen the three dollars that I could hand over to a strange man just for comin' and makin' a lot of screechin' noises on it all day; an' we're goin' to have a new carry-all to go to meetin' in—the old one is fair fallin' to pieces. The rest of the money we're goin' to lay by, an' if it keeps on comin' in, Thomas can go to the State Agricultural College in the fall, for a spell, anyway. We've told Sally that she can keep all she earns for her weddin' things, too, as long as Mrs. Cary stays."

"My, she's a reg'lar goose layin' a golden egg for you, ain't she? Well, I must be goin'; I'll be over again as soon as spring-cleanin' eases up a little, but I'm terrible druv just now. Maybe next time I can see her."

"You an' Joe an' Fred all come to dinner on Sunday—then you will."

Mrs. Elliott accepted with alacrity; but alas, for the eager guests! when Sunday came, Mrs. Cary had a severe headache and remained in bed all day.

She was so "simple and gentle," as Mrs. Gray said, that it came as a distinct shock when it was discovered that little as she talked, she observed a great deal. Austin was the first member of the family to find this out. All the others had gone to church, and he was lounging on the porch one Sunday morning, when she came out of the house, supposing that she was quite alone. On finding him there, she hesitated for a minute, and then sat quietly down on the steps, made one or two pleasant, commonplace remarks, and lapsed into silence, her chin resting on her hands, looking out towards the barns. Her expression was non-committal; but Austin's antagonistic spirit was quick to judge it to be critical.

"I suppose you've travelled a good deal, besides living in New York," he said, in the bitter tone that was fast becoming his usual one.

15

"Yes, to a certain extent. I've been around the world once, and to Europe several times, and I spent part of last winter South."

"How miserable and shabby this poverty-stricken place must look to you!"

She raised her head and leaned back against a post, looking fixedly at him for a minute. He was conscious, for the first time, that the pale face was extremely lovely, that the great dark eyes were not gray, as he had supposed, but a very deep blue, and that the slim throat and neck, left bare by the V-cut dress, were the color of a white rose. A swift current of feeling that he had never known before passed through him like an electric shock, bringing him involuntarily to his feet, in time to hear her say:

"It's shabby, but it isn't miserable. I don't believe any place is that, where there's a family, and enough food to eat and wood to burn—if the family is happy in itself. Besides, with two hours' work, and without spending one cent, you could make it much less shabby than it is; and by saving what you already have, you could stave off spending in the future."

She pointed, as she spoke, to the cluttered yard before them, to the unwashed wagons and rusty tools that had not been put away, to the shed-door half off its hinges, and the unpiled wood tossed carelessly inside the shed. He reddened, as much at the scorn in her gesture as at the words themselves, and answered angrily, as many persons do when they are ashamed:

"That's very true; but when you work just as hard as you can, anyway, you haven't much spirit left over for the frills."

16

"Excuse me; I didn't realize they were frills. No business man would have his office in an untidy condition, because it wouldn't pay; I shouldn't think it would pay on a farm either. Just as it seems to me—though, of course, I'm not in a position to judge—that if you sold all those tubercular grade cows, and bought a few good cattle, and kept them clean and fed them well, you'd get more milk, pay less for grain, and not have to work so hard looking after more animals than you can really handle well."

As she spoke, she began to unfasten her long, frilled, black sleeves, and rose with a smile so winning that it entirely robbed her speech of sharpness.

"Let's go to work," she said, "and see how much we could do in the way of making things look better before the others get home from church. We'll start here. Hand me that broom and I'll sweep while you stack up the milk-pails—don't stop to reason with me about it—that'll only use up time. If there's any hot water on the kitchen stove and you know where the mop is, I'll wash this porch as well as sweep it; put on some more water to heat if you take all there is."

When the Grays returned from church, their astonished eyes were met with the spectacle of their boarder, her cheeks glowing, her hair half down her back, and her silk dress irretrievably ruined, helping Austin to wash and oil the one wagon which still stood in the yard. She fled at their approach, leaving Austin to retail her conversation and explain her conduct as best he could, and to ponder over both all the afternoon himself.

"She's dead right about the cows," declared Thomas; "but what would be the use of getting good stock and

17

putting it in these barns? It would sicken in no time. We need new buildings, with proper ventilation, and concrete floors, and a silo."

"Why don't you say we need a million dollars, and be done with it? You might just as well," retorted his brother.

"Because we don't—but we need about ten thousand; half of it for buildings, and the rest for stock and utensils and fertilizers, and for what it would cost to clean up our stumpy old pastures, and make them worth something again."

At that moment Mrs. Cary entered the room for dinner, and the discussion of unpossessed resources came to an abrupt end. Her color was still high, and she ate her first hearty meal since her arrival; but her dress and her hair were irreproachably demure again, and she talked even less than usual.

That evening Molly begged off from doing her share with the dishes, and went to play on her newly tuned piano. She loved music dearly, and had genuine talent; but it seemed as if she had never realized half so keenly before how little she knew about it, and how much she needed help and instruction. A particularly unsuccessful struggle with a difficult passage finally proved too much for her courage, and shutting the piano with a bang, she leaned her head on it and burst out crying.

A moment later she sat up with a sudden jerk, realizing that the parlor door had opened and closed, and tried to wipe away the tears before any one saw them; then a hot blush of embarrassment and shame flooded her wet cheeks, as she realized that the intruder was not one of her sisters, but Mrs. Cary.

"What a good touch you have!" she said, sitting down by the piano, and apparently quite unaware of the storm. "I love music dearly, and I thought perhaps you'd let me come and listen to your playing for a little while. The fingering of that 'Serenade' is awfully hard, isn't it? I thought I should never get it, myself—never did, really well, in fact! Do you like your teacher?"

"I never had a lesson in my life," replied Molly, the sobs rising in her throat again; "there are two good ones in Wallacetown, but, you see, we never could af—"

"Well, some teachers do more harm than good," interrupted her visitor, "probably you've escaped a great deal. Play something else, won't you? Do you mind this dim light? I like it so much."

So Molly opened the piano and began again, doing her very best. She chose the simple things she knew by heart, and put all her will-power as well as all her skill into playing them well. It was only when she stopped, confessing that she knew no more, that Mrs. Cary stirred.

"I used to play a good deal myself," she said, speaking very low; "perhaps I could take it up again. Do you think you could help me, Molly?"

"*I!* help *you!* However in the world—"

"By letting *me* be your teacher! I'm getting rested now, and I find I've a lot of superfluous energy at my disposal—your brother had a dose of it this morning! I want something to do—something to keep me busy— something to keep me from thinking. I haven't half as much talent as you, but I've had more chances to learn. Listen! This is the way that 'Serenade' ought to go"— and Mrs. Cary began to play. The dusk turned to moonlight around them, and the Grays sat in the dining-room, hesitating to intrude, and listening with all their ears; and still she sat, talking, explaining, illustrating to Molly, and finally ended by playing, one after another, the old familiar hymns which they all loved.

"It's settled, then—I'll give you your first real lesson to-morrow, and send to New York at once for music. You'll have to do lots of scales and finger-exercises, I warn you! Now come into *my* parlor—there's something else I wanted to talk to you about."

"Do you see that great trunk?" she went on, after she had drawn Molly in after her and lighted the lamp; "I sent for it a week ago, but it only got here yesterday. It's full of all my—all the clothes I had to stop wearing a little while ago."

Molly's heart began to thump with excitement.

"You and Edith are little, like me," whispered Mrs. Cary. "If you would take the dresses and use them, it would be—be such a *favor* to me! Some of them are brand-new! Some of them wouldn't be useful or suitable for you, but there are firms in every big city that buy such things, so you could sell those, if you care to; and, besides the made-up clothes there are several dress-lengths—a piece of pink silk that would be sweet for Sally, and some embroidered linens, and—and so on. I'm going to bed now—I've had so much exercise to-day, and you've given me such a pleasant evening that I shan't have to read myself to sleep to-night, and when I've shut my bedroom door, if you truly would like the trunk, have your brothers come in and carry it off, and promise me never—never to speak about it again."

Monday and Tuesday passed by without further excitement; but Wednesday morning, while Mr. Gray was planting his newly ploughed vegetable-garden, Mrs. Cary sauntered out, and sat down beside the place where he was working, apparently oblivious of the fact that damp ground is supposed to be as detrimental to feminine wearing apparel as it is to feminine constitutions.

"I've been watching you from the window as long as I could stand it," she said, "now I've come to beg. I want a garden, too, a flower-garden. Do you mind if I dig up your front yard?"

He laughed, supposing that she was joking. "Dig all you want to," he said; "I don't believe you'll do much harm."

"Thanks. I'll try not to. Have I your full permission to try my hand and see?"

"You certainly have."

"Is there some boy in the village I could hire to do the first heavy work and the mowing, and pull up the weeds from time to time if they get ahead of me?"

Howard Gray leaned on his hoe. "You don't need to hire a boy," he said gravely; "we'll be only too glad to help you all you need."

"Thank you. But, you see, you've got too much to do already, and I can't add to your burdens, or feel free to ask favors, unless you'll let me do it in a business way."

Mr. Gray turned his hoe over, and began to hack at the ground. "I see how you feel," he began, "but—"

"If Thomas could do it evenings, at whatever the rate is around here by the hour, I should be very glad. If not, please find me a boy."

"She has a way of saying things," explained Howard Gray, who had faltered along in a state of dreary indecision for nearly sixty years, in telling his wife about it

21

afterwards,—"as if they were all settled already. What could I say, but 'Yes, Mrs. Cary'? And then she went on, as cool as a cucumber, 'As long as you've got an extra stall, may I send for one of my horses? The usual board around here is five dollars a week, isn't it?' And what could I say again but 'Yes, Mrs. Cary'? though you may believe I fairly itched to ask, 'Send *where?*' and, 'For the love of Heaven, how *many* horses have you?' "

"I could stand her actin' as if things was all settled," replied his wife; "I like to see folks up an' comin', even if I ain't made that way myself, an' it's a satisfaction to me to see the poor child kinder pickin' up an' takin' notice again; but what beats me is, she acts as if all these things were special favors to *her!* The garden an' the horse is all very well, but what do you think she lit into me to-day for? 'You'll let me stay all summer, won't you, Mrs. Gray?' she said, comin' into the kitchen, where I was ironin' away for dear life, liftin' a pile of sheets off a chair, an' settlin' down, comfortable-like. 'Bless your heart, you can stay forever, as far as I'm concerned,' says I. 'Well, perhaps I will,' says she, leanin' back an' laughin'—she's got a sweet-pretty laugh, hev you noticed, Howard?— 'and so you won't think I'm fault-findin' or discontented if I suggest a few little changes I'd like to make around, will you? I know it's awfully bold, in another person's house—an' such a *lovely* house, too, but—' "

"Well?" demanded her husband, as she paused for breath.

"Well, Howard Gray, the first of them little changes is to be a great big piazza to go across the whole front of the house! 'The kitchen porch is so small an' crowded,' says she, 'an' you can't see the river from there; I want a place to sit out evenings. Can't I have the fireplaces in my rooms unbricked,' she went on, 'an' the rooms repapered an' painted? An', oh,—I've never lived in a house where there wasn't a bathroom before, an' I want to make that big closet with a window off my bedroom into one. We'll have a door cut through it into the hall, too,' says she, 'an' isn't there a closet just like it overhead? If we can get a plumber here—they're such slippery customers—he might as well put in two bathrooms as one, while he's about it, an' you shan't do my great washin's any more without some good set-tubs. An' Mrs. Gray, kerosene lamps do heat up the rooms so in summer,—if there's an electrician anywhere around here—' 'Mrs. Cary,' says I, 'you're an angel right out of Heaven, but we can't accept all this from you. It means two thousand dollars, straight.' 'About what I should pay in two months for my living expenses anywhere else,' says she. 'Favors! It's you who are kind to let me stay here, an' not mind my tearin' your house all to pieces. Thomas is goin' to drive me up to Wallacetown this evenin' to see if we can find some mechanics'; an' she got up, an' kissed me, an' strolled off."

"Thomas thinks she's the eighth wonder of the world," said his father; "she can just wind him around her little finger."

"She's windin' us all," replied his wife, "an' we're standin' grateful-like, waitin' to be wound."

"That's so—all except Austin. Austin's mad as a hatter at what she got him to do Sunday morning; he doesn't like her, Mary."

"Humph!" said his wife.

CHAPTER III

"Good-bye, Mrs. Gray, I'm going for a ride."

"Good-bye, dearie; sure it ain't too hot?"

"Not a bit; it's rained so hard all this week that I haven't had a bit of exercise, and I'm getting cross."

"Cross! I'd like to see you once! It still looks kinder thunderous to me off in the West, so don't go far."

"I won't, I promise; I'll be back by supper-time. There's Austin, just up from the hayfield—I'll get him to saddle for me." And Sylvia ran quickly towards the barn.

"You don't mean to say you're going out this torrid day?" he demanded, lifting his head from the tin bucket in which he had submerged it as she voiced her request, and eyeing her black linen habit with disfavor.

"It's no hotter on the highroad than in the hayfield."

"Very true; but I have to go, and you don't. Being one of the favored few of this earth, there's no reason why you shouldn't sit on a shady porch all day, dressed in cool, pale-green muslin, and sipping iced drinks."

"Did you ever see me in a green muslin? I'll saddle Dolly myself, if you don't feel like it."

She spoke very quietly, but the immediate consciousness of his stupid break did not improve Austin's bad temper.

"Oh, I'll saddle for you, but the heat aside, I think you ought to understand that it isn't best for a woman to ride about on these lonely roads by herself. It was different a few years ago; but now, with all these Italian and Portuguese laborers around, it's a different story. I think you'd better stay at home."

The unwarranted and dictatorial tone of the last sentence spoiled the speech, which might otherwise, in spite of the surly manner in which it was uttered, have passed for an expression of solicitude. Sylvia, who was as headstrong as she was amiable, gathered up her reins quickly.

"By what right do you consider yourself in a position to dictate to me?" she demanded.

"By none at all; but it's only decent to tell you the risk you're running; now if you come to grief, I certainly shan't feel sorry."

"From your usual behavior, I shouldn't have supposed you would, anyway. Good-bye, Austin."

"Good-bye, Mrs. Cary."

"Why don't you call me Sylvia, as all the rest do?"

"It's not fitting."

"More dictation as to propriety! Well, as you please."

He watched her ride up the hill, almost with a feeling of satisfaction at having antagonized and hurt her, then turned to unharness and water his horses. He knew very well that his own behavior was the only blot on a summer, which but for that would have been almost perfect for every other member of the family, and yet he made no effort to alter it. In fact, only a few days before, his sullen resentment of the manner in which their long-prayed-for change of fortune had come had very nearly resulted disastrously for them all, and the more he brooded over it, the more sore and bitter he became.

By the first of August, the "Gray Homestead" had regained the proud distinction, which it had enjoyed in the days of its builder, of being one of the finest in the county. The house, with its wide and hospitable piazza, shone with white paint; the disorderly yard had become a smooth lawn; a flower-garden, riotous with color, stretched out towards the river, and the "back porch" was concealed with growing vines. Only the barns, which afforded Sylvia no reasonable excuse for meddling, remained as before, unsightly and dilapidated. Thomas, the practical farmer, had lamented this as he and Austin sat smoking their pipes one sultry evening after supper.

"Perhaps our credit has improved enough now so that we could borrow some money at the Wallacetown Bank," he said earnestly, "and if you and father weren't so averse to taking that good offer Weston made you last week for the south meadow, we'd have almost enough to rebuild, anyway. It's all very well to have this pride in 'keeping the whole farm just as grandfather left it to us,' but if we could sell part and take care of the rest properly, it would be a darned sight better business."

"Why don't you ask your precious Mrs. Cary for the money? She'd probably give it to you outright, same as she has for the house, and save you all that bother."

"Look here!" Thomas swung around sharply, laying a heavy hand on his brother's arm; "when you talk about her, you won't use that tone, if I know it."

Austin shrugged his shoulders. "Why shouldn't I?

26

What do you know about her that justifies you in resenting it? Nothing, absolutely nothing! She's been here four months, and none of us have any idea to this day where she comes from, or where all this money comes from. Ask her, if you dare to."

He got no further, for Thomas, always the mildest of lads, struck him on the mouth so violently that he tottered backwards, and in doing so, fell straight under the feet of Sylvia, who stood in the doorway watching them, as if rooted to the spot, her blue eyes full of tears, and her face as white as when she had first come to them.

"Thomas, how *could* you?" she cried. "Can't you understand Austin at all, and make allowances? And, oh, Austin, how could *you?* Both of you? please forgive me for overhearing—I couldn't help it!" And she was gone.

Thomas was on his feet and after her in a second, but she was too quick for him; her sitting-room door was locked before he reached it, and repeated knocking and calling brought no answer. Mr. and Mrs. Gray, who slept in the chamber opening from the dining-room, and back of Sylvia's, reported the next morning that something must be troubling the "blessed girl," for they had heard soft sobbing far into the night; but, after all, that had happened before, and was to be expected from one "whose heart was buried in the grave." Their sons made no comment, but both were immeasurably relieved when, after an entire day spent in her room, during which each, in his own way, had suffered intensely, she reappeared at supper as if nothing had happened. It was a glorious night, and she suggested, as she left the table, that Thomas might take her for a short paddle, a canoe being

27

among the many things which had been gradually arriving for her all summer. Molly and Edith went with them, and Austin smoked alone with his bitter reflections.

The thunder was rumbling in good earnest when Howard Gray and Thomas came clattering up with their last load of hay for the night, and the three men pitched it hastily into place together, and hurried into the house. Mrs. Gray was bustling about slamming windows, and the girls were bringing in the red-cushioned hammocks and piazza chairs, but the first great drops began to fall before they had finished, and the wind, seldom roused in the quiet valley, was blowing violently; Edith, stopping too long for a last pillow and a precious book, was drenched to the skin in an instant; the house was pitch dark before there was time to grope for lights, but was almost immediately illumined by a brilliant flash of lightning, followed by a loud report.

"My, but this storm is near! Usually, I don't mind 'em a bit, but, I declare, this is a regular rip-snorter! Edith, bring me—"

But Mrs. Gray was interrupted by the elements, and for fifteen minutes no one made any further effort to talk; the rain fell in sheets, the wind gathered greater and greater force, the lightning became constant and blinding, while each clap of thunder seemed nearer and more terrific than the one before it, when finally a deafening roar brought them all suddenly together, shouting frantically, "That certainly has struck here!"

It was true; before they could even reach it, the great north barn was in flames. There was no way of summoning outside help, even if any one could have reached

28

them in such a storm, and the wind was blowing the fire straight in the direction of the house; in less than an hour, most of the old and rotten outbuildings had burnt like tinder, and the rest had collapsed under the fury of the sweeping gale; but by eight o'clock the stricken Grays, almost too exhausted and overcome to speak, were beginning to realize that though all their hay and most of their stock were destroyed, a change of wind, combined with their own mighty efforts, had saved the beloved old house; it's window-panes were shattered, and its blinds were torn off, and its fresh paint smoked and defaced with wind-blown sand; but it was essentially unharmed. The hurricane changed to a steady downpour, the lightning grew dimmer and more distant, and vanished altogether; and Mrs. Gray, with a firm expression of countenance, in spite of the tears rolling down her cheeks, set about to finish the preparations for supper which the storm had so rudely interrupted three hours earlier.

"Eat an' keep up your strength, an' that'll help to keep up your courage," she said, patting her husband on the shoulder as she passed him. "Here, Katherine, take them biscuits out of the oven; an' Molly, go an' call the boys in; there ain't a mite of use in their stayin' out there any longer."

Austin was the last to appear; he opened the kitchen door, and stood for a moment leaning against the frame, a huge, gaunt figure, blackened with dirt and smoke, and so wet that the water dropped in little pools all about him. He glanced up and down the room, and gave a sharp exclamation.

"What's the matter, Austin?" asked his mother, stopping in the act of pouring out a steaming cup of tea.

"Come an' get some supper; you'll feel better directly. It ain't so bad but what it might be a sight worse."

"Come and get some supper!" he cried, striding towards her, and once more looking wildly around. "The thunderstorm has been over nearly two hours, plenty of time for her to get home—she never minds rain—or to telephone if she had taken shelter anywhere; and can any one tell me—has any one even thought—I didn't, till five minutes ago—*where is Sylvia?*"

CHAPTER IV

"Sylvia! Sylvia! Sylvia!"

The musical name echoed and reëchoed through the silent woods, but there was no other answer. Austin lighted a match, shielded it from the rain with his hand, and looked at his watch; it was just past midnight.

"Oh," he groaned, "where *can* she be? What has happened to her? If I only knew she was found, and unharmed, and safe at home again, I'd never ask for anything else as long as I lived."

He had knocked his lantern against a tree some time before, and broken it, and there was nothing to do but stumble blindly along in the darkness, hoping against hope. Howard Gray had gone north, Thomas east, and Austin south; before starting out, they had endeavored to telephone, but the storm had destroyed the wires in every direction. After travelling almost ten miles, Austin went home, thinking that by that time either his father or his brother must have been successful in his search, to be met only by the anxious despair of his mother and sisters.

"Don't you worry," he forced himself to say with a cheerfulness he was very far from feeling; "she may have gone down that old wood-road that leads out of the Elliotts' pasture. I heard her telling Thomas once that

31

she loved to explore, that they must walk down there some Sunday afternoon; maybe she decided to go alone. I'll stop at the house, and see if Fred happened to see her pass."

Fred had not; but Mrs. Elliott had; there was little that escaped her eager eyes.

"My, yes, I see her go tearin' past before the storm so much as begun; she's sure the queerest actin' widow-woman I ever heard of; Sally says she goes swimmin' in a bathin'-suit just like a boy's, an' floats an' dives like a fish—nice actions for a grievin' lady, if you ask me! Do set a moment, Austin; set down an' tell me about the fire; I ain't had no details at all, an' I'm feelin' real bad—" But the door had already slammed behind Austin's hurrying figure.

"Sylvia, Sylvia, where are you?"

He ploughed along for what seemed like endless miles, calling as he went, and hearing his own voice come back to him, over and over again, like a mocking spirit. The wind, the rain, and the darkness conspired together to make what was rough travelling in the daytime almost impassable; strong as he was, Austin sank down more than once for a few minutes on some fallen log over which he stumbled. At these times the vision of Sylvia standing in the midst of the still-smoking ruins of the buildings, which had been, in spite of their wretched condition, dear to him because they were almost all he had in the world, seemed to rise before him with horrible reality: Sylvia, dressed in her black, black clothes, with her soft dark hair, and her deep-blue eyes, and her vivid red lips which so seldom either drooped or smiled but lay tightly closed together, a crimson line in her white

32

face, which was no more sorrowful than it was mask-like. The expression was as pure and as sad and as gentle as that of a Mater Dolorosa he had chanced to see in a collection of prints at the Wallacetown Library, and yet —and yet—Austin knew instinctively that the dead husband, whoever he might have been, and his own brother Thomas were not the only men besides himself who had found it irresistibly alluring.

"I'm poorer than ever now," he groaned to himself, "and ignorant, and mean, and dirty, and a beast in every sense of the word; I can't ever atone for the way I've treated her—for the way I've—but if I could only find her and *try*, oh, I've got to! Sylvia, Sylvia, Sylvia—"

The rain struck about by the wind, which had risen again, lashed against the leaves of the trees, and the wet, swaying boughs struck against his face as he started on again; but the storm and his own footsteps were the only sounds he could hear.

It was growing rapidly colder, and he felt more than once in his pocket to make sure that the little flask of brandy he had brought with him was still safe, and tried to fasten his drenched coat more tightly about him. His teeth chattered, and he shivered; but this, he realized, was more with nervousness than with chill.

"If I'm cold, what must she be, in that linen habit? And she's so little and frail—" He pulled himself together. "I must stop worrying like this—of course, I'll find her,— alive and unharmed. Some things are too dreadful—they just can't happen. I've got to have a chance to beg her forgiveness for all I've said and done and thought; I've got to have something to give me courage to start all over again, and make a man of myself yet—to cleanse myself of ingratitude—and bitterness—and evil passions. Sylvia—Sylvia—Sylvia!"

It seemed as if he had called it a thousand times; suddenly he stopped short, listening, his heart beating like a hammer, then standing still in his breast. It couldn't be—but, oh, it was, it was—

"Austin! Is that you?"

"Yes, yes, yes, where are you?"

"I don't know, I'm sure—what a question!" And instantly a feeling of relief swept through him—she was *all right*—able to see the absurdity of his question—more than he could have done! "But wherever I am, we can't be far apart; keep on calling, follow my voice—Austin—Austin—Austin—"

"All right—coming—tell me—are you hurt?"

"No—that is, not much."

"How much?"

"Dolly was frightened by the storm, bolted, and threw me off; I must have been stunned for a few minutes. I'm afraid I've sprained my ankle in falling, for I can't walk; and, oh, Austin, I'm awfully cold—and wet—and tired!"

"I know; it's—it's been just hellish for you. Keep on speaking to me, I'm getting nearer."

"I'll put out my hands, and then, when you get here, you won't stumble over me. I'm sure you're very near; your footsteps sound so."

"How long have you been here, should you think?"

"Oh, hours and hours. I was riding on the main road, when just what you predicted happened. It served me right—I ought to have listened to you. And so—oh, here you are—*I knew, all the time,* you'd come."

34

He grasped the little cold, outstretched hands, and sank down beside her, chafing them in his own.

"Thank God, I've found you," he said huskily, and gulped hard, pressing his lips together; then forcing himself to speak quietly, he went on, "Sylvia—tell me exactly what happened—if you feel able; but first, you must drink some brandy—I've got some for you—"

"I don't believe I can. I was all right until a moment ago—but now everything seems to be going around—"

Austin put his arm around her, and forced the flask to her lips; then the soft head sank on his shoulder, and he realized that she had fainted. Very gently he laid her on the ground, and fumbled in the dark for the fastenings of her habit; when it was loosened, he pulled off his coat and flannel shirt, putting the coat over her, and the shirt under her head for a pillow; then listening anxiously for her breathing, felt again for her mouth, and poured more brandy between her lips. There were a few moments of anxious waiting; then she sighed, moved restlessly, and tried to sit up.

"Lie still, Sylvia; you fainted; you've got to keep very quiet for a few minutes."

"How stupid of me! But I'm all right now."

"I said, lie still."

"All right, all right, I will; but you'll frighten me out of my wits if you use that tone of voice."

"I didn't mean to frighten you; but you've got to keep quiet, for your own sake, Sylvia."

"I thought you said you wouldn't call me Sylvia."

"I've said a good many foolish things in the course of my life, and changed my mind about them afterwards."

"Or feel sorry if I came to grief—"

"And a good many untrue and wicked ones for which I have repented afterwards."

"Well, I did come to grief—or pretty nearly. I met three Polish workmen on the road. I think they were—intoxicated. Anyway, they tried to stop me. I was lucky in managing to turn in here—so quickly they didn't realize what I was going to do. If I hadn't been near the entrance to this wood-road—Austin, what makes you grip my hand so? You hurt."

"Promise me you'll never ride alone again," he said, his voice shaking.

"I certainly never shall."

"And could you possibly promise me, too, that you'll forgive the absolutely unforgivable way I've acted all summer, and give me a chance to show that I can do better—*Sylvia?*"

"Oh, yes, *yes!* Please don't feel badly about that. I—I—never misunderstood at all. I know you've had an awfully hard row to hoe, and that's made you bitter, and —any man hates to have a woman help—financially. Besides"—she hesitated, and went on with a humility very different from her usual sweet imperiousness—"I've been pretty unhappy myself, and it's made *me* self-willed and obstinate and dictatorial."

"You! You're—more like an angel than I ever dreamed any woman could be."

"Oh, I'm not, I'm not—please don't think so for a minute. Because, if you do, we'll start out on a false basis, and not be real friends, the way I hope we're going to be now—"

"Yes—"

"And, please, may I sit up now? And really, my hands

are warm"—he dropped them instantly—"and I would like to hear about the storm—whether it has done much damage, if you know."

"It has destroyed every building we owned except the house itself."

"Austin! You're not in earnest!"

"I never was more so."

"Oh, I'm sorry—more sorry than I can tell you!" One of the little hands that had been withdrawn a moment earlier groped for his in the darkness, and pressed it gently; she did not speak for some minutes, but finally she went on: "It seems a dreadful thing to say, but perhaps it may prove a blessing in disguise. I believe Thomas is right in thinking that a smaller farm, which you could manage easily and well without hiring help, would be more profitable; and now it will seem the most natural thing in the world to sell that great southern meadow to Mr. Weston."

"Yes, I suppose so; he offered us three thousand dollars for it; he doesn't care to buy the little brick cottage that goes with it—which isn't strange, for it has only five rooms, and is horribly out of repair. Grandfather used it for his foreman; but, of course, we've never needed it and never shall, so I wish he did want it."

"Oh, Austin—could *I* buy it? I've been *dying* for it ever since I first saw it! It could be made perfectly charming, and it's plenty big enough for me! I've sold my Fifth Avenue house, and I'm going to sell the one on Long Island too—great, hideous, barnlike places! Your mother won't want me forever, and I want a little place of my very own, and *I love* Hamstead—and the river—and the valley —I didn't dare suggest this—you all, except Thomas,

37

seemed so averse to disposing of any of the property, but—"

"If we sell the meadow to Weston, I am sure you can have the cottage and as much land as you want around it; but the trouble is—"

"You need a great deal more money; of course, I know that. Have you any insurance?"

"Very little."

For some moments she sat turning things over in her mind, and was quiet for so long that Austin began to fear that she was more badly hurt than she had admitted, and found it an effort to talk.

"Is anything the matter?" he asked at last, anxiously. "Are you in pain?"

"No—only thinking. Austin—if you cannot secure a loan at some local bank, would you be very averse to borrowing the money from me—whatever the sum is that you need? I am investing all the time, and I will ask the regular rates of interest. Are you offended with me for making such a suggestion?"

"I am not. I was too much moved to answer for a minute, that is all. It is beyond my comprehension how you could bring yourself to do it, after overhearing what you heard me say the other evening."

"Then you'll accept?"

"If father and Thomas think best, I will; and thank you, too, for not calling it a gift."

"Are you likely to be offended if I go on, and suggest something further?"

"No; but I am likely to be so overwhelmed that I shall not be of much practical use to you."

"Well, then, I'd like you to take a thousand dollars

more than you need for building, and spend it in travelling."

"In travelling!"

"Yes; Thomas is a born farmer, and the four years that he is going to have at the State Agricultural College are going to be exactly what he wants and needs. He isn't sensitive enough so that he'll mind being a little older than most of the fellows in his class. But, of course, for you, anything like that is entirely out of the question. How old are you, anyway?"

"Twenty-seven."

"Well, if you could get away from here for a time, and see other people, how they do things, how they make a little money go a long way, and a little land go still farther, how they work hard, and fail many times, and succeed in the end—not the science of farming that Thomas is going to learn, but the accomplished fact—I believe it would be the making of you. My Uncle Mat was one of the first importers of Holstein cattle in this country, and I'd like to have you do just what he did when he got through college. Of course, you can buy all the cows you want in the United States now, of every kind, sort, and description, and just as good as there are anywhere in the world; but I want you to go to Europe, nevertheless. Start right off while Thomas is still at home to help your father; take a steamer that goes direct to Holland; get into the interior with an interpreter. Then cross over to the Channel Islands. By that time you'll be in a position to decide whether you want to stock your farm with Holsteins, which have the strongest constitutions and give the most milk, or Jerseys, which give the richest. While you're over there, go to Paris and London for a few days

—and see something besides cows. Come home by Liverpool. I know the United States Minister to the Netherlands very well, and no end of people in Paris. I'll give you some letters of introduction, and you'll have a good time besides getting a practical education. The whole trip needn't take you more than eight weeks. Then next spring visit a few of the big farms in New York and the Middle West, and go to one of those big cattle auctions they hold in Syracuse in July. Then—"

"For Heaven's sake, Sylvia! Where did you pick up all this information about farming?"

"From Uncle Mat—but I'll tell you all about that some other time. The question is now, 'Will you go?'"

"God bless you, *yes!*"

"That's settled, then," she cried happily. "I was fairly trembling with fear that you'd refuse. Why *is* it so hard for you to accept things?"

"I don't know. I've been bitter all my life because I've had to go without so much, and this summer I've been equally bitter because things were changing. It must be just natural cussedness—but I'm honestly going to try to do better."

"We've got to stay here until morning, haven't we?"

"I'm afraid we have. You can't walk, and even if you could, the chances are ten to one against our finding the highroad in this Egyptian darkness! When the sun comes up, I can pick my own way along through the underbrush all right, and carry you at the same time. You must weigh about ninety pounds."

"I weigh one hundred and ten! The idea!—There's really no chance, then, of our moving for several hours?"

"I'm sorry—but you must see there is not. Does it seem

40

as if you couldn't bear being so dreadfully uncomfortable that much longer?"

"Not in the least. I'm all right. But—"

"Do you mind being here—alone with me?"

"No, *no, no!* Why on earth should I? Let me finish my sentence. I was only wondering if it might not help to pass the time if I told you a story? It's not a very pleasant one, but I think it might help you over some hard places yourself, if you heard it; and if you would tell part of it—as much as you think best—to your family after we get home, I should be very grateful. Some of it should, in all justice, have been told to you all long ago, since you were so good as to receive me when you knew nothing whatever about me, and the rest is—just for you."

"Is the telling going to be hard for you?"

"I don't think so—this way—in the dark—and alone. It has all seemed too unspeakably dreadful to talk about until just lately; but I've been growing so much happier —I think it may be a relief to tell some one now."

"Then do, by all means. I feel—"

"Yes—"

"More honored than I can tell you by your—confidence."

"Austin—when it's *in* you to say such nice things as you have several times to-night, *why* do you waste time saying disagreeable ones—the way you usually do to everybody?"

"I've just told you, I don't know, but I'm going to do better."

"Well—there was once a girl, whose father had died when she was a baby and who lived with her mother and a maid in a tiny flat in New York City. It was a pretty

41

little flat, and they had plenty to eat and to wear, and a good many pleasant friends and acquaintances; but they didn't have much money—that is, compared to the other people they knew. This girl went to a school where all her mates had ten times as much spending money as she did, who possessed hundreds of things which she coveted, and who were constantly showering favors upon her which she had no way of returning. So, from the earliest time that she could remember, she felt discontented and dissatisfied, and regarded herself as having been picked out by Providence for unusual misfortunes; and her mother agreed with her.

"I fancy it is never very pleasant to be poor. But if one can be frankly poor, in calico and overalls, the way you've been, I don't believe it's quite so hard as it is to be poor and try 'to keep up appearances'; as the saying is. This girl learned very early the meaning of that convenient phrase. She gave parties, and went without proper food for a week afterwards; she had pretty dresses to wear to dances, and wore shabby finery about the house; she bought theatre tickets and candy, but never had a cent to give to charity; she usually stayed in the sweltering city all summer, because there was not enough money to go away for the summer, and still have some left for the next winter's season; and she spent two years at miserable little second-rate 'pensions' in Europe—that pet economy of fashionable Americans who would not for one moment, in their own country, put up with the bad food, and the unsanitary quarters, and the vulgar associates which they endure there.

"Before she was sixteen years old this girl began to be 'attractive to men,' as another stock phrase goes. I may be mistaken, and I'll never have a chance now to find out whether I am or not, but I believe if I had a daughter like that, it would be my earnest wish to bring her up in some quiet country place where she could dress simply, and spend much time outdoors, and not see too many people until she was nineteen or twenty. But the mother I had been talking about didn't feel that way. She taught her daughter to make the most of her looks—her eyes and her mouth, and her figure; she showed her how to arrange her dress in a way which should seem simple—and really be alluring; she drilled her in the art of being flippant without being pert, of appearing gentle when she was only sly, of saying the right thing at the right time, and—what is much more important—keeping still at the right time. The pupil was docile because she was eager to learn and she was clever. She made very few mistakes, and she never made the same one twice.

"Of course, all this education had one aim and end—a rich husband. 'I hope I've brought you up too sensibly,' the mother used to say, 'for you to even think of throwing yourself away on the first attractive boy that proposes to you. Your type is just the kind to appeal to some big, heavy, oversated millionaire. Keep your eyes open for him.' The daughter was as obedient in listening to this counsel as she had been in regard to the others, for it fell in exactly with her own wishes; she was tired of being poor, of scrimping and saving and 'keeping up appearances.' The innumerable young bank clerks and journalists and teachers and college students who fluttered about her burnt their moth-wings to no avail. But that *rara avis*, a really rich man, found her very kind to him.

"Well, you can guess the result. When she was not

43

quite eighteen, a man who was beyond question a millionaire proposed to her, and she accepted him. He was nearly twenty years older than she was, and was certainly big, heavy, and oversated. Her uncle—her father's brother—came to her mother, and told her certain plain facts about this man, and his father and grandfather before him, and charged her to tell the child what she would be doing if she married him. Perhaps if the uncle had gone to the girl herself, it might have done some good—perhaps it wouldn't have—you see she was so tired of being poor that she thought nothing else mattered. Anyway, he felt a woman could break these ugly facts to a young girl better than a man, and he was right. Only, you see, the mother never told at all; not that she really feared that her daughter would be foolish and play false to her excellent training—but, still, it was just as well to be on the safe side. The millionaire was quite mad about his little fiancée; he was perfectly willing to pay—in advance—all the expenses for a big, fashionable wedding, with twelve bridesmaids and a wedding-breakfast at Sherry's; he was eager to load her with jewels, and settle a large sum of money upon her, and take her around the world for her honeymoon journey; he loved her little soft tricks of speech, the shy way in which she dropped her eyes, the curve of the simple white dress that fell away from her neck when she leaned towards him; and though she saw him drink—and drank with him more than once before her marriage—he took excellent care that it was not until several nights afterwards that she found him— really drunk; and they must have been married two months before she began to—really comprehend what she had done.

"There isn't much more to tell—that can be told. The woman who sells herself—with or without a wedding ring —has probably always existed, and probably always will; but I doubt whether any one of them ever has told—or ever will—the full price which she pays in her turn. She deserves all the censure she gets, and more—but, oh! she does deserve a little pity with it! When this girl had been married nearly a year, she heard her husband coming upstairs one night long after midnight, in a condition she had learned to recognize—and fear. She locked her bed-room door. When he discovered that, he was furiously angry; as I said before, he was a big man, and he was very strong. He knocked out a panel, put his hand through, and turned the key. When he reached her, he reminded her that she had been perfectly willing to marry him—that she was his wife, his property, anything you choose to call it; he struck her. The next day she was very ill, and the child which should have been born three months later came—and went—before evening. The next year she was not so fortunate; her second baby was born at the right time—her husband was away with another woman when it happened—a horrible, diseased little creature with staring, sightless eyes. Thank God! it lived only two weeks, and its mother, after a long period of suffering and agony during which she felt like a leper, recovered again, in time to see her husband die—after three nights, during which she got no sleep—of delirium tremens, leaving her with over two million dollars to spend as she chose—and the degradation of her body and the ruin of her soul to think of all the rest of her life!"

"Sylvia!"—the cry with which Austin broke his long silence came from the innermost depths of his being—

"Sylvia, Sylvia, you shan't say such things—they're not true. Don't throw yourself on the ground and cry that way." He bent over her, vainly trying to keep his own voice from trembling. "If I could have guessed what— telling this—this hideous story would mean to you, I never should have let you do it. And it's all my fault that you felt you ought to do it—partly because of those vile speeches I made the other evening, partly because I've let you see how wickedly discontented I've been myself, partly because you must have heard me urging my own sister to make practically this same kind of a marriage. Oh, if it's any comfort to you to know it, you haven't told me in vain! Sylvia, do speak to me, and tell me that you believe me, and that you forgive me!"

She managed to give him the assurance he sought, her desperate, passionate voice grown gentle and quiet again. But she was too tired and spent to be comforted. For a long time she lay so still that he became alarmed, thinking she must have fainted again, and drew closer to her to listen to her breathing; at first there was a little catch in it, betraying sobs not yet wholly controlled, then gradually it grew calm and even; she had fallen asleep from sheer exhaustion.

Austin, sitting motionless beside her, found the night one of purification and dedication. To men of Thomas's type, slow of wit, steady and stolid and unemotional, the soil gives much of her own peaceful wholesomeness. But those like Austin, with finer intellects, higher ambitions, and stronger passions, often fare ill at her hands. Their struggles towards education and the refinements of life are balked by poverty and the utter fatigue which comes from overwork; while their search for pleasure often ends

46

in a knowledge and experience of vices so crude and tawdry that men of greater wealth and more happy experience would turn from them in disgust, not because they were more moral, but because they could afford to be more fastidious. Between Broadway and the "main street" of Wallacetown, and other places of its type—small railroad or manufacturing centres, standing alone in an otherwise purely agricultural community—the odds in favor of virtue, not to say decency, are all in favor of Broadway; and Wallacetown, to the average youth of Hamstead, represents the one opportunity for a "show," "something to drink," and "life" in general. Sylvia had unlocked the door of material opportunity for Austin; but she had done far more than this. She had given him the vision of the higher things that lay beyond that, and the desire to attain them. Further than that, neither she nor any other woman could help him. The future, to make or mar, lay now within his own hands. And in the same spirit of consecration with which the knights of old prayed that they might attain true chivalry during the long vigil before their accolade, Austin kept his watch that night, and made his vow that the future, in spite of the discouragements and mistakes and failures which it must inevitably contain, should be undaunted by obstacles, and clean of lust and high of purpose.

The wind and rain ceased, the clouds grew less heavy, and at last, just before dawn, a few stars shone faintly in the clearing sky; then the sun rose in a blaze of glory. Sylvia had not moved, and lay with one arm under her dark head, the undried tears still on her cheeks. Austin lifted her gently, and started towards the highroad with her in his arms. She stirred slightly, opened her eyes and smiled, then lifted her hands and clasped them around his neck.

"It'll be easier to carry me that way," she murmured drowsily. "Austin—you're awfully good to me."

Her eyes closed again. A sheet of white fire, like that of which he had been conscious on the afternoon when they straightened out the yard together, only a thousand times more powerful, seemed to envelop him again. He looked down at the lovely, sleeping face, at the dark lashes curling over the white cheeks and the red, sweet lips. If he kissed her, what harm would be done—she would never even know—

Then he flung back his head. Sylvia was as far above him as those pale stars of the early dawn. It was clear to him that no one must ever guess how dearly he loved her; but he knew that it was far, far more essential that he, in his unworthiness, should not profane his own ideal. She was not for his touch, scarcely for his thoughts. The kiss which did not reach her lips burned into his soul instead, and cleansed it with its healing flame.

CHAPTER V

SYLVIA's sprain, as Austin had suspected, proved much more serious than she had admitted, but when the village doctor came about noon to dress her ankle, she insisted that she was none the worse for her long exposure, and that if she must lie still on a lounge for two weeks, the least the family could do would be to humor her in everything, and spend as much time as possible with her, or she would certainly die of boredom. She passed the entire day in making and unfolding plans, looking up the sailing dates of steamships, and writing letters of introduction for Austin. By night she had the satisfaction of knowing that Weston's offer for the south meadow had been accepted, that the Wallacetown Bank and the insurance money would furnish part of the needed funds, and that she was to be allowed to loan the rest, and that the little brick cottage belonged to her. The fact that Austin had had a long talk with his father and brother, and that his passage for Holland had been engaged by telegraph, seemed scarcely less of an achievement to her; but Mrs. Gray noticed, as she kissed her little benefactress after seeing her comfortably settled for the night, that her usually pale cheeks were very red and her eyes unnaturally bright, and worried over her all night long.

The next morning there could be no doubt of the fact that Sylvia was really ill, and two days later Dr. Wells shook his head with dissatisfaction after using his thermometer and stethoscope. He was a conscientious man who lacked self-confidence, and the look of things was disquieting to him.

"I think you ought to get a nurse," he said in the hall to Mrs. Gray as he went out, "and probably she would like to have her own doctor from the city in consultation, and some member of her family come to her. It looks to me very much as if we were in for bronchial pneumonia, and she's a delicate little thing at best."

Sylvia was laughing when Mrs. Gray, bent on being both firm and tactful, reëntered her room. "Tell Dr. Wells he must make his stage-whispers softer if he doesn't want me to overhear him," she said, "and don't think of ordering the funeral flowers just yet. I'm not delicate—I'm strong as an ox—if I weren't I shouldn't be alive at all. Get a nurse by all means if it will make things easier for you—that's the only reason I need one. They're usually more bother than they're worth, but I know of two or three who might do fairly well, if any one of them is free. My doctor is an old fogey, and I won't have him around. As for family, I'm not as greatly blessed—numerically or otherwise—in that respect as the Grays, but my Uncle Mat would love to come, I feel sure, as he's rather hurt at my runaway conduct." She gave the necessary addresses, and still persisting that they were making a great fuss about nothing, turned over on her pillow in a violent fit of coughing.

Sylvia was right in one thing: she was much stronger than Dr. Wells guessed, and though the next week proved an anxious one for every member of the household except herself, it was not a dismal one. Even if she were flat on her back, her spirit and her vitality remained contagious. Thomas, whose state of mind was by this time quite apparent to the family, though he imagined it to be a well-concealed secret, hung about outside her door, positive that she was going to die, and brought offerings in the shape of flowers, early apples, and pet animals which he thought might distract her. Austin, who shared his room, insisted that he could not sleep because Thomas groaned and sighed so all night; Molly pertly asked him why he did not try rabbits, as kittens did not seem to appeal to Sylvia, and his mother bantered him half-seriously for thinking of "any one so far above him" whose heart, moreover, was buried "in the grave." Austin's somewhat expurgated version of Sylvia's story put an end to the latter part of the protest, but sent his hearers into a new ferment of excitement and sympathy. Sally, who was all ready to start for a "ball" in Wallacetown with Fred when she heard it, declared she couldn't go one step, it made her feel "that low in her spirits," and Fred replied, by gosh, he didn't blame her one mite; whereat they wandered off and spent the evening at a very comfortable distance from the house, but fairly close together, revelling in a wealth of gruesome facts and suppositions. Katherine said she certainly never would marry at all, men were such dreadful creatures, and Molly said, yes, indeed, but what else *could* a girl marry?—while Edith determined to devote the rest of *her* life to attending and adoring the lovely, sad, drooping widow, whose existence was to be one long poem of beautiful seclusion; and she was so pleased with her own ideas, and her manner of expressing them, that she wept scalding tears into the broth she was making for Sylvia as she stirred it over the stove.

The presence of "Uncle Mat," greatly dreaded beforehand, proved an unexpected source of solace and delight. He was a quiet, shrewd little man, not unlike Sylvia in many ways, but with a merry twinkle in his eye, and a brisk manner of speech which she did not possess. He sized up the Gray family quickly, and apparently with satisfaction, for he talked quite freely of his niece to them, and they saw that they were not alone in their estimate of her.

"It certainly was a great stroke of luck all round—for her as well as for you—when she blew in here," he said, "but if you knew what an awful hole we think she's left behind her in New York you'd think yourselves doubly lucky to have her all to yourselves. There's more than one young man, I can tell you"—with a sly look at Thomas—"watching out for her return. You should have seen her at a party I gave for her three years ago or more, dressed in a pink frock looped up with roses, and with cheeks to match! She wasn't always this pale little shadow, I can tell you. Well, the boys were around her that night like bees round a honeysuckle bush—no denying there's something almighty irresistible about these little, soft-looking girls, now, is there? Ah! her roses didn't last long, poor child. Now you've given her a good, healthful place to live in, and something to think about and do—she'd have lost her reason without them, after all she's been through. But when you're tired of her, I want her. I'm a poor, forlorn lonely old bachelor, and I need her a great deal more than any of you. What do you say to a little walk, Mr. Gray, before we turn in? I want to have a look at your fine farm. I have a farm myself—no such grand old place as this, of course, but a neat little toy not far from the city, where I can run down Sundays. Sylvia used to be very fond of going down with me. It's from my foreman, a queer, scientific chap—Jenkins his name is —that she's picked up all these notions she's been unloading on you. Pretty good, most of them, aren't they, though? You must run down there some time, boys, and look things over—it's well to go about a bit when one's thinking of building and branching out—Sylvia's idea, exactly, isn't it?"

Mr. Gray and Thomas did "run down," seizing the opportunity while Austin was still at home, and while there was practically no farm-work to be done. Jenkins did the honors of Mr. Stevens's little place handsomely, and they returned with magnificent plans, from the erection of silos and the laying of concrete floors to the proper feeding of poultry. When "Uncle Mat" was obliged to return to his business, after staying over two weeks with the Grays, Austin went with him, for he suggested that he would be glad to have the boy as his guest in New York for a few days before he sailed.

"You better have a glimpse of the 'neat little toy,' too," he said, "and perhaps see something of a rather neat little city, too! You'll want to do a little shopping and so on, and I might be of assistance in that way."

"I don't see how you can go," said Thomas to Austin the night before he left, as they were undressing, "while Sylvia is still in bed, and won't be around for another week at least. She's responsible for all your tremendous good fortune, and you'll leave without even saying thank you and good-bye. You're a darned queer ungrateful cuss, and always were."

"I know it," said Austin, "and such being the 'nature of the beast,' don't bother trying to make me over. You can be grateful and devoted enough for both of us. Now, do shut up and let me go to sleep—I sure will be thankful to get a room to myself, if I'm not for anything else."

"I don't see how any one can help being crazy over her," continued Thomas, thumping his pillow as if he would like to pummel any one who disagreed with him.

"Don't you?" asked Austin.

The next night he was in New York with Mr. Stevens, trying hard to feel natural in a tiny flat which was only one of fifty in the same great house. A colored butler served an elaborate dinner at eight o'clock in the evening, and brought black coffee, liqueurs, and cigars into the living-room afterwards, and, worst of all, unpacked all his scanty belongings and laid them about his room. Austin really suffered, and the cold perspiration ran down his back, but he watched his host carefully and waited from one moment to another to see what would be expected of him next; he managed, too, before he went to bed, to ask a question which had been on his mind for some time.

"Would you mind telling me, sir, where Sylvia's mother is?"

Uncle Mat shot one of his keen little glances in Austin's direction. "Why, no, not at all, as nearly as I can," he said. "My brother, Austin, made a most unfortunate match; his wife was a mean, mercenary, greedy woman, as hard as nails, and as tough as leather—but handsome, oh, very handsome, as a girl, and clever, I assure you. I

54

have often been almost glad that my brother did not live long enough to see her in her real colors. She married, very soon after Sylvia herself, a worthless Englishman—discharged from the army, I believe, who had probably been her lover for some time. Cary gave her a check for a hundred thousand to get rid of her the day after his wedding to Sylvia, and the pair are probably living in great comfort on that at some second-rate French resort."

"Thank you for telling me; but it's rather awful, isn't it, that any one should have to think of her mother as Sylvia must? Why, my mother—" He stopped, flushing as he thought of how commonplace, how homely and ordinary, his mother had often seemed to him, how he had brooded over his father's "unfortunate match." "My mother has worked her fingers to the bone for all of us, and I believe she'd let herself be chopped in pieces to help us gladly any day."

"Yes," assented Mr. Stevens, "I know she would. There are—several different kinds of mothers in the world. It's a thousand pities Sylvia did not have a fair show at a job of that sort. She would have been one of the successful kind, I fancy."

"It would seem so," said Austin.

CHAPTER VI

New York City
August 25

DEAR MOTHER AND FATHER:

I'm going to lay in a stock of picture post-cards to send
you, for if things move at the same rate in Europe that
they do in New York, I certainly shan't have time to write
many letters. But I'll send a good long one to-night, anyhow. I always thought I'd like to live in the city, as you
know, but a few days of this has already given me a sort
of breathless feeling that I ought always to be on the
move, whether there's anything special to do or not. The
noise never stops for one minute, night or day, and the
streets are perfect miracles of light and dirt and *hurry*.
This whole flat could be put right into our dining-room,
and we'd hardly notice it at that, and *hot!* Mr. Stevens
says in the winter he nearly freezes to death, but I can't
believe it.

All day Friday he kept me tearing from shop to shop,
buying more clothes than I can wear out in a lifetime,
I believe, lots of them things I'd never even seen or heard
of before. Some of the suits had to be altered a little, so
in the afternoon we went back to the same places we'd
been to in the morning, and tried the blamed things on

again. How women can like that sort of thing is beyond me—I'd rather dig potatoes all day. By five o'clock I was so tired that I was ready to lie right down on Fifth Avenue, and let the passing crowds walk over me, if they liked. But Mr. Stevens hustled me into a huge hotel called the Waldorf for a hair-cut and "tea" (which isn't a good square meal, but a little something to drink along with a piece of bread-and-butter as thick through as tissue-paper) and then out again to see a few sights before we went home to dress for "an early dinner" (*seven o'clock!*) and go to the theatre in the evening. "Dressing" meant struggling into my new dress-suit. I hoped it wouldn't arrive in time, but Mr. Stevens had had it marked "rush," and it did. I felt like a fool when I got it on, and a pretty hot, uncomfortable fool to boot. Mr. Stevens apologized for the show, saying there was really nothing in town at this time of year, but you can imagine what it seemed like to me! I'd be almost willing to wear pink tights—same as a good many of the actresses did!— if it meant having such a glorious time.

It was almost ten o'clock Saturday morning when I waked up, and of course I felt like a fool again. But that is getting to be such a habitual state with me, that I don't need to keep wasting paper by mentioning it. By the time I was washed and shaved and dressed, Mr. Stevens had been to his office, transacted all the business necessary for the day, and was ready to see sights again. "It doesn't take long to do things when you get the hang of hustling," he said, referring to his own transactions; "come along. We've got a couple of hours before lunch, and then we'll take the 2.14 train down to my farm." So we shot downstairs about forty flights to the second in the elevator, hailed a passing taxicab, jumped in, and were tearing out Riverside Drive—much too fast to see anything—in no time. We had "lunch" at a big restaurant called Delmonico's, a great deal to eat and not half enough time to eat in, then took another taxi and made our train by catching on to the last car.

I don't need to tell you about the farm, because you know all about that already. I never left Jenkins's heels one second, and he said I was much more of a nuisance than Thomas, because Thomas caught on to things naturally, and I asked questions all the time. I don't believe I'll see anything in Europe to beat that place. When we get to milking our cows, and separating our cream, and doing our cleaning by electricity, it'll be something like, won't it?

We took a seven o'clock train back to New York this morning, so that Mr. Stevens could get to his office by nine, and he had me go with him and wait around until he was at leisure again. I certainly thought the stenographers' fingers would fly off, and all the office boys moved with a hop, skip, and jump; really, the slowest things in the rooms were the electric fans whizzing around. By half-past eleven Mr. Stevens had dictated about two hundred and fifty letters, sold several million dollars' worth of property (he's a real-estate broker), and was all ready to go out with me to buy more socks, neckties, handkerchiefs, etc., having decided that I didn't have enough. We had "lunch" at Sherry's—another swell restaurant—and took a trip up the Hudson in the afternoon, getting back at half-past ten—"Just in time," said Mr. Stevens, "to look in at a roof-garden before we go to bed." So we "looked," and it sure was worth a passing glance, and then some. It's one o'clock in the morning now, and I sail at nine, so I'm writing at this hour in desperation, or you won't get any letter at all.

Much love to everybody. I picture you all peacefully sleeping—except Thomas, of course—with no such word as "hurry" in your minds.

AUSTIN

S.S. Amsterdam
September 4

DEAR SALLY:

It doesn't seem possible that I'm going to land to-morrow! The first two days out were pretty dreadful, and I'll leave them to your imagination—there certainly wasn't much left of *me* except imagination! But by the third day I was beginning to sit up and take notice again, and by the fourth I was enjoying myself more than I ever did in all my life before.

There's a fellow on board named Arthur Brown, who has his sister Emily with him; they're both unmarried, and well over thirty, teachers in a small Western college, and are starting out on their "Sabbatical year." Seeing them together has made me think a lot about you, and wish you were along; they've very little money, and have never been to Europe before, and almost every night they sit down and figure out how they're going to get the most out of their trip, trying new plans and itineraries all the time. They get into such gales of laughter over it that you'd think being poor was the greatest fun in the world, and the tales they've told about working their way through high school and college, and saving up to come to Europe, would be pathetic if they weren't so screamingly funny. I haven't been gone very long yet, I know, but it's been long enough for me to decide that Sylvia sent me off, not primarily to buy cows and study agriculture, but to learn a few things that will be a darned sight better worth knowing than that even, and—*to have a good time!* In the hope, of course, that I'll come home, not only less green, but less cussedly disagreeable.

Mr. Stevens has crossed on this boat twice, and introduced me to both the captain and the chief engineer before I started; they've both been awfully kind to me, and I've seen the "inwards and outwards" of the ship from garret to cellar, so to speak, and learned enough about navigation and machinery to make me want to learn a lot more. But even without all this, there would have been plenty to do. This isn't a "fashionable line," so they say, but it's a good deal more fashionable than anything we ever saw in Hamstead, Vermont! There's dancing every evening—not a bit like what we have at home, and it really made me gasp a little at first—you thought I was hard to shock, too, didn't you? Well, believe me, I blushed the first time I discovered that I was expected to hold my partner so tight that you couldn't get a sheet of paper between us. However, I soon stopped blushing, and bent all my energies to the agreeable task of learning instead, and the girls are all so friendly and jolly, that I believe I'm getting the hang of the new ways pretty well. There are no square dances at all and very few waltzes or two-steps, but two newer ones, the one-step and fox-trot, hold the floor, literally and figuratively! I wish I could describe the girls' dresses to you, they're so pretty, but I can't a bit, except to say that they rather startled me at first, too; they appear to be made out of about one yard of material, and none of that yard goes to sleeves, and not much to waist. A very lively young lady sits next to me at the table, and I worried incessantly at first as to what would happen if her shoulder-straps should break; but apparently they are stronger than they look. When they—the girls, I mean—feel a little chilly on deck, they put on scarves of tulle—a gauzy stuff about half as thick as mosquito netting. I don't quite see why they're not all dead of pneumonia, but they seem to thrive.

I've also learned—or am trying to learn—to play a game of cards called "bridge"; it's along the same lines as good old bid-whist, but considerably dressed up. I like that, too, but feel pretty stupid at it, as most of the players can remember every two-spot for six hands back, and hold dreadful post-mortems of their opponents' mistakes at the end of the game. I've brought along the old French grammar I had in high school, as well as some new phrase-books that Mr. Stevens gave me, and take them to bed with me to study every night, for he told me that you could get along 'most anywhere if you knew French. There's a library aboard, too, so I've read several novels, and I'm getting used to my clothes—I don't believe I've got too many after all—and to taking a cold bath every morning and shaving at least once a day.

Make Fred toe the mark while I'm not there to look after you, but remember he's a good sort just the same; I was an awful fool ever to advise you not to stick to him, he's worth a dozen of his cousin. Tell Molly she'll have to do some practising to come up to the way some of the girls on this ship play, but I believe she's got more talent than all of them put together, if she'll only work hard enough to develop it. There's going to be an *extra* good time to-night, as it's the last one, and I'm looking forward to dancing my heels off. Love to you all, especially mother, and tell her I haven't seen a doughnut since I left home.

Affectionately your brother

AUSTIN

Paris, October 1

DEAR THOMAS:

I got here last night, and found the cable from father saying that the cattle and Dutch Peter had reached New York all right, and that he had met them there. I know you'll like Peter, and I hope we can keep him indefinitely, though I only hired him to take the cows over, and stay until those Holstein aristocrats were properly acclimated to the Homestead. I'm glad they've got there. And, gosh! I'm glad I've got *here!* I realize I've been a pretty poor correspondent, sending just picture postcards, and now and then a note to mother, but, you see, I've crowded every minute so darned full, and then I've never had much practice. So before I start out to "do" Paris, I'll practice a little on you.

I landed at Rotterdam, had twenty-four hours there with Emily and Arthur Brown—that brother and sister I met on shipboard—then we separated, they going to Antwerp, and I heading straight for The Hague to present Sylvia's letter of introduction to Mr. Little, the American Minister, shaking in my shoes, and cold perspiration running down my back, of course. But I needn't "have shook and sweat," as our friend Mrs. Elliott says, for he was expecting me and was kindness itself. He

62

found an interpreter to go through the farming district with me, and then he invited me to come and stay at his house for a few days before I started for the interior. He has a son about my age, who I imagine has suffered from the same form of heart disease with which you are afflicted at present, as he seemed to be somewhat affected every time Sylvia's name was mentioned; and a daughter Flora, an awfully friendly, jolly, pink-and-white creature. Fortunately she informed me promptly that she was engaged to a fellow in Paris, or I might have got heart disease, too. They kept me on the jump every minute—sight-seeing and parties, and excursions of all sorts, and one night we went to see a play of Shakespeare's, "The Two Gentlemen of Verona," given in Dutch. (I find that all Continentals admire him immensely, and give frequent performances of his works.) Get out our old copy and re-read it some rainy day; you're probably rusty on it, same as I was, but it's an interesting tale, and there's a song in it that can't help appealing to you. Here's the first verse:

"Who is Sylvia? What is she
    That all the swains commend her?
Holy, fair, and wise is she,
    The heavens such grace did lend her
That she might admired be."

I advise you to invest in doublet, hose, plumed hat, and guitar, and try the effect of a serenade under our Sylvia's—beg pardon, *your* Sylvia's window. The fellow in the play made a great hit, so there's no telling what you might accomplish.

I hated leaving the Littles', for the good time I had there sure beat the good time I had on shipboard "to a frazzle"; but I soon found out that the business part of the trip was going to be a good deal more interesting and absorbing than I had imagined it would be. My interpreter, Hans Roorda, a fellow several years younger than I am, can speak five languages, all equally well, and I kept him busy talking French to me. We were in the country almost three weeks. The farmers haven't half the mechanical conveniences that we considered absolutely necessary even in our least prosperous days, but are marvels of order and efficiency, for all that. I believe one of the greatest mistakes that we New England farmers have been making is to assume that farming is a mixture of three fourths muscle and one fourth brains—I'm beginning to think it's the other way around. As you have already learned, I followed Jenkins's advice, bought a dozen head of fine cattle, and hired Peter Kuyp, the son of one of the farmers I visited, to take care of them. Of course, this meant going back to Rotterdam to see them safely off, and I managed to get a glimpse of some of the other Dutch cities as well. When I got to Amsterdam I parted from Roorda with real regret, for I feel he's one of the many good friends I've already made. I found my first American mail in Amsterdam, among other letters one from you. The news from home in it was all fine. I'm glad father has sold that old Blue Hill pasture. It was too far off from the rest of our land to be of much real use to us, and I also think he was dead right to use the money he got from it to pay off old debts. Mr. Stevens writes me that he has sold Sylvia's Long Island house for her, and that her horses, carriages, sleighs, and motor are all going up to the Homestead. Now that the Holsteins are there, too, why don't you sell the few old cows and the two horses that we rescued from the fire, and use that money in paying off more debts? If the mortgage were only out of the way, with all the other improvements you speak of well started, I should think we were headed straight for millionaires' row.

I also found a letter from Mr. Little in Amsterdam, saying that Mrs. Little and Flora were about to start for Paris, and asking if I would care to act as their escort, since neither he nor his son could leave The Hague just then—simply a kind way of saying, "Here's another chance for you," of course! You can imagine the answer I telegraphed him! We "broke" the journey in Brussels and Antwerp, and I saw no end of new wonders, of course, and in Brussels we went to the opera. I did wish Molly was there, for she certainly would have thought she had struck Heaven, and I did, pretty nearly! I'm getting used to my dress-suit, and it isn't quite such an exquisite piece of torture to "do" my tie as it was at first, since Flora did it for me one night, and gave me some little hints for the future. She is really an awfully jolly girl.

We got to Paris late at night, and I never shall forget the long drive from the station, through the bright streets to the Fessendens' house, where the Littles were going to visit. Sylvia had given me a letter of introduction to them, too, but I didn't need to use it, for, of course, I got introduced to them then and there. There are three fellows—no girls—in the family, besides Mr. and Mrs. I knew beforehand that Flora was engaged to one of them, but I couldn't tell which, for they all fell upon her and embraced her with about equal enthusiasm. Then they all kissed Mrs. Little, and Mrs. Little and

Mrs. Fessenden hugged each other, and Mr. Fessenden hugged Flora. I began to think that perhaps I might be included—by mistake—but all my hopes were in vain. I was invited to come to dinner the next night, however, and then I took my leave, and drove round for an hour— it seemed like an hour in Fairyland—before I went back to my hotel.

You must be getting settled in college now—it must have been an awful wrench to tear yourself away from the Homestead, I know, but you'll have a great time after you get over the first pangs of separation, I'm sure, and don't forget that "absence makes the heart grow fonder." I refer, of course, to Sylvia's heart because you've made it sufficiently plain to all of us that yours *can't*. Well, the best of luck go with you.

AUSTIN

Southampton, October 27

DEAR SYLVIA:

I had a feeling in my bones when I woke up this morning that something extra pleasant was going to happen; and when I got down to breakfast, and saw, on the top of my pile of mail, a letter postmarked Hamstead, but in a strange handwriting, I knew that it *had* happened.

You begin by scolding me because I haven't written mother oftener. I know I deserve it, and I'll write her from now on, every Sunday, at least; but then you go on by asking why I've never written you, except the little note I sent back by the pilot, which you say is not a note at all, "but a series of repetitions of unmerited thanks." I haven't written because I didn't feel that you wanted to be bothered with me. And how can I write, and not say,

"Thank you, thank you, thank you," with every line? Why, I've learned more, enjoyed more, *lived* more, in these two months since I came to Europe than I had in all the rest of my life before! Sylvia—but I won't, if you don't like it!

Now, to answer your question, "What have I been doing all this time?" I feel sure you've seen what I have written, so you know what a wonderful trip I had from The Hague to Paris. I'm glad I haven't got to try to describe Paris to you, for of course you know it much better than I do; but I hope some day, when my mind's a little calmer, I can describe it to the rest of the family. Just now I'm not in any state yet to separate the details from the wild, magnificent jumble of picture galleries and churches, tombs and palaces, parks and gardens, wonderful broad, bright streets, theatres, cafés, and dinner-parties. Of course, all your letters were the main reason that every one was so nice to me. My first day of sight-seeing ended with a perfectly uproarious dinner at the Fessendens'; I never in my life ran into such a jolly crowd. I finally discovered which brother Flora belonged to—which had been puzzling me a good deal before—because about ten o'clock the other two suggested that we should go out and see if "we could have a little fun." I thought we were having a good deal right there, but of course I agreed, so we went; and we did.

Then—during the next ten days—I went to mass at the Madeleine, and to a ball at the American Embassy; I rode on the top of 'buses, and spun around in motors. We took some all-day trips out into the country, and saw not only the famous places, like Versailles and Fontaine-bleau, but lots of big, beautiful private estates with farms attached. There's none of the spotless shininess of Holland or the beautiful cattle there; but agriculture is developed to the nth degree for all that. Those French farmers wring more out of one acre than we do out of ten; but we're going to do some wringing in Hamstead, Vermont, in the future, I can tell you! The last night in Paris, I never went to bed at all. Twenty of us had dinner at the Café de la Paix—went to the theatre—saw the girls and fathers and mothers home—then went off with the other fellows to another show which lasted until three A.M. I had barely time to rush back to the hotel, collect my belongings, and catch my early train—for I'd made up my mind to do that so that I could stop off for two hours at Rouen on my way to Calais, and I was glad I did, though I must confess I yawned a good deal, even while I was looking at the Cathedral and the relics of Joan of Arc.

I had just a week in the Channel Islands, and though I didn't think beforehand that I could possibly get as much out of them as I did out of the country in Holland, of course, I found that I was mistaken. I bought six head of cattle, brought them to Southampton with me, and saw them safely embarked for America, as I cabled father. I suppose they've got there by now. They're beauties, but I believe I'm going to like the Holsteins better, just the same. They're larger and sturdier—less nervous—and give more milk, though it's not nearly so rich.

The Browns met me there, and I was awfully glad to see them again. I bought a knapsack, and, leaving all my good clothes behind me, started out with them on a week's walking trip through the Isle of Wight, getting back here only last night. We stopped overnight at any place we happened to be near, usually a farmhouse, and the next morning pursued our way again, with a lunch put up by our latest hostess in our pockets. Of course, the Browns didn't take the same interest in farming that I did, but they had a fine time, too. It's been a great thing for me to know them, especially Emily. She's not a bit pretty, or the sort that a fellow could get crazy over, or— well, I can't describe it, but you know what I mean. Every man who meets her must realize what a fine wife she'd make for somebody, and yet he wouldn't want her himself. But she's a wonderful friend. Do you know, I never had a woman friend before, or realized that there could be such a thing—for a man, I mean—unless there was some sentiment mixed up with it. This isn't the least of the valuable lessons I've learned.

After lunch to-day, we're going off again—not on foot this time, as it would take too long to see what we want to that way, but on hired bicycles. I'm sending my baggage ahead to London to "await arrival," but if the mild, though rather rainy, weather we've had so far holds, I hope to have two weeks more of *country* England before I go there; we have no definite plans, but expect to go to some of the cathedral towns, and to Oxford and Warwick at least.

And now I've overstayed the time you first thought I should be gone, already, and yet I'm going to close my letter by quoting the last lines in yours, "If you need more money, cable for it. (I don't; I haven't begun to spend all I had.) Don't hurry; see all you can comfortably and thoroughly; and if you decide you want to go somewhere that we didn't plan at first, or stay longer than you originally intended, please do. The family is well, the building going along finely, and Peter, your Dutch boy, most efficient—by the way, we all like him immensely. This is your chance. Take it."

Well, I'm going to. After the Browns leave London, they're going to Italy for the winter, and they want me to go with them, for a few weeks before I start home. I'll sail from Naples, getting home for Christmas, and what a Christmas it'll be! I know you'll tell me honestly if you think I ought not to do this, and I'll start for Liverpool at once, and without a regret; but if you cable "stay," I'll go towards Rome with an easy heart and a thankful soul.

I must stop, because I don't dare write any more. The "thank-you's" would surely begin to crop out.

Ever yours faithfully

AUSTIN GRAY

CHAPTER VII

THE first of October found a very quiet household at the old Gray Homestead. Austin was in Europe; Thomas had gone to college at Burlington, Molly to the Conservatory of Music in Boston. Sally had prudently decided to teach for another year before getting married, and now that she could keep all her earnings, was happily saving them for her modest trousseau; she "boarded" in Wallacetown, where she taught, coming home only for Saturdays and Sundays, while Katherine and Edith were in high school, and gone all day. Mrs. Gray declared that she hardly knew what to do with herself, she had so much spare time on her hands with so many "modern improvements," and such a small family in the house.

"Go with Mr. Gray on the 'fall excursion' to Boston," said Sylvia. "He told me that you hadn't been off together since you took your wedding trip. That will give you a chance to look in on Molly, too, and see how she's behaving—and you'll have a nice little spree besides. I'll look after the family, and Peter can look after the cows."

Sylvia had recovered rapidly from her illness, and her former shyness and aversion to seeing people were rapidly leaving her. She no longer lay in bed until noon, but was up with the rest of the family, insisting on doing

71

her share in the housework, and proving a very apt pupil in learning that useful and wrongly despised art; when callers came she always dropped in to chat with them a little while, and even the mail-carrier of the "rural delivery, route number two," the errand-boy on the wagon from Harrington's General Store, and all the agents for flavoring extracts and celluloid toilet sets and Bibles for miles around, were not infrequently found lingering on the "back porch" passing the time of day with her, whether they had any excuse of mail or merchandise or not. Not infrequently she went to spend the day with Mrs. Elliott or with Ruth, and to church on Sunday with all the family; and although perhaps she was not sorry at heart that her deep mourning gave her an excuse for not attending the village "parties" and "socials," she never said so. The Library, the Grange, and the Village Improvement Society all found her ready and eager to help them in their struggles to raise money, provide better quarters for themselves, or get up entertainments; and the Methodist minister was the first person to meet with a flat refusal to his demands upon her purse. He was far-famed as a successful "solicitor," and conceived the brilliant idea that Sylvia was probably sent by Providence to provide the needed repairs upon the church and parsonage and the increase in his own salary. He called upon her, and graciously informed her of his plan.

"The Lord has been pleased to make you the steward of great riches," he said unctuously, "and I feel sure there is no way you could spend them which would be more pleasing in his sight than that which I have just suggested."

"I agree with you perfectly that the church is in a disgraceful state of disrepair," said Sylvia calmly, "and that your salary is quite inadequate to live on properly. I have often wondered how your congregation could worship reverently in such a place, or allow their pastor to be so poorly housed. I believe the Bible commands us somewhere to do things decently and in order."

"You are quite right, Mrs. Cary, quite right. Then may I understand—"

"Wait just a minute. I have also wondered at the lack of proper pride your congregation seemed to show in such matters. It does not seem to me that it would really help matters very much if I, a complete outsider, not even a member of your communion, furnished all the necessary funds to do what you wish. Your flock would sit back harder than ever, and wait for some one else to turn up and do likewise when I have gone—and probably that second millionaire would never materialize, and you would be left worse off than before, even."

"My dear lady!" exclaimed the divine, amazed and distressed at the turn the conversation had taken, "most of the members of my congregation are in very moderate circumstances."

"I know—but they should do *their share*. And there are some, who, for a small village, are rich, and just plain stingy—why don't you go to them?"

"Unfortunately that would only result in the entire withdrawal of their support, I fear."

"And those are the worthy, struggling Christians whom you wish me to supply with everything to make their church beautiful and their minister comfortable—you want me to put a premium on stinginess! I shan't give you one cent under those conditions! Go to the three richest men in your church, and say to them, 'Whatever sum you will give, Mrs. Cary will double.' Appeal to your congregation as a whole, and tell it the same thing. Ask those who you know have no cash to spare to give some of their time, at whatever it is worth by the hour or the day. Set the children to arranging for a concert—I suppose you wouldn't approve of a little play—and see how the relatives and friends will flock to hear it. I'll gladly drill them. When you've tried all this, and the response has been generous and hearty, if still you haven't all you need, I'll gladly lend you the remainder of the sum without interest, and you may take your own time in discharging the debt."

"That is a young lady who gives a man much food for thought," remarked the minister to Mr. Gray, as, somewhat abashed, but greatly impressed, he was leaving the house a few minutes later.

"Very true—in more ways than one."

"Her person is not unpleasing and she seems to have an agile mind," continued Mr. Jessup.

Mr. Gray turned away to hide a smile. Later he teased Sylvia about her new conquest. "I am afraid," he said, his mouth twitching, "that you would flirt with a stone post."

"I didn't flirt with *him*," said Sylvia indignantly; "he ended the call by dropping on his knees, right there in my sitting-room, and saying, 'Let us pray—for new hearts!' Well, I've had lots of calls end with a prayer for a change of heart—"

"You little wretch! What did you do?"

"Do! I always strive to please! I knelt down beside him,

74

of course, and then he took my hand, so I— Honestly, I
don't care much what men *say*—if they only say it *right*—
but I draw the line at being *stroked!* If that's your idea
of a flirtation, it isn't mine!"

"Look out, my dear," warned Howard; "he's a widower
and a famous beggar." And Sylvia laughed with him.
During the first months she had never laughed. "I am
getting to love that child as if she were my own," he said
to his wife later. "Whatever shall we do when she goes
away? It won't be long now, you'll see."

"Mercy! Don't you even speak of it!" rejoined Mrs.
Gray. But she, too, was brooding over the possibility in
secret. "Are you sure you're quite contented here,
Sylvia?" she asked anxiously the next time they were
alone.

Sylvia laid down the dish she was wiping, and came
and laid her cheek, now growing softly pink again,
against Mrs. Gray's. "Contented," she echoed; "why, I'm
—I'm happy—I never was happy in my whole life before.
But I shall freeze to death here this winter, unless you'll
let me put a furnace in this great house; and I want to
glass in part of the big piazza, and have a tiny little conservatory for your plants built off the dining-room. Do
you mind if I tear up the place that much more—you've
been so patient about it so far."

Mrs. Gray could only throw up her hands.

The "spree" to Boston took place, and proved wonderfully delightful, and then they all settled down quietly
for the winter, looking forward to Christmas as the time
that was to bring the entire family together again. For
even James, the eldest son, had written that he was about
to be married, and should come home with his bride for

the holidays for his wedding trip; and as Sylvia still firmly refused to leave the farm, Mr. Stevens asked for permission to join Austin when he landed, and be with his niece over the great day. As the time drew near, the house was hung with garlands, and every window proudly displayed a great laurel wreath tied with a huge red bow. Sylvia moved all her belongings into her parlor, and decorated her bedroom for the bride and groom, and went about the house singing as she unpacked great boxes and trimmed a mammoth Christmas tree.

Four days before Christmas, Mr. and Mrs. James Gray arrived, and Mrs. James was promptly pronounced to be "all right" by her husband's family, though the poor girl, of course, underwent tortures before she was sure of their decision. Fred, who with his father and mother was to join in the great feast, brought Sally home from Wallace-town that same night, and took advantage of the mistle-toe which Sylvia had hung up, right before them all. Thomas and Molly, both wonderfully citified already, appeared during the course of the next afternoon from opposite directions, and Molly played, and Thomas expounded scientific farming, to the wonder of them all. And finally Mr. Gray went to meet the midnight train from New York at Wallacetown the night before Christmas Eve, and found himself being squeezed half to pieces by the bear hugs of Austin and the hearty handshakes of Mr. Stevens.

"Pile right into the sleigh," he managed to say at last when he was partially released, but still gasping for breath; "we mustn't stand fooling around here, with the thermometer at twenty below zero, and a whole house-ful waiting to treat you the same way you've treated me.

Austin, seems as if you were bigger than ever, and you've got a different look, same as Thomas and Molly have, only yours is more different."

"There was more room for improvement in my case," his son laughed back, throwing his arm around him again. "My, but it's good to see you! Talk about changes! You look ten years younger, doesn't he, Mr. Stevens? How's mother? And—and Thomas, and the girls? And—and Peter?"

"Yes, how is *Peter?*" said Mr. Stevens.

"Why, Peter's all right," returned Mr. Gray soberly; "what makes you ask? That sort is never sick and he's as good and steady a boy as I ever saw."

"I'm so glad to hear it," murmured Mr. Stevens in an interested voice.

"And we had the biggest creamery check this month, Austin," went on his father, "that we *ever* had—with just those few cows you sent! Peter tends them as if they were young girls being dressed up for their sweethearts. The hens are laying well, too, right through this cold weather—the poultry house is so clean and warm, they don't seem to know that it's winter. We have enough eggs for our own use, and some to sell besides—I guess there won't be any to sell *this* week, will there? You'll like James's wife, I'm sure, Austin, and you, too, Mr. Stevens—she's a nice, healthy, jolly girl with good sense, I'm sure. She's not as pretty as my girls, but, then, few are, of course, in my eyes. It's plain to see they just set their eye-teeth by each other—Sadie and James, I mean— and, of course, Fred is about most of the time; so with two pairs of lovers, it keeps things lively, I can tell you."

"Has Thomas recovered?" inquired Austin.

"Indeed, he hasn't! It's mean of us all to make fun of him—he's very much in earnest."

"How does Sylvia take it?" asked Sylvia's uncle.

"I don't think she notices."

"Oh, don't you?" said Mr. Stevens, in the same interested tone he had used before.

Mrs. Gray was standing in the door to receive them, even if it was twenty below zero, and was laughing and crying with her great boy in her arms before he was half out of the sleigh. The kissing that had taken place at the Fessendens' was nothing to that which now occurred at the Grays'; for when he had finished with his mother, Austin found all his sisters waiting for him, clamoring for the same welcome, and he ended with his new sister-in-law, and then began all over again. Meanwhile Mr. Stevens stood looking vainly about, and finally interrupted with "Where's *my* girl?"

"Oh, *there*, Mr. Stevens!" exclaimed Mrs. Gray, wiping her eyes, and settling her hair, "it was downright careless of me not to tell you right away, but I was so excited over Austin that I forgot all about it for a minute; of course, it's a dreadful disappointment to you, but it just couldn't seem to be helped. Frank—my son-in-law, you know, that lives in White Water—telephoned down this morning that the trained nurse had left, an' little Elsie was ailin', an' the hired girl so green, an' nothin' would do but that Sylvia must traipse up there to help Ruth before I could say 'Jack Robinson.' "

"What do you mean?" thundered Uncle Mat and Austin in the same breath; so Mrs. Gray tried again.

"Why, Ruth had a new baby a month ago, another little girl, an' the dearest child! They're all comin' home to-morrow, sure's the world, an' you'll see her then—they've named her Mary, for me, an' of course I'm real pleased. But as I was sayin'—it did seem as if some one had got to take hold an' help them get straightened out if they was goin' to put it through, an' of course, there's no one like Sylvia for jobs like that. Land! I don't know how we ever got along before she come! Anyway, she's up there now. Rode up with Hiram on the Rural Free Delivery—he was tickled most to death. She left her love, an' said maybe one of the boys would take the pair an' her big double sleigh, an' start up to get 'em all in real good season to-morrow mornin'."

"That means me, of course," said Thomas importantly.

"Of course," echoed both his brothers, quite unanimously.

Mr. Stevens said nothing, but calmly went up to bed, where he apparently slept well, as he did not reappear until after nine o'clock the following morning. He sought out Mrs. Gray in the sunny, shining kitchen, but did not evince as much surprise as she had expected when she told him, while she bustled about preparing fresh coffee and toast for him, that when Thomas, at seven o'clock, had gone to the barn to "hitch up" he had found that the double sleigh, the pair, and—Austin had all mysteriously vanished.

"Austin always was a dreadful tease," she ended, "but I can't help sayin' this is downright mean of him, when he knows how Thomas feels."

"My dear lady," said Mr. Stevens, cracking open the egg she had set before him with great care, "where are your eyes? What about Austin himself?"

Mrs. Gray set down the coffee-pot, looking at him in

bewilderment. "What do you mean?" she asked. "I hope Austin is grateful to her now—an' that he'll *say* so. At first he didn't like her at all, an' he's never taken to her same as the rest of us have—seems to feel she's bossy an' meddlesome. Howard an' I have spoken of it a thousand times. He began by resenting everything she did, an' then got so he didn't even mention her name."

"Exactly. I've noticed that myself. I don't pretend to be an infallible judge of human nature, but mark my words, Austin has cared for my Sylvia since the first moment he ever set eyes on her. No man likes to feel that the woman he's in love with is doing everything for him and his family, and that he can't—as he sees it—do anything in return. That's why he seems to resent her kindness, which I really think the rest of you have almost overestimated—if she's helped you in material ways, you've been her salvation in greater ways still. But there's still more to it than that: I think your son Austin has in him the makings of one of the finest men I ever knew, but he doesn't consider himself worthy of her. He'll try to conceal, and even to conquer, his feelings—just as long as he possibly can. I suppose he believes that'll be always. Of course, it won't. But naturally he can't bear to talk about her. Thomas has fallen in love with her face—which is pretty—and her manner—which is charming—after the manner of most men. But Austin has fallen in love with her mind—which is brilliant—and her soul—which, in spite of some little superficial faults that I believe he himself will unconsciously teach her to overcome, is beautiful—after the manner of very few men—and those men love but once, deeply and forever. And so, my dear Mrs. Gray, tease Thomas all you like, for

Sylvia will refuse Thomas when he asks for her, and he will be engaged to another girl within a year; but she will run away from Austin before he brings himself to tell her how he feels—and it will be many a long day before his heart is light again."

CHAPTER VIII

"I FAIRLY dread to have Christmas come for one reason," had said Mrs. Gray to her husband beforehand.

"Why? I thought you were counting the days!"

"So I am. But I hate to think of all the presents Sylvia's likely to load us down with. Seems as if she'd done enough. I don't want to be beholden to her for any more."

"Don't worry, Mary. Sylvia's got good sense, and delicate feelings as well as an almighty generous little heart. She'll be the first to think how we'd feel, herself."

Mr. Gray was right. When Christmas came there was a simple, inexpensive trinket for each of the girls, and slightly costlier ones for the bride and Mrs. Gray; little pocket calendars, all just alike, for the men; that was all. Mr. Stevens had taken pleasure in bringing great baskets of candy, adorned with elaborate bows of ribbon, and bunches of violets as big as their heads, to all the "children," a fine plant to Mrs. Gray, and books to Howard and his sons; and Austin's suit-case bulged with all sorts of little treasures, which tumbled out from between his clothes in the most unexpected places, as he unpacked it in the living-room, to the great delight of them all.

"Here's a dress-length of gray silk from Venice for

mother," he said, tossing the shimmering bundle into her lap; "I want her to have it made up to wear at Sally's wedding. And here's lace for Sadie and Sally both—the bride and the bride-to-be. Nothing much for the rest of you"—and out came strings of corals and beads, handkerchiefs and photographs, silk stockings and filagree work, until the floor was strewn with pretty things. After all the presents were distributed, it was time to begin to get dinner, and to decorate the great table laid for sixteen. There was a turkey, of course, and a huge chicken pie as well, not to mention mince pies and squash pies and apple pies, a plum pudding and vanilla ice-cream; angel cakes and fruit cakes and chocolate cakes; coffee and cider and blackberry cordial; and after they had all eaten until they could not hold another mouthful, and had "rested up" a little, Sylvia played while they danced the Virginia Reel, Mr. Stevens leading off with Mrs. Gray, and Mr. Gray with Sadie. And finally they all gathered around the piano and sang the good old carols, until it was time for the Elliotts to go home, and for Ruth to carry the sleepy babies up to bed.

Since early fall it had been Sylvia's custom to sit with the family for a time after the early supper was over, and the "dishes done up"; then she went to her own parlor, lighted her open fire, and sat down by herself to read or write letters. But she always left her door wide open, and it was understood that any one who wished to come to her was welcome. Austin was the last to start to bed on Christmas night, and seeing Sylvia still at her desk as he passed her room, he stopped and asked:

"Is it too late, or are you too tired and busy to let me come in for a few minutes?"

She glanced at the clock, smiling. "It isn't very late, I'm not a bit tired, and in a minute I shan't be too busy; I've been working over some stupid documents that I was bound to get through with to-night, but I'm all done now. Throw that rubbish into the fire for me, will you?" she continued, pointing to a pile of torn-up letters and printed matter, "and draw up two chairs in front of the fire. I'll join you in a minute."

He obeyed, then stood watching her as she straightened out her silver desk fixtures, gravely putting everything in perfect order before she turned to him.

"What a beau cavalier you have become," she said, smiling again, as he drew back to let her pass in front of him, and turned her chair to an angle at which the fire could not scorch her face; "what's become of the old Austin? I can't seem to find him at all!"

"Oh, I left him in the woods the night of the fire, I hope," returned Austin, laughing, "while you were asleep. I'm sure neither you nor any one else wants him back."

Sylvia settled herself comfortably, and smoothed out the folds of her dull-black silk dress. "Wouldn't you like to smoke?" she asked; "it's an awfully comfortable feeling —to watch a man smoking, in front of an open fire!"

"I'd love to, if you're sure you don't mind. I don't want to make the air in here heavy—for I suppose you've got to sleep here on this sofa, having allowed yourself to be turned out of your good bed."

She laughed. "I'm so small that I can curl up and sleep on almost anything, like a kitten," she said. "And its fine to think of being able to give my room to James and Sadie—they're so nice, and so happy together. I can open the windows wide for a few minutes after you've gone, and there won't be a trace of tobacco smoke left. If there were, I shouldn't mind it. Now, what is it, Austin?"

"I want to talk. I haven't seen you a single minute alone. And though the others are all interested, it isn't like telling things to a person who's done all the wonderful things and seen all the wonderful places that I just have. I've simply got to let loose on some one."

"Of course, you have. I thought that was it. Talk away, but not too loud. We mustn't disturb the others, who are all trying to go to sleep by this time. Tell me—which of the Italian cities did you like best—Rome—or Florence— or Naples?"

"Will you think me awfully queer if I say none of them, but after Venice, the little ones, like Assisi, Perugia, and Sienna. I'm so glad we took the time for them. Oh, *Sylvia*—" And he was off. The little clock on the mantel struck several times, unnoticed by either of them, and it was after one, when, glancing inadvertently at it, Austin sprang to his feet, apologizing for having kept her awake so long, and hastily bade her good-night.

"May I come again some evening and talk more?" he asked, with his hand on the door-handle, "or have I bored and tired you to death? You're a wonderful listener."

"Come as often as you like—I've been learning things, too, that I want to tell you about."

"For instance?"

"Oh, how to cook and sweep and sew—and how to be well and happy and at peace," she added in a lower voice. Then, speaking lightly again, "We'll try to keep up that French you've worked so hard at, together—I'm dreadfully out of practice, myself—and read some of Browning's Italian poems, if you would care to. Good-night, and again, Merry Christmas."

He left her, almost in a daze of excitement and happiness; and mounted the stairs, turning over everything that had been said and done during the two hours since he entered her room. As he reached the top, a sudden suspicion shot through him. He stopped short, almost breathlessly, then stood for several moments as if uncertain what to do, the suspicion gaining ground with every second; then suddenly, unable to bear the suspense it had created, ran down the stairs again. Sylvia's door was closed; he knocked.

"All right, just a minute," came the ready answer. A minute later the door was thrown open, and Sylvia stood in it, wrapped in a white satin dressing-gown edged with soft fur, her dark hair falling over her shoulders, her neck and arms bare. She drew back, the quick red color flooding her cheeks.

"*Austin!*" she exclaimed; "I never thought of your coming back—I supposed, of course, it was one of the girls. I can't—you mustn't—" But Sylvia was too much mistress of herself and woman of the world to remain embarrassed long in any situation. She recovered herself before Austin did.

"What has happened?" she asked quickly; "is any one ill?"

"No—Sylvia—what were those papers you gave me to burn?"

"Waste—rubbish. Go to bed, Austin, and don't frighten me out of my wits again by coming and asking me silly questions."

"What kind of waste paper? Please be a little more explicit."

"How did you happen to come back to ask me such a thing—what made you think of it?"

"I don't know—I just did. Tell me instantly, please."

"Don't dictate to me—the last time you did you were sorry."

"Yes—and you were sorry that you didn't listen to me, weren't you?"

"No!" she cried, "I wasn't—not in the end. If I hadn't gone out to ride that day, you never would have gone to Europe—and come back the man you have!"

She turned away from him, her eyes full of tears, her voice shaking. He was quite at a loss to understand her emotion, almost too excited himself to notice it; but he could not help being conscious of the tensity of the moment. He spoke more gently.

"Sylvia—don't think me presuming—I don't mean it that way; and you and I mustn't quarrel again. But I believe I have a right to ask what that document you gave me to burn up was. If you'll give me your word of honor that I haven't—I can only beg your forgiveness for having intruded upon you, and for my rudeness in speaking as I did."

She turned again slowly, and faced him. He wondered if it was the unshed tears that made her eyes so soft.

"You have a right," she said, "and *I* shouldn't have spoken as I did. You were fair, and I wasn't, as usual. I'll tell you. And will you promise me just to—to give this little slip of paper to your father—and never refer to the matter again, or let him?"

"I promise."

"Well, then," she went on hurriedly, "about a month ago I bought the mortgage on this farm. It seemed to me the only thing that stood in the way of your prosperity now—it hung around your father's neck like a millstone— just the thought that he couldn't feel that this wonderful old place was wholly his, the last years of his life, and that he couldn't leave it intact for you and Thomas and your children after you when he died. So I made up my mind it should be destroyed to-day, as my real Christmas present to you all. The transfer papers were all properly made out and recorded—this little memorandum will show you when and where. But Hiram Hutt's title to the property, and mine—and all the correspondence about them—are in that fireplace. That burden was too heavy for your father to carry—thank God, I've been the one to help lift it!"

In the moment of electrified silence that followed, Sylvia misinterpreted Austin's silence, just as he had failed to understand her tears. She came nearer to him, holding out her hands.

"Please don't be angry," she whispered; "I'll never give any of you anything again, if you don't want me to. I know you don't want—and you don't need—charity; but you did need and want—some one to help just a little— when things had been going badly with you for so long that it seemed as if they never could go right again. You'd lost your grip because there didn't seem to be anything to hang on to! It's meant new courage and hope and *life* to me to be able to stay here—I'd lost my grip, too. I don't think I could have held on much longer—to my *reason* even—if I hadn't had this respite. If I can accept all that from you, can't you accept the clear title to a few acres from me? Austin—don't stand there looking at me like that—tell me I haven't presumed too far."

"What made you think I was angry?" he said hoarsely. "Do men dare to be angry with angels sent from Heaven?" He took the little slip of paper which she still held in her extended hand. "I thought you had done something like this—that was why you made me burn the papers myself—in the name of my father—and of my children—God bless you." Without taking his eyes off her face, he drew a tiny box from his pocket. "Sylvia—would you take a present from *me*?"

"Why, yes. What—"

"It isn't really a present at all, of course, for it was bought with your money, and perhaps you won't like it, for I've noticed you never wear any jewelry. But I couldn't bear to come home without a single thing for you—and this represents—what you've been to me."

As he spoke, he slipped into her hand a delicate chain of gold, on which hung a tiny star; she turned it over two or three times without speaking, and her eyes filled with tears again. Then she said:

"It *is* a present, for this means you travelled third-class, and stayed at cheap hotels, and went without your lunches—or you couldn't have bought it. You had only enough money for the trip we originally planned, without those six weeks in Italy. I'll wear *this* piece of jewelry—and it will represent what *you've* been to *me*, in my mind. Will you put it on yourself?"

She held it towards him, bending forward, her head down. It seemed to Austin that her loveliness was like the fragrance of a flower. Involuntarily, the hands which clasped the little chain around her white throat, touching the warm, soft skin, fell to her shoulders, and drew her closer.

The swift and terrible change that went over Sylvia's face sent a thrust of horror through him. She shut her eyes, and shrank away, trembling all over, her face grown ashy white. Instantly he realized that the gesture must have recalled to her some ghastly experience in the past; that perhaps she had more than once been tricked into an embrace by a gift; that a man's love had meant but one thing to her, and that she now thought herself face to face with that thing again, from one whom she had helped and trusted. For an instant the grief with which this realization filled him, the fresh compassion for all she had suffered, the renewed love for all her goodness, were too much for him. He tried to speak, to take away his hands, to leave her. He seemed to be powerless. Then, blessedly, the realization of what he should do came to him.

"Open your eyes, Sylvia," he commanded.

Too startled to disobey, she did so. He looked into them for a full minute, smiling, and shook his head.

"You did not understand, dear lady," he said. And dropping on his knees before her, he took her hands, laid them against his cheek for a minute, touched them with his lips, and left her.

CHAPTER IX

UNCLE MAT made a determined effort to persuade Sylvia to return to New York with him; and though he was not successful, he was not altogether discouraged by her reply.

"I *have* been thinking of it," she said, "but I promised Mrs. Gray I'd stay here through the winter, and she'd be hurt and disappointed now if I didn't; besides, I don't feel quite ready for New York myself yet. I realize that I've remained—nearly long enough—and as soon as the warm weather comes, I'm going to have my own little house remodelled and put in order, and move there for the summer. It'll be such fun—just like doll's housekeeping! Then in the fall—I won't promise—but perhaps if you still want me, I'll come to you, at least until I decide what to do next."

"Come now for a visit, if you won't for the rest of the winter."

"Not yet; by spring I'm afraid I'll have to have some new clothes—I've had nothing since I came here except a fur coat, which arrived by parcel post! Sally wants to go away in the Easter vacation, and if you can squeeze us both into your little guest-room, perhaps we'll come together then."

"You're determined to have some sort of a bodyguard in the shape of your new friends to protect you from your old ones?"

"Not quite that. I'll come alone if you prefer it," said Sylvia quickly.

"No, no, my dear; I should be glad to have Sally. How about Austin, too? He could sleep on the living-room sofa, you know, and that would make four of us to go about together, which is always a pleasant number. Thomas would be home at that time, and Austin could probably leave more easily than at any other."

"Ask him by all means. I think he would be glad to go."

Austin was accordingly invited, and accepted with enthusiasm. Uncle Mat found him in the barn, where he was separating cream with the new electric separator, but he nodded, with a smile which showed all his white teeth, as his voice could not be heard above the noise of the machine.

"Indeed, I will," he said heartily, when the current was switched off again. "How unfortunate that Easter comes so late this year—but that will give us all the longer to look forward to it in! I hate to have you go back, Mr. Stevens, but I suppose the inevitable call of the siren city is too much for your easily tempted nature!"

Mr. Stevens laughed, and assented. "How that boy has changed!" he said to himself as he walked back to the house. "He fairly radiates enthusiasm and wholesomeness. Well, I'm sorry for him. I wish Sylvia would leave now instead of in the spring, in spite of her promises and scruples and what-not. And I wish, darn it all, that she were as easy to read as he is."

Austin's existence, just at that time, seemed even more rose-colored than Uncle Mat could suspect. The day after Christmas he pondered for a long time on the events of the night before, and gave some very anxious thought to his future line of conduct. At first he decided that it would be best to avoid Sylvia altogether, and thus show her that she had nothing to dread from him, for her sudden fear had been very hard to bear; but before night another and wiser course presented itself to him—the idea of going on exactly as if nothing had happened that was in the least extraordinary, and prove to her that he was to be trusted. Accordingly, assuming a calmness which he was very far from feeling, he stopped at her door again before going upstairs, saying cheerfully:

"Tell me to go away if you want to; if not, I've come for my first French lesson."

Sylvia looked up with a smile from the book she was reading. "Entrez, monsieur," she said gayly; "avez-vous apporté votre livre, votre cahier, et votre plume? Comment va l'oncle de votre ami? Le chat de votre mère, est-il noir?"

Austin burst out laughing at her mimicry of the typical conversation in a beginner's grammar, and she joined him. The critical moment had passed. He saw that he was welcome, that he had risen and not fallen in her regard, though he was far from guessing how much, and opening his book, drew another chair near the fire and sat down beside her.

"You must have some romances as well as this dry stuff," she said, when he had pegged away at Chardenal for over an hour. "We'll read Dumas together, beginning with the Valois romances, and going straight along in the proper order. You'll learn a lot of history, as well as considerable French. Some of it is rather indiscreet but—"

"Which of us do you think it is most likely to shock?" he asked, with such an expression of mock-alarm that they both burst out laughing again; and when they had sobered down, "Now may we have some Browning, please?"

So Sylvia reached for a volume from her shelf, and began to read aloud, while Austin smoked; she read extremely well, and she loved it. She went from "The Last Duchess" to "The Statue and the Bust," from "Fra Filippo Lippi" to "Andrea del Sarto." And Austin sat before the fire, smoking and listening, until the little clock again roused them to consciousness by striking twelve.

"This will never do!" he exclaimed, jumping up. "I must have regular hours, like any schoolboy. What do you say to Monday, Wednesday, and Friday evenings, from seven-thirty to ten? The other nights I'll bend my energies to preparing my lessons."

"A capital idea. Good-night, Austin."

"Good-night, Sylvia."

There were, however, no more French lessons that week. The next evening twenty young people went off together in sleighs, got their supper at White Water, danced there until midnight, and did not reach home until three in the morning. The following night there was a "show" in Wallacetown, and although they had all declared at their respective breakfast-tables—for breakfast is served anywhere from five-thirty to six-thirty in Hamstead, Vermont—that nothing would keep them out of bed after supper *that* night, off they all went again. A

94

"ball" followed the "show," and the memory of the first sleigh-ride proved so agreeable that another was undertaken. And finally, on New Year's Eve the Grays themselves gave a party, opening wide the doors of the fine old house for the first time in many years. Sylvia played for the others to dance on this occasion, as she had done at Christmas, but in the rest of the merry-making she naturally could take no part. Austin, however, proved the most enthusiastic reveller of all, put through his work like chain lightning, and was out and off before the plodding Thomas had fairly begun. Manlike, it did not occur to him to give up any of these festivities because Sylvia could not join in them. For years he had hungered and thirsted, as most boys do, for "a good time"—and done so in vain. For years his work had seemed so endless and yet so futile—for what was it all leading to?— that it had been heartlessly and hopelessly done, and when it was finished, it had left him so weary that he had no spirit for anything else much of the time. Now the old order had, indeed, changed, yielding place to new. Good looks, good health, and a good mind he had always possessed, but they had availed him little, as they have many another person, until good courage and high ideals had been added to them. He scarcely saw Sylvia for several days, and did not even realize it, they seemed so full and so delightful; then coming out of the house early one afternoon intending to go to the barn to do some little odd jobs of cleaning up, he met her, coming towards him on snowshoes, her cheeks glowing, and her eyes sparkling. She waved her hand and hurried towards him.

"Oh, *Austin!* Are you awfully busy?"

"No, not at all. Why?"

"I've just been over to my house, for the first time—you know in the fall, I couldn't walk, and then I lost the key, and—well, one thing after another has kept me away—lately the deep snow. But these last few days I got to thinking about it—you've all been gone so much I've been alone, you see—so I decided to try getting there on snow-shoes—just think of having a house that's so quiet that there isn't even a *road* to it any more! It was quite a tramp, but I made it and went in, and, oh! it's so *wonderful*—so exactly like what I hoped it was going to be—that I hurried back to see if you wouldn't come and see it too, and let me tell you everything I'm planning to do to it?"

She stopped, entirely out of breath. In a flash, Austin realized, first, that she had been lonely and neglected in the midst of the good times that all the others had been having; realized, too, that he had never before seen her so full of vitality and enthusiasm; and then, that, without being even conscious of it, she had come instinctively to him to share her new-found joy, while he had almost forgotten her in his. He was not sufficiently versed in the study of human nature to know that it has always been thus with men and women, since Eve tried to share her apple with Adam and only got blamed for her pains. Austin blamed himself, bitterly and resentfully, and decided afresh that he was the most utterly ungrateful and unworthy of men. His reflections made him slow in answering.

"Don't you *want* to come?"

"Of course I want to come! I was just thinking—wait a second, I'll get my snowshoes."

"I'm going to tear down a partition," she went on

96

excitedly as they ploughed through the snow together, "and have one big living-room on the left of the front door; on the right of it a big bedroom—I've always *pined* for a downstairs bedroom—I don't know why, but I never had one till I came to your house—with a bathroom and dressing-room behind it; the dining-room and kitchen will be in the ell. I'm sure I can make that unfinished attic into three more bedrooms, and another bathroom, but I want to see what you think. I'm going to have a great deep piazza all around it, and a flower-garden—and—"

She could hardly wait to get there. Her enthusiasm was contagious. Austin soon found himself making suggestions, helping her in her plans. They went through every nook and corner of the tiny cottage; he had not dreamed that it possessed the possibilities that Sylvia immediately found in it. They stayed a long time, and walked home over fields of snow which the sinking sun was turning rosy in its glowing light. That evening Austin came for his lesson again.

By the second of January, the last of the visitors had gone, and the old Gray place was restored to the order and quiet which had reigned before the holidays began. Mrs. Gray was lonely, but her mind was at ease. She had been watching Austin closely, and it seemed quite clear to her that Uncle Mat was mistaken about him. The idea that her favorite son was going to be made unhappy was quickly dismissed; and in her rejoicing over the first payment on their debt at the bank, and in the new position of importance and consequence which her husband was beginning to occupy in the neighborhood, it was soon completely forgotten. The succeeding months seemed to prove her right; and the all-absorbing interest in the family was Mr. Gray's election to the Presidency of the Coöperative Creamery Association of Hamstead, and his probable chances of being nominated as First Selectman —in place of Silas Jones, recently deceased—at March Town Meeting.

CHAPTER X

WALLACETOWN, the railroad centre which lay five miles south of Hamstead across the Connecticut River, was generally regarded by the agricultural community in its vicinity as a den of iniquity. This opinion was not deserved. Wallacetown was progressive and prosperous; its high school ranked with the best in the State, its shops were excellent, its buildings, both public and private, neat and attractive. There were several reasons, however, for the "slams" which its neighbors gave it. Its population, instead of being composed largely of farmers, the sons, grandsons, and great-grandsons of the "old families" who had first settled the valley, was made up of railway employees and officials, and of merchants who had come there at a later date. Close team-work between them and the dwellers in Hamstead, White Water, and other villages near at hand, would have worked out for the advantage of both. But unfortunately they did not realize this. Wallacetown was also the only town in the vicinity where a man "could raise a thirst" as Austin put it, Vermont being "dry," and New Hampshire, at this time, "local option." Probably, from the earliest era, young men have been thirsty, and their parents have bemoaned the fact. It is not hard to imagine Eve wringing her hands over Cain and Abel when they first sampled generously the beverage they had made from the purple grapes which grew so plentifully near the Garden of Eden. Wallacetown also offered "balls," not occasionally, but two or three times a week. The Elks Hall, the Opera House, and even the Parish House were constantly being thrown open, and a local orchestra flourished. These "balls" were usually quite as innocent as those that took place in larger cities, under more elegant and exclusive surroundings; but the stricter Methodists and Congregationalists of the countryside did not believe in dancing at all, especially when there might be a "ginger-ale highball" or a glass of ale connected with it. Besides, there were two poolrooms and a wide street paved with asphalt, and brilliantly lighted down both sides. Trains ran—and stopped—by night as well as by day, and Sundays as well as week-days. In short, Wallacetown was up-to-date. That alone, in the eyes of Hamstead, was enough to condemn it. And when an enterprising citizen opened a Moving-Picture Palace, and promptly made an enormous success of it, Mrs. Elliott could no longer restrain herself.

"It's something scandalous," she declared, "to see the boys an' girls who would be goin' to Christian Endeavor or Epworth League if they'd ben brought up right, crowdin' 'round the entrance doors lookin' at the posters, an' payin' out good money that ought to go into the missionary boxes for the heathen in the Sandwich Islands, to go an' see filums of wimmen without half enough clothes on. We read in the *Wallacetown Bugle* that there was goin' to be a picture called 'The Serpent of the Nile' an' Joe an' I thought we could risk that, it sounded kinder geographical an' instructive. Of course we went mostly to see the new buildin' an' who else would be there, anyway. But land! the serpent was a girl dressed in the main in beads an' a pleasant smile. She loafed around on hard-lookin' sofas that was set right out in the open air, an' seemed to have more beaux than wimmen-friends. I'm always suspicious of that kind of a woman. I wanted to leave right away, as soon as I see what it was goin' to be like, but Joe wouldn't. He wanted to set right there until it was over. He seemed to feel afraid some one might see us comin' out, an' that maybe we better stay until the very end, so's we wouldn't be noticed, slippin' out with the crowd.—Have you took cold, Sylvia? You seem to have a real bad cough."

Sylvia, who had been sewing peacefully beside the sunny kitchen window filled with geraniums, rose hastily, and left Mrs. Gray alone with her friend. Having gained the hall in safety, she sank down on the stairs, and laughed until the tears rolled down her cheeks. And here Austin, coming in a moment later, found her.

"What on earth—?" he began, and then, without even pursuing his question, sat down beside her and joined in her laugh. "What would you do?" he said at last, when some semblance of order had been restored, "without Mrs. Elliott? Considering the quiet life you lead, you must be simply pining for amusement."

"I am," said Sylvia. "Austin—let's go to the movies in Wallacetown to-morrow night."

Austin, suddenly grave, shook his head. "Shows" in Wallacetown were associated in his mind with a period in his life when he had very nearly broken his mother's heart, and which he had now put definitely behind him.

101

The idea of connecting Sylvia, even in the most remote way, with that period, was abhorrent to him.

"Why not?" she asked defiantly.

"Well, for one thing, the roads are awful. This combination in March of melting snow and mud is worse than anything I know of—ruts and holes and slush. It would take us over an hour to get there."

"And three to get back, I suppose," said Sylvia pertly; "we could go in my motor."

"I haven't taken out the new license for this year yet. Besides, though I believe the movies are very good for a place the size of Wallacetown, of course, they can't be equal to what you'll be seeing in New York pretty soon. Wait and go there."

"I won't!" said Sylvia, springing up. "I'll get Thomas to take me. You always have some excuse when I want you to do anything. Why don't you say right out that you don't care to go?"

Sylvia expected denials and protestations. She was disappointed. Thomas had arrived home for his long spring vacation a few days before, and had promptly begun to follow Sylvia about like a shadow. Austin, who never sought her out except for his French lessons, had endeavored to remonstrate with his younger brother. The boy flared up, with such unusual and unreasonable anger, that Austin had decided it was wiser not to try to spare him any longer, but to let "him make a fool of himself and have it over with." When Sylvia made her tart speech, it suddenly flashed through his mind that a ten-mile ride, without possibility of interruption, was an excellent opportunity for this. He therefore grinned so cheerfully that Sylvia was more puzzled and piqued than ever.

"I'm sure Thomas would be tickled to death to take you," he said enthusiastically; "I'll get the car registered the first thing in the morning, and he can spend the afternoon washing and oiling it. It really needs a pretty thorough going-over. It'll do my heart good to see him in his old clothes for once. He seems to have entirely overlooked the fact that he was to spend this vacation being pretty useful on the farm, and not sighing at your heels dressed in the height of fashion as he understands it. He's wearing out the mat in front of the bureau, he stands there so much, and I've hardly had a chance for a shave or a tub since he got here. He locks himself in the bathroom and spends hours manicuring his nails and putting bay-rum on his hair. He— All right, I won't if you say so! But, Sylvia, you ought to make a real spree of this, and go in to the drug-store for an ice-cream soda after the show."

"Is that the usual thing?"

"It's the most usual thing that I should recommend to you. Of course, there are others—"

"Austin, you are really getting to be the limit. Go tell Thomas I want him."

"With pleasure. I haven't," murmured Austin, "had a chance to tell him that so far. He's never been far enough off—except when he was getting ready to come. That's probably what he's doing now. I'll go upstairs and see."

Austin had guessed right. Thomas stood in front of the mirror, shining with cleanliness, knotting a red silk tie. He had reached that stage in a young man's life when clothes were temporarily of supreme importance. Gone was the shy and shabby ploughboy of a year before. This self-assertive young gentleman was clad in a checked

103

suit in which green was a predominating color, a black-and-white striped shirt, and chocolate-colored shoes. His hair, still dripping with moisture, was brushed straight back from his forehead and the smell of perfumed soap hung heavy about him.

"Hullo," he said, eyeing his brother's intrusion with disfavor, "how dirty you are!"

Austin, whose khaki and corduroy garments made him look more than ever like a splendid bronze statue, nodded cheerfully.

"I know. But some one's got to work. We can't have two lilies of the field on the same farm.—Sylvia wants to speak to you."

"Do you know why?" asked Thomas, promptly displaying more dispatch.

"I think she intends to suggest that you should take her to the moving-pictures in Wallacetown to-morrow night. She doesn't get much amusement here, and now that she's feeling so much stronger again, I think she rather craves it."

"Of course she does," said Thomas, "and if you weren't the most selfish, pig-headed, blind bat that ever flew, you'd have seen that she got it, long before this. Where is she?"

It seemed to the impatient Thomas that the next evening would never arrive. All night, and all the next day, he planned for it exultantly. He was to have the chance which the ungrateful Austin had seen fit to cast away. He would show Sylvia how much he appreciated it. Through the long afternoon, suddenly grown unseasonably warm, he toiled on the motor until it was spick and span from top to bottom and from end to end. He was careful to start his labors early enough to allow a full hour to dress before supper, cautioned his mother a dozen times to be sure there was enough hot water left in the boiler for a deep bath, and laid out fresh and gorgeous garments on the bed before he began his ablutions. He was amazed to find, when he came downstairs, that Sylvia, who had tramped over to the brick cottage that afternoon, was still in the short muddy skirt and woolly sweater that she had worn then, poking around in the yard testing the earth for possibilities of early gardening.

"The frost has come out a good deal to-day," she said, wiping grimy little hands on an equally grimy handkerchief; "I expect the mud will be awful these next few weeks, but I can get in sweet peas and ever-bearing strawberries pretty soon now."

"We'll have to start right after supper," said Thomas, by way of a delicate hint. He did not feel that it was proper for him to suggest to Sylvia that her present costume was scarcely suitable to wear if she were to accompany him to a "show."

"Start?" Sylvia looked puzzled. Then she remembered that in a moment of pique with Austin she had arranged to go to Wallacetown with Thomas. As she thought it over, it appealed to her less and less. "You mean to Wallacetown? I'm afraid I'd forgotten all about it, I've been so busy to-day. I wonder if we'd better try it? The warmth to-day won't have improved the roads any, and they were pretty bad before."

Thomas felt as if he should choke. That she should treat so casually the evening towards which he had been counting the moments for twenty-four hours seemed almost unbearable. He strove, however, to maintain his dignified composure.

"Just as you say, of course," he replied with hurt coolness.

Sylvia glanced at him covertly, and the corners of her mouth twitched.

"I suppose we may as well try it," she said. "Do you suppose some of the others would like to come with us? There's plenty of room for everybody."

Again Thomas choked. This was the last thing that he desired. How was he to disclose to Sylvia the wonderful secret that he adored her with the whole family sitting on the back seat?

"I don't believe they could get ready now," he said; "they didn't know you expected them to go, you see, and there's really awfully little time." He took out his watch.

Sylvia fled. Twenty minutes later she appeared at the supper-table, clad in a soft black lace dress, slightly low in the neck, her arms only partially concealed by transparent, flowing sleeves, her waving hair coiled about her head like a crown. She had on no jewels—only the little star that Austin had given her—and the gown was the sort of demi-toilette which two years before she would have considered hardly elaborate enough for dinner alone in her own house. To the Grays, however, her costume represented the zenith of elegance, and Thomas began vaguely to feel that there was something the matter with his own appearance.

"Ought I to have put on my dress-suit?" he asked Austin in a stage-whisper, as Sylvia left the room to get her wraps.

The mere thought of a dress-suit at the Wallacetown "movies" was comic to the last degree, but the merciless Austin jumped at the suggestion.

"Why don't you? You won't be very late if you change quickly. You won't need to take another bath, will you? I'll bring round the car."

He showed himself, indeed, all that was helpful and amiable. He not only brought around the car, he went up and helped Thomas with stubborn studs and a refractory tie. He stood respectfully aside to let his brother wrap Sylvia's coat around her, and held open the door of the car.

"Have a good time!" he shouted after them, as they plunged out of sight, somewhat jerkily, for Thomas, who had not driven a great deal, was not a master of gear-shifting. His mother looked at him anxiously.

"I can't help feelin' you're up to some deviltry, Austin," she said uneasily, "though I don't know just what 'tis. I'm kinder nervous about this plan of them goin' off to Wallacetown."

"I'm not," said Austin with a wicked grin, and took out his French dictionary.

The first part of the evening, however, seemed to indicate that Mrs. Gray's fears were groundless. Sylvia and Thomas reached the Moving-Picture Palace without mishap, though they had left the Homestead so late owing to the latter's change of attire and the slow rate at which the mud and his lack of skill had obliged them to ride, that the audience was already assembled, and "The Terror of the Plains," a stirring tale of an imaginary West, was in full progress before they were seated. Thomas's dress-suit did not fail to attract immediate attention and

107

equally immediate remarks, and Sylvia, who hated to be conspicuous, felt her cheeks beginning to burn. But— more sincerely than Mr. Elliott—she decided that it was better to wait until the entertainment was over than to attract further notice by going out at once. Thomas, less sensitive than she, enjoyed himself thoroughly.

"We have splendid pictures in Burlington," he announced, "but this is good for a place of this size, isn't it, Sylvia?"

"Yes. Don't talk so loudly."

"I can't talk any softer and have you hear unless I put my head up closer. Can I?"

"Of course, you may not. Don't be so silly."

"I didn't mean to be fresh. You're not cross, are you, Sylvia?"

It seemed to her as if the "show" would never end. Chagrin and resentment overcame her. What had possessed her to come to this hot, stuffy place with Thomas, instead of reading French in her peaceful, pleasant sitting-room with Austin? Why didn't Austin show more eagerness to be with her, anyway? She liked to be with him—ever and ever so much—didn't see half so much of him as she wanted to. There was no use beating about the bush. It was perfectly true. She was growing fonder of him, and more dependent on him, every day. And every other man she had ever known had been grateful for her least favor, while he— Her hurt pride seemed to stifle her. She was very close to tears. She was jerked back to composure by the happy voice of Thomas.

"My, but that was a thriller! Come on over to the drugstore, Sylvia, and have an ice-cream cone."

"I'm not hungry," said Sylvia, rising, "and it must

be getting awfully late. I'd rather go straight home."

Thomas, though disappointed, saw no choice. But once off the brilliantly lighted "Main Street," and lumbering down the road towards Hamstead, he decided not to put off the great moment, for which he had been waiting, any longer. Wondering why his stomach seemed to be caving in so, he tactfully began.

"Did you know I was going to be twenty-one next month, Sylvia?" he asked.

"No," said Sylvia absently; "that is, I had forgotten. You seem more like eighteen to me."

This was a somewhat crushing beginning. But Thomas was not daunted.

"I suppose that is because I was older than most when I went to college," he said cheerfully, "but though you're a little bit older, I'm nearer your age than any of the others—much nearer than Austin. Had you ever thought of that?"

"No," said Sylvia again, still more absently. "Why should I? I feel about a thousand."

"Well, you *look* about sixteen! Honest, Sylvia, no one would guess you're a day over that, you're so pretty. Has any one ever told you how pretty you are?"

"Well, it has been mentioned," said Sylvia dryly, "but I have always thought that it was one of those things that was greatly overestimated."

"Why, it couldn't be! You're perfectly lovely! There isn't a girl in Burlington that can hold a candle to you. I've been going out, socially, a lot all winter, and I know. I've been to hops and whist-parties and church-suppers. The girls over there have made quite a little of me, Sylvia, but I've never—"

There was a deafening report. Thomas, cursing inwardly, interrupted himself.

"We must have had a blow-out," he said, bringing the car to a noisy stop. "Wait a second, while I get out and see."

It was all too true. A large nail had passed straight through one of the front tires. He stripped off his ulster, and the coat of his dress-suit, and turned up his immaculate trousers.

"You'll have to get up for a minute, while I get the tools from under the seat, Sylvia. I'm awfully sorry.— It's pretty dark, isn't it?—I never changed a tire but once before. Austin's always done that."

"Austin's always done almost everything," snapped Sylvia. Then, peering around to the back of the car, "Why don't *you do* something? What *is* the matter now?"

"The lock on the extra wheel's rusted—you see it hasn't been undone all winter. I can't get it off."

"Well, *smash* it, then! We can't stay here all night."

"I haven't got anything to smash it *with*. I must have forgotten to put part of the tools back when I cleaned the car."

"Oh, Thomas, you are the most *inefficient* boy about everything except farming that I ever saw! Let me see if I can't help."

She jumped out, her feet, clad in silk stockings and satin slippers, sinking into the mud as she did so. Together for fifteen minutes, rapidly growing hot and angry, they wrestled with the refractory lock. At the end of that time they were no nearer success than they had been in the beginning.

"We'll have to crawl home on a flat tire," she said at

last disgustedly; "I hope we'll get there for breakfast."

Thomas had never seen her temper ruffled before. Her imperiousness was always sweet, and it was Heaven to be dictated to by her. The fact that he believed her to be comparing him in her mind to Austin did not help matters. Austin, as he knew very well, would have managed some way to get that tire changed. For some time they rode along in silence, the mud churning up on either side of the guards with every rod that they advanced. At last, realizing that his precious moments were slipping rapidly away, and that though, in Sylvia's present mood, it was hardly a favorable time to go on with his declaration, the morrow would be even less so, Thomas summoned up his courage once more.

"Is your back tired?" he asked. "It's awfully jolty, going over these ruts. I could steer all right with one hand, if you would let me put my other arm around you."

"You're not steering any too well as it is," remarked Sylvia tartly. "*Thomas!* What are you thinking of? Don't you touch me!—There, now you've done it!"

Thomas certainly had "done it." Sylvia, at his first movement, had slapped him in the face with no gentle tap. And Thomas, with only one hand on the wheel, and too amazed to keep his wits about him, had allowed the car to slide down the side of the road into the deep, muddy gutter, straight in front of the Elliotts' house.

Late as it was, a light was snapped on in the entrance without delay. Electricity had been installed here before any other place in the village had been blessed with it, for the owners never missed a chance of seeing anything, and Mrs. Elliott seemed to sleep with one eye and one ear open. She appeared now in the doorway, dressed

111

in a long, gray flannel "wrapper," her hair securely fastened in metal clasps all about her head, against the "crimps" for the next day.

"Who is it?" she cried sharply—"and what do you want?"

Of all persons in the world, this was the last one whom either Sylvia or Thomas desired to see. Neither answered. Nothing dismayed, Mrs. Elliott advanced down the walk. Her carpet-slippers flapped as she came.

"Come on, Joe," she called over her shoulder to her less intrepid spouse. "Are you goin' to leave me alone to face these desperate drunkards, lurchin' around in the dead of night, an' makin' the road unsafe for doctors who might be out on some errand of mercy—they're the only *respectable* people who wouldn't be abed at this hour of the night. You better get right to the telephone, an' notify Jack Weston. He ain't much of a police officer, to be sure, but I guess he can deal with bums like these—too stewed to answer me, even!" Then, as she drew nearer, she gave a shriek that might well have been heard almost as far off as Wallacetown, "Land of mercy! It's Sylvia an' Thomas!"

Thomas cowered. No other word could express it. But Sylvia got out, slamming the door behind her.

"We've been to Wallacetown to a moving-picture show," she said with a dignity which she was very far from feeling, "and we've been unfortunate in having tire-trouble on the way home. And now we seem to be stuck in the mud. I had no idea the roads were in such a condition, or of course I shouldn't have gone. We can't possibly pry the motor up in this darkness, so I think we may as well leave it where it is, first as last until morning, and walk the rest of the way home. Come on, Thomas."

"I wouldn't ha' b'lieved," said Mrs. Elliott severely, "that you would ha' done such a thing. Prayer-meetin' night, too! Well, it's fortunate no one seen you but me an' Joe. If I was gossipy, like some, it would be all over town in no time, but you know I never open my lips. But, land sakes! here comes a *team*. Who can this be?"

Eagerly she peered out through the darkness. Then she turned again to the unfortunate pair.

"It's Austin in the carryall," she cried excitedly; "now, ain't that a piece of luck? You won't have to walk home, after all. Though what *he's* out for, either, at this hour—"

Austin reined in his horse. "Because I knew Sylvia and Thomas must have got into some difficulty," he said quietly. Considering the pitch at which it had been uttered, it had not been hard to overhear Mrs. Elliott's speech. "Pretty bad travelling, wasn't it? I'm sorry. Tires, too? Well, that was hard luck. But we'll be home in no time now, and of course the show was worth it. You didn't hurt your dress-suit any, did you, Thomas? I worried a little about that. You drive—I'll get in on the back seat with Sylvia, and make sure the robe's tucked around her all right. It seems to be coming off cold again, doesn't it? Good-night, Mrs. Elliott—thank you for your sympathy."

Conversation languished. Austin, unseen by the miserable Thomas on the front seat, and unreproved by the weary and chilly Sylvia, "tucked the robe around her" and then, apparently, forgot to take his arm away. Moreover, he searched in the darkness for her small, cold fingers, and gathered them into his free hand, which was warm and big and strong. As they neared the house, he spoke to her.

"The next time you want to go to 'a show' I guess I'd better take you myself, after all," he whispered. "You'll find a hot-water bag in your bed, and hot lemonade in the thermos bottle on the little table beside it. I put a small 'stick' in it—oh, just a twig! And I've kept the kitchen fire up. The water in the tank's almost boiling, if you happen to feel like a good tub—"

He helped her out, and held open the front door for her gravely. Then, closing it behind her, he turned to Thomas.

"You'd better run along, too," he said, with a slight drawl; "I'll put the horse up."

"Oh, go to hell!" sobbed Thomas.

CHAPTER XI

"So you refused Weston's offer of three hundred dollars for Frieda?"

"Yes, father. Do you think I was wrong?"

"Well, I don't know. That's a good deal of money, Austin."

"I know, but think what she cost to import, and the record she's making! I told him he might have two of the brand-new bull calves at seventy-five apiece."

"What did he say?"

"Jumped at the chance. He's coming *for* the calves, and *with* the cash early to-morrow morning. I said he might have a look at Dorothy, too. Peter thinks she isn't quite up to our standard, and I'm inclined to agree with him, though I imagine his opinion is based partly on the fact that she's a Jersey! If Weston will give three hundred for *her,* right on the spot, I think we'd better let her go."

"Did you do any other special business in Wallace-town?"

"I took ten dozen more eggs to Hassan's Grocery, and he paid me for the last two months. Thirty dollars. Pretty good, but we ought to do better yet, though, of course, we eat a great many ourselves. How's the tax assessing coming along? I suppose you've been out all day, too."

"Yes. I'm so green at it I find it rather hard work. It's hard luck that both of the listers should be sick just now, though in New Hampshire the selectmen always have to do the assessing. But I've had some funny experiences to-day. I found one woman terribly distressed because her husband wasn't at home 'He waited 'round all yesterday afternoon for you, thinkin' you'd probably be here,' she said, 'but he's gone to White Water to-day.' 'Well,' I said, 'let's see if we can't get along just as well without him. Have you a horse?' 'Yes, but he's over age—he can't be taxed.' 'Any cows?' 'Just two heifers—they're too young.' 'Any money on deposit?' 'Lord, no!' 'Then there's only the poll-tax?' I suggested. 'Bless you, he's seventy-six years old—there ain't no poll-tax!' she rejoined. And the long and short of it was that they weren't taxable for a single thing!"

Austin laughed. "How much longer are you going to be at this, father?" he asked, as he turned to go away.

"All through April, I'm afraid. I'm sorry it makes things so much harder for you on the farm, Austin, but it means three dollars a day. I'm so glad Katherine and Edith could go on the high school trip to Washington—your mother had her first letter this noon. You'll want to read it—they're having a wonderful time. I'm trying to figure out whether we can possibly let Katherine go to Wellesley next year. She's got her heart just set on it, and Edith seems perfectly willing to stay at home, so we shan't be put to any extra expense for her."

"I guess when the time comes we can find a way to help Katherine if she helps herself as much as Thomas and Molly are doing. By the way, has it occurred to you

116

that there may be some reason for Edith's sudden turn towards domesticity?"

"Why, no—what do you mean?"

"Peter."

"Peter!" echoed Mr. Gray, aghast; "why the child isn't seventeen yet, and he can't be more than a couple of years older!"

"I know. But such things do sometimes happen."

"You don't consider Peter a suitable match for one of your sisters?" went on the horrified father; "why, she's oceans above him."

"Any farther than Sylvia is above Thomas? You seem to be taking that rather hard."

For Thomas, in spite of Austin's warnings, and his chastening experience on the night of the expedition to the Moving-Picture Palace, had broken bounds again and openly declared himself. Sylvia, who already reproached herself for her ill-temper on that occasion, was very kind and very sweet, and had the tact and wisdom not to treat the matter as a joke; but she was as definite and firm in her "no" as she was considerate in the way she put it. Thomas was as usual quite unable to conceal his feelings, and his parents were grieving for him almost as much as he was for himself, although they had never expected any other outcome to his first love-affair, and were somewhat amazed at his presumption.

"You never thought of this yourself," went on the bewildered parent, ignoring Austin's last remark, feeling that his children were treating him most unfairly by indulging in so many affairs of the heart which could not possibly have a fortunate outcome. "I haven't noticed a thing, and I'm sure your mother hasn't, or she would

117

have spoken about it to me. Why, Edith's hardly out of her cradle."

"It would take a pretty flexible cradle to hold Edith nowadays," returned Austin dryly; "she's running around all over the countryside, and she has more partners at a dance than all the other girls put together. She isn't as nice as Molly, or half so interesting as Katherine, but she has a little way with her that—well, I don't know just *what* it is, but I see the attraction myself. I thought I'd tell you so that if you didn't like it, we could try to scrimp a little harder, and send her off for a year or so, too—she never could get into college, but she might go to some school of Domestic Science. No—I didn't notice Peter's state of mind myself at first."

"Sylvia!" said his father sharply. "She didn't approve, of course."

"On the contrary, very highly. She says that the sooner a girl of Edith's type is married—to the right sort of a man, of course—the better, and I'm inclined to think that she's right. Then she pointed out that Peter had gone doggedly to school all winter, struggling with a foreign language, and enduring the gibes he gets from being in a class with boys much younger than himself, with very good grace. She mentioned how faithful and competent he was in his work, and how interested in it; asked if I had noticed the excellency of his handwriting, his accounts—and his manners! And finally she said that a boy who would promise his mother to go to church once a fortnight at least, and keep the promise, was doing pretty well."

"Speaking of church," said Mr. Gray uneasily, as if forced to agree with all Austin said, yet anxious to change the subject, "Mr. Jessup is calling. He comes pretty frequently."

"Yes—I had noticed *that* for myself! I don't think Sylvia particularly likes it."

"Then I imagine she can stop it without much outside help," said his father, somewhat ruefully. "Well, we must get to work, and not sit here talking all the rest of the afternoon—not that there's so very much afternoon left! What are you going to do next, Austin?"

"Change my clothes, and then start burning the rubbish-pile—there's a good moon, so I can finish it after the milking's done."

"That means you'll be up until midnight—and you were out in the barn at five!" exclaimed Mr. Gray. "I don't see where you get all your energy."

"From ambition!" laughed Austin, starting away. "This is going to be the finest farm in the county again, if I have anything to do about it." As he entered the house, and went through the hall, he could hear voices in Sylvia's parlor, and though the door was ajar, he went past it, contrary to his custom. His father was right. If she did not like the minister's visits, she was quite competent to stop them without outside help. Was it possible—*could* it be?—that she *did* like them? He flung off his business clothes and got into his overalls with a sort of savage haste—after all, what difference ought it to make to him whether she liked them or not? She was going away almost immediately, would inevitably marry some one before very long, Mr. Jessup at least held a dignified position and possessed a good education, and if she married him, she would come back to Hamstead, they could see her once in a while— Having tried to comfort

119

himself with these cheering reflections, he started down the stairs, inwardly cursing. Then he heard something which made him stop short.

"Please go away," Sylvia was saying, in the low, penetrating voice he knew so well, "and I think it would be better if you didn't come any more. How dare you speak to me like that! And how can a clergyman so lose his sense of dignity as to behave like any common fortune-hunter?"

Austin pushed open the door without stopping to knock, and walked in.

"Good-afternoon, Mr. Jessup," he said coolly, "my father told me we were having the pleasure of a call from you. I'm just going out to milk—won't you come with me, and see the cattle? They're really a fine sight, tied up ready for the night."

Mr. Jessup picked up his hat, and Austin held the door open for him to pass out, leaving Sylvia standing, an erect, scornful little black figure, with very red cheeks, her angry eyes growing rapidly soft as she looked straight past the minister at Austin.

The results of Mr. Jessup's visit were several. The most immediate one was that Austin's work was so delayed by the interruption it received that it was nearly nine o'clock before he was able to start his bonfire. Thomas joined him, but after an hour declared he was too sleepy to work another minute, and strolled off to bed. Austin's next visitor was his father, who merely came to see how things were getting along and to say good-night. And finally, when he had settled down to a period of laborious solitude, he was amazed to see Sylvia open and shut the front door very quietly, and come towards him in the moonlight, carrying a white bundle so large that she could hardly manage it.

"For Heaven's sake!" he exclaimed, hurrying to help her, "you ought to have been asleep hours ago! What have you got here?"

"Something to add to your bonfire," she said savagely, and as he took the great package from her, the white wrapping fell open, showing the contents to be inky black. "All the crêpe I own! I won't wear it another day! I've been respectful to death—even if I couldn't be to the dead—and to convention long enough. I've swathed myself in that stuff for nearly fifteen months! I won't be such a hypocrite as to wear it another day! And if Thomas—and—and—Mr. Jessup and—and everybody—are going to pester the life out of me, I might just as well be in New York as here. I'm glad I'm going away."

"No one else is going to pester you," said Austin quietly, "and they won't any more. But you'll have a good time in New York—I think it's fine that you're going." He tossed the bundle into the very midst of the burning pile, and tried to speak lightly, pretending not to notice the excitement of her manner and the undried tears on her flushed cheeks. "I think you're just right about that stuff, too. Will this mean all sorts of fluffy pink and blue things, like what Flora Little wears? I should think you would look great in them!"

"No—but it means lots and lots of pure white dresses and plain black suits and hats, without any crêpe. Then in the fall, lavender, and gray, and so on."

"I see—a gradual improvement. Won't you sit down a few minutes? It's a wonderful night."

"Thank you. Austin—you and Sally will have to help

121

me shop when I get to New York—Heaven knows what I can wear to travel down in."

Austin stopped raking, and flung himself down on the grass beside her. "Sylvia," he said quickly, "I'm awfully sorry, but I can't go."

"Can't go! Why not?" she exclaimed, with so much disappointment in her voice that he was amazed.

"Father's a selectman now, you know, and away all day just at this time on town business. There's too much farmwork for Thomas and Peter to manage alone. I didn't foresee this, of course, when I accepted your uncle's invitation. I can't tell you how much it means to me to give it up, but you must see that I've got to."

"Yes, I see," she said gravely, and sat silently for some minutes, fingering the frill on her sleeve. Then she went on: "Uncle Mat wants me to stay a month or six weeks with him, and I think I ought to, after deserting him for so long. When I come back, my own little house will be ready for me, and it will be warm enough for me to move in there, so I think these last few days will be 'good-bye.' Your family has let me stay a year—the happiest year of all my life—and I know your mother loves me —almost as much as I love her—and hates to have me go. But all families are better off by themselves, and in one way I think I've stayed too long already."

"You mean Thomas?"

She nodded, her eyes full of tears. "I ought to have gone before it happened," she said penitently; "any woman with a grain of sense can usually see that—that sort of thing coming, and ward it off beforehand. But I didn't think he was quite so serious, or expect it quite so soon."

"The young donkey! To annoy you so!"

"*Annoy* me! Surely you don't think *Thomas* was thinking of the money?"

"Good Lord, no, it never entered his head! Neither did it enter his head what an unpardonable piece of presumption it was on his part to ask you to marry him. A great, ignorant, overgrown, farmer boy!"

"You are mistaken," said Sylvia quietly; "I do not love Thomas, but if I did, the answer would have had to be 'no' just the same. The presumption would be all on my part, if I allowed any clean, wholesome, honest boy, in a moment of passion, to throw away his life on a woman like me. Thomas must marry a girl, as fresh as he is himself—not a woman with a past like mine behind her."

For nearly a year Austin had exercised a good deal of self-control for a man little trained in that valuable quality. At Sylvia's speech it gave way suddenly, and without warning. Entirely forgetting his resolution never to touch her, he leaned forward, seizing her arm, and speaking vehemently.

"I wish you would get rid of your false, gloomy thoughts about yourself as easily as you have got rid of your false, gloomy clothing," he said, passionately. "The mother and husband who made your life what it was are both where they can never hurt you again. Your character they never did touch, except in the most superficial way. When you told me your story, that night in the woods, you tried to make me think that you did voluntarily—what you did. You lied to me. I thought so then. I know it now. You were flattered and bullied, cajoled and coerced—a girl scarcely older than my sister Edith, whom we consider a child, whose father is distressed to even think of her as marriageable. It is time to stop feeling repentance for sins you never committed, and to look at yourself sanely and happily—if you must be introspective at all. No braver, lovelier, purer woman ever lived, or one more obviously intended to be a wife and mother. The sooner you become both, the better."

There was a moment of tense silence. Sylvia made no effort to draw away from him; at last she asked, in a voice which was almost pleading in its quality:

"Is that what you think of me?"

Austin dropped his hand. "Good God, Sylvia!" he said hoarsely; "don't you know by this time what I think of you?"

"Then you mean—that you want me to marry you?"

"No, no, no!" he cried. "Why are you so bound to misunderstand and misjudge me? I beg you not to ride by yourself, and you tell me I am 'dictating.' I go for months without hearing from you for fear of annoying you, and you accuse me of 'indifference.' I bring you a gift as a vassal might have done to his liege lady—and you shrink away from me in terror. I try to show you what manner of woman you really are, and you believe that I am displaying the same presumption which I have just condemned in my own brother. Are you so warped and embittered by one experience—a horrible one, but, thank Heaven, quickly and safely over with!—that you cannot believe me when I tell you that the best part of a decent man's love is not passion, but reverence? His greatest desire, not possession, but protection? His ultimate aim, not gratification, but sacrifice?"

He bent over her. She was sitting quite motionless, her head bowed, her face hidden in her hands; she was trembling from head to foot. He put his arm around her.

"Don't!" he said, his voice breaking; "don't, Sylvia. I've been rough and violent—lost my grip on myself— but it's all over now—I give you my word of honor that it is. Please lift your head up, and tell me that you forgive me!" He waited until it seemed as if his very reason would leave him if she did not answer him; then at last she dropped her hands, and raised her head. The moon shone full on her upturned face, and the look that Austin saw there was not one of forgiveness, but of something so much greater that he caught his breath before she moved or spoke to him.

"Are you blind?" she whispered. "Can't you see how I have felt—since Christmas night, even if you couldn't long before that? Don't you know why I just couldn't go away? But I thought you didn't care for me—that you couldn't possibly have kept away from me so long if you did—that you thought I wasn't good enough— Oh, my dear, my dear—" She laid both hands on his shoulders.

The next instant she was in his arms, his lips against hers, all the sorrow and bitterness of their lives lost forever in the glory of their first kiss.

CHAPTER XII

WHEN, two days later, Sylvia and Sally left for New York, none of the Grays had been told, much less had they suspected, what had happened. A certain new shyness, which Austin found very attractive, had come over Sylvia, and she seemed to wish to keep their engagement a secret for a time, and also to keep to her plan of going away, with the added reason that she now "wanted a chance to think things over."

"To think whether you really love me?" asked Austin gravely.

"Haven't I convinced you that I don't need to think that over any more?" she said, with a look and a blush that expressed so much that the conversation was near to being abruptly ended.

Austin controlled himself, however, and merely said: "I'm going down to our little cemetery this afternoon to put it in good order for the spring; I know you've always said you didn't want to go there, but perhaps you'll feel differently now. All the Grays are buried there, and no one else, and in spite of all the other things we've neglected, we've kept that as it should be kept; and it's so peaceful and pretty—always shady in summer, when it's hot, and sheltered in winter, when it's cold! I thought you could take a blanket and a book, and sit and read while I worked. Afterwards we can walk over to your house if you like—you may want to give me some final directions about the work that's to be done there while you're gone."

"I'd love to go to the cemetery—or anywhere else, for that matter—with you," said Sylvia, "and afterwards—to *our* house. Perhaps you'll want to give some directions yourself!"

The tiny graveyard lay in the hollow of one of the wooded slopes which broke the great, undulating meadow which stretched from the Homestead to the river, a wall made of the stones picked up on the place around it, a plain granite shaft erected by the first Gray in the centre, and grouped about the shaft the quaint tablets of the century before, with old-fashioned names spelled in an old-fashioned manner, and with homely rhymes and trite sayings underneath; farther off, the newer gravestones, more ornate and less appealing. The elms were just beginning to bud, and the cold April wind whistled through them, but the pines were as green and sheltering as always, and Sylvia spread her blanket under one of them, and worked away at the sewing she had brought instead of a book, while Austin burned the grass and dug and pruned, whistling under his breath all the time. He stopped once to call her attention to a robin, the first they had seen that spring, and finally, when the sacred little place was in perfect order, came with a handful of trailing arbutus for her, and sat down beside her.

"I thought I remembered seeing some of this on the bank," he said; "it's always grown there—will you take

127

it for your 'bouquet des fiançailles,' Sylvia? I remember how surprised we all were last year because you liked the little wild flowers best, and went around searching for them, when your rooms were full of carnations and hothouse roses. And because you used to go out to walk, just to see the sunsets. Do you still love sunsets, too?"

"Yes, more than ever. In the fall while you were gone, I used to go down to the river nearly every afternoon, and watch the color spread over the fields. There's something about a sunset in the late autumn that's unlike those at any other time of year—have you ever noticed? It's not rosy, but a deep, deep golden yellow—spreading over the dull, bare earth like the glory from the diadem of a saint—one of those gray Fathers of early Italy, for instance."

"I know what you mean—but they seem to me more like the glory that comes into any dull, bare life," said Austin,—"the kind of glory you've been to me. It worries me to hear you say you want to go away to 'think things over.' What is there to think over—if you're sure you care?"

"There are lots of details to a thing of this sort."

"A thing of what sort?"

"Oh, Austin, how stupid you are! A—a marriage, of course."

"I thought all that was necessary were two willing victims, a license, and a parson."

"Well, there's a good deal more to it than that. Besides, your family would surely guess if I stayed here. I want to keep it just to ourselves for a little while."

"I see. It's all right, dear. Take all the time you want."

"What would you tell them, anyway?" she went on lightly,—"that I proposed to you, and that you accepted me? Or, to be more exact, that you didn't accept me, but said, 'No, no, no!' most decidedly, and went on repeating it, with variations, until I threw myself into your arms? It was an awful blow to my pride—considering that heretofore I've certainly had my fair share of attention, and even a little more than that—to have to do *all* the lovemaking, and I'm certainly not going to go brag about it—" This time the conversation really did get interrupted, for Austin would not for one instant submit to such a "garbling of statistics" and took the quickest means in his power to put an end to it.

He had the wisdom, however, greater, perhaps, than might have been expected, not to oppose any of her wishes just then, and it was Sylvia herself who at the last minute felt her heart beginning to fail her, and called him to the farther end of the station platform, on the pretext of consulting him about some baggage.

"I don't see how I can say good-bye—in just an ordinary way," she whispered, "and I'm beginning to miss you dreadfully already. If I can't stand it, away from you, you must arrange to come down for at least a day or two."

It was beginning to sprinkle, and, taking her umbrella, he opened it and handed it to her, leaning forward and kissing her as soon as she was hidden by it.

"I never meant to say good-bye 'in an ordinary way,'" he said cheerfully, "whatever your intentions were! And, of course, I'll manage to come to town for a day or two, if you find you really want me. Fred would be glad to help me out for that long, I'm sure. On the other hand,

129

if it's a relief to be rid of me for a while, and New York looks pretty good to you, don't hurry back— you've been away for a whole year, remember. I'll understand."

In spite of his cheerful words and matter-of-course manner, Austin stood watching the train go out with a heavy heart. He was very sincere in feeling that his presumption had been great, and that he had taken advantage of feelings which mere youth and loneliness might have awakened in Sylvia, and from which she would recover as soon as she was with her own friends again. And yet he loved her so dearly that it was hard— even though he acknowledged that it was best—to let her go back to the world by whose standards he felt he fell short in every way.

"If I lose her," he said to himself, "I must remember that—of course I ought to. King Cophetua and the beggar maid makes a very pretty story—but it doesn't sound so well the other way around. And then she's given me such a tremendous amount already—if I never get any more, I must be thankful for that."

Sally spent a rapturous week in New York, and came home with her modest trousseau all bought and glowing accounts of the good times she had had.

"The very first thing Sylvia did, the morning after we got there," she said, "was to buy a new limousine and hire a man to run it. My, you ought to see it! It's lined with pearl gray, and Sylvia keeps a gold vase with orchids—fresh ones every day—in it! She helped me choose all my things, and I never could have got half so much for my money, or had half such pretty things if she hadn't; and she began right off to get the most *elegant* clothes for herself, too! I knew Sylvia was pretty, but I never knew *how* pretty until I saw her in a low-necked white dress! We went to the theatre almost every evening, and saw all the sights, besides—it didn't take long to get around in that automobile, I can tell you! Perfect rafts of people kept coming to see her all the time, telling her how glad they were to see her back, and teasing her to do things with them. I bet she'll get married again in no time—there were *dozens* of men, all awfully rich and attractive and apparently just *crazy* about her! We went out twice to lunch, and once to dinner, at the grandest houses I ever even imagined, and every one was lovely to me, too, but of course it was only Sylvia they really cared about. I was about wild, I got so excited, but it didn't make any more impression on Sylvia than water rolling off a duck's back—she didn't seem the least bit different from when she was here, helping mother wash the supper dishes, and teaching Austin French. She took it all as a matter of course. I guess we didn't any of us realize how important she was."

"I did," said Austin.

"You!" exclaimed his sister, with withering scorn. "You've never been even civil to her, much less respectful or attentive! If you could see the way other men treat her—"

"I don't want to," said Austin, with more truth than his sister guessed.

A young, lovely, and agreeable widow, with a great deal of money, and no "impediments" in the way of either parents or children, is apt to find life made extremely pleasant for her by her friends; and every one felt, moreover, that "Sylvia had behaved so very well." For two months after her husband's death, she had lived in the greatest seclusion, too ill, too disillusioned and horror-stricken, too shattered in body and soul—as they all knew only too well—to see even her dearest friends. Then she had gone to the country, remaining there quietly for a year, regaining her health and spirits, and had now returned to her uncle's home, lightening her mourning, going out a little, taking up her old interests again one by one—a fitting and dignified prelude for a new establishment of her own. She could not help being pleased and gratified at the warmth of her reception; and she found, as Austin had predicted, that "New York looked pretty good to her." It is doubtful whether the taste for luxury, once acquired, is ever wholly lost, even though it may be temporarily cast aside; and Sylvia was too young and too human, as well as too healthy and happy again, not to enjoy herself very much, indeed.

For nearly a month she found each day so full and so delightful as it came, that she had no time to be lonely, and no thought of going away; but gradually she came to a realization of the fact that the days were *too* full; that there were no opportunities for resting and reading and "thinking things over"; that the quiet little dinners and luncheons of four and six, given in her honor, were gradually but surely becoming larger, more formal and more elaborate; that her circle of callers was no longer confined to her most intimate friends; that her telephone rang in and out of season; that the city was growing hot and dusty and tawdry, and that she herself was getting tired and nervous again. And when she waked one morning at eleven o'clock, after being up most of the night before, her head aching, her whole being weary and confused, it needed neither the insistent and disagreeable memory of a little incident of the previous evening, nor the letter from Austin that her maid brought in on her breakfast-tray, to make her realize that the tinsel of her gayety was getting tarnished.

DEAREST (the letter ran):

It is midnight, and—as you know—I am always up at five, but I must send you just a few words before I go to bed, for these last two days have been so full that it has seemed to be impossible to find a moment in which to write you. "Business is rushing" at the Gray Homestead these days, and everything going finely. The chickens and ducklings are all coming along well—about four hundred of them—and we've had three beautiful new heifer calves this week. Peter is beside himself with joy, for they're all Holsteins. I went to Wallacetown yesterday afternoon, and made another $200 payment on our note at the bank—at this rate we'll have that halfway behind us soon.

To-day I've been over at your house every minute that I could spare and succeeded in getting the last workman out—for good—at eight o'clock this evening. (I bribed him to stay overtime. There are a few little odd jobs left, but I can work those in myself in odd moments.) There is no reason now why you shouldn't begin to send furniture any time you like. I never would have believed that it would be possible to get three such good bedrooms—not to mention a bathroom and closets—out of the attic, or that tearing out partitions and unblocking fireplaces would work such wonders downstairs. It's all just as you planned it that first day we tramped over in the snow to see it—do you remember?—and it's all lovely, especially your bedroom on the right of the front door, and the big living-room on the left. The papers you chose are exactly right for the walls, and the white paint looks so fresh and clean, and I'm sure the piazza is deep enough to suit even you. I've ploughed and planted your flower- and vegetable-gardens, as well as those at the Homestead, and this warm, early spring is helping along the vegetation finely, so I think things will soon be coming up. We've decided to try both wheat and alfalfa as experiments this year, and I can hardly wait to see whether they'll turn out all right.

Katherine graduates from high school the eighteenth of June, and as Sally's teaching ends the same day, and Fred's patience has finally given out with a bang, she has fixed the twenty-fifth for her wedding. Won't she be busy, with just one week to get ready to be a bride, after she stops being a schoolmarm? But, of course, we'll all turn to and help her, and Molly will be home from the Conservatory ten days before that—you know how efficient she is. By the way, has she written you the good news about her scholarship? We may have a famous musician in the family yet, if some mere man doesn't step in and intervene. Speaking of lovers, Peter is teaching Edith Dutch! And when mother remonstrated with her, she flared up and asked if it was any different from having you teach me French! (I sometimes believe "the baby" is "onto us," though all the others are still entirely unsuspicious, and keep right on telling me I never half appreciated you!) So they spend a good deal of time

134

at the living-room table, with their heads rather close together, but I haven't yet heard Edith conversing fluently in that useful and musical foreign language which she is supposed to be acquiring.

I haven't had a letter from you in nearly a week, but I'm sure, if you weren't well and happy, Mr. Stevens would let us know. I'm glad you're having such a good time—you certainly deserve it after being cooped up so long. Sorry you think it isn't suitable for you to dance yet, for, of course, you would enjoy that a lot, but you can pretty soon, can't you?

Good-night, darling. God bless you always!

AUSTIN

There was something in the quiet, restrained tone of the letter, with its details of homely, everyday news, and the tidings of his care and interest in her little house, that touched Sylvia far more than many pages of passionate outpouring of loneliness and longing could have done. She knew that the loneliness and longing were there, even though he would not say so, and she turned from the great bunch of American Beauties which had also come in with her breakfast-tray, with something akin almost to disgust as she thought of Austin's tiny bunch of arbutus—his "bouquet des fiançailles," as he had called it—the only thing, besides the little star, that he had ever given her. She called her maid, and announced that in the future she would never be at home to a certain caller; then she reached for the telephone beside her bed and cancelled all her engagements for the next few days, on the plea of not feeling well, which was perfectly true; and then she called up Western Union, and dispatched a long telegram, after which she indulged in a comforting and salutary outburst of tears.

"It will serve me quite right if he won't come," she sobbed. "I wouldn't if I were he, not one step—and he's just as stubborn as I am. I never was half good enough for him, and now I've neglected him, and frittered away my time, and even flirted with other men—when I'd scratch out the eyes of any other woman if she dared to look at him. It's to be hoped that he doesn't find out what a frivolous, empty-headed, silly, vain little fool I am— though it probably would be better for him in the end if he did."

Sylvia passed a very unhappy day, as she richly deserved to do. For the woman who gives a man a new ideal to live for, and then, carelessly, herself falls short of the standard she has set for him, often does as great and incalculable harm as the woman who has no standards at all.

Uncle Mat received a distinct shock when he reached his apartment that night, to find that his niece, dressed in a severely plain black gown, was dining at home alone with him. Before he finished his soup he received another shock.

"Austin Gray is coming to New York," she said, coolly, buttering a cracker; "I have just had a telegram saying he will take a night train, and get in early in the morning —eight o'clock, I believe. I think I'll go and meet him at the station. Are you willing he should come here, and sleep on the living-room sofa, as you suggested once before, or shall I take him to a hotel?"

"Bring him here by all means," returned her bewildered relative; "I like that boy immensely. What streak of good luck is setting him loose? I thought he was tied hand and foot by bucolic occupations."

"Apparently he has found some means of escape," said Sylvia; "would you care to read aloud to me this evening?"

CHAPTER XIII

"Why, Sylvia, my dear! I never dreamed that you would come to meet me!"

Austin was, indeed, almost beside himself with surprise and delight when, as he left the train and walked down the long platform in the Grand Central Station, he saw Sylvia, dressed in pure white serge, standing near the gate. He waved his hat like a schoolboy, and hurried forward, setting down his suit-case to grip her hands in both of his.

"Have you had any breakfast?" she asked, as they started off.

"Yes, indeed, an hour ago."

"Then where would you like to go first? I have the motor here, and we're both entirely at your disposal."

He hesitated a moment, and then said, laughing, "It didn't occur to me that you'd come to the station, and I fully intended to go somewhere and get a hair-cut that wouldn't proclaim me as coming straight from Hamstead, Vermont, and replenish the wardrobe that looked so inexhaustible to me last fall, before I presented myself to you."

Sylvia joined in his laugh. "Go ahead. I'll sit in the

motor and wait for you. Afterwards we'll go shopping together."

"To buy things like these?" he asked, eyeing her costume with approval.

"No. I have enough clothes now. I was going to begin choosing our furniture—and thought you might be interested. Get in, dear, this is ours," she said, walking up to the limousine which Sally had described with such enthusiasm, and which now stood waiting for her, its door held open by a French chauffeur, who was smiling with true Gallic appreciation of his mistress's "affaire de cœur," "and here," she added, after they were comfortably seated inside, taking a gardenia from the flower-holder, "is a posy I've got for you."

"Thank you. Have you anything else?" he asked, folding his hand over hers as she pinned it on.

"Oh, Austin, you're such a funny lover!"

"Why?"

"Because you nearly always—ask beforehand. Why don't you take what you've a perfect right to—if you want it?"

"Possibly because I don't feel I have a perfect right to—or sure that I have any right at all," he answered gravely, "and I can't believe it's really real yet, anyway. You see, I only had two days with you—the new way—before you left, and I had no means of knowing when I should have any more—and a good deal of doubt as to whether I deserved any."

There was no reproach in the words at all, but so much genuine humility and patience that Sylvia realized more keenly than ever how selfish she had been.

"You'll make me cry if you talk to me like that!" she

139

said quickly. "Oh, Austin, I've countless things to say to you, but first of all I want to tell you that I'll never leave you like this again, that it's—just as real as *I am*, that you can have just as many days as you care to now, and that I'll spend them all showing you how much right you have!" And she threw her arms around his neck and drew his face down to hers, oblivious alike of André on the front seat and all the passing crowds on Fifth Avenue.

"Don't," Austin said after a moment. "We mustn't kiss each other like that when some one might see us—I forgot, for a minute, that there *was* any one else in the world! Besides, I'm afraid, if we do, I'll let myself go more than I mean to—it's all been stifled inside me so long—and be almost rough, and startle or hurt you. I couldn't bear to have that happen to you—again. I want you always to feel safe and shielded with me."

"Safe! I hope I'll be as safe in heaven as I am with you! Don't you think I know what you've been through this last year?"

"No, I don't," he said passionately; "I hope not, anyway. And that was before I ever touched you, besides. It's different now. I shan't kiss you again to-day, my dear, except"—raising her hand to his lips—"like this. Are you going to wait for me here?" he ended quietly, as the motor began to slow down in front of the Waldorf.

"No," she said, her voice trembling; "I'm going to church, 'to thank God, kneeling, for a good man's love.' Come for me there, when you're ready."

"Are you in earnest?"

"I never was more so."

He joined her at St. Bartholomew's an hour later, and

140

seeking her out, knelt beside her in the quiet, dim church, empty except for themselves. She felt for his hand, and gripping it hard, whispered with downcast eyes and flushed cheeks:

"Austin, I have a confession to make."

"Of course, you have—I knew that from the moment I got your telegram. Well, how bad is it?" he said, trying to make his voice sound as light as possible. But her courage had apparently failed her, for she did not answer, so at last he went on:

"You didn't miss me much, at first, did you? When you thought of me I seemed a little—not much, of course, but quite an important little—out of focus on the only horizon that your own world sees. Well, I knew that was bound to happen, and that if you really cared for me as much as you thought you did at the farm, it was just as well that it should—for you'd soon find out how much your own horizon had broadened and beautified. Don't blame yourself too much for that. I suppose the worst confession, however, is that something occurred to make you long, just a little, to have me with you again—just as you were glad to see me come into the room the last day our minister called. What was it?"

"Austin! How can you guess so much?"

"Because I care so much. Go on."

"People began to make love to me," she faltered, "and at first I did—like it. I—flirted just a little. Then—oh, Austin, don't make me tell you!"

"I never imagined," he said grimly, "that Thomas and Mr. Jessup were the only men who would ever look at you twice. I suppose I've got to expect that men are going to *try* to make love to you always—unless I lock

141

you up where no one but me can see you, and that doesn't seem very practical in this day and generation! But I don't see any reason—if you love me—why you should *let* them. You have certainly got to tell me, Sylvia."

"I will not, if you speak to me that way,". she flashed back. "Why should I? You wouldn't tell me all the foolish things you ever did!"

"Yes, Sylvia, I will," he said gravely, "as far as I can without incriminating anybody else—no man has a right to kiss—or do more than that—and tell, in such a way as to betray any woman—no matter what sort she is. Some of the things I've done wouldn't be pleasant, either to say or to hear; for a man who is as hopeless as I was before you came to us is often weak enough to be perilously near being wicked. But if you wish to be told, you have every right to. And so have I a right to an answer to my question. No one knows better than I do that I'm not worthy of you in any way. But you must think I am or you wouldn't marry me, and if you're going to be my wife, you've got to help me to keep you—as sacred to me as you are now. Shall I tell first, or will you? A church is a wonderful place for a confession, you know, and it would be much better to have it behind us."

"You needn't tell at all," she said, lifting her face and showing as she did so the tears rolling down her cheeks. "*Weak!* You're as strong as steel! If all men were like you, there wouldn't be anything for me to tell either. But they're not. The night before I telegraphed you, an old friend brought me home after a dinner and theatre party. We had all had an awfully gay time, and—well, I think it was a little *too* gay. This man wanted to marry me long ago, and I think, perhaps, I would have accepted him once—if he'd—had any money. But he didn't then— he's made a lot since. He began to pay me a good deal of attention again the instant I got back to New York, and I was glad to see him again, and— Of course, I ought to have told him about you right off, but some way, I didn't. I always liked him a lot, and I enjoyed—just having him round again. I thought that if he began to show signs of—getting restive—I could tell him I was engaged, and that would put an end to it. But he didn't show any signs—any *preliminary* signs, I mean, the way men usually do. He simply—suddenly broke loose on the way home that night, and when I refused him, he said most dreadful things to me, and—"

"Took you in his arms by force, and kissed you, in spite of yourself." Austin finished the sentence for her, speaking very quietly.

"Oh, Austin, *please* don't look at me like that! I couldn't help it!"

"Couldn't help it! No, I suppose you struggled and fought and called him all kinds of hard names, and then you sent for me, expecting me to go to him and do the same. Well, I shan't do anything of the sort. I think you were twice as much to blame as he was. And if you ever —let yourself in for such an experience again, I'll never kiss you again—that's perfectly certain."

"*Austin!*"

"Well, I mean it—just that. I don't know much about society, but I know something about women. There are women who are just plain bad, and women who are harmless enough, and attractive, in a way, but so cheap and tawdry that they never attract very deeply or very long, and women who are good as gold, but who haven't a particle of—allure—I don't know how else to put it—Emily Brown's one of them. Then there are women like you, who are fine, and pure, and—irresistibly lovely as well; who never do or say or even think anything that is indelicate, but whom no man can look at without—wanting—and who—consciously or unconsciously—I hope the latter—tempt him all the time. You apparently feel free to—play with fire—feeling sure you won't get even scorched yourself, and not caring a rap whether any one else gets burnt; and then you're awfully surprised and insulted and all that if the—the victim of the fire, in his first pain, turns on you. 'Said dreadful things to you'—I should think he would have, poor devil! Perhaps young girls don't realize; but a woman over twenty, especially if she's been married, has only herself to blame if a man loses his head. Were you sweet and tender and—*aloof,* just because you were sick and disgusted and disillusioned, instead of because that was the real *you*—are you going to prove true to your mother's training, after all, now that you're happy and well and safe again? If you have shown me heaven—only to prove to me that it was a mirage—you might much better have left me in what I knew was hell!"

He left her, so abruptly that she could not tell in which direction he had turned, nor at first believe that he had really gone. Then she knelt for what seemed to her like hours, the knowledge of the justice of all he had said growing clearer every minute, the grief that she had hurt him so growing more and more intolerable, the hopelessness of asking his forgiveness seeming greater and greater. It did not occur to her to try to find him, or to ex-

144

pect that he would come back—she must stay there until she could control her tears, and then she must go home. A few women, taking advantage of the blessed custom which keeps nearly all Anglican and Roman churches open all day for rest, meditation, and prayer, came in, stayed a few minutes, and left again. At eleven o'clock there was a short service, the daily Morning Prayer, sparsely attended. Sylvia knelt and stood, mechanically, with the other worshippers. Then suddenly, just before the benediction was pronounced, Austin slid into the seat beside her, and groped for her hand. Neither spoke, nor could have spoken; indeed, there seemed no need of words between them. A very great love is usually too powerful to brook the interference of a question of forgiveness. The clergyman's voice rose clear and comforting over them:

" 'The grace of our Lord Jesus Christ, and the love of God, and the fellowship of the Holy Ghost, be with us all ever more. Amen.' "

"Is there a flower-shop near here?" was the perfectly commonplace question Austin asked as they went down the church steps together into the spring sunshine.

"Yes, just a few steps away. Why?"

"I want to buy you some violets—the biggest bunch I can get."

"Aren't you rather extravagant?"

"Not at all. The truth is, I've come into a large fortune!"

"Austin! What do you mean?"

He evaded her question, smiling, bought her an enormous bouquet, and then suggested that if her destination was not too far away they should walk. She dismissed

the smiling André, and walked beside Austin in silence
for a few minutes hoping that he would explain without
being asked again.

"Did you say you were going to Tiffany's to buy furniture—I thought Tiffany's was a jewelry store, and in
the opposite direction?"

"It is. I'm going to the Tiffany Studios—quite a different place. Austin—don't tease me—do tell me what you
mean?"

"Why? Surely you're not marrying me for my money!"

"Good gracious, you plague like a little boy! Please!"

"Well, a great-aunt who lived in Seattle, and whom I
haven't seen in ten years, has died and left me all her
property!"

"How much?"

"Mercy, Sylvia, how mercenary you are! Enough so
you won't have to buy my cigars and shoe-strings—aren't
you glad?"

"Of course, but I wish you'd stop fooling and tell me
all about it."

"Well, I shan't—if I did you'd make fun of me, because it would seem so small to you, and I want to be
just as lavish and extravagant as I like with it all the
time I'm in New York—you'll have to let me 'treat' now!
And just think! I'll be able to pay my own expenses when
I take that trip to Syracuse which you seem to think is
going to complete my agricultural education. Peter's
going with me, and I imagine we'll be a cheerful couple!"

"How are things going in that quarter?"

"Rather rapidly, I imagine. I've given father one warning, and I shan't interfere again, bless their hearts! I

caught him kissing her on the back stairs the other night, but I walked straight on and pretended not to see."

"Thereby earning their everlasting gratitude, of course, poor babies!"

"How many years older than Edith are you?"

"Never mind, you saucy boy! Here we are—have you any suggestions you may not care to make before the clerks as to what kind of furniture I shall buy?"

"None at all. I want to see for myself how much sense you have in certain directions, and if I don't like your selections, I warn you beforehand that the offending articles will be used for kindling wood."

"Do be careful what you say. They know me here."

"Careful what *I* say! I shall be a regular wooden image. They'll think I'm your second cousin from Minnesota, being shown the sights."

He did, indeed, display such stony indifference, and maintain such an expression of stolid stupidity, that Sylvia could hardly keep her face straight, and having chosen a big sofa and a rug for her living-room, and her dining-room table, she announced that she "would come in again" and graciously departed.

"I have a good mind to shake you!" she said as they went down the steps. "I had no idea you were such a good actor—we'll have to get up some dramatics when we get home. Did you like my selections?"

"Very much, as far as they went. Where are you going now—I see that your grinning Frenchman and upholstered palace on wheels are waiting for you again."

"Well, I can't walk *all* day—I'm going to Macy's to buy kitchen-ware. You'd better do something else—I'm afraid you'll criticize my brooms and saucepans!"

"All right, go alone. I'm going to the real Tiffany's."

"What for?"

"To squander my fortune, Pauline Pry. I'll meet you at Sherry's at one-thirty. I suppose some kindly policeman will guide my faltering footsteps in the right direction. Good-bye." And he closed the door of the car in her radiant face.

They had a merry lunch an hour later, Austin ordering the meal and paying for it with such evident pleasure that Sylvia could not help being touched at his joy over his little legacy. Then he proposed that, although they were a little late, they might go to a matinée, and afterwards insisted on walking up Fifth Avenue and stopping for tea at the Plaza.

"I've seen more beautiful cities than New York," he said, as they sauntered along, much more slowly than most of the hurrying throng,—"Paris, for instance—fairly alive with loveliness! But I don't believe there's a place in the world that gives you the feeling of *power* that this does—especially just at this time of day, when the lights are coming on, and all these multitudes of people going home after their day's work or pleasure. It's tremendous —lifts you off your feet—do you know what I mean?"

They reached home a little after six, to find Uncle Mat, whose existence they had completely forgotten, waiting for them with his eyes glued to the clock.

"I was about to have the Hudson River dragged for you two," he said, as Austin wrung his hand and Sylvia kissed him penitently. "Where *have* you been? I came home to lunch, and made several appointments to introduce Austin to some very influential men, who I think would make valuable acquaintances for him. It's inex-

148

cusable, Sylvia, for you to monopolize him this way."

The happy culprits exchanged glances, and then Sylvia linked her arm in Austin's and got down on her knees, dragging him after her.

"I suppose we may as well confess," she said, "because you'd guess it inside of five minutes, anyway. Please don't be very angry with us."

"What *are* you talking about? Austin, can you explain? Has Sylvia taken leave of her senses?"

"I'm afraid so, sir," said Austin, with mock gravity; "it certainly looks that way. For about six weeks ago she told me that—some time in the dim future, of course—she might possibly be prevailed upon to marry me!"

Uncle Mat declared afterwards that this last shock was too much for him, and that he swooned away. But all that Austin and Sylvia could remember was that after a moment of electrified silence, he embraced them both, exclaiming, "Bless my stars! I never for one moment suspected that she had that much sense!"

CHAPTER XIV

"Are you two young idiots going out again this evening?" asked Uncle Mat as the three were eating their dessert, glancing from Sylvia's low-necked white gown to Austin's immaculate dress-suit.

"No. This is entirely in each other's honor. But I hope you are, for I want to talk to Austin."

"Good gracious! What have you been doing all day? What do you expect *me* to do?"

"You can go to your club and have five nice long rubbers of bridge," said Sylvia mercilessly, "and when you come back, please cough in the hall."

"I want to write a few lines to my mother, after I've had a little talk with Mr. Stevens—then I'm entirely at your disposal," said Austin, as she lighted their cigars and rose to leave them.

"I'm glad some one wants to talk to me," murmured Uncle Mat meekly.

Sylvia hugged him and kissed the top of his head. "You dear jealous old thing! I've got some telephoning and notes to attend to myself. Come and knock on my door when you're ready, Austin."

"You have a good deal of courage," remarked Uncle

Mat, nodding in Sylvia's direction as she went down the hall.

"Perhaps you think effrontery would be the better word."

"Not at all, my dear boy—you misunderstand me completely. Sylvia's the dearest thing in the world to me, and I've been worrying a good deal about her remarriage, which I knew was bound to come sooner or later. I'm more than satisfied and pleased at her choice—I'm relieved."

"Thank you. It's good to know you feel that way, even if I don't deserve it."

"You do deserve it. In speaking of courage, I meant that the poor husband of a rich wife always has a good deal to contend with; and aside from the money question, you're supersensitive about what you consider your lack of advantages and polish—though Heaven knows you don't need to be!" he added, glancing with satisfaction at the handsome, well-groomed figure stretched out before him. "I never saw any one pick up the veneer of good society, so called, as rapidly as you have. It shows that real good breeding was back of it all the time."

"I guess I'd better go and write my letter," laughed Austin, "before you flatter me into having an awfully swelled head. But I want to tell you first—I'm not a pauper any more. I've got twenty thousand dollars of my own—an old aunt has died and left most of her will in my favor. I've taken capital, and paid off all our debts—except what we owe to Sylvia. She can give me that for a wedding present if she wants to. It's queer how much less sore I am about her money now that I've got a little of my own! There are one or two things that I want to buy for her, and I want to pay my own expenses and Peter's on a trip through western New York farms this summer. The rest I must invest as well as I can, to bring me in a little regular income. I'm sure, now that the farm and the family are perfectly free of debt, that I can earn enough to add quite a little to it every year. If Sylvia lost every cent she had, we could get married just the same, and though she'd have to live simply and quietly, she wouldn't suffer. I thought you would help me with investments—or take me to some other man who would."

"I will, indeed—if you don't spend *all* your time, as Sylvia fully intends you shall, making love to her. This changes the outlook wonderfully—clears the sky for both of you! It's bad for a man to be wholly dependent on his wife, and scarcely less bad for her. But there's another matter—"

"Yes, sir?"

"I don't want you to think I'm meddling—or under-estimating Sylvia—"

"I won't think that, no matter what you say."

"How long have you and she been in love with each other? Wasn't it pretty nearly a case of 'first sight'?"

Austin flushed. "It certainly was with me," he said quietly.

"And haven't you—quarrelled from the very beginning, too?"

The boy's flush deepened. "Yes," he said, still more quietly, "we seemed to misunderstand—and antagonize each other."

"Even to-day?"— Then as Austin did not answer, "Now, tell me truthfully—whose fault is it?"

"The first time it was mine," said Austin quickly. "She

152

made me clean up the yard—it needed it, too!—and I was furious! And I was rude—worse than rude—to her for a long time. But since then—"

"You needn't be afraid to say it was hers," remarked Sylvia's uncle dryly. "She wants an absolutely free hand, which isn't good for her to have—she's only twenty-two now, pretty as a picture, and still absolutely inexperienced about many things. She can't bear the thought of dictation, and you're both young and self-willed and proud, and very much in love—which makes the whole thing harder, not easier, as I suppose you imagine. Now, some women, even in these days, aren't fit to live with until—figuratively speaking—they've been beaten over the head with a club. Sylvia's not that kind. She's not only got to respect her husband's wishes, she's got to *want* to—and I believe you can make her want to! I think you're absolutely just—and unusually decent. If I didn't I shouldn't dare say all this to you—or let you have her at all, if I could help it. And besides being fair, you know how to express yourself—which some poor fellows unfortunately can't do—they're absolutely tongue-tied. In fact, you're perfectly capable of taking things into your own hands every way, and making a success of it—and if you don't before you're married, neither of you can possibly hope to be happy afterwards."

"There's one thing you're overlooking, Mr. Stevens, which I should have had to tell you to-night, anyway."

"What is it?"

"I'm not worthy of tying up Sylvia's shoes—much less of marrying her. I've been straight as a string since she came to the farm, but before that—any one in Hamstead would tell you. It was town talk. I can't, knowing that, act as I would if I—didn't have that to remember. It's all very well to say that a man—*gets through* with all that, absolutely—I've heard them say it dozens of times! But how can he be sure he is through—that the old sins won't crop up again? I love Sylvia more than—than I can possibly talk about, and I'm *afraid*—afraid that I won't be worthy of her, and that if she gave in absolutely—that I'd abuse my position."

Uncle Mat glanced up quietly from his cigar. There were tears in the boy's eyes, his voice trembled. The older man, for a moment, felt powerless to speak before the penitent sincerity of Austin's confession, the humility of his bared soul.

"As long as you feel that way," he said at last, a trifle huskily, "I don't believe there's very much danger—for either of you. And remember this—lots of good people make mistakes, but if they're made of the right stuff, they don't make the same mistake but once. And sometimes they gain more than they lose from a slip-up. You certainly are made of the right stuff. Perhaps you will go through some experience like what you're dreading, though I can't foresee what form it will take. Meanwhile remember that Sylvia's been through an awful ordeal, and be very gentle with her, though you take the reins in your hands, as you should do. I'm thankful that she has such a bright prospect for happiness ahead of her now—but don't forget that you have a right to be happy, too. Don't be too grateful and too humble. She's done you some favors in the past, but she isn't doing you one now—she never would have accepted you if she hadn't been head over heels in love with you. Now write your letter, and then go to her. But to-morrow I want you all

154

the morning—we must look into the acquaintances I spoke about, and the investments you spoke about. Meanwhile, the best of luck—you deserve it!"

Austin smoked thoughtfully for some minutes after Uncle Mat left him, and finally, roused from his brown study by the striking of a clock, went hurriedly to the desk and began his letter. Before he had finished, Sylvia's patience had quite given out, and she came and stood behind him, with her arm over his shoulder as he wrote. He acknowledged the caress with a nod and a smile, but went on writing, and did not speak until the letter was sealed and stamped.

"Sorry to have kept you waiting, dear. Now, then, what is it?"

"I've been thinking things over."

"So I supposed. Well, what have you thought, honey?"

"First, that I want you to have these. I've been going through my jewelry lately, and have had Uncle Mat sell everything except a few little trinkets I had before I—was married, and the pearls he gave me then. In my sorting process, I came across these things that were my father's. I never offered them to—to—any one before. But I want you to wear them, if you will."

She handed him a little worn leather box as she spoke, and on opening it he found, besides a few pins and studs of no great value, a handsome, old-fashioned watch and a signet ring.

"Thank you very much, dear. I'll wear them with great pride and pleasure, and this will be an exchange of gifts, for I've got something for you, too—that's what my shopping was this morning."

He took her left hand in his, slipped off her wedding

155

ring, and slid another on her finger—a circle of beautiful diamonds sunk in a platinum band delicately chased.

"*Austin!* How exquisite! I never had—such a lovely ring! How did you happen to choose—just this?"

"Largely because I thought you could use it for both an engagement ring now, and a wedding ring when we get married—which was what I wanted." And without another word, he took the discarded gold circle and threw it into the fire. "And partly," he went on quite calmly—as if nothing unusual had happened, and as if it was an everyday occurrence to burn up ladies' property without consulting them—"because I thought it was beautiful, and—suitable, like the little star."

"And you expect me to wear it, publicly, now?"

"I shall put it a little stronger than that—I shall insist upon your doing so."

She looked up in surprise, her cheeks flushing at his tone, but he went on quietly:

"I've just written my mother, and asked her to tell the rest of the family, that we are engaged. They have as much right to know as your uncle. You can do as you please about telling other people, of course. But you can't wear another man's ring any longer. And it seems to me, as we shall no longer be living in the same house, and as I shall be coming constantly to see you after you come back to Hamstead, that it would be much more dignified if I could do so openly, in the rôle of your prospective husband. While as far as your friends here are concerned—after what you told me this morning—I think you must agree with me that it is much fairer to let them know at once how things stand with you, and introduce me to them."

"I don't want to use up these few precious days giving parties. I want you to myself."

"I know, dear—that's what I'd prefer, in one way, too. But I have got to take some time for business, and later on your friends will feel that you were ashamed of me— and be justified in feeling so—when they learn that we are to be married, and that you were not willing to have me meet them when I was here."

Sylvia did not answer, but sat with her eyes downcast, biting her lips, and pulling the new ring back and forth on her finger.

"That is, of course, unless you *are* ashamed—are you perfectly sure of your own mind? If not, my letter isn't posted yet, and it is very easy to tell your uncle that you have found you were mistaken in your feelings."

"What would you do if I should?" she asked defiantly.

"Do? Why, nothing. Tell him the same thing, of course, pack my suit-case, and start back to Hamstead as soon as I had met the men I came to see on business."

"Oh, Austin, how can you talk so! I don't believe you really want me, after all!"

"Don't you?" he asked in an absolutely expressionless voice, and pushing back his chair he walked over to the window, turning his back on her completely.

She was beside him in an instant, promising to do whatever he wished and begging his forgiveness. But it was so long before he answered her, or even looked at her, that she knew that for the second time that day she had wounded him almost beyond endurance.

"If you ever say that to me again, no power on earth will make me marry you," he said, in a voice that was not in the least threatening, but so decisive that there could be no doubt that he meant what he said; "and we've got to think up some way of getting along together without quarrelling all the time unless you have your own way about everything, whether it's fair that you should or not. Now, tell me what you wanted to talk to me about, and we'll try to do better—those troublesome details you mentioned before you left the farm? Perhaps I can straighten out some of them for you, if you'll only let me."

"The first one is—money."

"I thought so. It's a rather large obstacle, I admit. But things are not going to be so hard to adjust in that quarter as I feared. I'll tell you now about the little legacy I mentioned this morning." And he repeated his conversation with Uncle Mat. "You can do what you please with your own money, of course—take care of your own personal expenses, and run the house, and give all the presents you like to the girls—but you can't ever give me another cent, unless you want to call the family indebtedness to you your wedding present to me."

"You can't get everything you want on the income of ten thousand dollars—which is about all the capital you'll have left when you've paid all these first expenses you mention."

"I can have everything I *need*—with that and what I'll earn. What's your next 'detail'?"

"I suppose I'll have to give in about the money—but will you mind, very much, if we have—a long engagement?"

"I certainly shall. As I told you before, I think too much has been sacrificed to convention already."

"It isn't that."

"What, then?"

"I don't know how to tell you, and still have you believe I love you dearly."

"You mean, that for some reason, you're not ready to marry me yet?" And as she nodded without speaking, her eyes filling with tears, he asked very gently, "Why not, Sylvia?"

"I'm afraid."

"Afraid—*of me?*"

"No—that is, not of you personally—but of marriage itself. I can't bear yet—the thought of facing—passion."

The hand that had been stroking her hair dropped suddenly, and she felt him draw away from her, with something almost like a groan, and put her arms around his neck, clinging to him with all her strength.

"*Don't*—I love you—and love you—and *love you*—oh, can't I make you see? Are you very angry with me, Austin?"

"No, darling, I'm not angry at all. How could I be? But I'm just beginning to realize—though I thought I knew before—what a perfect hell you've been through —and wondering if I can ever make it up to you."

"Then this doesn't seem to you dreadful—to have me ask for this?"

"Not half so dreadful as it would to have you look at me as you did on Christmas night."

He began stroking her hair again, speaking reassuringly, his voice full of sympathy.

"Don't cry, dearest—it's all right. There's nothing to worry over. It's right that you should have your way about this—it's *my* way, too, as long as you feel like this. I hope you won't *too* long—for—I love you, and want you, and—and need you so much—and—I've waited a year for you already. But I promise never to force—or even urge —you in any way, if you'll promise me that when you *are* ready—you'll tell me."

"I will," she sobbed, with her head hidden on his shoulder.

"Then that's settled, and needn't even be brought up again. Don't cry so, honey. Is there anything else?"

"Just one thing more; and in a way, it's the hardest to say of any."

"Well, tell me, anyway; perhaps I may be able to help."

"My baby," she said, speaking with great difficulty,— "the poor little thing that only lived two weeks. It's buried in the same lot with—its father—at Greenwood. I never can go near that place again. I've paid some one to take care of it, and Uncle Mat has promised me to see that it's done. I think some day you and I—will have a son—more than one, I hope—and he will *live!* But if this—this baby—could be taken away from where he is now, and buried in that little cemetery, you know—I could go sometimes, quite happily, and stay with him, and put flowers on his little grave; and later on there could be a stone which said, merely, 'Harold, infant son of Sylvia—Gray.'"

Apparently Austin forgot what he had said that morning, for long before she had finished he took her in his arms; but the kisses with which he covered her face and hair were like those he would have given to a little child, and there was no need of an answer this time. For a long while she lay there, clinging to him and crying, until she was utterly spent with emotion, as she had been on the night when they had stayed in the wood; and at last, just as she had done then, she dropped suddenly and quietly to sleep. Through the tears which still blinded his own eyes, Austin half-smiled, remembering how he had longed to kiss her as he carried her home, rejoicing that his conscience no longer needed to stand like an iron barrier between his lips and hers. He waited until he was sure that she was sleeping so soundly that there would be little danger of waking her, then lifted her, took her down the hall to her room, and laid her on the big, four-posted bed.

"That's the second time you've been to sleep in my arms, darling," he whispered, bending over to kiss her before he left her; "the third time will be on our wedding night—God grant that isn't very far away!"

CHAPTER XV

"GRADUATION from high school" ranks second in importance only to a wedding in rural New England families. For not only the "Graduating Exercises" themselves, with their "Salutatory" and "Valedictory" addresses, their "Class History" and "Class Prophecy," their essays and songs, constitute a great occasion, but there is also the all-day excursion of picnic character; the "Baccalaureate Sermon" in the largest church; the "Prize Speaking" in the nearest "Opera House"; and last, but not least, the "Graduation Ball" in the Town Hall. The boys suffer agonies in patent-leather boots, high, stiff collars and blue serge suits; the girls suffer torments of jealousy over the fortunate few whose white organdie dresses come "ready-made" straight from Boston. The Valedictorian, the winner at "Prize Speaking," the belle of the parties, are great and glorious beings somewhat set apart from the rest of the graduates; and long after housework and farming are peacefully resumed again, the success of "our class" is a topic of enduring interest.

A wedding brings even more in its train. The bride's house, where the marriage service, as well as the wedding reception, generally takes place, must be swept and scoured from attic to cellar, and, if possible, painted and papered as well. Guest-rooms must be set in order for visiting members of the family, and the bridal feast prepared and served without the help of caterers. The express office is haunted for incoming wedding presents, and though the destination of "the trip"—generally to Montreal or Niagara Falls if the happy pair can afford it—is a well-guarded secret, the trousseau and the gifts, as they arrive, stand in proud display for the neighbors to run in and admire, and the prospective bride and groom, self-conscious and blushing, attend divine service together in the face of a smiling and whispering congregation.

It was small wonder, then, that the Gray family, with the prospect of a graduation and a wedding within a few days of each other before it, was thrown into a ferment of excitement compared to which the hilarity of the Christmas holidays was but a mild ripple. Molly had won a scholarship at the Conservatory, and was beginning to show some talent for musical composition; Katherine was the Valedictorian of her class; Edith had every dance engaged for the ball; and though Thomas had not distinguished himself in any special way, he had kept a good average all the year in his studies, and managed to be very nearly self-supporting by the outside "chores" he had done at college, and it was felt that he, too, deserved much credit, and that his home-coming would be a joyful event. He was trying out "practical experiments" with his class, and could promise only to arrive "just in time"; but Molly, who headed her letters with the notes of the wedding march, and said that she was practicing it every night, wrote that she would be home *plenty* long enough beforehand to help with *every-thing*, and that mother *simply mustn't* get all worn out working too hard with the house-cleaning; Sadie and James were coming home for a week, to take in both festivities, though Sadie must be "careful not to overdo just now." Katherine was entirely absorbed in her determination to get "over ninety" in every one of her final examinations; and Mr. and Mrs. Gray were both so busy and so preoccupied that Edith and Peter were left to pursue the course of true love unobserved and undisturbed.

The effect which Austin's letter to his mother, written the night after he reached New York, produced in a household already pitched so high, may readily be imagined. A thunderbolt casually exploding in their midst could not have effected half such a shock of surprise, or the gift of all the riches of the Orient so much joy. And when, a week later, he came home bringing Sylvia with him—a new Sylvia, laughing, crying, blushing, as shy as a girl surprised at her first tête-à-tête, Mr. and Mrs. Gray welcomed the little lady they loved so well as their daughter.

Those were great days for Mrs. Elliott, who, as mother of the prospective bridegroom, as well as Mrs. Gray's most intimate friend, enjoyed special privileges; and as she was not averse to sharing her information and experiences, the entire village joyfully fell upon the morsels of choice gossip with which she regaled them.

"I don't believe any house in the village ever held so many elegant clothes at once," she declared. "For besides all Sally's things, which are just too sweet for anything, there's Katherine's graduation dress an' ball-dress, an a third one, mind, to wear when she's bridesmaid—most girls would think they was pretty lucky to have any one of the three! Edith has a bridesmaid's dress just like hers, an' a bright yellow one for the ball, an' Molly's maid-of-honor's outfit is handsomest of all—pale pink silk, draped over kind of careless-like with chif*fon*, an' shoes an' silk stockin's to match. An' Mis' Gray, besides that pearl-colored satin Austin brought her from Europe, has a lavender brocade! 'I didn't feel to need it at all,' she told me, 'but Sylvia just insisted. "Two nice dresses aren't a bit too many for you to have," says Sylvia; "the gray one will be lovely for church all summer, an' after Sally's weddin', you can put away the lavender for—Austin's," she finished up, blushin' like a rose.' 'Have you any idea when that's goin' to be?' I couldn't help askin'. 'No,' says Mis' Gray, 'I wish I had. Howard an' I tried to persuade her to be married the same night as Sally! I've always admired a double-weddin'. But she wouldn't hear of it, an' I must say I was surprised to see her so set against it, an' that Austin didn't urge her a bit, either, for they just set their eyes by each other, any one can see that, an' there ain't a thing to hinder 'em from gettin' married to-morrow, that I know of, if they want to—unless perhaps they think it's too soon,' she ended up, kinder meanin'-like."

"The presents are somethin' wonderful," Mrs. Elliott related on another occasion. "Sally's uncle out in Seattle —widower of her that left Austin all that money—has sent her a whole dinner-set, white with pink roses on it—twelve dozen pieces in all, countin' vegetable dishes, bone-plates, an' a soup-tureen. She's had sixteen pickle-forks, ten bon-bon spoons, an' eight cut-glass whipped-cream bowls, but I dare say they'll all come in handy, one way or another, an' it makes you feel good to have so many generous friends. Austin's insisted on givin' her one of them Hol*steen* cows he fetched over from Holland, an' Fred says it's one of the most valuable things she's got, though I should feel as if any good bossy, raised right here in Hamstead, would probably do 'em just as well, an' that he might have chosen somethin' a little more tasty. Ain't men queer? Sylvia? Oh, she's given her a whackin' big check—enough so Sally can pay all her 'personal expenses,' as she calls 'em all her life, an' never touch the principal at that; an' a big box of knives an' forks an' spoons—'a chest of flat silver' she calls it, an' a silver tea-set to match—awful plain pattern they are, but Sally likes 'em. Yes, it's nice of her, but it ain't any more than I expected. She's got plenty of money—why shouldn't she spend it?"

Only once did Mrs. Elliott say anything unpleasant, and the village, knowing her usually sharp tongue, thought she did remarkably well, and took but little stock in this particular speech.

"I'm glad it's Sally Fred picked out, an' not one of the other girls," she declared; "she's twenty-nine years old now—a good, sensible age—pleasant an' easy-goin', same's her mother is, an' yet real capable. Ruth always was a silly, incompetent little thing—she has to hire help most of the time, with nothin' in the world to do but cook for Frank, look after that little tiny house, take care of them two babies, an' go into the store off an' on when business is rushin'. Molly's head is full of nothin' but music, an' Katherine's of books. As to that pretty little fool, Edith,

I'm glad she ain't my daughter, runnin' round all the time with that Dutch boy, an' her parents both so possessed with the idea that she ain't out of her cradle yet—she bein' the youngest—that they can't see it. Peter ain't the only one she keeps company with either—if he was, it wouldn't be so bad, for I guess he's a good enough boy, though I can't understand a mortal word he says, an' them foreigners all have a kinder vacant look, to me. But the other night I was took awful sudden with one of them horrible attacks of indigestion I'm subject to—we'd had rhubarb pie for supper, an' 'twas just elegant, but I guess I ate too much of it, an' the telephone wouldn't work on account of the thunderstorm we'd had that day—seems like that there'd been a lot of them this season—so Joe had to hitch up an' go for the doctor. As he went past the cemetery, he see Edith leanin' over the fence with that no-count Jack Weston—an' it was past midnight, too!"

In the midst of such general satisfaction, it was perhaps inevitable that at least one person should not be pleased. And that person, as will be readily guessed, was Thomas. Sylvia, thinking the blow might fall more bearably from his brother's hand than from hers, relegated the task of writing him to Austin; and Austin, with a wicked twinkle in his eye, wrote him in this wise:

DEAR THOMAS:

When you made that little break that I warned you against this spring, Sylvia probably offered to be a sister to you. I believe that is usual on such occasions. You have doubtless noticed that she is exceptionally truthful

167

for a girl, so—largely to keep her word to you, perhaps—she decided a little while ago to marry me. Of course, I tried to dissuade her from this plan, but you know she is also stubborn. There seems to be nothing for me to do but to fall in with it. I don't know yet when the execution is going to take place, and though, of course, it would be a relief in a way if I did, I am not finding the death sentence without its compensations. Why don't you come home over some Sunday, and see how well I am bearing up? Sylvia told me to ask you, with her love, or I should not bother, for I am naturally a little loath, even now, to have so dangerous a rival, as you proved yourself in your spring vacation, too much in evidence.

Your affectionate brother

AUSTIN

P.S. Have you taken any more ladies to Moving-Picture Palaces lately?

Needless to say, if Sylvia had seen this epistle, it would not have gone. But she did not. Austin took good care of that. And Thomas did come home—without waiting for Sunday. He rushed to the Dean's office, and told him there had been a death in the family. It is probable that, at the moment, he felt that this was true. At any rate, the Dean, looking at the boy's flushed cheeks and heavy eyes, did not doubt it for an instant.

"Of course, you must go home at once," he said kindly; "wait a minute, my Ford's at the door. I'll run you down to the station—you can just catch the one o'clock. I'll tell one of the fellows to express a suit-case to you this evening."

Travel on the Central Vermont Railroad is safe, but

its best friend cannot maintain that it is swift. To get from Lake Champlain to the Connecticut River requires several changes, much patient waiting in small and uninteresting stations for connections, and the consumption of considerable time. It was a little after seven when Thomas, dinnerless and supperless, reached Hamstead, and plodding doggedly up the road in a heavy rain, met Mr. and Mrs. Elliott just starting out in their buggy for Thursday evening prayer meeting.

"Pull up, Joe," the latter said excitedly, as she spied the boy advancing towards them. "I do declare, there's Thomas Gray comin' up the road. I wonder if he's been expelled, or only suspended. I must find out, so's I can tell the folks about it after meetin', an' go down an' comfort Mary the first thing in the mornin' after I get them tomato plants set out. I always thought Thomas was some steadier than Austin, but Burlington's a gay place, an' he's probably got in with wild companions up there. Do you suppose it's some cheap little show girl, or gettin' in liquor by express from over in New York State, or forgin' a check on account of gamblin' debts? I know how boys spend their time while they're gettin' educated, you can't tell me. Or maybe he hasn't passed some examination. He never was extra bright. Failed everything, probably.—Good-evenin', Thomas, it's nice to see you back, but quite a surprise, it not bein' vacation time or nothin'. I suppose everything's goin' fine at college, ain't it?'

Thomas had never loved Mrs. Elliott, and lately he had come as near hating her as he was capable of hating anybody. He longed inexpressibly to cast a withering scowl in her direction, and pass on without answering.

169

But his inborn civility was greater than his aversion. He pulled off his cap and stopped.

"Yes, everything's all right—I guess," he said, rather stupidly. Then a brilliant inspiration struck him. "I've been doing so well in my studies that they've given me a few days off to come home. That doesn't often happen —they made an exception in my case."

It was seldom that the slow-witted Thomas was blessed with one of these flights of fancy. For a minute he felt almost cheered. Mrs. Elliott was baffled.

"Do tell," she exclaimed. "It must be a rare thing— I never hear the like of it before. I'm most surprised you didn't take advantage of such a chance to go down to Boston an' see Molly. Didn't feel's you could afford it, I suppose. I guess she's kinder lonely down there. She don't seem to get acquainted real fast. You'd think, with all the people there *are* in Boston, she wouldn't ha' had much trouble, but then Molly's manner ain't in her favor, an' I suppose folks in the city is real busy—must be awful hard to keep house, livin' the way they do. I don't think much of city life. The last time Joe an' I went down on the excursion, we see the Charles River, an' the Old Ladies' Home, an' the Chamber of Horrors down on Washington Street, but we was real glad to come home. There was somethin' the matter with the lock to our suit-case, an' we couldn't get it undone all the time we was there, but fortunately it was real warm weather, so we really didn't suffer none. I thought by this time Molly might have a beau, but then, Molly's real plain. If the looks could ha' ben divided up more even between her an' Edith, same's the brains between you an' Austin, 'twould ha' ben a good thing, wouldn't it? But then you

170

say you're gettin' on well now, an' in time some man may marry her, so's he can set an' listen to her play when he comes in tired from his chores at night. I've heard of sech things. An' then there's quite a bunch of love-affairs in the family already, ain't there?"

"Yes," said Thomas angrily, "there is."

Mrs. Elliott was quick to mark his tone. She nudged her husband.

"Well, well," she said playfully, "Austin's cut you out, ain't he? Mr. Jessup was in the race for a while, too, an' I thought he was runnin' pretty good, but you know we read in the Bible it don't always go to the swift. An' Austin may not get her after all—I hear there's several in New York as well an' she might change her mind. I never set much stock in young men marryin' widows myself. Seems like there's plenty of nice girls as ought to have a chance. An' Sylvia's awful high-toned, an' stubborn as a mule—I dunno's she an' Austin will be able to stick it out, he's some set himself. I shouldn't wonder if it all got broke off, an' I'm not sayin' it mightn't be for the best if it was. But I don't deny Sylvia's real pretty an' generous, an' I like her spunk. I was tellin' Joe only yesterday—"

"I'm afraid I'm keeping you from meeting," said Thomas desperately, and strode off down the road.

The barn—the beautiful new barn that Sylvia had made possible and that had filled his heart with such joy and pride—was still lighted. He walked straight to it, and met Peter coming out of the door. Peter stared his surprise.

"Where's my brother?" said Thomas roughly.

"Mr. Gray ben still in the barn vorking. It's too bad

171

he haf so much to do—he don't get much time mit de missus—den she tink he don't vant to come. I'm glad you're back, Mr. Thomas. I vas yust gon in to get ve herd book for him. I took it in to show Edit' someting I vant to explain to her, and left it in ve house. Most dum."

"You needn't bring it back. I want to see him alone."

Peter nodded, his bewilderment growing, and disappeared. Thomas flung himself down the long stable, without once glancing at the row of beautiful cows, his footsteps echoing on the concrete, to the office at the farther end. The door was open, and Austin sat at the roll-top desk, which was littered with account books, transfer sheets, and pedigree cards, typewriting vigorously. He sprang up in surprise.

"Why, Thomas!" he exclaimed cordially. "Where did you drop from? I'm awfully glad to see you!"

"You damned mean deceitful skunk!" cried the boy, slamming the door behind him, and ignoring his brother's outstretched hand. "I'd like to smash every bone in your body until there wasn't a piece as big as a toothpick left of you! You made me think you didn't care a rap about her—you said I wasn't worthy of her—that I was an ignorant farmer and she was a great lady. That's true enough—but I'm just as good as you are, every bit! I know you've done all sorts of rotten things I never have! But just the same this is the first time I ever thought that you—or any Gray—wasn't *square!* And then you write me a letter about her like that—as if she'd flung herself at your head—*Sylvia!*"

Austin's conscience smote him. He had never seen Thomas's side before; and neither he nor any other

172

member of the family had guessed how much their incessant teasing had hurt, or how hard the younger brother had been hit. In the extremely unsentimental way common in New England, these two were very fond of each other, and he realized that Thomas's affection, which was very precious to him, would be gone forever if he did not set him right at once.

"Look here," he said, forcing Thomas into the swivel chair, and seating himself on the desk, ignoring the papers that fell fluttering to the floor, "you listen to me. You've got everything crooked, and it's my fault, and I'm darned sorry. I never told you I cared for Sylvia, not because I wanted to deceive you, but because I cared so everlasting *much*, from the first moment I set eyes on her, that I couldn't talk about it. No one else guessed either— you weren't the only one. The funny part of it is, that *she* didn't! She thought, because I steered pretty clear of her, out of a sense of duty, that I didn't like her especially. Imagine—not liking Sylvia! Ever hear of any one who didn't like roses, Thomas? But I never dreamed that she'd have me—or even of asking her to! As to throwing herself at my head—well, she put it that way herself once, and I shut her up pretty quick—you'll find out how to do it yourself some day, with some other girl, though, of course, it doesn't look that way to you now—but I can't give you that treatment! I guess I'll have to tell you —though I never expected to tell a living soul—just how it did happen. It's—it's the sort of thing that is too sacred to share with any one, even any one that I think as much of as I do of you—but I've got to make you believe that, five minutes beforehand, I had no idea it was going to occur." And as briefly and honestly as he could, he told

Thomas how Sylvia had come to him while he was making his bonfire, and what had taken place afterwards. Then, with still greater feeling in his voice, he went on: "There's something else I haven't told any one else either, and that is, that I can't for a single instant get away from the thought that, even now, I'm not going to get her. I know I haven't any right to her, and I don't feel sure that I can make her happy—that she can respect me as much as a girl ought to respect the man she's going to marry. I certainly don't think I'm any worthier of her than you— or as worthy—never did for a minute. I *have* done lots of rotten things, and you've always been as straight as a string—and you'd better thank the Lord you have! When you get engaged you won't have to go through what I have! But you see the difference is, as far as Sylvia and you and I are concerned"—he hesitated, his throat growing rough, his ready eloquence checked—"Sylvia likes you ever so much; she thinks you're a fine boy, and that by and by you'll want to marry a fine girl; but I'm a man already, and young as she is, Sylvia's a woman— and God knows why—she loves me!"

Austin glanced at Thomas. The anger was dying out of the boy's face, and unashamed tears were standing in his eyes.

"A lot," added Austin huskily. Then, after a long pause: "Won't you have a whiskey-and-soda with me—I've got some in the cupboard here for emergencies, while we talk over some of this business I was deep in when you came in? There are any number of things I've been anxious to get your opinion on—you've got lots of practical ability and good judgment in places where I'm weak, and I miss you no end when you're where I can't get at

174

you—I certainly shall be glad when you're through your course, and home for good! And after we get this mess straightened out"—he bent over to pick up the scattered sheets—"we'd better go in together and find Sylvia, hadn't we?"

CHAPTER XVI

STRANGELY enough, Sylvia and Austin were perhaps less happy at this time than any of the other dwellers at the Homestead. After the first day, the week in New York had been a period of great happiness to both of them, and Austin had proved such an immediate success, both among Sylvia's friends and Uncle Mat's business associates, that both were immensely gratified. But after the return to the country, matters seemed to go less and less well. During the year in which they had "loved and longed in secret," each had exalted the other to the position of a martyr and a saint. The intimacy of their engagement was rapidly revealing the fact that, after all, they were merely ordinary human beings, and the discovery was something of a shock to both. Austin had thought over Uncle Mat's advice, and found it good; he was gentle and considerate, and showed himself perfectly willing to submit to Sylvia's wishes in most important decisions, but he refused to be dictated to in little things. She was so accustomed, by this time, to having her slightest whim not only respected, but admired, by all the adoring Gray family, and most of her world at large besides, that she was apt to behave like a spoiled child when Austin thwarted her. She nearly always had to admit, afterwards, that he had been right, and this did not make it any easier for her. His "incessant obstinacy," as she called it, was rapidly "getting on her nerves," while it seemed to him that they could never meet that she did not have some fresh grievance, or disagree with him radically about something. She wanted him at her side all the time; he had a thousand other interests. She saw no reason why, after they were married, they should live in the country all the year, and every year; he saw no reason why they should do anything else. And so it went with every subject that arose.

If Sylvia had been less idle, she would have had no time to think about "nerves." But the manservant and his wife whom she had installed in the little brick house were well-trained and competent to the last degree, and the ménage ran like clock-work without any help from her. She was debarred from riding or driving alone, and the girls at the farm had no time to go with her, and it was still an almost unheard-of thing in that locality for a woman to run a motor. She could not fill an hour a day working in her little garden, and she had no special taste for sewing. The only thing for her to do seemed to be to sit around and wait for Austin to appear, and Austin was not only very busy, but extremely absorbed in his work. It was impossible for him to come to see her every night, and when he did come, he was so thoroughly and wholesomely tired and sleepy, that his visits were short. On Sundays he had more leisure; but Mr. and Mrs. Gray seemed to take it for granted that Sylvia would still go to church with them in the morning, and spend the rest of the day at their house. She could not bring herself to the point of disappointing them, though she rebelled inwardly; but she complained to Austin, as they were walking back to her house together after a day spent in this manner, that she never saw him alone at all.

"It's not only the family," she said, "but Peter, and Fred, and Mr. and Mrs. Elliott are around all the time, and to-day there were Ruth and Frank and those two fussy babies needing something done for them every single minute besides! It was perfect bedlam. I want you to myself once in a while."

"You can have me to yourself, for good and all, whenever you want me," replied Austin.

This was so undeniable a statement that Sylvia changed the subject abruptly.

"There is no earthly need of your working so hard, and you know it."

"But Sylvia, I like to work; and I'm awfully anxious to make a success of things, now that we've got such a wonderful start at last."

"Are you more interested in this stupid old farm than you are in me?"

"Why, Sylvia, it isn't a 'stupid old farm' to me! It's the place my great-grandfather built, and that all the Grays have lived in and loved for four generations! I thought you liked it, too."

"I do, but I'm jealous of it."

"You ought not to be. You know that there's nothing in the world so dear to me as you are."

"Then let me pay for another hired man, so that you'll have more time for yourself—and for me."

"Indeed, I will not. You'll never pay for another thing on this farm if I can help it. No one could be more grateful than I am for all you've done, but the time is over for that."

"Won't you come in?" she asked, as they reached her garden, and she noticed that he stopped at the gate.

"Not to-night—we've had a good walk together, and you know I have to get up pretty early in the morning. Good-night, dear," and he raised her fingers to his lips.

She snatched them away, lifting her lovely face. "Oh, Austin!" she cried, "how can you be so calm and cold? I think sometimes you're made of stone! If you must go, don't say good-night like that—act as if you were made of flesh and blood!"

"I'm acting in the only sane way for both of us. If you don't like it, I had better not come at all."

And he went home without giving her even the caress he had originally intended, and slept soundly and well all night; but Sylvia tossed about for hours, and finally, at dawn, cried herself to sleep.

The first serious disagreement, however, came just before Katherine's graduation. Austin, who loved to dance, was looking forward to his clever sister's "ball" with a great deal of pride and pleasure, and was genuinely amazed when Sylvia objected violently to his going, saying that as she could not dance, and as all the rest of the family would be there, Katherine did not need him, and that he had much better stay at home with her.

"But, Sylvia," protested Austin, "I *want* to go. I'm awfully proud of Katherine, and I wouldn't miss it for anything. Why don't you come, too? I don't see any reason why you shouldn't."

"Of course you don't. You weren't brought up among people who know what's proper in such matters."

"I know it, Sylvia. But if that's going to trouble you, you should have thought of it sooner. My knowledge of etiquette is very slight, I admit, but my common-sense tells me that announcing one's engagement should be equivalent to stopping all former observances of mourning."

"I didn't want to announce it. It was you that insisted upon that, too."

"Well, you know why," said Austin with some meaning.

"All right, then," burst out Sylvia angrily, "go to your old ball. You seem to think you are an authority on everything. I'm sure I don't want to go, anyway, and dance with a lot of awkward farmers who smell of the cowstable. I shouldn't think you would care about it either, now that you've had a chance to see things properly done."

"I care a good deal about my sister, Sylvia, and about my friends here, too. There are no better people on the face of the earth—I've heard you say so, yourself! It's only a chance that I'm a little less awkward than some of the others."

The result of this conversation was that Austin did not go near Sylvia for several days. He was deeply hurt, but that was not all. He began to wonder, even more than he ever had before, whether his comparative poverty, his lack of education, his farmer family and traditions and friends, were not very real barriers between himself and a girl like Sylvia. What was more, he questioned whether a strong, passionate, determined man, who felt that he knew his own best course and proposed to take it, could ever make such a delicate, self-willed little creature

180

happy, even if there were no other obstacles in their path than those of warring disposition. Something of his old sullenness of manner returned, and his mother, after worrying in silence over him for a time finally asked him what the trouble was. At first he denied that there was anything, next stubbornly refused to tell her what it was, and at last, like a hurt schoolboy, blurted out his grievance. To his amazement and grief, Mrs. Gray took Sylvia's part. This was the last straw. He jerked himself away from her, and went out, slamming the front door after him. It was evening, and he was tired and hot and dirty. The rest of the family had almost finished supper when he reached the table, an unexpected delay having arisen in the barn, and he had eaten the unappetizing scraps that remained hurriedly, without taking time to shave and bathe and change his clothes. He had never gone to Sylvia in this manner before; but he strode down the path to her house with a bitter satisfaction in his heart that she was to see him when he was looking and feeling his worst, and that she would have to take him as he was, or not at all. He found her in her garden cutting roses, a picture of dainty elegance in her delicate white fabrics. She greeted him somewhat coolly, as if to punish him for his lack of deference to her on his last visit, and his subsequent neglect, and glanced at his costume with a disapproval which she was at no pains to conceal. Then with a sarcasm and lack of tact which she had never shown before, she gave voice to her general dissatisfaction.

"*Really, Austin,* don't come near me, please; you're altogether too *barny*. Don't you think you're carrying your devotion to the nobility of labor a little too far, and your devotion to me—if you still have any—not quite far enough? You're slipping straight back to your old slovenly, disagreeable ways—without the excuse that you formerly had that they were practically the only ways open to you. If you're too proud to accept my money and the freedom that it can give you, and so stubborn that you make a scene and then won't come near me for days because I refuse to go to a cheap little public dance with you—"

She got no farther. Austin interrupted her with a violence of which she would not have believed him capable.

"*If!* If you're too stubborn to go with me to my sister's *graduation ball,* and too proud to accept the fact that I'm a *farmer,* with a farmer's friends and family and work, and that *I'm damned glad of it,* and won't give them up, or be supported by any woman on the face of the earth, or let her make a pet lap-dog of me, you can go straight back to the life you came from, for all me! You seem to prefer it, after all, and I believe it's all you deserve. If you don't—don't ask my forgiveness for the things you've said the last two times I've seen you, and say *you'll go to that party* with me, and be just as darned pleasant to every one there as you know how to be—and promise to stop quarrelling, and keep your promise—I'll never come near you again. You're making my life utterly miserable. You won't marry me, and yet you are bound to have me make love to you all the time, when I'm doing my best to keep my hands off you—and I'd rather be shot *than* marry you, on the terms you're putting up to me at present! You've got two days to think it over in, and if you don't send for me before it's time to start for the ball, and tell me you're sorry, you won't get another chance to send for me again as long as you live. I'm either not worth having at all, or I'm worth treating better than you've seen fit to do lately!"

He left her, without even looking at her again, in a white heat of fury. But before the hot dawn of another June day had given him an excuse to get up and try to work off his feelings with the most strenuous labor that he could find, he had spent a horrible sleepless night which he was never to forget as long as he lived. His anger gave way first to misery, and then to a panic of fear. Suppose she took him literally—though he had meant every word when he said it—suppose he lost her? What would the rest of his life be worth to him, alone, haunted, not only by his senseless folly in casting away such a precious treasure, but by his ingratitude, his presumption, and his own unworthiness? A dozen times he started towards her house, only to turn back again. She *hadn't* been fair. They *couldn't* be happy that way. If he gave in now, he would have to do it all the rest of his life, and she would despise him for it. As the time which he had stipulated went by, and no message came, he suffered more and more intensely—hoped, savagely, that she was suffering, too, and decided that she could not be, or that he would have heard from her; but resolved, more and more decidedly, with every hour that passed, that he would fight this battle out to the bitter end.

It was even later than usual when he came in on the night of the ball, and when he entered, every one in the house was hurrying about in the inevitable confusion which precedes a "great occasion." Edith, the only one who seemed to be ready, was standing in the middle of the living-room, fresh and glowing as a yellow rose in her bright dress, Peter beside her buttoning her gloves.

183

She glanced at her grimy brother with a feeble interest.

"Mercy, Austin, you'd better hurry! We're going to leave in five minutes."

"Well, *I'm* not going to leave in five minutes! I've got to get out of these clothes and have a bath and—"

"It's hardly necessary to tell me all that—one glance at you is sufficient," said Edith flippantly.

"Well, I can come on later alone, I suppose. Where's mother?"

"Still dressing. Why?"

"Do you happen to know whether—Sylvia's been over here this afternoon—or sent a telephone message or a note?"

"I'm perfectly sure she hasn't. Why?"

"Nothing," said Austin grimly, and left the room.

Like most people who try to dress in a hurry when they are angry, Austin found that everything went wrong. There was no hot water left, and he had to heat some himself for shaving while he took a cold bath; his mother usually got his clothes ready for him when she knew he was detained, but this time she had apparently been too rushed herself. He couldn't find his evening shoes; he couldn't get his studs into his stiff shirt until he had had a struggle that raised his temperature several degrees higher than it was already; the big, jolly teamful departed while he was rummaging through his top drawer for fresh handkerchiefs; and he was vainly trying to adjust his white tie satisfactorily, when a knock at the door informed him that he was not alone in the house after all; he said "come in" crossly, and without turning, and went on with his futile attempts.

"Has every one else gone? I didn't know I was so late
184

—but I've been all through the house downstairs calling, and couldn't get any answer. Let me do that for you—let's take a fresh one—"

He wheeled sharply around, and found Sylvia standing beside him—Sylvia, dressed in shell-pink, shimmering satin and foamy lace, with pearls in her dark hair and golden slippers on her feet, her neck and arms white and bare and gleaming. With a little sound that was half a sob, and half a cry of joy, she flung her arms around his neck and drew his face down to hers.

"Austin—I'm—I'm sorry—I do—beg your forgiveness from the bottom of my heart. I promise—and I'll keep my promise—to be reasonable—and kind—and fair—to stop making you miserable. It's been all my fault that we've quarrelled, every bit—and we never will again. I've come to tell you—not just that I'll go to the party with you, gladly, if you're still willing to take me, but that there's nothing that matters to me in the whole world—except you—"

The first touch of Sylvia's arms set Austin's brain seething; after the hungry misery of the past few days, it acted like wine offered to a starving man, suddenly snatched and drunk. Her words, her tears, her utter self-abandonment of voice and manner, annihilated in one instant the restraint in which he had held himself for months. He caught the delicate little creature to him with all his strength, burying his face in the white fragrance of her neck. He forgot everything in the world except that she was in his arms—alone with him—that nothing was to come between them again as long as they lived. He could feel her heart beating against his under the soft lace on her breast, her cool cheeks and mouth growing warm under the kisses that he rained on them until his own lips stung. At first she returned his embrace with an ardor that equalled his own; then, as if conscious that she was being carried away by the might of a power which she could neither measure nor control, she tried to turn her face away and strove to free herself.

"Don't," she panted; "let me go! You—you—hurt me, Austin."

"I can't help it—I shan't let you go! I'm going to kiss you this time until I get ready to stop."

For a moment she struggled vainly. Austin's arms tightened about her like bands of steel. She gave a little sigh, and lifted her face again.

"I can't seem to—kiss back any more," she whispered, "but if this is what you want—if it will make up to you for these last weeks—it doesn't matter whether you hurt or not."

Every particle of resistance had left her. Austin had wished for an unconditional surrender, and he had certainly attained it. There could never again be any question of which should rule. She had come and laid her sweet, proud, rebellious spirit at his very feet, begging his forgiveness that it had not sooner recognized its master. A wonderful surge of triumph at his victory swept over him—and then, suddenly—he was sick and cold with shame and contrition. He released her, so abruptly that she staggered, catching hold of a chair to steady herself, and raising one small clenched hand to her lips, as if to press away their smarting. As she did so, he saw a deep red mark on her bare white arm. He winced, as if he had been struck, at the gesture and what it disclosed, but it needed neither to show him that she was bruised and hurt from the violence of his embrace; and dreadful as he instantly realized this to be, it seemed to matter very little if he could only learn that she was not hurt beyond all healing by divining the desire and intention which for one sacrilegious moment had almost mastered him.

A gauzy scarf which she had carried when she entered the room had fallen to the floor. He stooped and picked it up, and stood looking at it, running it through his hands, his head bent. It was white and sheer, a mere gossamer—he must have stepped on it, for in one place it was torn, in another slightly soiled. Sylvia, watching him, holding her breath, could see the muscles of his white face growing tenser and tenser around his set mouth, and still he did not glance at her or speak to her. At last he unfolded it to its full size, and wrapped it about her, his eyes giving her the smile which his lips could not.

"Nothing matters to me in the whole world either—except you," he said brokenly. "I think these last few—dreadful days—have shown us both how much we need each other, and that the memory of them will keep us closer together all our lives. If there's any question of forgiveness between us, it's all on my side now, not yours, and I don't think I can—talk about it now. But I'll never forget how you came to me to-night, and, please God, some day I'll be more worthy of—of your love and—and your *trust* than I've shown myself now. Until I am—" He stopped, and, lifting her arm, kissed the bruise which his own roughness had made there. "What can I do—to make that better?" he managed to say.

"It didn't hurt—much—before—and it's all healed—

187

now," she said, smiling up at him; "didn't your mother ever 'kiss the place to make it well' when you were a little boy, and didn't it always work like a charm? It won't show at all, either, under my glove."

"Your glove?" he asked stupidly; and then, suddenly remembering what he had entirely forgotten—"Oh—we were going to a ball together. You came to tell me you would, after all. But surely you won't want to now—"

"Why not? We can take the motor—we won't be so very late—the others went in the carryall, you know."

He drew a long breath, and looked away from her. "All right," he said at last. "Go downstairs and get your cloak, if you left it there. I'll be with you in a minute."

She obeyed, without a word, but waited so long that she grew alarmed, and finally, unable to endure her anxiety any longer, she went back upstairs. Austin's door was open into the hall, but it was dark in his room, and, genuinely frightened, she groped her way towards the electric switch. In doing so she stumbled against the bed, and her hand fell on Austin's shoulder. He was kneeling there, his whole body shaking, his head buried in his arms. Instantly she was on her knees beside him.

"My darling boy, what is it? Austin, *don't!* You'll break my heart."

"The marvel is—if I haven't—just now. I told your uncle that I was afraid I would some time—that I knew I hadn't any right to you. But I didn't think—that even I was bad enough—to fail you—like *this*—"

"You *haven't* failed me—you *have* a right to me—I never loved you so much in all my life—" she hurried on, almost incoherently, searching for words of comfort.

188

"Dearest—will it make you feel any better—if I say I'll marry you—right away?"

"What do you mean? When?"

"To-night, if you like. Oh, Austin, I love you so that it doesn't matter a bit—whether I'm afraid or not. The only thing that really counts—is to have you happy! And since I've realized that—I find that I'm not afraid of anything in the whole world—and that I want to belong to you as much—and as soon—as you can possibly want to have me!"

It was many months before Hamstead stopped talking about the "Graduation Ball of that year." It surpassed, to an almost extraordinary degree, any that had ever been held there. But the event upon which the village best loved to dwell was the entrance of Sylvia Cary, the loveliest vision it had ever beheld, on Austin Gray's arm, when all the other guests were already there, and everyone had despaired of their coming. Following the unwritten law in country places, which decrees that all persons engaged, married, or "keeping company," must have their "first dance" together, she gave that to Austin. Then Thomas and James, Frank and Fred, Peter, and even Mr. Gray and Mr. Elliott, all claimed their turn, and by that time Austin was waiting impatiently again. But country parties are long, and before the night was over, all the men and boys, who had been watching her in church, and bowing when they met her in the road, and seizing every possible chance to speak to her when they went to the Homestead on errands—or excuses for errands—had demanded and been given a dance. She was lighter than thistledown—indeed, there were moments when she

189

seemed scarcely a woman at all, but a mere essence of fragile beauty and sweetness and graciousness. It had been generally conceded beforehand that the honors of the ball would all go to Edith, but even Edith herself admitted that she took a second place, and that she was glad to take it.

Dawn was turning the quiet valley and distant mountains into a riotous rosy glory, when, as they drove slowly up to her house, Austin gently raised the gossamer scarf which had blown over Sylvia's face, half-hiding it from him. She looked up with a smile to answer his.

"Are you very tired, dear?"

"Not at all—just too happy to talk much, that's all."

"Sylvia—"

"Yes, darling—"

"You know I have planned to start West with Peter three days after Sally's wedding—"

"Yes—"

"Would you rather I didn't go?"

"No; I'm glad you're going—I mean, I'm glad you have decided to keep to your plan."

"What makes you think I have?"

"Because, being you, you couldn't do otherwise."

"But when I come back—"

Her fingers tightened in his.

"I want two months all alone with you in this little house," he whispered. "Send the servants away—it won't be very hard to do the work—for just us two—I'll help. That's—that's—*marriage*—a big wedding and a public honeymoon—and—all that go with them—are just a cheap imitation—of the real thing. Then, later on, if you like, this first winter, we'll go away together—to Spain or Italy

or the South of France—or wherever you wish—but first—
we'll begin together here. Will you marry me—the first of
September, Sylvia?"

Austin drove home in the broad daylight of four o'clock
on a June morning. Then, after the motor was put away,
he took his working clothes over his arm, went to the
river, and plunged in. When he came back, with damp
hair, cool skin, and a heart singing with peace and joy,
he found Peter, whistling, starting towards the barn with
his milk-pail over his arm. It was the beginning of a new
day.

CHAPTER XVII

"I, SARAH, take thee, Frederick, to my wedded husband, to have and to hold from this day forward, for better for worse, for richer for poorer, in sickness and in health, to love, cherish, and to obey, till death us do part, according to God's holy ordinance. And thereto I give thee my troth."

The old clock in the corner was ticking very distinctly; the scent of roses in the crowded room made the air heavy with sweetness; the candles on the mantelpiece flickered in the breeze from the open window; outside a whip-poor-will was singing in the lilac bushes.

"With this ring I thee wed, and with all my worldly goods I thee endow: In the name of the Father, and of the Son, and of the Holy Ghost. Amen."

An involuntary tear rolled down Mrs. Gray's cheek, to be hastily concealed and wiped away with her new lace handkerchief; her husband was looking straight ahead of him, very hard, at nothing; Ruth adjusted the big white bow on little Elsie's curls; Sylvia felt for Austin's hand behind the folds of her dress, and found it groping for hers.

Then suddenly the spell was broken. The minister was shaking hands with the bride and groom, Sally was taking

192

her bouquet from Molly, every one was laughing and talking at once, crowding up to offer congratulations, handling, admiring, and discussing the wedding presents, half-falling over each other with haste and excitement. Delicious smells began to issue from the kitchen, and the long dining-table was quickly laden down. Sylvia took her place at one end, behind the coffee-urn, Molly at the other end, behind the strawberries and ice-cream. Katherine, Edith, and the boys flew around passing plates, cakes of all kinds, great sugared doughnuts and fat cookies. Sally was borne into the room triumphant on a "chair" made of her brothers' arms to cut and distribute the "bride's cake." Then, when every one had eaten as much as was humanly possible, the piano was moved out to the great new barn, with its fine concrete floors swept and scoured as only Peter could do it, and its every stall festooned with white crepe paper by Sylvia, and the dancing began—for this time the crowd was too great to permit it in the house, in spite of the spacious rooms. Molly and Sylvia took turns in playing, and each found several eager partners waiting for her, every time the "shift" occurred. Finally, about midnight, the bride went upstairs to change her dress, and the girls gathered around the banisters to be ready to catch the bouquet when she came down, laughing and teasing each other while they waited. Great shouts arose, and much joking began, when Edith—and not Sylvia as every one had privately hoped—caught the huge bunch of flowers and ribbon, and ran with it in her arms out on the wide piazza, all the others behind her, to be ready to pelt Sally and Fred with rice when they appeared. Thomas was to drive them to the station, and Sylvia's motor was bedecked with white garlands and bows, slippers and bells, from one end of it to the other. At last the rush came; and the happy victims, showered and dishevelled, waving their handkerchiefs and shouting good-bye, were whisked up the hill, and out of sight.

Sylvia insisted on staying, to begin "straightening out the worst of the mess" as soon as the last guest had gone, and on remaining overnight, sleeping in Sally's old room with Molly, to be on hand and go on with the good work the first thing in the morning. Sadie and James had to leave on the afternoon train, as James had stretched his leave of absence from business to the very last degree already; so by evening the house was painfully tidy again, and so quiet that Mrs. Gray declared it "gave her the blues just to listen to it."

The next night was to be Austin's last one at home, and he had promised Sylvia to go and take supper with her, but just before six o'clock the telephone rang, and she knew that something had happened to disappoint her.

"Is that you, Sylvia?"

"Yes, dear."

"Mr. Carter—the President of the Wallacetown Bank, you know—has just called me up. There's going to be a meeting of the bank officers just after the fourth, as they've decided to enlarge their board of directors, and add at least one 'rising young farmer' as he put it— And oh, Sylvia, he asked if I would allow my name to be proposed! Just think—after all the years when we couldn't get a *cent* from them at any rate of interest, to have that come! It's every bit due to you!"

"It isn't either—it's due to the splendid work you've done this last year."

194

"Well, we won't stop to discuss that now. He wants me to drive up and see him about it right away. Do you mind if I take the motor? I can make so much better time, and get back to you so much more quickly—but I can't come to supper—you must forgive me if I go."

"I never should forgive you if you didn't—that's wonderful news! Don't hurry—I'll be glad to see you whatever time you get back."

She hung up the receiver, and sat motionless beside the instrument, too thrilled for the moment to move. What a man he was proving himself—her farmer! And yet—how each new responsibility, well fulfilled, was going to take him more and more from her! She sighed involuntarily, and was about to rise, when the bell sounded again.

"Hullo," she said courteously, but tonelessly. The bottom of the evening had dropped out for her. It mattered very little how she spent it now until Austin arrived.

"Land, Sylvia, you sound as if there'd ben a death in the family! Do perk up a little! Yes, this is Mrs. Elliott—Maybe if some of the folks on this line that's taken their receivers down so's they'll know who I'm talkin' to an' what I'm sayin' will hang up you can hear me a little more plain." (This timely remark resulted in several little clicks.) "There, that's better. I see Austin tearin' past like mad in your otter, and I says to Joe, 'That means Sylvia's all alone again, same as usual; I'm goin' to call her up an' visit with her a spell!' Hot, ain't it? Yes, I always suffer considerable with the heat. I sez this mornin' to Joe, 'Joe, it's goin' to be a hot day,' and he sez, 'Yes, Eliza, I'm afraid it is,' an' I sez, 'Well, we've got to stand it,' an' he—"

"I hope you have," interrupted Sylvia politely.

"Yes, as well as could be expected—you know I ain't over an' above strong this season. My old trouble. But then, I don't complain any—only as I said to Joe, it is awful tryin'. Have you heard how the new minister's wife is doin'? She ain't ben to evenin' meetin' at all regular sence she got here, an' she made an angel cake, just for her own family, last Wednesday. She puts her washin' out, too. I got it straight from Mrs. Jones, next door to her. I went there the other evenin' to get a nightgown pattern she thought was real tasty. I don't know as I shall like it, though. It's supposed to have a yoke made out of crochet or tattin' at the top, an' I ain't got anything of the kind on hand just now, an' no time to make any. Besides, I've never thought these new-fangled garments was just the thing for a respectable woman—there ain't enough to 'em. When I was young they was made of good thick cotton, long-sleeved an' high-necked, trimmed with Hamburg edgin' an' buttoned down the front. Speakin' of nightgowns, how are you gettin' on with your trousseau? Have you decided what you're goin' to wear for a weddin' dress? I was readin' in the paper the other day about some widow that got married down in Boston, an' she wore a pink chiffon dress. I was real shocked. If she'd ben a divorced person, I should have expected some such thing, but there warn't anything of the kind in this case—she was a decent young woman, an' real pretty, judgin' from her picture. But I should have thought she'd have wore gray or lavender, wouldn't you? There oughtn't to be anything gay about a second weddin'! Well, as I was sayin' to Joe about the minister's wife — What's that? You think they're both real nice, an' you're glad he's got *some* sort of a wife? Now, Sylvia, I always did think you was a little mite hard on Mr. Jessup. I says to Joe, 'Joe, Sylvia's a nice girl, but she's a flirt, sure as you're settin' there,' an' Joe says—"

"Have you heard from Fred and Sally yet?"

"Yes, they've sent us three picture post-cards. Real pretty. There ain't much space for news on 'em, though —they just show a bridge, an' a park, an' a railroad station. Still, of course, we was glad to get 'em, an' they seem to be havin' a fine time. I heard to-day that Ruth's baby was sick again. Delicate, ain't it? I shouldn't be a mite surprised if Ruth couldn't raise her. 'Blue around the eyes,' I says to Joe the first time I ever clapped eyes on her. An' then Ruth ain't got no get-up-and-get to her. Shiftless, same's Howard is, though she's just as well-meanin'. I hear she's thinkin' of keepin' a hired girl all summer. Frank's business don't warrant it. He has a real hard time gettin' along. He's too easy-goin' with his customers. Gives long credit when they're hard up, an' all that. Of course it's nice to be charitable if you can afford it, but—"

"Frank isn't going to pay the hired girl."

"There you go again, Sylvia! You kinder remind me of the widow's cruse, never failin'. 'Tain't many families gets hold of anything like you. Well, I must be sayin' good-night—there seems to be several people tryin' to butt in an' use this line, though probably they don't want it for anything important at all. I've got no patience with folks that uses the telephone as a means of gossip, an' interfere with those that really needs it. Besides, though I'd be glad to talk with you a little longer, I'm plum tuckered out with the heat, as I said before. I ben makin'

197

currant jelly, too. It come out fine—a little too hard, if anything. But, as I says to Joe, 'Druv as I am, I'm a-goin' to call up that poor lonely girl, an' help her pass the evenin'.' Come over an' bring your sewin' an' set with me some day soon, won't you, Sylvia? You know I'm always real pleased to see you. Good-night."

"Good-night." Sylvia leaned back, laughing.

Mrs. Elliott, who infuriated Thomas, and exasperated Austin, was a never-failing source of enjoyment to her. She went back to the porch to wait for Austin, still chuckling.

After the conversation she had had with him, she was greatly surprised, when, a little after eight o'clock, the garden gate clicked. She ran down the steps hurriedly with his name on her lips. But the figure coming towards her through the dusk was much smaller than Austin's and a voice answered her, in broken English, "It ain't Mr. Gray, missus. It's me."

"Why, Peter!" she said in amazement; "is anything the matter at the farm?"

"No, missus; not vat you'd call *vrong.*"

"What is it, then? Will you come up and sit down?"

He stood fumbling at his hat for a minute, and then settled himself awkwardly on the steps at her feet. His yellow hair was sleekly brushed, his face shone with soap and water, and he had on his best clothes. It was quite evident that he had come with the distinct purpose of making a call.

"Can dose domestics hear vat ve say?" he asked at length, turning his wide blue eyes upon her, after some minutes of heavy silence.

"Not a word."

"Vell den—you know Mr. Gray and I goin' away to-morrow."

"Yes, Peter."

"To be gone much as a mont', Mr. Gray say."

"I believe so."

"Mrs. Cary, dear missus,—vill you look after Edit' vile I'm gone?"

"Why, yes, Peter," she said warmly, "I always see a good deal of Edith—we're great friends, you know."

"Yes, missus, that's vone reason vy I come—Edit' t'ink no vone like you—ever vas, ever shall be. But den—I'm vorried 'bout Edit'."

"Worried? Why, Peter? She's well and strong."

"Oh, yes, she's vell—ver' vell. But Edit' love to have a good time—'vun' she say. If I go mit, she come mit me—ven not, mit some vone else."

"I see—you're jealous, Peter."

"No, no, missus, not jealous, only vorried, ver' vorried. Edit' she's young, but not baby, like Mr. and Missus Gray t'ink. I don't like Mr. Yon Veston, missus, nod ad all—and Edit' go out mit him, ev'y chance she get. An' Mr. Hugh Elliott, cousin to Miss Sally's husband, dey say he liked Miss Sally vonce—he's back here now, he looks hard at Edit' ev'y time he see her. He's that kind of man, missus, vat does look ver' hard."

Sylvia could not help being touched. "I'll do my best, Peter, but I can't promise anything. Edith is the kind of girl, as you say, that likes to have 'fun' and I have no real authority over her."

As if the object of his visit was entirely accomplished, Peter rose to leave. "I t'ank you ver' much, missus," he said politely. "It's a ver' varm evening, not? Good-night."

For a few minutes after Peter left, Sylvia sat thinking over what he had said, and her own face grew "vorried" too. Then the garden gate clicked again, and for the next two hours she was too happy for trouble of any kind to touch her. Austin's interview with Mr. Carter had proved a great success, and after that had been thoroughly discussed, they found a great deal to say about their own plans for September. For the moment, she quite forgot all that Peter had said.

It came back to her, vividly enough, a few nights later. She had sat up very late, writing to Austin, and was still lying awake, long after midnight, when she heard the whirr of a motor near by, and a moment later a soft voice calling under her window. She threw a negligee about her, and ran to the front door; as she unlatched it, Edith slipped in, her finger on her lips.

"Hush! Don't let the servants hear! Oh, Sylvia, I've had such a lark—will you keep me overnight!"

"I would gladly, but your mother would be worried to death."

"No, she won't. You see, I found, two hours ago, that it would be a long time before I got back, and I telephoned her saying I was going to spend the night with you. Don't you understand? She thought I was here then."

"Edith—you didn't lie to your mother!"

"Now, Sylvia, don't begin to scold at this hour, when I'm tired and sleepy as I can be! It wasn't my fault we burst two tires, was it? But mother's prejudiced against Hugh, just because Sally, who's a perfect prude, didn't happen to like him. Lend me one of your delicious nightdresses, do, and let me cuddle down beside you—the bed's so big, you'll never know I'm there."

Sylvia mechanically opened a drawer and handed her the garment she requested.

"Gracious, Sylvia, it's like a cobweb—perhaps if I marry a rich man, I can have things like this! What an angel you look in yours! Austin will certainly think he's struck heaven when he sees you like that! I never could understand what a little thing like you wanted this huge bed for, but, of course, you knew when you bought it—"

"Edith," interrupted Sylvia sharply, "be quiet! In the morning I want to talk with you a little."

But as she lay awake long after the young girl had fallen into a deep, quiet sleep, she felt sadly puzzled to know what she could, with wisdom and helpfulness, say. It was so usual in the country for young girls to ride about alone at night with their admirers, so much the accepted custom, of which no harm seemed to come, that however much she might personally disapprove of such a course, she could not reasonably find fault with it. It was probably her own sense of outraged delicacy, she tried to think, after Edith's careless speech, that made her feel that the child lacked the innate good-breeding and quiet attractiveness, which her sisters, all less pretty than she, possessed to such a marked extent, in spite of their lack of polish. She tried to think that it was only to-night she had noticed how red and full Edith's pouting lips were growing, how careless she was about the depth of her V-cut blouses, how unusually lacking in shyness and restraint for one so young. In the morning, she said nothing and Edith was secretly much relieved; but she went and asked Mrs. Gray if she could not spare her youngest daughter for a visit while Austin was away, "to ward off loneliness." She found the good lady out in the garden, weeding her petunias, and bent over to help her as she made her request.

"There, dearie, don't you bother—you'll get your pretty dress all grass-stain, and it looks to me like another new one! I wouldn't have thought baby-blue would be so becomin' to you, Sylvia. I always fancied it for a blonde, mostly, but there! you've got such lovely skin, anything looks well on you. Do you like petunias? Scarcely anyone has them, an' cinnamon pinks, an' johnnie-jump-ups any more—it's all sweet-peas, an' nasturtiums, an' such! But to me there ain't any flower any handsomer than a big purple petunia."

"I like them too—and it doesn't matter if my dress does get dirty—it'll wash. Now about Edith—"

"Why, Sylvia, you know how I hate to deny you anything, but I don't see how I can spare her! Here it is hayin'-time, the busiest time of the year, an' Austin an' Peter both gone. I haven't a word to say against them young fellows that Thomas has fetched home from college to help while our boys are gone, they're well-spoken, obligin' chaps as I ever see, but the work don't go the same as it do when your own folks is doin' it, just the same. Besides, Sally's not here to help like she's always been before, summers, an' it makes a pile of difference, I can tell you. Molly can play the piano somethin' wonderful, an' Katherine can spout poetry to beat anything I ever heard, but Edith can get out a whole week's washin' while either one of 'em is a-wonderin' where she's goin' to get the hot water to do it with, an' she's a real good

202

cook! I never see a girl of her years more capable, if I do say so, an' she always looks as neat an' pretty as a new pin, whatever she's doin', too. Why don't you come over to us, if you're lonely? We'd all admire to have you! There, we've got that row cleaned out real good—s'posin' we tackle the candytuft, now, if you feel like it."

Sylvia would gladly have offered to pay for a competent "hired girl," but she did not dare to, for fear of displeasing Austin. So she wrote to Uncle Mat to postpone his prospective visit, to the great disappointment of them both, and filled her tiny house with young friends instead, urging Edith to spend as much time helping her "amuse" them as she could, to the latter's great delight. Unfortunately the girl and one of the boys whom she had invited were already so much interested in each other that they had eyes for no one else, and the other fellow was a quiet, studious chap, who vastly preferred reading aloud to Sylvia to canoeing with Edith. The girl was somewhat piqued by this lack of appreciation, and quickly deserted Sylvia's guests for the more lively charms of Hugh Elliott's red motor and Jack Weston's spruce runabout. Mr. and Mrs. Gray saw no harm in their pet's escapades, but, on the contrary, secretly rejoiced that the humble Peter was at least temporarily removed and other and richer suitors occupying the foreground. They were far from being worldly people, but two of their daughters having already married poor men, they, having had more than their own fair share of drudgery, could not help hoping that this pretty butterfly might be spared the coarser labors of life.

Sylvia longed to write Austin all about it, but she could not bring herself to spoil his trip by speaking slightingly, and perhaps unjustly, of his favorite sister's conduct. As she had rather feared, the short trip originally planned proved so instructive and delightful that it was lengthened, first by a few days and then by a fortnight, so that one week in August was already gone before he returned. He came back in holiday spirits, bubbling over with enthusiasm about his trip, full of new plans and arrangements. His enthusiasm was contagious, and he would talk of nothing and allow her to talk of nothing except themselves.

"My, but it's good to be back! I don't see how I ever stayed away so long."

"You didn't seem to have much difficulty—every time you wrote it was to say you'd be gone a little longer. I suppose some of those New York farmers have pretty daughters?"

"You'd better be careful, or I'll box your ears! What mischief have *you* been up to? I've heard rumors about some bookish chap, who read Keats's sonnets, and sighed at the moon. You see I'm informed. I'll take care how I leave you again."

"You had better. I won't promise to wait for you so patiently next time."

"Don't talk to me about patient waiting! Sylvia, is it really, honestly true I've only got three more weeks of it?"

"It's really, honestly true. Good-night, darling, you *must* go home."

"And *you've* only got three weeks more of being able to say that! I suppose I must obey—but remember, *you'll* have to promise to obey pretty soon."

"I'll be glad to, Austin—"

"Yes, dear—Sylvia, I think your cheeks are softer than ever—"

"I don't think Edith looks very well, do you?"

"Why, I thought she never was so pretty! But now you speak of it she *does* seem a little fagged—not fresh, the way you always are! Too much gadding, I'm afraid."

"I'm afraid so. Couldn't you—?"

"My dear girl, leave all that to Peter—I've got *my* hands full, keeping *you* in order. Sylvia, there's one thing this trip has convinced me we've got to have, right away, and that's more motors. We've got the land, we've got the buildings, and we've got the stock, but we simply must stop wasting time and grain on so many horses—its terribly out of date, to say nothing else against it. We need a touring-car for the family, and a runabout for you and me,—do sell that great ark of yours, and get something you can learn to run yourself, and that won't use half the gasoline,—and a tractor to plough with, and a truck to take the cream to the creamery."

"Well, I suppose you'll let me give these various things for Christmas presents, won't you? You're so awfully afraid that I'll contribute the least little bit to the success of the farm that I hardly dare ask. But I could bestow the tractor on Thomas, the truck on your father, and the touring-car on the girls, and certainly we'll need the runabout for all-day trips on Sundays—after the first of September."

"All right. I'll concede the motors as your share. Now, what will you give me for a reward for being so docile?"

She watched him down the path with a heart overflowing with happiness. Twice he turned back to wave his hand to her, then disappeared, whistling into the darkness. She knelt beside her bed for a long time that night, and finally fell into a deep, quiet sleep, her hand clasping the little star that hung about her throat.

Three hours later she was abruptly awakened, and sat up, confused and startled, to find Austin leaning over her, shaking her gently, and calling her name in a low, troubled voice.

"What is it? What has happened?" she murmured drowsily, reaching instinctively for the dressing-gown which lay at the foot of the bed. Austin had already begun to wrap it around her.

"Forgive me, sweetheart, for disturbing you—and for coming in like this. I tried the telephone, and called you over and over again outside your window—you must have been awfully sound asleep. I was at my wits' end, and couldn't think of anything to do but this—are you very angry with me?"

"No, no—why did you need me?"

"Oh, Sylvia, it's Edith! She's terribly sick, and she keeps begging for you so that I just *had* to come and get you! She was all right at supper-time—it's so sudden and violent that—"

Sylvia had slipped out of bed as if hardly conscious that he was beside her. "Go out on the porch and wait for me," she commanded breathlessly; "you've got the motor, haven't you? I won't be but a minute.

She was, indeed, scarcely longer than that. They were almost instantly speeding down the road together, while she asked, "Have you sent for the doctor?"

"Yes, but there isn't any there yet. Dr. Wells was off on a confinement case, and we've had to telephone to Wallacetown—she was perfectly determined not to have one, anyway. Oh, Sylvia, what can it be? And why should she want you so?"

"I don't know yet, dear."

"Do you suppose she's going to die?

"No, I'm afraid—I mean I don't think she is. Why didn't I take better care of her? Austin, can't you drive any faster?"

As they reached the house, she broke away from him, and ran swiftly up the stairs. Mr. and Mrs. Gray were both standing, white and helpless with terror, beside their daughter's bed. She was lying quite still when Sylvia entered, but suddenly a violent spasm of pain shook her like a leaf, and she flung her hands above her head, groaning between her clenched teeth. Sylvia bent over her and took her in her arms.

"My dear little sister," she said.

CHAPTER XVIII

When the long, hideous night was over, and Edith lay, very white and still, her wide, frightened eyes never leaving Sylvia's face, the doctor, gathering up his belongings, touched the latter lightly on the arm.

"She'll have to have constant care for several days, perfect quiet for two weeks at least. But if I send for a nurse—"

"I know. I'm sure I can do everything necessary for her. I've had some experience with sickness before."

The doctor nodded, a look of relief and satisfaction passing over his face. "I see that you have. Get her to drink this. She must have some sleep at once."

But when Sylvia, left alone with her, held the glass to Edith's lips, she shrank back in terror.

"No, no, no! I don't want to go to sleep—I mustn't—I shall dream!"

"Dear child, you won't—and if you do, I shall be right here beside you, holding your hand like this, and you can feel it, and know that, after all, dreams are slight things."

"You promise me?"

"Indeed I do."

"Oh, Sylvia, you're so brave—you told the doctor you'd taken care of some one that was sick before—who was it?"

It was Sylvia's turn to shudder, but she controlled it quickly, and spoke very quietly.

"I was married for two years to a man who finally died of delirium tremens. No paid nurse—would have stayed with him—through certain times. I can't tell you about it, dear, and I'm trying hard to forget it—you won't ask me about it again, will you?"

"Oh, *Sylvia!* Please forgive me! I—I didn't guess—I'll drink the medicine—or do anything else you say!"

So Edith fell asleep, and when she woke again, the sun was setting, and Sylvia still sat beside her, their fingers intertwined. Sylvia looked down, smiling.

"The doctor has been here to see you, but you didn't wake, and we both felt it was better not to disturb you. He thinks that all is going well with you. Will you drink some milk, and let me bathe your face and hands?"

"No—not—yet. Have you really been here—all these hours?"

"Yes, dear."

"With no rest—nothing to eat or drink?"

"Oh, yes, Austin brought me my dinner, but I ate it sitting beside you, and wouldn't let him stay—he's so big, he can't help making a noise."

"Does he know?"

"Not yet."

"And father and mother?"

Sylvia was silent.

"Oh, Sylvia, I'm a wicked, wicked girl, but I'm not what you must think! I'm not a—a murderess! Peter came up behind me on the stairs in the dark last night, and spoke to me suddenly. It startled me—everything seems to have startled me lately—and I slipped, and fell, and hurt myself—I didn't do it on purpose."

"You poor child—you don't need to tell me that—I never would have believed it of you for a single instant." Then she added, in the strained voice which she could not help using on the very rare occasions when she forced herself to speak of something that had occurred during her marriage, but still as if she felt that no word which might give comfort should be left unsaid, "Perhaps your mother has told you that the little baby who died when it was two weeks old wasn't the first that I—expected. A fall or—or a blow—or any shock of—fear or grief—often ends—in a disaster like this."

"Will the others believe me, too?"

"Of course they will. Don't talk, dear, it's going to be all right."

"I must talk. I've got to tell—I've got to tell *you*. And you can explain—to the family. You always understand everything—and you never blame anybody. I often wonder why it is—you're so good yourself—and yet you never say a word against any living creature, or let anybody else do it when you're around; but lots of girls, who've—done just what I have—and didn't happen to get found out—are the ones who speak most bitterly and cruelly—I know two or three who will be just *glad* if they know—"

"They're not going to know."

"Then you will listen, and—and believe me—and *help?*"

"Yes, Edith."

"I thought it happened only in books, or when girls had no one to take care of them—not to girls with fathers and mothers and good homes—didn't you, Sylvia?"

"No, dear. I knew it happened sometimes—oh, more often than *sometimes*—to girls—just like you."

"And what happens afterwards?"

Sylvia shuddered, but it was too dark in the carefully shuttered room for Edith to see her. She said quite quietly:

"That depends. In many cases—nothing dreadful."

"Ever anything good?"

"Yes, yes, *good* things can happen. They can be *made* to."

"Will you make good things happen to me?"

"I will, indeed I will."

"And not hate me?"

"Never that."

"May I tell you now?"

"If you believe that it will make you feel better; and if you will promise, after you have told me, to let me give you the treatment you need."

"I promise— Do you remember that in the spring Hugh Elliott came to spend a couple of months with Fred?"

Sylvia's fingers twitched, but all she said was, "Yes, Edith."

"He used to be in love with Sally; but he got all over that. He said he was in love with me. I thought he was— he certainly acted that way. Saying—fresh things, and— and always trying to touch me—and—that's the way men usually do when they begin to fall in love, isn't it, Sylvia?"

"No, darling, not *usually*—not—some kinds of men." And Sylvia's thoughts flew back, for one happy instant, to the man who had knelt at her feet on Christmas night. "But—I know what you mean—"

"And—I liked it. I mean, I thought the talk was fun

211

to listen to, and that the—rest was—oh, Sylvia, do you understand—"

"Yes, dear, I understand."

"And he was awfully jolly, and gave me such a good time. I felt flattered to think he didn't treat me like a child, that he paid me more attention than the older girls."

"Yes, Edith."

"And I thought what fun it would be to marry him, instead of some slow, poky farmer, and have a beautiful house, and servants, and lovely clothes. I kept thinking, every night, he would ask me to; but he didn't. And finally, one time, just before we got home after a dance, he said—he was going away in the morning."

"Yes, Edith."

"Oh, I was so disappointed, and sore, and—angry! That was it, just plain angry. I had been going with Jack all along when Hugh didn't come for me, and Jack came the very night after Hugh went away, and took me for a long ride. He told me how terribly jealous he had been, and how thankful he was that Hugh was out of the way at last, and that Peter was going, too. So I laughed, and said that Peter didn't count at all, and that I hated Hugh —of course neither of those things was true, but I was so hurt, I felt *I'd* like to hurt somebody, too. And finally, I blurted out how mean Hugh had been, to make me think he cared for me, when he was just—having a good time. Then Jack said, 'Well, *I* care about you—I'm just crazy over you.' 'I don't believe you,' I said; 'I'll never believe any man again.' Just to tease him—that was all. 'I'll show you whether I love you,' he said, and began to kiss me. I think he had been drinking—he does, you know.

Of course, I ought to have stopped him, but I—had let Hugh—it meant a lot to me, too—the first time. But after I found it didn't mean anything to him—it didn't seem to matter—if some one else *did*—kiss me—I was flattered —and pleased—and—comforted. You mustn't think that what—happened afterwards—was all Jack's fault. I think I could have stopped it even then—if he'd been sober, anyway. But I didn't guess—I never dreamed—how far you could—get carried away—and how quickly. Oh, Sylvia, why didn't somebody tell me? At home—in the sunshine—with people all around you—it's like another world —you're like another person—than when there's nothing but stillness and darkness everywhere, and a man who loves you, pleading, with his arms around you—

"And afterwards, I thought no one would ever know. Jack thought so, too. Besides, you see, he is crazy to marry me—he'd give anything to. But I wouldn't marry him for anything in the world—whatever happened—the great ignorant, dirty drunkard! Only he isn't unkind—or cowardly—don't think that—or let the others think so! He's willing to take his share of the blame—he's *sorry*—

"Then, just a little while ago—I began to be afraid of— what had happened. But I didn't know much about that, either. I thought, some way, I might be mistaken—I hoped so, anyhow. I wanted to come—and tell you all about it—but I didn't dare. I never saw you kiss Austin but once—you're so quiet when you're with him, Sylvia, and other people are around—and it was—it was just like —*a prayer*. After seeing that, I *couldn't* come to you— with my story—unless *I had* to—I felt as if it would be just like throwing mud on a flower.

"Then, yesterday, after the work was done, Peter asked

213

me to go to walk with him. It was so late, when he and Austin got home, that I had scarcely seen him. I was going upstairs, in the dark, and I didn't know that he was anywhere near—it frightened me when he called. So—so I slipped—and fell—all the way down. I knew, right away, that I was hurt; but, of course, I didn't guess how much. I went to walk with him just the same, because it seemed as if it—would feel good to be with Peter —he's always been so—well, I can't explain—*so square*. And while we were out, I began to feel sick—and now, of course, he'll never be willing—to take me to walk— to be seen anywhere with me again! I can't bear it! I mind —not having been square to him—more than anything else—more than half-killing mother, even! Oh, Sylvia, tell them, please, *quickly!* and have it over with—tell them, too, that it was my own fault—don't forget that part! And then take me away with you, where I won't see them— or any one else I know—and teach me to be good—even if you can't help me to forget!"

Two hours later, when Edith was sleeping again, Mrs. Gray came into the room with a mute, haggard expression on her kind, homely face which Sylvia never forgot, and put her arms around the younger woman.

"Austin's askin' for you, dearie. It's been a hard day for him, too—I think you ought to go to him. I'll sit here until you come back."

Sylvia nodded, and stole silently out of the room. Austin was waiting for her at the foot of the stairs, his smile of welcome changing to an expression of stern solic- itude as he looked at her.

"Have you been seeing ghosts? You're whiter than

chalk—no wonder, shut up in that hot, dark room all day, without any rest and almost without any food! No matter if Edith does want you most, you'll have to take turns with mother after this. Come out with me where it's cool for a little while—and then you must have some supper, and a bath, and Sally's room to sleep in—if you won't go home, which is really the best place for you."

She allowed him to lead her, without saying a word, to the sheltered slope of the river, and sat down under a great elm, while he flung himself down beside her, laying his head in her lap.

"Sylvia—just think—less than three weeks now! It's been running through my head all day—I've almost got it down to hours, minutes, and seconds— What's the matter with Edith, anyway? Father and mother are as dumb as posts."

"The matter is—oh, my darling boy—I might as well tell you at once—we can't—I've got to go away with Edith. Austin, you must wait for me—another year—" And her courage giving out completely, she threw herself into his arms, and sobbed out the tragic story.

CHAPTER XIX

"Sylvia, I won't give you up—*I can't!*"

"Darling, it isn't giving me up—its only waiting a little longer for me."

"Don't you think I've waited long enough already?"

"Yes, Austin, but— Perhaps I won't have to stay away a whole year—perhaps by spring—or we might be married now, just as we planned, and take Edith with us."

"No, no!" he cried; "you know I wouldn't do that—I want you all to myself!" Then, still more passionately, "You're only twenty-two yourself—you shan't darken your own youth with—this—this horrible thing. You've seen sorrow and sin enough—far, far too much! You've a right to be happy now, to live your own life—and so have I."

"And hasn't Edith any right?"

"No—she's forfeited hers."

"Do you really think so? Do you believe that a young, innocent, sheltered girl, so pretty and so magnetic that she attracts immediate attention wherever she goes, who has starved for pretty things and a good time, and suddenly finds them within her reach, whose parents wilfully shut their eyes to the fact that she's growing up, and boast that 'they've kept everything from her'—and then let her go wherever she chooses, with that pitiful lack of armor, doesn't deserve another chance? And I think if you had stayed with her through last night—and seen the change that suffering—and shame—and hopelessness have wrought in that little gay, lovely, thoughtless creature, you'd feel that she had paid a pitifully large forfeit already —and realize that no matter how much we help her, she'll have to go on paying it as long as she lives."

Austin was silent for a moment; then he muttered:

"Well, why doesn't she marry Jack Weston? She admits that it was half her fault—and that he really does care for her."

"*Marry* him!" Sylvia cried—"*after that!* He cares for her as much as it is in him to care for anybody—but you know perfectly well what he is! Do you want her to tie herself forever to an ignorant, intemperate, sensual man? Put herself where the nightmare of her folly would stare her perpetually in the face? Where he'd throw it in her teeth every time he was angry with her, that he married her out of charity—and probably tell the whole country-side the same thing the first time he went to Wallacetown on a Saturday evening and began to 'celebrate'? How much chance for hope and salvation would be left for her then? Have you forgotten something you said to me once —something which wiped away in one instant all the bitterness and agony of three years, and sent me—straight into your arms? 'The best part of a decent man's love is not passion, but reverence; his greatest desire, not possession, but protection; his ultimate aim, not gratification, but sacrifice.'"

"I didn't guess then what a beautiful and wonderful thing passion could be—I'd only seen the other side of it."

Sylvia winced, but she only said, very gently: "Then can you, with that knowledge, wish Edith to keep on seeing it all her life? It's—it's pretty dreadful, I think—remember I've seen it too."

"Good God, Sylvia, do stop talking as if the cases were synonymous! *You were married!* It's revolting to me to hear you keep saying that you 'understand.' There's no more likeness between you and Edith than there is between a lily growing in a queen's garden and a sweet-brier rose springing up on a dusty highroad."

"I know how you feel, dear; but remember, the sweet-brier rose isn't a *weed!* They're both flowers—and fragrant—and—and fragile, aren't they?" Then, very softly: "Besides, the lily growing in the queen's garden, even though the wicked king may own it for a time, is usually picked in the end—by the fairy prince—to adorn his palace; while the little sweet-brier rose any tramp may pluck and stick in his hat—and fling away when it is faded. And if it was really the property of an honest woodman and his wife, and the highroad ran very close to the border of a sheltered wood, where their cottage was—wouldn't they feel very badly when they found their rose was gone?"

"You plead very well," said Austin almost roughly, "and you're pleading for every one *but me*—for Edith and father and mother, who've all done wrong—and now you want to take the burden of their wrongdoing on your own innocent shoulders, and make me help you—no matter how *I* suffer! *I've* tried to do *right*—never so hard in all my life—and mostly—I've succeeded. You've helped—I never could have done it without you—but a lot of it has been pulling myself up by my own bootstraps. Now

I've reached the end of my rope—and I suppose, instead of thinking of that—the next thing you do will be to make excuses for Jack Weston."

"Yes," said Sylvia, very gently, "that's just what I'm going to do. I know how hard you've tried—I know how well you've succeeded. I know there aren't many men like you—*as good as you*—in the whole world. I'm not saying that because I'm in love with you—I'm not saying it to encourage you—I'm saying it because it's true. You've conquered—all along the line. It's so wonderful—and so glorious—that sometimes it almost takes my breath away. Darling—you know I've never reproached you—even in my own mind—for anything that may have happened before you knew me—and *I* know, that much as you wish now it never had happened—still you can comfort yourself with the old platitudes of 'the double standard.' 'All men do this some time—or nearly all men. I haven't been any worse than lots of others—and I've always respected *good* women'—oh, I've heard it all, hundreds of times! Some day I hope you'll feel differently about that, too—that you won't teach *your* son to argue that way—not only because it's wrong, but because it's dangerous—and very much out of date, besides. This isn't the time to go into all that—but I wonder if you would be willing to tell me everything that went through your mind for five minutes—when I came to you the night of the Graduation Ball, and you took me in your arms?"

"*Sylvia!*" The cry came from the hidden depths of Austin's soul, wrung with grief and shame. "I thought you never guessed— Since you did—how could you go on loving me so—how can you say what you just have—about my—*goodness?*"

"Darling, *don't!* I never would have let you know that I guessed—if everything else I said hadn't failed! That wasn't a reproach! 'Go on loving you'—how could I help loving you a thousand times more than ever—when you won the greatest fight of all? It's no sin to be tempted—I'm glad you're strong enough—and human enough—for that. And I'm thankful from the bottom of my heart—that you're strong enough—and *divine* enough—to resist temptation. But you know—even a man like you—what a sorceress plain human nature can be. What chance has a weakling like Jack Weston against her, when she leads him in the same path?"

For all answer, he buried his face in the folds of her dress, and lay with it hidden, while she stroked his hair with soft and soothing fingers; she knew that she had wounded him to the quick, knew that this battle was the hardest of all, knew most surely that it was his last one, and that he would win it. Meanwhile there was nothing for her to do but to wait, unable to help him, and forced to bear alone the burden of weariness and sacrifice which was nearly crushing her. Should Austin sense, even dimly, how the sight of Edith's suffering through the long, sleepless night had brought back her own, by its reawakened memories of agony which he had taught her to forget; should divine that she, too, had counted the days to their marriage, and rejoiced that the long waiting was over, she knew that Edith's cause would be lost. She counted on the strength of the belief that most men hold—they never guess how mistakenly—that fatigue and pain are matters of slight importance among the really big things of life, and that women do not feel as strongly as they do, that there is less passion in the giving than in the taking, that mother-love is the greatest thing they ever know. Some day, she would convince him that he was wrong; but now— At last he looked up, with an expression in his eyes, dimly seen in the starlight, which brought fresh tears to hers, but new courage to her tired heart.

"If you do love me, and I know you do," he said brokenly, "never speak to me about that again. You've forgiven it—you forgive everything—but I never shall forgive myself, or feel that I can atone, for what I meant —for that one moment—to do, as long as I live. On Christmas night, when there was no evil in my heart, you thought you saw it there, because your trust had been betrayed before; I vowed then that I would teach you at least that I was worthy of your confidence, and that most men were; and when I had taught you, not only to trust me, but to love me, so that you saw no evil even when it existed—I very nearly betrayed you. It wasn't my strength that saved us *both*—it was your wonderful love and faith. There's no desire in the world that would profane such an altar of holiness as you unveiled before me that night." He lifted her soft dress, and kissed the hem of her skirt. "I haven't forgiven myself about—what happened before I knew you, either," he whispered; "you're wrong there. I used those arguments, once, myself, but I can't any more. We'll teach—*our son*—better, won't we, so that he'll have a cleaner heritage to offer his wife than I've got for mine—but he won't love her any more. Now, darling, go back to the house, and get some rest, if you can, but before you go to sleep, pray for me— that when Edith doesn't need you any more—I may have you for my own. And now, please, leave me—I've got to be alone—"

"Dat," said a voice out of the darkness, "is just vat she must nod do."

Austin sprang to his feet. It was too dark to see more than a few feet. But there could be no doubt that the speaker was very near, and the accent was unmistakable. Austin's voice was heavy with anger.

"Eavesdropping, Peter?"

"No—pardon, missus; pardon, Mr. Gray. Frieda is sick. I been lookin' ev'ywhere for Mr. Gray to tell him. At last I hear him speak out here, I come to find. Then I over-hear—I cannot help it. I try—vat you say—interrupt—it vas my vish. Beliefe me, please. But somet'ing hold me—here." He put his hand to his throat. "I could not. I ver' sorry. But as it is so I haf heard—I haf also some few words to speak.

"Dere vas vonce a grade lady," he said, coming up closer to them, "who vas so good, and so lofly, and so sveet, that no vone who saw her could help lofing her; and she vas glad to help ev'y vone, and gif to ev'y vone, and she vas so rich and vise dat she could help and gif a great deal.

"And dere vas a poor boy who vas stupid and homely and poor, and he did nodings for any vone. But it hap-pened vone time dat dis boy t'ought dat he and the grade lady could help the same person. So he vent to her and say—but ver' respectful, like he alvays felt to her, 'Dis is my turn. Please, missus, let me haf it.'"

"What do you mean, Peter?" asked Sylvia gently.

He came closer still. It was not too dark, as he did so, to see the furrows which fresh tears had made on his grimy face, to be conscious of his soiled and stained working clothes, and his clumsiness of manner and carriage; but the earnest voice went on, more doggedly than sadly:

"Vat I heard 'bout Edit' to-night, I guessed dis long time ago. Missus—if you hear that Mr. Gray done som ver' vrong t'ing—even *dis* ver' vrong t'ing—"

"I know," said Sylvia quickly; "it wouldn't make any difference now—I care too much. I'd want him—if he still wanted me—just the same. I'd be hurt—oh, dreadfully hurt—but I wouldn't feel angry—or revengeful—that's what you mean, isn't it, Peter?"

"Ya-as," said Peter gratefully, "dats yust it, missus, only, of course I couldn't say it like dat. I t'ank you, missus. Vell, den, I lof Edit' ever since I come here last fall, ver' much, yust like you lof Mr. Gray—only, of course, you can't believe dat, missus."

"Yes, I can," said Sylvia.

"So I say," went on Peter, looking only at Sylvia now, "Edit' need you, but Mr. Gray, he need you, too. No vone in t'e vorld need me but Edit'. You shall say, 'Peter's fat'er haf sent for him, Peter go back to Holland ver' quick'—vat you say, suddenly. 'Let Edit' marry Peter and go mit.' Ve stay all vinter mit my fat'er and moder—"

"You'll travel," interrupted Sylvia. "Edith will have the same dowry from me that Sally had for a wedding present. She won't be poor. You can take her everywhere—oh, Peter, you can—*give her a good time!*"

Peter bowed his head. There was a humble grace about the gesture which Sylvia never forgot.

"You ver' yust lady, missus," he said simply; "dat must be for you to say. Vell, den, after my fat'er and moder haf welcomed her, ve shall travel. Den in de spring if you need me for de cows—Mr. Gray—if you don't t'ink shame to haf boy like me for your broder—ve come back. If nod, ve'll stay in Holland. You need no fear to haf— I vill make Edit' happy—"

Some way, Austin found Peter's hand. He was beyond speech. But Sylvia asked one more question.

"Edith thinks you can't possibly love her any more," she said—"that you won't even be willing to see her again. If she thought you were marrying her out of charity, she'd die before she'd let you. How are you going to convince her that you want to marry her because you love her?"

"Vill you gif me one chance to try?" replied Peter, looking straight into her eyes.

CHAPTER XX

"WELL, I declare it's so sudden like, I should think your breath would be took away."

Mrs. Gray smiled at Mrs. Elliott, and went on with her sewing, rocking back and forth placidly in her favorite chair. If the latter had been a woman who talked less and observed more, she would have noticed how drawn and furrowed her old friend's rosy, peaceful face had grown, how much repression there was about the lips which smiled so bravely. But these details escaped her.

" 'Course it does look that way to an outsider," said Mrs. Gray, slowly, as if rehearsing a part which had been carefully taught her, "but when you come to know the facts, it ain't so strange, after all."

"Would you feel to tell them?" asked Mrs. Elliott eagerly.

"Why, sure. Edith an' Peter's been sort of engaged this long time back, but they was so young we urged 'em to wait. Then Peter's father wrote sayin' he was so poorly, he wished Peter could fix it so's to come home, through the cold weather, an' Edith took on terrible at bein' separated from him, an' Peter declared he wouldn't leave without her; an' then—well, Sylvia sided with 'em, an' that settled it."

Mrs. Elliott nodded. "You'd never think that little soft-lookin' creature could be so set an' determined, now, would you?" she asked. "I never see any one to beat her. An' mum! She shuts her mouth tighter'n a steel trap!"

"If any family ever had a livin' blessin' showered on 'em right out of heaven," said Mrs. Gray, "we did, the day Sylvia come here. Funny, Austin's the only one of us can see's she's got a single fault. He says she's got lots of 'em, just like any other woman—but I bet he'd cut the tongue out of any one else who said so. Seems as if I couldn't wait for the third of September to come so's she'll really be my daughter, though I haven't got one that seems any dearer to me, even now."

"Speakin' of weddin's," said Mrs. Elliott, "why didn't you have a regular one for Edith, same as for Sally?"

"Land! I can't spend my whole time workin' up weddin's! Seems like they was some kind of contagious disease in this family. James was married only last December, an' even if we wasn't to that, we got all het up over it just the same. An' now we've hardly got our breath since Sally's, an' Austin's is starin' us in the face! I couldn't see my way clear to house-cleanin' this whole great ark in dog-days for nobody, an' Edith an' Peter's got to leave the very day after Sylvia'n Austin get married. Peter was hangin' round outside Edith's door the whole blessed time, after her fall—"

"Strange she should be so sick, just from a fall, ain't it?"

"Yes, 'tis, but the doctor says they're often more serious than you'd think for. Well, as I was sayin', Sylvia come out of Edith's room an' found Peter settin' on top of the stairs for the third time that day, an' she flared right up, an' says, 'For Heaven's sake, why don't you get

married right off—now—to-day—then you can go in an'
out as you like!' And before we half knew what she was
up to she had telephoned the new minister. Austin said
he wished she'd shown more of that haste about gettin'
married herself, an' she answered him right back, if she'd
been lucky enough to get as good a feller as Peter, maybe
she might have. It's real fun to hear 'em tease each other.
Sylvia likes the new minister. She says the best thing
about the Methodist Church that she knows of is the way
it shifts its pastors around—nothin' like variety, she says—
an' a new one once in three years keeps things hummin'.
She says as long as so many Methodists don't believe in
cards an' dancin' an' such, they deserve to have a little
fun some way, an'—"

"You was talkin' about Edith," interrupted Mrs. Elliott,
rather tartly, "you've got kinder switched off."

"Excuse me, Eliza—so I have. Well, Sylvia got Edith
up onto the couch (the doctor had said she might get up
for a little while that day, anyhow) an' give her one of
her prettiest wrappers—"

"What color? White?"

"No, Sylvia thought she was too pale. It was a lovely
yellow, like the dress she wore to the Graduation Ball.
We all scurried 'round an' changed our clothes—Austin's
the most stunnin'-lookin' thing in that white flannel suit
of his, Sylvia wants he should wear it to his own weddin',
'stead of a dress-suit—an' I wore my gray— Well, it was
all over before you could say 'Jack Robinson' an' I never
sweat a drop gettin' ready for it, either! I shall miss Edith
somethin' terrible this winter, but she'll have an elegant
trip, same as she's always wanted to, an' Peter says he
knows his parents'll be tickled to death to have such a
pretty daughter-in-law!"

227

"Don't you feel disappointed any," Mrs. Elliott could not help asking, "to have a feller like Peter in the family?"

Mrs. Gray bit her thread. "I don't know what you got against Peter," she said; "I look to like him the best of my son-in-laws, so far."

But that evening, as she sat with her husband beside the old reading-lamp which all the electricity that Sylvia had installed had not caused them to give up, her courage deserted her. Howard, sensing that something was wrong, looked up from "Hoard's Dairyman," which he was eagerly devouring, to see that the *Wallacetown Bugle* had slipped to her knees, and that she sat staring straight ahead of her, the tears rolling down her cheeks.

"Why, Mary," he said in amazement—"Mary—"

The old-fashioned New Englander is as unemotional as he is undemonstrative. For a moment Howard, always slow of speech and action, was too nonplussed to know what to do, deeply sorry as he felt for his wife. Then he leaned over and patted her hand—the hand that was scarcely less rough and scarred than his own—with his big calloused one.

"You must stop grieving over Edith," he said gently, "and blaming yourself for what's happened. You've been a wonderful mother—there aren't many like you in the world. Think how well the other seven children are coming along, instead of how the eighth slipped up. Think how blessed we've been never to lose a single one of them by death. Think—"

"I do think, Howard." Mrs. Gray pressed his hand in return, smiling bravely through her tears. "I'm an old fool to give way like this, an' a worse one to let you catch me at it. But it ain't wholly Edith I'm cryin' about. Land,

228

every time I start to curse the devil for Jack Weston, I get interrupted because I have to stop an' thank the Lord for Peter. An' all the angels in heaven together singin' Halleluiah led by Gabriel for choirmaster, couldn't half express my feelin's for Sylvia! I guess 'twould always be that way if we'd stop to think. Our blessin's is so much thicker than our troubles, that the troubles don't show up no more than a little yellow mustard growin' up in a fine piece of oats—unless we're bound to look at the mustard instead of the oats. As it happens, I wasn't thinkin' of Edith at all at that moment, or really grievin' either. It was just—"

"Yes?" asked Howard.

"This room," said Mrs. Gray, gulping a little, "is about the only one in the house that ain't changed a mite. The others are improved somethin' wonderful, but I'm kinder glad we've kept this just as it was. There's the braided rugs on the floor that I made when you was courtin' me, Howard, an' we used to set out on the doorstep together. An' the fringed tidies over the chairs an' sofa that Eliza give me for a weddin' present—they're faded considerable, but that good red wool never wears out. There's the crayon portraits we had done when we was on our honeymoon, an' the ones of James an' Sally when they was babies. Do you remember how I took it to heart because we couldn't scrape together the money no way to get one of Austin when he come along? He was the prettiest baby we ever had, too, except—except Edith, of course. An' after Austin we didn't even bring up the subject again— we was pretty well occupied wonderin' how we was goin' to feed an' clothe 'em all, let alone havin' pictures of 'em. Then there's the wax flowers on the mantelpiece. I always trembled for fear one of the youngsters would knock 'em off an' break the glass shade to smithereens, but they never did. An' there's your Grandfather Gray's clock. I was a little disappointed at first because it had a brass face, 'stead o' bein' white with scenes on it, like they usually was—an' then it was such a chore, with everything else there was to do, to keep it shinin' like it ought to. But now I think I like it better than the other kind, an' it's tickin' away, same as it has this last hundred years an' more. Do you remember when we began to wind it up, Saturday nights, together?— All this is the same, praise be, but—"

"Yes?" asked Howard Gray again.

"For years, evenin's," went on Mrs. Gray, "this room was full of kids. There was generally a baby sleepin'—or refusin', rather loud, to sleep!—in the cradle over in the corner. The older ones was settin' around doin' sums on their slates, or playin' checkers an' cat's-cradle. They quarrelled considerable, an' they was pretty shabby, an' I never had a chance to set down an' read the *Bugle* quiet-like, after supper, because the mendin'-basket was always waitin' for me, piled right up to the brim. Saturday nights, what a job it was all winter to get enough water het to fill the hat-tub over an' over again, an' fetch in front of the air-tight. Often I was tempted to wash two or three of 'em in the same water, but, as you know, I never done it. Thank goodness, we'd never heard of such a thing as takin' a bath every day then! I don't deny it's a comfort, with all the elegant plumbin' we've got now, not to feel you've got to wait for a certain day to come 'round to take a good soak when you're hot or dirty, but it would have been an awful strain on my conscience an' my back both in them days. I used to think sometimes, 'Oh, how glad I shall be when this pack of unruly youngsters is grown up an' out of the way, an' Howard an' I can have a little peace.' An' now that time's come, an' I set here feelin' lonely, an' thinkin' the old room *ain't* the same, in spite of the fact, as I said before, that it ain't changed a mite, because we haven't got the whole eight tumblin' 'round under our heels. I know they're doin' well—they're doin' most *too* well. I'm scared the time's comin' when they'll look down on us, Howard, me especially. Not that they'll mean to—but they're all gettin' so —so different. You had a good education, an' talk right, but I can't even do that. I found an old grammar the other day, an' set down an' tried to learn somethin' out of it, but it warn't no use—I couldn't make head or tail of it. An' then they're all away—an' they're goin' to keep on bein' away. James is South, an' Thomas is at college, an' Molly's studyin' music in Boston, an' before we know it Katherine'll be at college too, an' Edith an' Austin in Europe. That leaves just Ruth an' Sally near us, an' they're both married. I don't begrudge it to 'em one bit. I'm glad an' thankful they're all havin' a better chance than we did. If I could just feel that some day they'd all come back to the Homestead, an' to us—an' come because they *wanted* to—"

Howard put his arm around his wife, and drew her down beside him on the old horsehair sofa. One of the precious red wool tidies slipped to the floor, and lay there unnoticed. Slowly, while Mrs. Gray had been talking, the full depth of her trouble became clear to him, and the words to comfort her rose to his lips.

"They will, Mary," he said; "they will; you wait and

231

see. How could you think for one moment that our children could look down on their mother? It's mighty seldom, let me tell you, that any boy or girl does that, and only with pretty good reason then—never when they've been blessed with one like you. I haven't been able to do what I wanted for ours, but at least I gave them the best thing they possibly could have—a good mother—and with that I don't think the hardships have hurt them much! Have you forgotten—you mustn't think I'm sacrilegious, dear—that the greatest mother we know anything about was just a poor carpenter's wife—and how much her Great Son loved her? Her name was Mary, too—I'm glad we gave Molly that name—she's a good girl—somehow it seems to me it always carries a halo of sacredness with it, even now!— Then, besides—Thomas and Austin are both going to be farmers, and live right here on the old place. Austin's so smart, he may do other things besides, but this will always be his home and Sylvia's. Peter and Edith'll be here, too, and Sally and Ruth aren't more than a stone's-throw off, as you might say. That makes four out of the eight—more than most parents get. The others will come back, fast enough, to visit, with us and them here! And think of the grandchildren coming along! Why, in the next generation, there'll be more kids piling in and out of this living-room than you could lug water and mend socks for if you never turned your hand to another thing! And, thank God, you won't have to do that now— you can just sit back and take solid comfort with them. You had to work so hard when our own children were babies, Mary, that you never could do that. But with Ruth's and Austin's and Sally's—"

He paused, smiling, as he looked into the future. Then

he kissed her, almost as shyly as he had first done more than thirty years before.

"Besides," he said, "I'm disappointed if you're lonely here with me, just for a little while, because I'm enjoying it a whole lot. Haven't you ever noticed that when two people that love each other first get married, there's a kind of *glow* to their happiness, like the glow of a sunrise? It's mighty beautiful and splendid. Then the burden and heat of the day, as the Bible says, come along. It doesn't mean that they don't care for each other any more. But they're so tired and so pressed and so worried that they don't say much about their feelings, and sometimes they even avoid talking to each other, or quarrel. But when the hard hours are over, and the sun's gone down—not so bright as it was in the morning, maybe, but softer, and spreading its color over the whole sky—the stars come out—and they know the best part of the day's ahead of them still. They can take time then to sit down, and take each other's hands, and thank God for all his blessings, but most of all for the life of a man and a woman together. Austin and Sylvia think they're going to have the best part now, in the little brick cottage. But they're not. They'll be having it thirty years from now, just as you and I are, in the Old Gray Homestead."

Mary Gray wiped her eyes. "Why, Howard," she said, "you used to say you wanted to be a poet, but I never knew till now that you *was* one! I'd rather you'd ha' said all that to me than—than to have been married to Shakespeare!" she ended with a happy sob, and put her white head down on his shoulder.

CHAPTER XXI

UNCLE MAT, whose long-postponed visit was at last taking place, sat talking in front of the fire in Sylvia's livingroom with the "new minister." The room was bright with many candles, and early fall flowers from her own garden stood about in clear glass vases. In the dining-room beyond, they could see the two servants moving around the table, laid for supper. A man's voice, whistling, and the sound of rapidly approaching footsteps, came up the footpath from the Homestead. And at the same moment, the door of Sylvia's own room opened and shut and there was the rustle of silk and the scent of roses in the hall.

A moment later she came in, her arm on Austin's. Her neck and arms were bare, as he loved to see them, and her white silk dress, brocaded in tiny pink rosebuds, swept soft and full about her. A single string of great pearls fell over the lace on her breast, and almost down to her waist, and there was a high, jewelled comb in her low-dressed hair. She leaned over her uncle's chair.

"Austin says the others are on their way. Am I all right, do you think, Uncle Mat?"

"You look to me as if you had stepped out of an old French painting," he said, pinching her rosy cheek; "I'm satisfied with you. But the question arises, is Austin? He's so fussy."

Austin laughed, straightening his tie. "I can't fuss about this dress," he said, "for I chose it myself. But I'm not half the tyrant you all make me out—I'm wearing white flannel to please her. Is there plenty of supper, Sylvia? I'm almost starved."

"I know enough to expect a man to be hungry, even if he's going to be hanged—or married," she retorted, "but I'll run out to the kitchen once more, just to make sure that everything is all right."

The third of September had come at last. There was no question, this time, of a wedding in St. Bartholomew's Church, with twelve bridesmaids and a breakfast at Sherry's; no wonderful jewels, no press notices, almost no trousseau. Austin's family, Uncle Mat, and a few close friends came to Sylvia's own little house, and when the small circle was complete, she took her uncle's arm and stood by Austin's side, while the "new minister" married them. Thomas was best man; Molly, for the second time that summer, maid-of-honor. Sadie and James were missing, but as "a wedding present" came a telegram, announcing the safe arrival of a nine-pound baby-girl. Edith was not there, either, and the date of sailing for Holland had been postponed. She had gained less rapidly than they had hoped, and still lay, very pale and quiet, on the sofa between the big windows in her room. But she was not left alone when the rest of the family departed for Sylvia's house; for Peter sat beside her in the twilight, his big rough fingers clasping her thin white ones.

There proved to be "plenty of supper," and soon after it was finished the guests began to leave, Uncle Mat with many imprecations at Sylvia's "lack of hospitality in turning them out, such a cold night." Even the two capable servants, having removed all traces of the feast, came to her with many expressions of good-will, and the assurance of "comin' back next season if they was wanted," and departed to take the night train from Wallacetown for New York. By ten o'clock the white-panelled front door with its brass knocker had opened and shut for the last time, and Austin bolted it, and turned to Sylvia, smiling.

"Well, *Mrs. Gray*," he said, "you're locked in now—far from all the sights and sounds that made your youth happy—shop-windows, and hotel dining-rooms, the slamming of limousine doors, and the clinking of ice in cocktail-shakers. Your last chance of escape is gone—you've signed and sealed your own death-warrant."

"Austin! don't joke—to-night!"

"My dear," he asked, lifting her face in his hands, "did you never joke because you were afraid—to show how much you really felt?"

"Yes," she replied, "very often. But there's nothing in the whole world for me to be afraid of now."

"So you're really ready for me at last?" he whispered.

Whatever she answered—or even if she did not answer at all—to all appearances, Austin was satisfied. His mother, seeing him for the first time three days later, was almost startled at the radiance in his face. It was, perhaps, a strange honeymoon. But those who thought so had felt, and rightly, that it was a strange marriage. After the first few days, Austin spent every day at the farm, as usual, walking back to the little brick cottage for his noonday dinner, and leaving after the milking was done at night; and Sylvia, dressed in blue gingham, cooked and cleaned and sewed, and put her garden in shape for the winter. In spite of her year's training at Mrs. Gray's capable hands, she made mistakes; she burnt the grape jelly, and forgot to put the brown sugar into the sweet pickle, and took the varnish off the dining-room table by polishing it with raw linseed oil, and boiled the color out of her sheerest chiffon blouse; and they laughed together over her blunders. Then, when evening came, she was all in white again, and there was the simple supper served by candle-light in the little dining-room, and the quiet hours in front of the glowing fire afterwards, and the long, still nights with the soft stars shining in, and the cool air blowing through the open windows of their room.

Then, when the Old Gray Homestead had settled down to the blessed peacefulness and security which, the harvest safely in, the snows still a long way off, comes to every New England farm in the late fall, they closed their white-panelled front door behind them, and sailed away together, as Austin had wished to do. There were a few gay weeks in London and Paris, The Hague and Rome— "enough," wrote Sylvia, "so that we won't forget there *is* any one else in the world, and use the wrong fork when we go out to dine." There was a fortnight at the little Dutch house where by this time Peter and Edith were spending the winter with Peter's parents—"where our bed," wrote Sylvia, "was a great big box built into the wall, but, oh! so soft and comfortable; with another box for the very best cow just around the corner from it, and the music of Peter's mother's scrubbing-brush for our morning hymn." And then there were several months of wandering—"without undue haste, but otherwise just like any other tourists," wrote Sylvia. They went leisurely from place to place, as the weather dictated and their own inclinations advised. Part of the time Edith and Peter were with them, but even then they were nearly always alone, for Edith was not strong enough to keep up, even with their moderate pace. They revisited places dear to both of them, they sought out many new ones; early spring found them in Paris; and it was here that there finally came an evening when Austin put his arms around his wife's shoulders—they had made a longer day of sight-seeing than usual, and she looked pale and tired, as having finished dressing earlier than he she sat in the window, looking down at the brilliant street beneath them, waiting for him to take her down to dinner—and spoke in the unmistakably firm tone that he so seldom used.

"It's time you were at home, Sylvia—we're overstaying our holiday. I'll make sailing arrangements to-morrow."

So, by the end of May, they were back in the little brick cottage again, and the two capable servants were there, too, for there must be no danger, now, of Sylvia's getting over-tired. Those were days when Austin seldom left his wife for long if he could help it; found it hard, indeed, not to watch her constantly, and to keep the expression of anxiety and dread from his eyes. He had not proved to be among those men, who, as some French cynic, more clever than wise, has expressed it, find "the chase the best part of the game." His engagement had been a period containing much joy, it is true, but also, much doubt, much self-adjusting and repression—his marriage had not held one imperfect hour. Sylvia, as his wife, with all the petty barriers which social inequality and money and restraint had reared between them broken down by the very weight of their love, was a being even much more desired and hallowed than the pale, black-robed, unattainable lady of his first worship had been; that Sylvia should suffer, because of him, was horrible; that he might possibly lose her altogether was a fear which grew as the days went on. It fell to her to dispel that, as she had so many others.

"Why do you look at me so?" she asked, very quietly, as, according to their old custom, they sat by the river-bank watching the sun go down.

"I don't mean to. But sometimes it seems as if I couldn't bear all this that's coming. Nothing on earth can be worth it."

"You don't know," said Sylvia softly. "You won't feel that way—after you've seen him. You'll know then—that whatever price we pay—our life wouldn't have been complete without this."

"I can't understand why men should have all the pleasure—and women all the pain."

"My darling boy, they don't! That's only an old false theory, that exploded years ago, along with the one about everlasting damnation, and several other abominable ones of like ilk. Do you honestly believe—if you will think sanely for a moment—that you have had more joy than I? Or that you are not suffering twice as much as I am, or ever shall?"

"You say all that to comfort me, because you're twice as brave as I am."

"I say it to make you realize the truth, because I'm honest."

239

Molly and Katherine were busy at the Homestead in those days, Sally and Ruth in their own little houses; but Edith was at the brick cottage a great deal. In spite of all Peter's loving care, and the treatment of a great doctor whom Sylvia had insisted she should see in London, she was not very strong, and found that she must still let the long days slip by quietly, while the white hands, that had once been so plump and brown, grew steadily whiter and slimmer. She came upon Sylvia one sultry afternoon, folding and sorting little clothes, arranging them in neat, tiny piles in the scented, silk-lined drawers of a new bureau, and after she had helped her put them all in order, with hardly a word, she leaned her head against Sylvia's and whispered:

"I do wish there were some for me."

"I know, dear; but you're very young yet. Many wives are glad when this doesn't happen right away. Sally is."

"I know. But, you see, I feel that perhaps there never will be any for me—and that seems really only fair—doesn't it?"

Sylvia was silent. Her sympathy would not allow her to tell all the London doctor had said to her about her young sister-in-law; neither would it allow her to be untruthful. But certain phrases he had used came back to her with tragic intensity.

"Many a woman who can recuperate almost miraculously from organic disease fails to rally from shock—we've been overlooking that too long."—"Every sleepless night undoes the good that the sunshine during the daytime has wrought, and after many sleepless nights the days become simply horrible preludes to more terrors."—"I can't drug a child like that to a long life of uselessness

240

—make her as happy as you can, but let her have it over with as quickly as Nature will allow it—or take her to some other man—I can't in charity to her tell you anything else."

So Sylvia and Peter made her "as happy as they could," and that they hoped at times was very happy, indeed; but the look of dread never left her eyes for long, and the tired smile which had replaced her ringing laugh came less and less often to her pale lips.

There was another faithful visitor at the brick cottage that summer, for after the end of June, Thomas, who came home from college at that time, seemed to be on hand a good deal. He, as well as Austin, had proved false to Uncle Mat's prophecy; for far from falling in love with another girl within a year, he showed not the slightest indication of doing so, but seemed to find perfect satisfaction in the society of his own family, especially that portion of it in which Sylvia was, for the moment, to be found. Austin at first marvelled at the ease with which he had accepted her for a sister; but the boy's perfect transparency of behavior made it impossible to feel that the new and totally different affection which he now felt for her was a pose. Gradually he grew to depend on Thomas to "look after Sylvia" when, for one reason or another, he was called away. His interests at the bank took him more and more frequently to Wallacetown; there were cattle auctions, too important to neglect, a day's journey from home; there was even a tiny opening beginning to loom up on the political horizon. Austin was too bound by every tie of blood and affection to the Homestead ever to build his hearth-fire permanently elsewhere; but he was also rapidly growing too big to be confined by it to the exclusion of the new opportunities which seemed to be offering themselves to him in such rapid succession in every direction.

Coming in very late one evening in August after one of these necessary absences, he found Sylvia already in bed, their room dark. She had never failed to wait up for him before. He felt a sudden pang of anxiety and contrition.

"Are you ill, darling? I didn't mean to be so late."

"No, not ill—just a little more tired than usual." She drew his head down to her breast, and for some minutes they held each other so, silently, their hearts beating together. "But I think it would be better if we sent for the doctor now—I didn't want to until you came home."

She slipped out of bed, and walked over to the open window, his arm still around her. The river shone like a ribbon of silver in the moonlight; the green meadows lay in soft shadows for miles around it; in the distance the Homestead stood silhouetted against the starlit sky.

"What a year it's been!" she whispered, "for you and me alone together! And how many years there are before us—and our children—and the Homestead—and all that we stand for—as long as the New England farms and the Great Glorious Spirit which watches over them shall endure!"

A cloud passed over the moon dimming its brightness. It brought them to the realization that the long, hard hours of the night were before them both, to be faced and conquered. The New York doctor, whom Sylvia had once before refused to send for, and the fresh-faced, rosy nurse, who had both been staying at the brick cottage for the last few days, were called, the servants roused to activity. There came a time when Austin, impotent to serve Sylvia, marvelling at her bravery, wrung by her suffering, felt that such agony was beyond endurance, beyond hope, beyond anything in life worth gaining. But when the breathless, horrible night had dragged its interminable black length up to the skirts of the radiant dawn, the mist rose slowly from the quiet river and still more quiet mountains, the first singing of the birds broke the heavy stillness, and Austin and Sylvia kissed each other and their first-born son in the glory of the golden morning.

THE END

THE CAREER OF DAVID NOBLE

To

HENRY WILDER KEYES

WHOSE CAREER, FROM SELECTMAN OF HAVERHILL, NEW
HAMPSHIRE, TO UNITED STATES SENATOR FROM NEW HAMP-
SHIRE, HAS BEEN A SOURCE OF GREAT PRIDE AND DEEP JOY
TO THOSE WHO KNOW HIM, BUT MOST OF ALL TO HIS WIFE,
THIS STORY OF A NEW ENGLAND BOY IS DEDICATED WITH
MUCH LOVE.

CONTENTS

PART ONE

PART TWO

PART THREE

Part One

CHAPTER I

IN WHICH TWO FAMILIES DECIDE TO MOVE TO HAMSTEAD

IT WAS a raw, cold night, as March nights are apt to be in Vermont, the snow piled in great drifts about the house and along the silent road, the wind blowing fiercely from the south—that cold south wind which portends to any intelligent Vermonter at that time of year, a thaw, followed, if the Fates are propitious, by "a sugar snow," and then by "mud-time"—the kind of night, in short, which makes you glad that winter is almost over, and at the same time gives you a feeling of dread for the disagreeable season that lies between you and real spring weather still.

Hiram Noble, who had driven ten miles over the hills to Hamstead that afternoon, banged the kitchen door behind him with a sense of weary satisfaction, and threw a number of packages done up in pink paper on the table that stood near it. The kitchen was not cold. On the contrary, the thermometer, had there been such an unnecessary luxury in the Noble establishment, would certainly have registered eighty-five. On the whole, the scene was one of comfort and good cheer. Mrs. Noble, dressed in a gray calico wrapper, partially covered by an apron of brown print, stood by the red-hot stove,

1

frying potatoes and salt pork, which gave forth sharp, hissing sounds, and smelled most fragrantly. The larger kitchen table, covered, like the one near the door, with a red tablecloth, was already set with the remainder of the evening meal—a great plate of bread, a smaller one of cake, a dish of maple syrup and another of pickles. In the further corner of the room, around a lamp with a purple shade set upon an old-fashioned desk, sat four boys, the eldest apparently about fourteen, the youngest seven or eight, who were alternately studying and quarreling; while near the stove, her attention about equally divided between a doughnut and a rubber pacifier, was a baby girl in a high-chair.

Mrs. Noble shoved back her frying pan, and turned to greet her husband with characteristic New England demonstration.

"Wal, here ye be at last," she said, wiping her hands on her apron, "I'd about decided you wuz a-goin' to spend the night in the pool-room, or some sech den of iniquity. Did you get all them things I told ye to? I s'pose likely you forgot more'n half! Leon, don't you touch them pickles! You wait for the rest to git to the table, and then take your proper share. There now! You've et up most of what I had laid out already! Sam, pull up the baby. I don't s'pose David wants any supper—he can go right on readin'—he won't be missed none."

The various individuals thus pleasantly addressed, responded promptly. Leon, the boy of eight, swallowed the last offending pickle hurriedly, and without answering. Sam shoved his slate aside, walked over to the baby, and removing the pacifier and doughnut stub with a tactfulness which plainly showed that he was used to

2

much dealing with infants, put her at her proper place at the family board. David, the eldest boy, glanced up, and still holding his finger in his book, reluctantly moved towards the table; while Mr. Noble, deep in ablutions from the tin basin in the sink, was the only one that replied.

"Left Hamstead at four o'clock," he said, "an' the pool-room ain't open until seven. I wouldn't ha' ben so long if you hadn't given me so many fool errands to do. Land! When do you think Susie's goin' to wear out all them clothes? I notice you didn't send for nothin' for the boys."

"The boys didn't need nothin'," said his wife, sharply. "Here, Harry, wake up! Is that the way you do your sums? You won't never get through grammar school at this rate."

"There you go again," said Hiram good-naturedly, "always scoldin' Harry because book-learnin' don't seem to come just natural to him, good boy as he is at his chores and around the farm. And forever lightin' into David because he won't do nothin' much *but* read and study, when he's at the head of his class, and always has ben. What you got there now, David?"

"It's some plays," replied the boy, looking up with glowing eyes, "written by a man named Shakespeare. There's a story of his life in the front of the book. He lived in England ever so long ago, in a little place no bigger than Wallacetown, but he went away from there to London, and— Oh, they're great! Do you suppose they're ever acted at any of the entertainments down in Hamstead? I wish—"

"And I wish," interrupted his mother, "that you'd fill

3

the wood-box a little more regular, and not waste your time on such trash. Plays! I don't see where you ever got such notions! I'm sure all my family is respectable, God-fearin' people, that has nothin' to do with Shakespeare and sech. You must get your taste from your father's folks. Them plays is immoral as can be, like as not!"

"They're ever so much more respectable than the Old Testament," retorted the boy, "and you don't mind hearin' that read, right out in meetin', if you don't ever read a word of anything yourself. No, Susie, you can't have that book to tear up."

" 'Twould be the best use 'twas ever put to if she did," said his mother, "but then you don't care nothin' about pleasin' her, and never did—and she the only girl I've got left, out of three, with all you boys livin' right on and thrivin' and eatin' your heads off, let alone bein' pert and lazy."

"There, there," interposed Hiram again, soothingly, "don't sass your ma, Dave, and don't rub the boy the wrong way all the time, Lizzie. I hearn a great piece of news down to Hamstead to-day. What do you s'pose it was?"

"Nothin' good, I'll be bound," said Mrs. Noble. "I knew perfectly well you wasn't doin' errands all that time. Standin' around the air-tight in the post-office gossipin'! No, Leon, you can't have any more syrup—you are the greediest boy I ever see."

"Well, 'taint bad news, anyway," went on her husband, "do you remember the Huntington family, Lizzie?"

"Do I? Do I remember that gamblin', drinkin', young reprobate and his high and mighty old pa that treated every one as if they wasn't good enough to lick the blackin' off his boots? I should say I do!"

4

"Come, Lizzie, they wasn't so bad as all that. Hal Huntington was what you might call a little lively, but he was always awfully generous and good-hearted, and I liked him. We was about the same age, you know, and I used to see quite a lot of him, when he used to come up here summers from Boston. There warn't nothin' high and mighty about *him*. He was friends with everybody, even if he did get all the boys in the village into scrapes. You wouldn't remember that as well as I do, bein' a little older."

"All the *boys!* How about all the *girls!*" cried Mrs. Noble with unmistakable meaning, wiping the baby's mouth and taking her in her lap, "lucky for me I *was* older. You needn't always be flingin' that in my face, neither. There ain't but four years' difference between us, and I don't know where you'd ha' been today, if you hadn't had a good prudent wife to look after you, shiftless like you've always ben. Wal, whatever become of Hal Huntington? Nothin' good, I'll warrant."

"Wal, you know old Huntington allus thought the sun rose and set on Hal's head," went on Hiram. " 'Twan't but natural, bein' all he had in the world. Hal went to Harvard College, down to Cambridge, Mass., and wuz invited to leave before he was really quite due to be through. So he and his father went to Europe, and I never heard from that day to this what happened to 'em after that."

"What did?" asked Mrs. Noble, trying to suppress the eagerness in her voice, and wondering how she would ever be able to wait until the next meeting of the Ladies' Aid to pass along this thrilling story.

"They went to Paris," said her husband, in much the

5

same tone that a clergyman of the old school used in speaking of the infernal regions, "and Hal fooled 'round for a spell, enjoyin' himself like he always did. Then he took-up kinder pointed with a French actress, the kind that's called a *ballette* dancer, that wears pink tights, and awful short petticoats."

"Don' speak of such things too loud before the boys," admonished his wife. "I told you nothin' good would ever come of him. What next?"

"He took sick with typhoid fever, and when the doctor told him right out plain there warn't any hope for him, he sent for the girl and married her. His father came into Hal's room and found her settin' by the bed, dressed jest like any other woman, and Hal says, 'This is my wife.'"

"Hiram Noble! You're makin' this up!"

"Land! You don't suppose I've got brains enough to make up an unlikely story like this, do you? Wal, the old man swore something awful, and vowed there weren't a word of truth in it and all that. But Hal told his father he was dying and that they wuz married fast enough by the American minister, but the girl bein' a Catholic, wanted to get his consent, so they could be married over again by a priest, and accordin' to French law—it seems you can't do that way without the parents is willin'. Then he told the old man why they'd got to be good to her— Hal warn't all bad, Lizzie. And Mr. Huntington see that he wuz dying sure enough, and he promised to see that she was looked after all right, finally, and give in about them havin' another ceremony, too.

"He didn't see her again for some months after the funeral. Then she sent for him. She wuz livin' in a place called Fontainebleau that ain't far from Paris. He'd kept

6

track of her actions, and had had his lawyer send her enough money to live on. Well, he went, when he got her message and wuz met at the door by one of them Catholic women called nuns, or sisters, or somethin' of the sort, and she told him that Hal's widow couldn't live 'til mornin', and that there was a baby girl a few days old. I guess there must have ben some good in the girl, and she was pretty, and she was dyin', and Mr. Huntington promised her he would take the baby, and bring her up a lady.

"He never felt much like goin' back to Boston; so he's ben wanderin' around Europe all these years. Now he's gettin' old, and he's tired of that—wants to settle down. So he's comin' to Hamstead to live—not just summers, but all year round. The old house is bein' fixed up for him—land, you never see such goin's on!"

"What they doin' to it? I should think 'twas good enough for any one, the way 'twas—the best in the country, now that the old Gray place has got so awful run down."

"Wal, 'twarn't good enough for him. I went all over it this afternoon with his confidential agent—the same as told me this yarn," said Hiram with a chuckle, "Sunday I'm a-goin' to get out the carryall and hitch up, and take you in to see it, too, Lizzie. My, but it's tasty! There's a steam-heat furnace, and hard-wood floors everywhere, and four bath-rooms. Sol Daniels is paintin' with three men to help him, and Tony Smith is buildin' a new piazza for the help. It's rumored 'round some that they're goin' to have one of them new machines called an ottermobile, but I guess there ain't no truth in that. The stable's bein' fixed up for three horses, though, and there's a pony for

7

the little girl, too. She's most twelve years old now, and pretty as a picture, they say, with a heathenish foreign name that nobody can't pronounce."

"She'll grow up a lost creature, like as not, with such a father and mother," said his wife cheerfully, rising from the table with Susie, who had gone to sleep with her thumb in her mouth. "Boys, clear off the table and wash up the dishes, while I put the baby to bed."

" 'Twon't take you long to lay her in her cradle—she's asleep already," muttered David. "Father, are they awful rich?"

"Who, the Huntingtons? Lord, yes, I s'pose there wouldn't be no countin' their money, there's so much of it!"

"I s'pose the little girl has all the books she wants to read, don't you? I s'pose she can go to High School in Hamstead, and to the University of Vermont afterward, don't you?"

"Like as not. I did hear tell she had a French woman called a governor—no, that warn't the word, but 'twas somethin' like that—to teach her, but of course it ain't to be expected that she gets much of an education that way."

Mr. Noble lighted his pipe, put his feet in the oven, and unfolded his favorite periodical, the *"Rural Outlook."* Mrs. Noble remained in the bedroom that led out of the kitchen with the baby. David buried himself in his book again, and the three younger boys, after remarking scornfully that they would rather get along without his help than having him "bossin' round," washed and wiped the dishes, set the table for breakfast and swept up the kitchen, then went upstairs to bed. He read on, undisturbed, his cheeks, growing brighter, his lips parted with excitement, until finally, conscious that some one was watching him, he started up, to see his father standing beside him with an unusual expression on his face.

"Dave," he began haltingly, and stopped, visibly embarrassed. "Dave,—"

"Yes, Dad—I forgot about the wood—honest, I did—I didn't leave it a-purpose. I'll get it now."

"I warn't thinkin' about the wood," said Hiram Noble. "Set where you be a minute. You're a good boy, and I hate to see your ma so down on you. You ain't as handy about the farm as some, but once you make up your mind to a thing, you hang on to it like grim death, and you work real hard—and I swear you're awful smart at your books. What you want to be when you're grown up—a farmer?"

"I s'pose of course I have to be," the boy muttered sullenly. Then without warning, the smothered resentment of years broke out. "But I hate it! Loathe it! Maybe if we'd had one of them nice valley farms down by the river, it wouldn't be so bad. That's good fertile land, and there's schools around, and—and shows once in a while; but here, out back—what's a fellow got ahead of him but plowin' up rocks all his life, and tryin' to get a livin' off 'em? What chance has he ever got to *learn* anything?"

"Now Dave, it ain't fitten to speak ill of your own home—"

"You asked me. I've *tried* to like it, honest, I have, Dad, and the other boys do; but if I could only get away—"

The boy drew a long breath. Looking at him, his father

9

was surprised to see that his eyes were full of rebellious and angry tears.

"Well, sposin' you could?" he said, hardly less excitedly than David himself.

"I'd clear out so quick you couldn't see me for the dust. And I'd learn to be a doctor—the kind that cuts people up and sews 'em up again—a surgeon. And I'd have an ottermobile—I've ben readin' about 'em in a magazine that I picked up in the road—some one must have dropped it out of a team. And a whole houseful of books. And—and everything," he ended weakly.

"Wal,—" said his father slowly, "I don't know but what you would, give you half a chance. What do you think would be the first step to take to get all them little fixin's?"

"To go to High School in Hamstead," replied the boy promptly.

"Wal, Dave," Mr. Noble spoke slowly, but his voice quivered with emotion. "Wal, Dave—set down and listen to me. The Huntington family ain't the only one that's a-goin' to move into Hamstead. The Noble family's a-goin' too, and you kin go to High School."

Shakespeare slid to the floor, and lay there, disregarded. David fairly sprang at his father.

"You're joking," he gasped— "Oh, what'll mother say?"

Hiram cast an uneasy glance in the direction of the bedroom, and lowered his voice, but he spoke none the less firmly for all that. "She won't say nothing about it," he declared softly, but decisively. "Your ma's a good woman, but she's ben sayin' for a spell of about sixteen years, and I reckon it's time for me to do a little talkin' myself. Anyway, it won't do her no good if she does make a fuss now. I've sold my farm to a fool from New York who wants to come into the country and lead the simple life, and I've bought Daniel's house right next to the post-office. I've ben savin' quite a little money sence you boys got big enough to help me, and I ain't had to have no hired man; and I've got about three times what this place is worth from that crazy dude, on account of the view. I guess he'll find views ain't real nourishin', if he ever gets down to hard tacks. I've taken my turn plowin' up stones, just as you say, and my father and grandfather before me—now I want you should do somethin' else if you kin, and I kinder think you kin. You kin go to High School anyway, and the other boys too, when they get big enough. I'm kinder hopin' to get an appointment for postmaster. That would tickle your ma—she could help out there and get a chance to see what mail every one in town had. Jake French don't care to have it again on account of his liver trouble, and he said he'd like real well to have me get it, so I know he'll use his influence for me, and he's got considerable. And maybe, if you're smart and hire out regular for chores round, in school time, and work out at something summers, I wouldn't be a mite surprised if you could lay by enough to go to the University of Vermont by and by and learn to be a doctor."

CHAPTER II

JACQUELINE DÉSIRÉE

It was a stifling hot afternoon in mid-July, but a slight breeze stirred the leaves of the willow-trees along the bank, the swift current made cool rushing sounds, and the shadows grew long in the late afternoon sun. David Noble, stretched at full length in the shade, threw his arms over his head and shut his eyes. His hair was wet from a swim in the river, and lay close and thick about his thin tanned face; his bare feet and legs shone golden brown; as to his costume, few words suffice to describe it, for it consisted solely of a calico shirt, and a pair of shabby trousers.

He had been to church that morning, not because he wanted to—for indeed, there was nothing in the bare, close building or the gaunt unloving minister which could possibly attract the boy—but after the manner of New England children, because he was expected or forced to go. The minister and his wife had come to dinner afterwards. It was the first time the Nobles had had company since they moved to Hamstead, six weeks earlier, for Mrs. Noble entertained, after the manner of the New England housewife of her time and station, seldom and profusely. In fact, the dinner left nothing to be de-

sired. There were fricasseed chicken and mashed pota-
toes, and the first green peas from the garden, there
were currant jelly, and sweet pickles and hot biscuit;
there were custard pie and vanilla ice-cream and three
kinds of cake; there were coffee and molasses candy. But
afterwards, when they had sat in the parlor—which had
been opened for the occasion, but still suggested funerals
rather than sociability—in uncomfortable state for over
an hour, David watched his chance and slipped from the
room, beckoning Sam after him.

"If you'll do my chores tonight," he whispered, "I'll
give you a dime. I'm goin' down to the river—goin' in
swimmin'."

"But it's Sunday," Sam whispered back in amazement.

"I don't care if 'tis—I'm just as hot as if 'twas Monday.
I'm goin' to change my clothes, and take that book I got
outter the liberry yesterday, and skin outter the back
door. Don't you tell until it's too late to get holt to me,
and I'll give you the dime tomorrow mornin'. See?" And
Sam saw.

David had been by the river now for almost two hours,
reading in undisturbed bliss, and swimming to his heart's
content. He was growing drowsy. In another five minutes he would have been fast asleep, when suddenly the
sound of a singing voice, growing nearer and nearer,
made him sit up, rubbing his eyes and listening intently.

It was a child's voice, very sweet and clear, but he was
greatly puzzled by the fact that distinctly as each syllable seemed to be pronounced, he could not understand
a single word of it; neither did it sound in the least like
a hymn, the only kind of a song he had ever heard on

13

Sunday. It was half gay and half sad and altogether teasing. He jumped to his feet and looked around him, then stood staring with his mouth wide open, first in surprise and then in reluctant fascination.

Half a dozen rods away was a little girl, coming nearer and nearer, singing, and dancing as she sang. She was so light, so exquisitely rapid and graceful in every movement, that she seemed hardly to touch the ground. David had never seen anything like her before. She had on a very full white dress, which reached scarcely to her knees, leaving her legs quite bare except for short white socks and bronze ankle-ties. There was a great pink bow on the top of her head, and her hair, shining in the sun, fell around her rosy face in a mass of brown curls. He held his breath, involuntarily taking a step nearer her. This was the first vision of loveliness and charm which his barren life had held. Suddenly she caught sight of the boy, waved her hand as if in welcome, and when she was quite close to him stopped dancing and singing, and gave him a friendly smile.

"Hello," she said pleasantly.

"Hello," muttered David, watching her furtively. Now that she no longer danced and sang, the spell was broken; he was ashamed of having been so swayed by something he did not understand, and was not at all sure that he admired her, after all.

"It's a nice day, isn't it?" she went on with persistent amiability.

"Kinder hot," vouchsafed David grudgingly.

"Yes, but it's lovely here. Grandfather went to sleep after dinner, and Mademoiselle was in her room, so I ran away. I came down a lane that leads right back of our

14

house. I think I'll come quite often after this, it's so cool and pleasant."

David made no answer. If the child beside him felt no embarrassment, as was quite evident, he was shy enough for two. Never had he seen a little girl who talked and acted like this one. He stood twisting his bare toe until it made a hole in the ground, regarding her sidewise, suspiciously. Apparently oblivious of his lack of cordiality, she sat down on the grass near him, her white skirts spreading out like a fan around her, and picked up the book he had been reading.

" 'The Last of the Mohicans' " she exclaimed, "Oh, isn't it splendid? Grandfather's just finished reading it to me. How far are you?"

"Not very far."

"You're rather hard to talk to, aren't you?" said the little girl cheerfully. "Are you always this way? If you are, you ought to practice, by yourself, I mean, and look straight at any one, too, when you're speaking—grandfather says that's very important. Where do you live? How old are you? What's your name?"

David, crimson with bashfulness and resentment, but stung by her remark about practicing, sat down beside her.

"I've always lived out back—"

"Out—? Excuse me?"

"Back—over the hills. West Hamstead, you know. But now I live in Hamstead. My name's David Noble, and I'm fourteen."

"I live in Hamstead too, now. I've always lived in Paris before this. Except sometimes, this last year or two, grandfather's taken me on trips to Italy and Switzerland in the summer-time. I'm eleven. I just had a birthday. This locket was my birthday present. It has pictures of my father and mother inside. My name's Jacqueline Désirée Huntington—why, what's the matter?"

A sudden light broke upon David. He looked her full in the face at last, overcome with excitement.

"Are you the little girl who lives in the Big House with dozens of servants and hundreds of books?" he cried, "whose father—" he stopped abruptly.

"What about my father?" she asked quickly, as if thirsty for information. "He died ever so long ago—before I was born."

David's training along lines of tactfulness had been limited, to say the least. He had no wish to hurt the friendly child's feelings, and he knew that he had made a stupid break, that there was little good that he could say of either of her parents.

"My father used to know him when they was both boys," he said, awkwardly, "He used to come up here in the summer-time. They went fishin' and swimmin' together. And dad says he was—real kind and generous."

Désirée's eyes shone with pleasure. "I'm awfully glad I found you," she said, "It's hard to get any one to talk about him. Grandfather doesn't like to, he still feels so badly because he died. This is the first time I've ever had a picture of him—or my mother. It's lonely here, after Paris. I haven't had a soul—a young soul, I mean—to speak to since I left the convent."

"The what?"

"The convent—where I went to school, you know."

"Are you a Catholic?"

If he had asked her if she were a leper, his tone could

hardly have conveyed more horror. He drew his clean bare legs further away from possible contact with her frilly skirts.

"Do you—mind?" she asked wistfully. Her voice sank, the fresh gaiety gone from it. "Grandfather minds too, but he tries not to let me see. He promised my mother, before she died, that I should be one, you see. She wanted me to be. I don't understand why any one should —think it's queer. I was awfully happy with the Sisters, and I miss it all so much—the incense and the music and the stained-glass windows, and that feeling of being all good and happy, the minute you get inside the chapel and hear the organ playing. We took turns, helping with the altar flowers—and at Christmas time there was always the crêche, and the Holy Child in it, and we stayed up for midnight mass. I made my first Communion before I left—I'm glad of that. But I'm sorry not to please grandfather. It's hard, isn't it, when the things you love best don't please some one you care for?"

A thousand conflicting thoughts were racing through David's bewildered brain. Was it possible there were Catholics in the world who were *good?* That there were children who *loved* to go to church, and grieved because they were deprived of doing so? Half of the little girl's words were incomprehensible to him, but her feeling was clear enough. Hamstead, the Mecca of his dreams, represented Egyptian exile to her.

"What do you *do* all the time here?" she went on bravely after a minute, "Besides being no churches—real churches, I mean—there are no shops, and no parks, and no theatres, and no *people*. Nothing but grass and trees!"

He laughed, a little bitterly. "If you'd ben fetched up

out back instead of to Paris," he said, not unkindly, "you'd think this was quite a place. It looks awful good to me. When I get a chance I read; but mostly I do chores for people—weed gardens, and drive cows, and milk 'em afterwards. Now that hayin's come, I hope I can get some money ridin' the rake. I'm trying to earn enough money to go to the University of Vermont by and by and learn to be a doctor—I'm goin' to, too!"

He spoke with a sort of savage superiority. Poor and ragged and ignorant though he knew himself to be, he felt vastly superior to this little French "heathen" with her changing moods, her quick gestures and many questions, and her self-assurance. Suddenly it occurred to him, that in spite of the fact that she was so generally unsatisfactory, she might be a means to an end. He jerked out an embarrassed query.

"Say—your grandfather don't want any extra help, does he?"

"Help—about what?"

"Some one to work. You don't s'pose he'd let me come and live at his house and do odd jobs after school hours— and read his books, do you?"

Jacqueline shook her head. "I'll lend you all the books you want," she said, "but I don't believe he needs any more servants. I'd love to have you come though—come back to supper with me, and we'll ask him." Then noting his look of dismay at the mere suggestion, "Oh, do! I'm so lonely, I shall die here pretty soon! And I've got a big box of chocolates that have just come from Maillard's— and—and there's a skeleton—a real live skeleton—I mean a real dead one—well, anyway, a *bone* skeleton up in the attic. I'll show him to you."

David's face kindled. "Mother'd lick me good," he said thoughtfully, "if I went anywheres on Sunday—barefoot, too. But—a big one, is it?" he wavered, and Jacqueline, with the precocious instinct of her sex, saw it—knew too, that he longed to go, not to comfort her loneliness, but for the sake of the possible "job," and the certain cheer of chocolates and skeleton. It caused her a slight pang; nevertheless, like Eve, she held out her apple bravely.

"Oh, yes—an awfully big one," she murmured, and she began to hum again, that little tilting, merry song, with the words that David could not understand, as she turned and danced away from him, looking back to wave her hand, and smile over her shoulder.

Without another word he followed her.

CHAPTER III

You've brought a friend home to supper, Désirée? I didn't know you had made friends here—in fact, I fear there are no suitable playmates for you in this place."

The man laid down the book he was reading, and drew the breathless child on his knee, smoothing back her mass of curls, and kissing her flushed little face. His own seemed as finely tempered, as clear-cut, and as cold as a steel rapier, but it softened slightly as she threw her arms around his neck.

"Well, he's not a very old friend. I ran away after dinner—"

"We hunted everywhere for you—you have given us a most anxious afternoon. Promise me you'll never do it again, my dear."

"Well, we'll talk about that later," she said, settling herself comfortably on his lap and kissing his nose. "I found a lovely lane leading to the meadow, behind the big barns, and I walked down it to the river. It's beautiful down there. And I found a boy."

"Jacqueline—" The little girl had no way of guessing the bitter memories and still more bitter dread for the future which her impulsiveness stirred in the man. Where

20

was heredity to lead this gay and wayward little dancer who had become so unspeakably precious to him? His one instinct was to cage her, above all to keep her to himself. She rippled on, either ignoring the anxious severity of his face, or unconscious of it.

"His name's David Noble—and, oh, grandfather, he says his daddy used to go fishing with mine. He has awfully bad manners, and dirty finger nails, and he's barefoot, but somehow I like him. He wants to be a doctor some day, and is trying to find some kind of horrid work he calls 'chores' so that he can earn enough money. He asked me if you needed any more help. I was surprised, because I thought *he* needed the help, and I do so want to give it to him! He's waiting out in the hall until I say David. I'm going to say it now—David."

If Jacqueline had given the boy a new vision of femininity, no less did this wonderful house give him a new ideal of a dwelling place. The hall in which he stood waiting was wainscotted in mahogany, there were thick soft rugs in rich colors on the polished floors, and draperies at doors and windows even softer and richer; paintings in heavy gold frames hung on the walls, and there were ornaments of burnished copper on either side of a great gilt clock which stood on the mantel-piece; through an open door he could see into a white panelled dining-room, with side-boards laden with silver and crystal; a man-servant, dressed in livery, was laying a fine embroidered cloth, edged with lace, on the large round table in the middle of the room, and putting a bowl of crimson roses in the center of it. On the stair-landing, against a red velvet curtain, stood the gleaming white statue of a beautiful, undraped woman. Through the

21

dazed bewilderment of David's brain, a new determination took shape.

"And when I get to be a doctor," he promised himself, "I'll have a house just like this—only much handsomer."

When Jacqueline called, he started, and pushing aside the brocaded portière, entered the library. The dream of the future was rudely shattered by the agonizing reality of the present. He took a few steps forward, then stopped abruptly, his shabby cap in his hands, his head hanging; he could feel the redness of his cheeks, the length and bareness of his legs, the raggedness of his clothes, with a consciousness that was painful to a degree of torture. But for the sake of plenty of books, the sight of a real skeleton, and even the possibility of a "steady job" he was prepared to suffer much.

Mr. Huntington's greeting was hardly of the nature to be reassuring. He swept the boy from head to foot with a glance that pierced through him like a March wind, and spoke in a voice as cold and cutting as the thin March ice that gathers so quickly towards evening on the little pools of water bravely melting in the brief sunshine of a March day.

"Miss Huntington," he said, "has no authority to engage my servants for me. When I require them, I select them from reliable sources, I do not pick them up from the highways and byways. Moreover, my present needs are quite filled. Neither has Miss Huntington the age nor the discretion to select her own companions, and the fact that your father and hers—if it is a fact—were acquainted does not interest me. My son was not always fortunate in his choice of friends. I shall endeavor to assure myself that his daughter does not consort with tramps and beggars."

"Grandfather!" cried Jacqueline passionately, but David interrupted her. He pushed her aside, and strode forward, his hot, bashful face raised as if by magic, his voice blazing with anger.

"I ain't a tramp or a beggar," he cried. "I didn't ask to come to your house—I come because she plagued me so I couldn't get out of it. But I'm ten times as respectable as she is—I ain't got a drunkard for a father nor a cheap actress who had to be married out of pity for a mother, neither. I'll never set foot in here again, not if it was to save your life nor hers—they ain't worth it."

He plunged out of the room and through the front door, slamming it after him; but Jacqueline, too quick for her grandfather, was beside him before he reached the walk. She caught hold of his arm.

"Grandfather wasn't fair," she cried. "You needn't ever come there again, until he takes back all the hateful things he said. But you shall have the books just the same —I'll bring them down to the river—and the skeleton too, if I can manage. But tell me—whose father was a drunkard, and whose mother was an actress? Don't people get married because they love each other? David—you're not angry with me, are you?"

He did not answer her, but shaking her off roughly, started down the dusty street on a dead run. She could easily have caught up with him; but her wounded pride, and her bruised and bewildered mind, drove her back to the house. She flung herself into her grandfather's arms in a torrent of rage and tears. Before she would be pacified, he was obliged to tell her, for the first time, something of her parentage, to promise her a certain amount of freedom of movement, and to pour such other balm as he could on her outraged little heart, himself furious with resentment that his own hasty speech had indirectly brought about such a necessity.

As to David's parents, their anger knew no bounds, when the boy, too enraged and insulted to maintain his customary reticence, hurled out the story of his afternoon; and it would be difficult to tell which of the two families went to bed that night with the bitterer feelings against the other.

CHAPTER IV

THE FIRST RUNG OF THE LADDER

DAVID kept his word rather better than most people do; for it was nearly five years before he entered Mr. Huntington's house again.

Jacqueline kept her word a great deal better than most people do; she managed not only to take the books but the skeleton down to the river, and after going there on three successive afternoons without finding David, she went to his father's house.

Mrs. Noble opened the door in response to her gentle rap, and looked out at her through the narrow crack with sour disapproval.

"You kin run right along," she said sharply, "whether you're sellin' soap for a premium or solicitin' for a fair, it's all the same to me; I ain't got no time to trifle away with you."

"I don't understand," said the child, much puzzled, "I'm Jacqueline Huntington, and I've come to see David. I've brought him the books I promised him, and when he's read these, I'll bring some more."

"Well, if you're Jackaleen Huntington, I certainly shan't let you in," was the furious answer, "David's a perfectly decent, self-respectin' boy, and it won't do you no good to run after him and try to pervert him, you little furrin' heathen!" and the door slammed in the little girl's face.

Mrs. Noble happened to be in a frame of mind compared with which her usual acidity was sweet indeed. It is a mistake to overestimate the feeling of democracy in small villages, and she had that afternoon been mercilessly snubbed at a meeting of the Ladies' Aid, by Miss Manning, one of Hamstead's aristocrats. Of course the family at the Big House "didn't count"—they were simply "summer people" and Hamstead never "called" unless it wanted a subscription to Foreign Missions or a contribution to the Annual Church Supper, or something of that nature. But the Mannings and the Grays and the Elliotts and the Westons—the families, in short, whose ancestors had founded the village and those about it, and had lived there, in the same houses which their great-grandfathers had built, ever since—were apt to look down on new-comers, especially if they came from "out back" with a superiority such as Boston itself feels over its humbler suburbs. It did not matter that Miss Manning was so homely and so "peppery" that no man had been known to "keep company" with her; that the Grays were as poor as church mice, and their handsome son, Austin, as "wild as a hawk"; that Mrs. Elliott was a tireless gossip, and that the Westons, father and son, drank too much—any more than the same failings would have mattered on the Back Bay—where, as a matter of fact, they exist quite as frequently. These same persons had their good qualities too, Miss Manning was generous to the point of bounty, Austin had a wonderful mind, the Westons had dispositions like sunshine. They formed the society of Hamstead, and the rest of the village recognized it. So, when Mrs. Noble and Miss Manning disagreed as to the number of eggs that should go into an angel cake, the Ladies' Aid promptly and unanimously sided with Miss Manning, though she was but an indifferent cook, and Mrs. Noble an unusually good one. Even through the long shut-in winters in the little cottage at West Hamstead, when most women would have found it well-nigh impossible to set a good table, Hiram's family was remarkably well-fed. This undeserved slight was too much for human nature to stand.

"I never used more'n eight eggs in my life, and I never had one fall yet. I've heard the remark passed lots of times that no one had such luck with angel cakes as I have."

"Well, some women do well that way, but I was brought up to use the best of everything, and plenty of it. (Pass me the bastin' thread, will you, Mis' Gray? Does that hem look even to you?) I wouldn't dream of greasin' the pan with anything except butter, either."

"I don't grease my pan at all, and I don't have a mite of trouble with its stickin'. To my way of thinkin', a good cook can manage with a few things a sight better than a poor one can just by bein' extravagant. Don't you think so, Mis' Gray?"

"Land! It's so long since I've felt I could afford one at all, I've forgotten how I used to do. But Miss Manning always sets an elegant table. You'll say so yourself, when you've been here a little longer, Mis' Noble."

"We all know what Miss Manning's tea-parties are like," said Mrs. Elliott with a simper.

"All of us that gets invited to them, of course you

mean," added Mrs. Weston. "I've always thought your cakes was remarkable, Jane."

"I don't wonder that woman's husband drinks," snorted Mrs. Noble, in an audible whisper to Mrs. Gray. "She's the worst toady I ever see in my life."

"Oh, no she ain't—she's real nice," the good-natured Mrs. Gray hastened to whisper back. "It's natural she should agree with Miss Manning—they've been real intimate always, same as their mothers was before 'em. Heathen wear more clothes than you'd think, judgin' from some of the accounts in the missionary papers, don't they? My back is most broke runnin' that machine this hot day."

Bitter as it was to have to "swallow Miss Manning's angel cake whole—and I'll bet it was a fallen angel cake at that," as Mrs. Noble said in relating the experience to her husband—this was not all. Not a single woman had noticed—or at all events mentioned—the calla lily and Martha Washington geranium in her parlor window, though she had raised one of the shades in that sacred apartment—at the incalculable risk of fading the carpet —because there was no other place where they would "show to the street" as the earnest workers went past to the vestry. Her skill with flowers was as noteworthy as it was with cookery—that, too, had been overlooked— probably on account of Miss Manning's old-fashioned garden! Immeasurably wounded herself, it was like balm of Gilead to Mrs. Noble to be able to turn Jacqueline, hurt and bewildered, from her door.

But Hiram took another view of it when his wife related the episode with pride that night at the supper table.

"Wal, I admire her for keepin' her promise," he said, pausing in the act of pouring his tea from cup to saucer before drinking it. "I never s'posed she meant a word of it. She must have to do some plannin' to get 'round that grandfather of hers. But Sol Daniels says she's real cute that way—not exactly what you'd call sly—but she manages! He see quite a lot of her when he was finishin' the last of the paintin', and he says every one on the place just worships her, and she twists all that gang of foreign servants round her little finger till they don't know whether they're a-foot or a-horseback. And that kind and thoughtful and generous, Sol says, that she'd take the shoes off her feet and give 'em to you if she thought you needed 'em. Next time you see her go by on horseback, I'd stop her if I wuz you, David, and thank her. Pass me a few more of them cucumbers, Lizzie, seems as if they wuz unusual tasty tonight."

Mrs. Noble's spirits revived at this well-merited praise of the garden products which she had striven so hard to raise. The events of the afternoon were momentarily forgotten in the pleasing remembrance of the morning, during which she had taken her husband's place at the post-office for a couple of hours while he went "out back" to confer with the seeker for simplicity from New York in regard to further purchases of land.

"There was an uncommon large mail come in on the ten o'clock," she remarked as she complied with his request, "I dunno when I've seen so heavy a bag. I dunno but what we shall soon be havin' two, they take so many papers and magazines up to the Big House. Sol Daniels says he got a stitch in his side luggin' it all in one. And the Grays always have more readin' matter comin' to them

than their means warrant. Austin is writin' real regular
to a girl up in Wallacetown, too. He might better save
the money that goes into postage. She writes back on
pink paper. Thomas come in for the mail this mornin' and
I blushed to hand him such a lookin' envelope. Austin
ought to think more of the awful example he's settin'
those younger brothers and sisters of his. They're all
smelled up, too. Stop your snickerin', David, you know
perfectly well it was the pink letters I was talkin' about,
and not. . . . Miss Mannin' had two mail order cata-
logues from firms in New York City, but land! with that
face on her, it don't make much odds where she buys her
clothes, she can't look no different. Jack Weston had a
postal from a feller in White Water askin' him to come
up and spend Sunday with him and go fishin'. You can
talk about the depravity of the heathen, but I couldn't
help thinkin' when I see that, we've got our hands full
with depravity right here in Hamstead. Fishin' itself
would be bad enough, of course, but we all know what
goes with it. I hope he'll get sobered off before he comes
home. Well, just as I was glancin' at the postal to make
sure who 'twas for—of course it would have been an
awful thing to put it in the wrong box—Mis' Elliott come
in and wanted to know what was on it. I do hate a curi-
ous woman, above all things, but of course I had to give
her the gist of it, so's not to have trouble. I suppose it'll
be all over town in no time now, but I done my best to
stop it. I told her I should feel awful if it got around.
Then right on top of that she says, 'Ain't it too bad about
old Mis' Brown?' and when I says, 'Why, what's the
matter with her?' she says, 'Why, that's what I'm tryin'
to find out.' She does beat all. She told me she just got

back from her cousin's funeral, down in Maine. 'Twas the handsomest she'd ever see. A mahogany coffin, and two floral harps and a pillow with "Rest in Peace" on it, besides lots of ordinary tributes, of course. He was real well-off, she may get a little something herself, though the widow is awful graspin', seems to think he'll leave practically everything to her, as long as there weren't no children. I don't know when I've enjoyed hearin' about anything so much—. Well, maybe you're right about that French young one. David kin do as he likes for all me."

David had already decided that he had been somewhat too rash in flinging away the possibilities which a friendship with Jacqueline might possess, and the revelation that his father would not disapprove of the acquaintance offered a ready excuse to his pride for trying to get in touch with her again. She rode nearly every day, accompanied sometimes by her grandfather, but more often by a groom, who kept at a respectful distance; and the next afternoon David met her with the latter, as he was driving home Sol Daniels' cows—one of the "chores" which was slowly but surely, in quarters and dimes, bringing in the precious money that was in time to send him to the University of Vermont. She seemed to bear him no malice for his mother's rudeness, for she stopped, jumped off her pony, and held out her hand, saving him the embarrassment of speaking first.

"I've been to the river every Sunday," she said, "but you did not come. So finally I went to your house, but a cross woman in a gray wrapper slammed the door in my face, when she heard what I wanted. You ought to tell your mother to get rid of that servant."

"I'll come to the river next Sunday," said David, "that

warn't a servant—we don't keep no hired girl. It was my mother."

"Oh, I'm sorry! I didn't guess—please forgive me! I wouldn't say anything—against any one's mother—for anything in the world."

David's conscience smote him. "That's all right," he said awkwardly, "I know you didn't mean nothin'. I must get along now, but I'll see you next Sunday, sure."

Jacqueline turned to the waiting groom. "Oh, Thomas," she said casually, "lead Frou-Frou home, will you please? I think I'll walk. You may meet me at the foot of the driveway with her in half an hour."

"Very good, Miss. A little this side of the driveway, perhaps?"

He was perfectly grave, but the corners of his mouth twitched.

"You always understand me perfectly," said Jacqueline soberly. Then, as the man rode off, she turned to David coolly, "Which way do you go? I'll walk along with you a little way—I think I have a better plan than the river now."

David felt as if the leaping of his heart must surely be visible in his face. "What is it?" he said, with elaborate unconcern.

"You know grandfather has a farm, and a foreman to run it. He lives in the lodge."

"The—"

"The little house down by the big gate. Sheldon's his name. He's an awfully pleasant man."

"Well?"

"Well, I heard him talking to grandfather the other day, and he said he needed more workmen—'help,' he

32

called it, just as you do. 'If you'd let me hire men around here, Mr. Huntington,' he said, 'they'd be more contented than the ones you get from the city, and understand their work much better. I could get more out of them.'"

"Well?"

"Grandfather said all right, to do as he thought best. Of course Sheldon has nothing to do with the house-servants, or the men in our own stable. Thomas's father, Grimes, is coachman, and they both live with Mrs. Grimes in the cottage by the coachhouse. They don't 'mix' with the farm hands at all. And Sheldon hires all of those himself. Oh, David, why don't you see if he wouldn't hire you?

"He wants a boy," she went on breathlessly, "to sleep in the big barn. It's really a lovely barn, and there's a nice little room in it on purpose for you—for some boy, I mean. You see he wants some one right there nights, with all those valuable work-horses, and cows, and—things," she added hurriedly, and a little vaguely, unconsciously admitting to David that her agricultural education had been much neglected, in spite of her superior wisdom on many other subjects. "I know Sheldon hasn't found one yet, for he said he wanted to be sure to get one who wouldn't all the time be running off to balls in Wallacetown, and you wouldn't do that, would you, David, because you aren't old enough, and besides you want to study? And grandfather goes to sleep every evening right after dinner, and Mademoiselle goes to her room to write to her relations in France as soon as she's put me to bed—and then I can get up again, and slip down to see you, and bring you books—and you can have the skeleton for company."

Perhaps it was this last attractive appeal that carried the day. At any rate, David went to see Sheldon.

Less than a week later he was installed as "general boy" on Mr. Huntington's farm. The village, which, of course, immediately heard of this, did not entirely approve. And Mrs. Elliott, with her usual lack of delay, decided to tell Mrs. Noble so, in case—as she had reason to hope—no one else had forestalled her in this agreeable task. She accordingly sought out her new neighbor after supper, and found her in the garden, picking string-beans for canning, assisted by two of her younger sons, while Susie, her thumb in her mouth, and a sugar cookie in her free hand, hitched up and down on the path with one foot tucked under her.

"Good evenin'," said Mrs. Elliott, breathless with haste, "Warm, ain't it? Awful tryin' weather we've had this season."

Mrs. Noble wasted no time in greetings. "I ben so druv I ain't noticed the weather," she responded, snapping off a bean.

"Well, I sh'd think you'd need all your family to home to help ye, busy like you are."

"I dunno's a woman's family's always a help to her," said Mrs. Noble, going on down the trim line of vegetables without stopping, "I kin git more done when I ain't hampered too much by anybody in the family—or out of it, as fur as that goes."

Mrs. Elliott had never heard of *double entendre;* nevertheless, at that moment, though she could not have called it by name, she became vaguely and uncomfortably conscious that there was such a thing.

"But I make 'em work when I kin," went on Mrs. Noble

vigorously, after a slight pause, "though 'tain't much, of course. Sam! take that bushel basketful inter the kitchen, and tell Leon to start in stringin'. Don't trip over Susie and *spill* it! If your father's in from the post-office tell him I want he should make sure there's plenty of wood in the fire, and that it's kept so. I can't keep a-runnin' in all the time. And then you hurry right back, and help Harry to start fillin' the basket agin down to the other end of the garden. I guess that second batch I planted is ready, too. . . . Hev you done much cannin' this summer, Mis' Elliott? I've put up over a hundred quarts of vegetables so far, and that's a fair beginnin', with strawberries an' currants, an' raspberries besides, of course! But I can't do as much as I used to do on the farm now that I hev to be in the post-office so much—an' hev neighbors runnin' in all the time."

Still uncomfortable, Mrs. Elliott decided that the only thing to do was to take the bull by the horns.

"I hear," she said sternly, "that your boy has gone up to the Big House to work."

"Which boy?" inquired Mrs. Noble, as if this was the first time she had heard of it.

"Land! David, of course!"

"Get out from under my feet, Susie!" cried Mrs. Noble, sharply and suddenly, "I 'most fell over you. Here—take a carrot an' chew on that awhile, now your cookie's gone."

"It's true, ain't it? insisted Mrs. Elliott, perspiring slightly.

Mrs. Noble wiped the carrot on her gingham apron, and handed it to her daughter.

"There! . . . Kitty'd like a taste, too, ef she comes

35

around! . . . Why yes, it's true. Has any one said it ain't?"

"Not as I know of. Leastways—but no one could hardly believe it. I'm sure *I* couldn't. I shouldn't want a son of mine to go there, and everyone feels the same way. The minister is real surprised. I shouldn't wonder a mite ef he spoke about it in prayer-meetin'. There's all kinds of queer stories about the Big House, and the folks that lives there. Likely some of 'em ain't true. But I've heard—"

"I've heard it, too," said Mrs. Noble crisply.

"Heard what?"

"The same as you hev, I s'pose. But it don't frighten me none."

"But I ain't told you yet *what* I heard."

"I know you ain't. You don't need to. It don't frighten me none, whether I know what 'tis or not."

"Oh," gasped Mrs. Elliott, looking a little frightened herself, "Well, as I sez before, I shouldn't want a son of mine to go there—that's all. I sez to Joe, the minute I heard, 'I must go right down an' tell that boy's mother how sorry I feel for her. I know he's an awful stubborn boy. I know he's hard for her to handle. I kin tell by the look of him. His looks ain't like my Fred's at all—' "

"I've noticed that myself," said Mrs. Noble.

"But, I sez to Joe, 'Maybe she'd think of some way she could stop him, ef she had a chance to talk it over with some other woman.' And Joe sez, just as kind, 'Yes, why don't you go down an' pass the evenin' with Mis' Noble?' He's real unselfish—some men wouldn't feel they could spare their wives a whole evenin', that way. But he urged me to come right along, and not to hurry back. He's settin' on the back kitchen porch readin' last week's

Wallacetown Bugle. He makes it a point not to read the paper till it's a week old, so's he kin hev the pleasure of hearin' the news first from the neighbors."

"Well," said Mrs. Noble, straightening herself up suddenly, "you kin go home an' tell him a piece of news from me, which, so fur as I know, ain't in the paper yet: And that is that I don't blame him a mite for wantin' to hev peace once in a while, but that I don't feel no call to help him git it by stoppin' my work to let you tell me what to let my young ones do, and what not to let 'em do. I've had seven of my own to your one, an' I wuz the eldest of ten myself, so I've had some practice in raisin' 'em. Dave didn't consult me none in makin' his plans, but I don't know as I'd hev hindered him much ef he had. He's fourteen years old, an' when a boy gits to that age, he's kinder apt to take the bit in his teeth, one way or another. If it happens to be a curb bit, it cuts him up some, an' he goes round with a bloody mouth for a while, but them wounds don't last. Not as *I've* noticed."

She tucked Susie under one arm, and lifted her brimming pail with the other.

"On your way home," she said tartly, "you might run in an' tell Mis' Weston it's a pity Jack drinks so. An' then go an' ask Mis' Gray if she knows where Austin is tonight—an' who with—an' what time she expects him back. That'd give yer husband time to read his paper real thorough, an' I'm sure them other women would be grateful to hear what you think of their sons, and the success they've had bringin' 'em up,—same as I'm grateful to hear what you think of mine. I'm sorry to leave you. But I cal'-late to get all them beans ready for the stove before I go to bed, and some of 'em on tonight, so's I kin git the job finished the first thing in the morning. Good-night, Mis' Elliott!"

Hiram was pushing a stick of wood into the already crowded stove when his wife entered the kitchen. "I see you hev had a caller," he said with interest, turning.

Mrs. Noble set down her baby and her pail, and slammed the lid, which her husband had lifted, back into its place.

"Yes, an' I guess we're likely to have some more," she retorted. "I told you what sort of things was bound to happen if you left the farm. But if any of them callers trick you inter sayin' you don't admire David for gittin' up an' startin' to *do* somethin', 'stead of sittin' on the post-office steps all the time tellin' what he thinks some one else ought to do—well, you'll hear from me, Hiram Noble, sure as that's your name! I'd a sight rather see a son of mine wearin' out the soles of his shoes than the seat of his pants!"

Mr. Noble stared at his wife, open-mouthed.

"Why, Lizzie," he stammered, "when you first heard David was agoin' to the Big House—I mean that he had *gone*—you was so mad you said you'd lick the hide off'n him, the first time you could lay your hands on him. What's come over you?"

But Mrs. Noble did not even deign to reply. She snorted, and began to string her beans.

. . . .

So, as we have said before, David was installed as general utility boy on Mr. Huntington's farm, with the acknowledged privilege of going to school in term-time, eating at the farm house, sleeping and studying in the comfortable little room at the end of the long line of stalls,—and the unacknowledged one of seeing Jacqueline very often indeed. Night after night, after she had been warmly tucked up and was supposed to be soundly sleeping, she stole through the gardens and across the wide lawns, easily concealed by the abundant shrubbery, down the shaded paths that led to the big barn. Sheldon, discovering, as was perhaps inevitable, the state of friendliness between the two children, not only never mentioned it, but guarded it from the detection of others. David did his work with a kind of fierce thoroughness that was a marvel of speed and efficiency, and when it was done, he never stirred off the place, but sat "with his nose in his books" until all hours of the night. Sheldon, after years of bitter and aggravating experience with flighty and stupid "general boys" knew that it would be a long day before he would find such a treasure again, and realized that anything that contributed to his content must be looked upon with a lenient eye. Moreover, he was quick to realize that Jacqueline was always the seeker, that David never presumed upon her favors, and was at times almost impatient at her interruptions. Had things been the other way around, Sheldon's conscience might have troubled him—as it was, he sincerely rejoiced that the lonely child had found some one to amuse and cheer her. Mr. Huntington, who had grown old before his time, took but little personal interest in his estate; he seldom saw David, and failed to recognize, in the unobtrusive and exemplary young farm hand, the ragged boy whom Jacqueline had once so thoughtlessly introduced to the seclusion of his library, into which he retired more and more. David's parents, blissfully ignorant that he came into any contact with the family at the Big

House, and more than gratified at the wages he drew from the big purse, were supremely content. And so matters drifted on uneventfully enough until David was in his last year in the Hamstead High School, and nearly nineteen years old, and Jacqueline, who did not go to school at all, but taught David almost everything worth knowing that he knew, was not quite three years younger.

It could hardly be expected that they would drift much longer.

CHAPTER V

THE AWAKENING

It was a mild, starry evening in mid-May, and David, who had been up most of the night before with a sick cow, had nearly fallen asleep over his books. They were piled high around him, a motley collection. There were his school books, almost falling to pieces from hard use, for several other pupils at the High School had had them before him; there were the daily papers, slightly out of date, for they went from the Big House to the farm house, and from the farm house to the little room in the barn; there were several agricultural periodicals—*Hoards Dairyman, The Holstein-Friesian World, The Rural Outlook*—which he read conscientiously from cover to cover, before he turned to devour the two old medical books, sadly behind the times, which the village doctor had discarded as no longer useful, and given to him; and finally there were two or three shabby novels from the Hamstead Public Library.

The window of the little room was wide open, and David, yawning and stretching his arms above his head walked over to it, and stood looking out into the calm and silent night, feeling vaguely restless and lonely. Jacqueline was in New York. As she grew older, her grandfather became daily more proud of her, and at last he shook off his inertia and desire for solitude, and began to seek out his old friends again, that he might have the satisfaction of displaying his treasure. He had buried himself in shame because of his son; he was emerging with pride because of his grandchild. The success of the first venture into his old world after an absence of many years was so great that it was soon and often repeated. Jacqueline was personally too lovely and winning, and financially too great a prize for the dimming remembrance of the scandal connected with her parents to carry much weight. Occasionally some matron whose own daughter lacked partners at a party remarked acidly that of course it was not surprising that Désirée Huntington danced so well, or some father whose son failed to make even the most halting progress with his books sought public consolation in the statement that Hal Huntington's girl was naturally a good linguist; but for the most part, if they spoke of the matter at all, everyone said that of course there was likely to be a black sheep in every family, and the Huntington family was no exception to the rule, but still, it was a fine family just the same, one of the best—and yes, indeed, the child had wonderful charm, and it was easy to see that she was going to be a great beauty. The Big House, which for years had been so quiet, was filled with guests much of the time, and trips to New York, to Washington and Baltimore, and even to Boston, which Mr. Huntington had expected never to visit again, became more and more frequent. David had seen less and less of her these last two years. It was now six weeks since she had been in Hamstead at all, and there had been no intimation of when she was likely to return; in fact, there had been some talk before she left of the possibility that she might enter a fashionable boarding school for the spring months.

Sheldon, who by this time loved David as if he were his own son, could not help boasting about him from time to time to the less fortunate farmers in his vicinity, whose "hired men" were the vexation of their lives. There was just cause for his satisfaction. The boy worked hard and faithfully, and he saved his wages. The account at the Wallacetown bank, started four years earlier with a grimy dollar-bill, had crept up until it had already passed the thousand-dollar mark. He spent nothing on amusements, little on clothes, yet his appearance was always creditable. He had shot up tall and slim and he carried himself well, neither slouching nor stalking. The determination of his mind seemed reflected in his body— the strong shoulders were flung back, the dark, lean face and head of heavy black hair rose defiantly above them. Almost any man can look well in broadcloth and fine linen; this one contrived to give grace and dignity to a pair of cotton overalls. His record at school, moreover, was excellent. He was to graduate in a few weeks, valedictorian of his class.

"And he's as straight," Sheldon invariably wound up, "as a ramrod; as clean as a whistle."

This was true. However, David deserved less credit on this score than Sheldon and his audience gave him. He had a single-track mind, and the train that ran on it was an express to the city of material success. It made no stops at the way-stations of idleness and folly largely because he had no inclination to do so—they would have used up valuable time. Moreover, the boy worked, physically and mentally, from five o'clock in the morning until late at night. He was too tired when evening came, and still had too much ahead of him before he could go to bed, if he were not only to reach the goal ahead of him, but live up to the standard he had already set, to "run with the crowd." He had gained much by the course he had chosen; but he had also lost something as well. He had made few friends, and if there were no evil in the boy, neither was there much unselfishness, or gentleness, or human sympathy.

None of the girls in his class at school had interested or attracted him in the least; and when he thought of Jacqueline at all, which was seldom, it was with a sense of passing and grudging gratitude for the fact that without her help he should not have been able to travel so far already on his single-track railway. He never missed her when she was gone; sometimes, when she appeared at the barn, he was glad to see her, for she was merry company, and he had no other; at other times, he was merely impatient with the unwelcome interruption of his work. If he had analyzed her at all, he would have admitted that she was pretty, that she was loyal and generous, that she was tender of heart. But he had never done so— never until he stood by his window on that May night, feeling dissatisfied with himself and all the world. Then suddenly, he realized it all. He felt, with the realization, that he would give anything in the world to see her, that he was hungry and thirsty for something he had never wanted before, and that only she could give him—and, as he stared out into the starlight, he saw her coming towards him, and caught his breath, a flame of violent feeling sweeping through him.

She was clad in a soft muslin dressing-gown, that fell to her feet, showing, as she moved, almost every line of her exquisitely slender and graceful figure; the wide flowing sleeves hung away from her arms, leaving them bare far above the elbow; the deep cut V of the waist showed her throat and neck gleaming white and bare; her hair was gathered into a great knot at the nape of her neck, and escaped in delicate curls about her lifted face. She was singing softly, a little French song, as she had been the day he first saw her. He could understand the words readily enough now, but they meant nothing to him. All that mattered was that she was there, that she was coming towards him, that he wanted her more than anything else in the world. . . . Pallas Athene, draped in the garments of wisdom, helmeted, spear in hand, had advanced sternly towards him through the groves of learning during five years of steady toil. He had accepted her challenge, and won her grudging favor; she was no longer a stranger to him, but a friend and mentor; but when he first knew her well, he could not have told, nor did he care. But Aphrodite rose suddenly from the sea-foam, where an instant before there had been only the calm and sunny water of a blue ocean, dazzling in her unashamed loveliness, pearly-white and beautiful as the shell upon which she stood, a smile of invitation on her parted lips. . . .

Jacqueline caught sight of him. She nodded; waved her hand, and walked nearer without hurrying; then with a sudden impulse, ran to the window, and caught his hand in hers.

"Oh, I'm so glad to see you!" she cried. "We came home on the evening train; but we only decided to do

45

it at the last moment, so that our telegram saying we were coming reached Grimes barely in time to meet us at the station—you didn't know, did you? We had dinner, and after I had seen that grandfather was comfortable for the night—he was pretty tired, for he isn't very strong —I got out of my traveling clothes, and had a bath, intending to go right to bed myself, when suddenly it came over me that I couldn't wait another minute to see you. So I slipped into the quickest thing I could and came out. Isn't it a heavenly night? Lift me up, David, so that I won't have to go around through the barn!"

It was a request that she had made dozens of times before. To come in through the window saved considerable time, and greatly lessened the danger of discovery. He leaned over and took her in his arms; then instead of releasing her as soon as her feet touched the floor, he crushed her to him with all his strength. She flung her arms around his neck with the candid and affectionate embrace of a happy child.

"My, but you're strong," she said admiringly, "let go, David, you hurt. I'm sure Cyril Wainwright couldn't pick me up like that."

He released her, almost savagely. She did not understand—did not even see how he felt. His sudden passion had been so unreasoning that he had blindly taken for granted an instant response to his own emotion. And there she stood, looking at him with clear, smiling eyes, telling him that he hurt, and speaking to him about another man.

"Who is Cyril Wainwright?" he asked thickly.

"A boy I met this spring. Oh, David, I've had such a good time! I haven't been to school after all, just visiting and doing the nicest things all the time! But I'm going next fall, for a year, and after that I'm going to 'come out' in New York, and then grandfather's going to take me to London to be presented. Won't it be wonderful?"

"Is Cyril Wainwright going, too?"

Jacqueline burst out laughing. "I don't know—but just at present he seems to manage to go everywhere that I do, so perhaps he will. Anyway, he's coming here to spend next Sunday with his grandfather, who was a great friend of my grandfather when they were in college. His father and mother are both dead, just like mine. You see we have lots of things in common. He's ever so old—twenty-one, and a senior at Harvard. He—David, are you sick, or what's the matter with you?"

"I was up almost all last night—I'm sleepy."

"Too sleepy to be glad to see me?"

"I'm glad to see you," he said fiercely, "only—"

"Well, I must say you don't *seem* very enthusiastic—" she turned towards the window. He stepped in front of it.

"Jacqueline," he said, "don't—"

"Don't *what?* I'm going back to the house, I'm sleepy myself—but I'll come again tomorrow night if I can manage to. You're right in my way—that's better—why, no, I can jump down all right alone! I always do."

He watched her out of sight, then sat down, and tried to force his seething brain to map out a plan of action, too unsophisticated to know that he was by no means the first man to find his desires and his sense of elementary righteousness as far apart as the two poles. Jacqueline had gone away hurt, he knew, by his strange reception, and very far, he saw also, from guessing the cause of it. And proposing to come again the next evening! These lonely,

47

intimate visits must stop instantly—that was his very first decision. Sooner or later he would be bound to betray himself, and now that he reasoned the matter out, he saw with tardy gratitude that it would be the worst possible return for all her goodness to ask her to wait indefinitely for a man who was not fit to tie up her shoes, who had, indeed, for several years, been her servant, milked her cows and groomed her horses! Besides, what would he gain by telling her that he loved her? She would laugh, and ask him how old he thought he was, anyway? Inquire if it was not a little sudden, considering that he had only tolerated her, all this time, for the sake of a skeleton? Point out to him that ladies were not in the habit of marrying their stable boys; and come again the next evening as if nothing had happened. And if he persisted, told her that some day he would surely be worthy of her, forced her to see how he felt, tried to touch her—that, he knew, would mean instant and disgraceful dismissal, and the complete overthrow of all his hopes. Daylight found him no nearer a solution of his troubles—he went to his work after a second sleepless night, though for a very different cause than his first one.

It was hard enough to be not quite nineteen, and know that you were poor and ignorant and in love; but how much worse this condition of things could be made by the power of jealousy, David was shortly to discover also.

Jacqueline did not come to see him the next evening after all. Cyril Wainwright and his grandfather came several days sooner than they were expected, and arrived that afternoon; but she saw David, very unexpectedly, the next morning. Thomas was away on his vacation, and Grimes was smitten with sudden illness; he telephoned down to the big barn, and asked Sheldon if he could send his chore-boy up to the stable to do the morning work, and take Frou-Frou and Sophie around to the Big House for Miss Jacqueline's morning ride.

She was standing with her back to the path as he came up, laughing and talking with her guest, a slim fair youth, irreproachably dressed in London riding togs, who was smoking a cigarette, and smiling at the girl with an expression half-amused and half-provoked. She was quite evidently teasing him.

"I'll make you take back that speech before we get home!" he warned her, lazily.

"You'll keep me out forever then!"

"I'd like nothing better."

"Pshaw! You'd be keen for it until about lunch time. Then you would be ready enough to come home."

"We might take lunch with us; something we could put in our pockets. Haven't you ever heard of feasting on bread and cheese, and kisses?"

"Yes, but I don't care for bread and cheese, and I don't think you can put kisses in your pocket— *Why, David!*"

"Grimes is sick, and Thomas is away, you know."

"I hadn't heard. No, thank you, Mr. Wainwright will help me up. That's all, thank you."

"You had better have that boy discharged, Jacqueline," Cyril said, as they started off, quite loudly enough for David to hear, "awfully bad form, you know, coming to the door in overalls like that, and not even touching his hat and calling you 'miss.'"

He did not hear the girl's reply; she was off at full gallop, laughing. Laughing—as if it were an amusing thing to have that long-legged, tow-headed dude talk

49

about keeping her out forever, and feeding her with
kisses, and offering her advice on the subject of her
affairs! It was all right for him to lift—not help—her into
her saddle, and be damned slow about it—she didn't tell
him to let go, that he hurt! All day long David thought
about it, and the longer he thought, the more unfair and
intolerable it seemed to him; and when evening came,
for the first time in his life, he asked Sheldon for a "team"
to go to Wallacetown.

Sheldon hesitated.

"I don't begrudge you a horse and buggy, Dave," he
said kindly, "you ain't asked many favors sense you ben
here, and you've done a good many. I ain't one of those
that thinks Wallacetown's the den of iniquity that some
does, either—it's a real smart, up-and-comin' place. Still,
'tain't just the spot I'd choose first to turn a boy of your
age loose in, and it's pleased me considerable that you
ain't never seemed to care to go there. I kinder hate to
see you start in."

"You don't expect to see me shut up with a pile of
books for company every night for the rest of my life,
do you?" said the boy, hotly. He seemed to be unable,
these last few horrible days, to escape for one instant
from his newly wakened, throbbing senses. If they could
not be satisfied in the way for which they seemed to cry
aloud, perhaps there was some chance of surfeiting or
deadening them. And because he was hurt himself, he
wanted, desperately, to strike back—to hurt some one
himself, by doing something foolish, or wild, or wicked—

"No, I expect to see you make your mark in the world.
There ain't many young fellers, David, has got your talents and your grit, and I look to see you do better with

them qualities than throw them away in the pool-rooms and saloons in Wallacetown; but you kin have the team."

Sheldon waited up for him in the little room in the barn that had so long proved so safe a sanctuary. David was both surprised and insulted to find him there. It was a rainy night, and he was soaked to the skin; he did not know how to dance, and the "ball" he had attended had bored him to extinction. He was not the first person to return more out of temper than injured by his maiden attempt to "see life."

"Did you think I'd be so drunk I couldn't get to bed alone?" he asked with bitter sarcasm; and after the kindly farmer had departed with awkward apologies, he muttered to himself, "But I will be next time, if no one thinks any better of me than that."

The events of the following day did not tend to improve David's frame of mind, or to raise his spirits. He was set to weeding flower-beds and clipping shrubbery, and his work took him—and kept him—near the deep veranda of the big house, where, the weather having become suddenly unseasonably hot, Jacqueline and her guest had ensconced themselves in big willow chairs, with a frosted pitcher of lemonade and two tall, slim glasses between them, and several volumes of poetry for company. The "general boy," dirty, dishevelled, and perspiring, could not lose sight for one moment of the vision of Cyril Wainwright, clad in white trousers, white tennis shoes, white silk shirt, silk socks and blue coat, not a hair of his sleek blond head out of place, a fragrant rosebud —presumably pinned there by Jacqueline—in his buttonhole, a cigarette between his long, slim fingers. What was worse, he could not escape from Jacqueline's voice. Her

51

"education" had reached that point where the English poets, by means of diagrams and synopses, were being "taken up"; and, given this dry and meager opening, her own temperament, tastes and talents, were causing her to drink far more deeply from these wellsprings of beauty and emotion than her teachers would have either imagined or approved. With her usual impulse of wishing to share with some one else that which she herself enjoyed, she insisted on reading aloud to Cyril; and though he cared very little for the rhapsodies of Shelley or the melting sequences of Keats he enjoyed tremendously the effortless hours passed on the shady piazza with Jacqueline beside him, and, to secure and retain these, he would have listened without objection if she had seen fit to read to him pages from Webster's dictionary—and would have derived about as much inspiration from them. But to David the poetry, overheard from the bushes, meant something very different; and when the girl, after reading "Bright Star, would I were constant as thou art," closed her book and sat looking out over the meadows with an expression of hushed joy on her face, while Cyril murmured politely, "Well, that chap *did* know how to write, didn't he?" David flung down his scissors with a muttered oath, and crept up closer to where the others were sitting.

"Think you could be as constant as all that?" drawled Cyril after a comfortable pause, reaching for a fresh cigarette.

Jacqueline gave a slight start, colored quickly, and drew in her breath. "Oh, *yes*—" she breathed, "if—if—I ever loved any one the way Keats loved Fanny, you know! And Fanny didn't love Keats! It seems so strange!

She treated him dreadfully! I'm sure I should feel more like Juliet."

"A funeral vault, eh? Faithful unto death and all the rest of it. Well, I think you might brighten up even a tomb considerably. You're the most *alive* kid I ever saw! — Light this for me, will you? I can't reach the matches."

"The funeral vault of course—if—if that had to be part of it—but I was thinking of something else." She picked up another book, and, her fingers trembling with excitement, began turning the pages rapidly. Then she read,

" 'Romeo: Oh, will you leave me thus unsatisfied?' "

" 'Juliet: What satisfaction canst thou have tonight?' "

" 'Romeo: The exchange of thy love's faithful vows with mine.' "

" 'Juliet: I gave thee mine before thou didst request it. And yet I would it were to give again. . . .
My bounty is as boundless as the sea;
My love as deep; the more I give to thee
The more I have—for both are infinite.' "

"Go on," said Cyril encouragingly, "that's a pretty scene, when it's well acted. Ever seen it played? I suppose you haven't—I keep forgetting how young you are. I'll take you to it sometime."

"No, you won't," answered Jacqueline slowly, "And I don't want to read any more. You don't feel the same way about it that I do. You don't feel it *at all!*"

"But it's only a silly story about two mooning idiots, after all, you know—"

"It isn't! It isn't! I don't quite understand it, of course, but it's *real*—and it's—a sort of *creed*—"

"Oh, good Lord," interrupted Cyril, flinging down his cigarette and bending over her, "You take things too seriously, baby. I feel enough for *you*, anyway, you cute little thing—"

David picked up his shears, got to his feet, and strode away. That night he asked for a "team" again.

But it was not until Sheldon, undeterred by the boy's ingratitude on the first occasion, had seen him come back three times in the grey of early dawn exhausted and intoxicated and profane, that he decided he must have immediate help if David were to be made to behave himself; and with the unreasoning but unerring instinct of real affection, it was to Jacqueline that he turned for assistance. Cyril had departed. Sheldon felt sure that before long she would go to the barn. He deliberately lay in wait for her in the garden, and he did not have to wait long.

"David ain't home," he said abruptly, as she approached, "if you wuz thinkin' of tryin' to see him. And I guess I shall have to discharge him."

"*David!* Why, I thought he was the apple of your eye! What's the trouble?"

"He goes to Wallacetown every evenin'."

Jacqueline laughed.

"Is that all?"

"That's enough."

"Because he takes the horses too often, you mean?"

"No—but because of the places the horses take him to." The foreman blushed, a deep, honest brick-red. "It's hard to speak to a young lady about such things; but I know you've always been real friendly to Dave. Maybe a word from you—"

There is something in the intelligence back of a young girl's innocence that senses the black things she does not know. Jacqueline came nearer to Sheldon, and he saw that there were tears in her eyes.

"I know," she said, "that is, I'd heard—that men—but not *David!*" She stopped, her lips quivering. It was the old cry, her woman's heritage from the centuries that had gone before her. Other men may sin, but not this one whom I trust! "I'll try—to help. You—you love David, don't you, Sheldon?"

"Love," like "God"—are we not told that the two are synonymous—is a word seldom used in rural New England. Sheldon's blush deepened.

"Yes," he muttered shyly.

"So do I," said Jacqueline quietly.

CHAPTER VI

THE ROAD TO WALLACETOWN

"Say, I guess you don't remember me—I met you at the ball last Thursday night."

David, who was standing on the curb-stone opposite the Wallacetown station, watching the arrival of the New York express, turned to see a girl of twenty-one or thereabouts beside him, and holding out her hand. She was short and plump, with a mass of lusterless black hair, much puffed out under a sailor hat, bright red cheeks, and small snapping black eyes, and was dressed in a cloth skirt and a pink silk blouse, not very fresh and trimmed with cheap lace.

"I'm afraid I don't," he said, vaguely polite, "I don't dance much; but I want to learn; and I'm real—I mean, very—glad to meet you again. What was your name?"

"It was, and *is,* Elsie French," the girl responded with a laugh and a coquettish toss of the head. "Seems as if I'd seen you round here several times lately—aren't you gettin' more sociable than you used to be?"

"I never have been much in Wallacetown," David responded.

"There's an awfully jolly set, once you get acquainted," said Elsie. "Course we don't like to pick up with any one

56

that comes along, so there's some that says we're stuck up, but there ain't a word of truth in it. We'd be real pleased to see you any time. I work in Sawyer's store, and I'm going to meet some of the crowd at the drug store for an ice-cream soda, and then go to the show at the Opera House. It's a real show, not home-talent, 'Out in Idaho,' and from the posters I should say 'twas just grand. What do you say to comin' along with us?"

"I'd like to," he said, "let me treat you to the soda, won't you? That's the drug-store, you mean, right over there, isn't it?"

While he was speaking, the door of the apothecary's shop was thrown open, and a girl came out and stood on the step, looking up and down the bright street with eager interest. Wallacetown was at that time the only place in the vicinity which boasted electric street lights and concrete pavements, and two or three of the leading citizens had already invested in automobiles, and were driving back and forth doing their Saturday evening shopping. The crowds from the train were pouring across the street, and the restaurant near the drug-store was doing a lively business, while the town band, a short distance off, was playing the airs that had been popular in New York six months before. She was bareheaded, and dressed in a white linen habit, her slender figure clearly silhouetted against the dark door behind her. Elsie stared at her with curiosity.

"I wonder who that girl is," she said. "My, but she's got a swell figure! She seems to be all alone, don't she? It won't take any one as good-lookin' as she is long to pick up a feller, though; likely she's waitin' for some one now."

David's heart leapt to his throat. "I'm afraid you'll have

to excuse me," he said hurriedly, "that's—that's Miss Huntington, from Hamstead. I work at her grandfather's farm, you know—something must be the matter—" and without waiting for an answer, he strode towards the drug-store. "Jacqueline," he said thickly, "what are you doing here?"

"Why, David," she said, turning with cordial surprise, "what are *you* doing here? I supposed of course you were grinding away as usual, only too thankful not to be interrupted! Grandfather is ailing again, and out of his pet tonic, so as I wanted to ride anyway, I came up here to get it! It's such a relief not to have Mademoiselle dodging every footstep I take, you can't imagine! If I'd realized how much more satisfactory a lady's maid would be than a governess, I'd have managed to make this change for the better long ago! I supposed I'd get home earlier than this, of course, but Sophie went lame, and I had to walk her the last half of the way!"

She went across the pavement as she spoke, towards the hitching post where Sophie was tied.

"I'd like to stay here a little while," she continued. "I've hardly ever been here, and never in the evening— it's like a little city, isn't it? I love the country now—do you remember how I hated it at first?—but I'll never outgrow my early taste for lights and music and people, I'm afraid! But I suppose it's just as well that I get back before any one finds out I'm gone—and begins to worry." She laughed. "I saddled myself—I wish I'd taken Frou-Frou instead—I haven't liked the look of Sophie's foot for days! Now I'm afraid I'll have to lead her all the way home, and walk myself. Unless you'd let me ride back with you—if you weren't doing anything special?"

David untied the waiting horse. "Get on," he said, vainly trying to steady his voice, "and ride until we can get out of this place. She can't be too lame for that. I'm on foot myself tonight—I've had a team several times lately, and I didn't want to ask again—so I can't drive you home. But I'm coming with you, of course."

He lifted her into the saddle, as he had seen Cyril Wainwright do it, handed her the reins, and started out beside her in silence. Twice before they were off the bright street, he stumbled, and he took hold of the bridle and gripped it; the third time that it happened, they had already reached the dusty highway. He glanced up at Jacqueline. She was looking straight down the moonlit road.

"Jacqueline," he said.

She turned and smiled down at him.

"Yes, David," she said gently.

"I want to tell you something."

She put her hand on his shoulder. "Yes, David," she said again.

"I couldn't let you come home alone—promise me you won't ever go out—this way again. But I haven't any right to be with you. I've—I've been drinking, Jacqueline."

The girl slipped from her horse, and thrust a small, cool hand between his hot clenched ones.

"I knew that all the time," she said quietly.

He wrenched his hand away, and turned his head. Of what stuff was this girl made? He knew only too well the torrent of abuse, the lamentation, the sour recrimination, that such a confession would have called forth if he had made it to his mother. An overpowering sense of shame for what he had already done, a sickening fear of what might have happened if he had not met her when he did, seemed to surge about him, and drag him under and drown him. He tried to shake it off, to reason that she was there with him now, that nothing was strong enough to prevail against her presence—it was of no use—he seemed actually to hear the roar of the waves—

"Let's sit down for a minute," Jacqueline was saying. "I love this curve in the road, don't you? There's no better place to see the mountains, and the river, and the valley, all at once—it's almost beautiful enough to be Heaven, in the moonlight, isn't it?"

He sank down beside her, gratefully, on the green bank. Gradually the roaring ceased. He reached for her hand again.

"I want to tell you something else," he said, "when I saw you I was just going into the drug-store with a girl I didn't know. I was going to treat her to an ice-cream soda, and take her to a show, and—"

"There!" said Jacqueline, " I knew I was spoiling some kind of a good time! Why didn't you tell me before, and let me come home alone? I wouldn't have minded a bit."

"Oh!" he said, and set his teeth. There is no one in the world more unwilling to bruise the fragrant blossom of a young girl's innocence than the boy who loves her. "You don't understand. I didn't know her. She spoke to me on the street. She—"

"Oh, David," cried the girl, "it breaks my heart to see you so dreadfully unhappy! You *didn't* go with her—everything's all right!"

There was silence for several moments. He clasped the

hand that he held to his heart, and held it there—Jacqueline could feel the beating. When he spoke again, his voice was clear and steady.

"I promise you," he said, "that I will never drink too much again—or do anything else that you would be ashamed of."

"I know you won't," she said. She made no attempt to take away her hand, and he gripped it hard. The worst was over—he had sinned, confessed, been forgiven, and started afresh; but he knew, that before he could be happy again, he must rid himself of jealousy as well as shame.

"Would you tell me something, too?" he asked.

"Anything you like."

"Did Cyril Wainwright kiss you that day you went out riding with him—or any other time that he was here?"

For a moment the girl sat very still. He felt her hand tremble a little in his. There was no anger in her voice when she answered him, but there was more reserve than he had ever heard before.

"Don't you know without asking me?" she said.

"You and he were joking—"

"Oh, *that!* People say all kinds of things! It's rather puzzling, but I'm learning. It's only the way they talk—in society. It doesn't mean anything."

"Then he didn't? He or any one else?"

"Of course not," she said; she drew her hand away. "Come," she said, very quietly, "we must go home."

Something like a sob rose in the boy's throat. She had trusted him far, far beyond the measure of his deserving, and he had rewarded the sweetness of her charity only by doubting her dignity, grieving her to the heart; still, even though he should hurt her yet more, he could not let it rest there.

"No," he said, snatching her hand back again, "no— I can't—not until—I'm going to kiss you myself—I'm going to be the first—"

Then suddenly he poured it all out—unworthiness, jealousy, longing, love. Incoherent words, broken sentences, came tumbling through his quivering lips. He hadn't meant to tell her—honestly, he hadn't—not for years and years—until he was rich and great—and then not like this. He wasn't telling her himself, really; it was telling itself. . . .

"And you thought I wasn't glad to see you," he cried at last, "when I didn't—didn't dare—to let you know—" He swept her into his arms. "But I've got to now—"

When at last, trembling in every limb, he raised his head, Jacqueline lifted hers, clinging to him, and the light that he saw shining in her eyes told him that at the first touch of his hungry lips she, too, had been granted the vision of Aphrodite, rising pearly-white and beautiful from the calm and sunny sea.

CHAPTER VII

THE BOUNDLESS SEA

ON THE morning following the evening that Jacqueline and David had spent together on the road to Wallace-town, the boy walked up and down the vegetable garden, between trim rows of infant potato-plants, spraying them with Paris Green. A less congenial—not to say less romantic—occupation for one who had recently and exultantly become an accepted lover would be hard to imagine. He was tired—weary, for the first time in his life, to the point of exhaustion, not only from the hard "spring work" on the farm, which always lay heavily upon his shoulders, and from the almost sleepless nights which, for more than a week, he had been passing, but from the inevitable reaction after the excitement and triumph through which he had passed. His head and back ached, with a dull, stupefying pain, his eyes smarted, his throat felt choked and dry; his overwrought brain seemed stubbornly to refuse to work at all, much less to be spurred into increased activity, as he had vaguely expected it would be, by sensations of ambition fulfilled and desire gratified. He had "got what he wanted"—something equally despaired of, and longed for—and instead of being overcome with joy and rapture he was overcome with discouragement and fatigue. The events of the night before, viewed in the light of a blazing and relentless sun instead of a silvering and sheltering moon, seemed to take on a very different aspect. His sudden and overpowering passion for Jacqueline appeared not only presumptuous and hopeless, but senseless as well. His vision blurred, and two or three scalding tears fell quickly on the grimy hands holding the sprayer. He dropped to the ground, and threw his arm across his face . . .

At the further end of the garden, he could hear Sheldon talking to some one. The foreman seemed to be in high humor—his loud, jovial voice and raucous laugh grated on the boy's nerves—well, in a minute he would stop roaring and guffawing, when he came down the path and found his farm-hand literally—"lying down on his job." And of course it would all be laid to those trips to Wallacetown, when he had asked for the "team"—to *all* the trips to Wallacetown, which had, after all, been harmless and even boring, except that last one. . . . He would probably be fired. It didn't matter—nothing mattered, so long as this deadly weariness following his wild folly—a folly that was as ridiculous as it was wicked —a folly that would ruin his career—had taken possession of him. Then he realized that it was to Jacqueline that Sheldon was talking. . . . And still he did not move, even when the sound of her footsteps, coming in his direction, told him that she was getting nearer, that she was hunting for him. She called him twice, but he did not answer. Probably she wanted to tell him that she, too, realized the madness of what had taken place the night before, the utter impossibility of his remaining at the

Big House. Well, he would get ahead of her—he would tell her himself, first, when she found him. But he wouldn't bother to *help* her find him. . . . Then, suddenly, he felt her arms around his shoulders, her cheek laid against his. . . .

"Oh, David," she was whispering, "isn't it wonderful to wake up—the morning after—and find that it isn't just a beautiful dream—that it's all true?"

Mechanically, he turned his head towards her, blinking back his stupid tears, and gulping as he did so.

"Do—do you think so?" he asked numbly.

"Do I *think* so? *Oh, David!* . . . And what do you suppose? You're going to have a day off—a whole day—and we're going back to that heavenly bend in the road where—where we sat last night—and see it all over again."

He pulled himself free, almost roughly, and got to his feet.

"Some one may see you," he said in a hard voice. "You mustn't touch me like that. Besides, you'll get all dirty—I'm covered with every sort of filth. And I can't have the day off—I never do. The work's way behind as it is. Sheldon wouldn't listen to it for a minute."

"He has listened," said Jacqueline calmly. "Quite pleasantly. About five minutes ago. Sheldon always listens when I talk to him."

"You mean you've asked him already?"

"Of course. And packed the lunch. Chicken salad and olives and sandwiches and angel cake. And lemonade in one of those queer new bottles that keeps things hot or cold, just as you want them to. Have you ever seen one?— Well, you'll be interested; they're quite ingenious.

65

And grandfather's very miserable this morning," she ended cheerfully, "a splitting headache. There's not the slightest chance of his feeling any better until the sun goes down, and he won't ask for me before that—and then we'll be home. I'll devote the evening to him—except, of course, for running out, for a minute, to say good night to you."

David hesitated for a minute; then, without replying, he picked up his sprayer and resumed his work.

"Do you think I care," asked Jacqueline softly, "how much dirt there is on the outside of your clothes—as long as you're *inside*? And as for being afraid that any one will see me touching you—oh, how I wish I could tell the whole world that—you really do love me! I've been so afraid that you didn't! And I've loved you—ever since I can remember!"

"Jacqueline," began the boy desperately, "you—I— we've got to talk this thing over a little. Last night—we couldn't."

"Of course we couldn't! And of course we must! That's exactly why I've made this lovely plan for us to spend the day together—so that we can! And then you raise objections! Why don't you stop—delaying things, and put those hateful tools in the barn and come along—I left the lunch basket in your room."

But even when, the dusty highway behind them, they had climbed the little hill overlooking the river where they had sat the night before, and had eaten the dainty lunch from the English tea-basket, David still found himself unable to talk, and Jacqueline, apparently, had no wish to do so. She looked more like a little girl than at any time that he had seen her that spring, dressed in a

66

frilled sunbonnet, a straight yellow smock of crisp linen, a short white skirt and heelless white canvas shoes; the loveliness of her figure, which the flowing negligée and the tight-fitting habit had both so effectually, though so differently, revealed, was completely hidden, to David's vaguely-felt relief. And her sunny contentment, her calm acceptance of their changed relations and her joy in them, seemed unpenetrated and impenetrable by the doubts and fears that were assailing him. He watched her, without offering to help, while, singing under her breath, she repacked the remains of their lunch carefully and neatly in the basket, and then sat stolidly beside her, staring away from her, without the power to break the silence which was rapidly becoming intolerable to him, until, for the second time that day, Jacqueline laid her cheek against his. He turned his head and kissed her, not because he especially wished to do so, but because he realized that she must be wondering why he had not done so before.

"You're a little dear," he managed to say, huskily, "I— I think a lot of you. And I want to talk to you, ever so much. But I can't seem to get the words out—or to do anything, but sit here like a bump on a log! I'm dog-tired —I can't imagine why; and I can't think of anything except how tired I am—and how I wish I could go to sleep, and forget—about everything for a while."

"Wouldn't you like to lay your head down on my lap and try to go to sleep?" she asked, gently. "We've lots of time, and I'm sure I could make you comfortable. When you get rested, then we can talk." She held out both arms — "Please—dear—"

"I'd—I'd hate to muss you up, you're so clean and pretty—"

Jacqueline laughed. "I've told you once before today that I don't mind about *your* clothes," she said, "I'm sorry if you care so much about mine. Won't you come?"

Suddenly David knew that there was nothing on earth he wanted to do so much as what she was urging. He almost tumbled into her arms, and buried his face in the cool soft fabric of her dress. Then he felt her fingers, stroking, ever so gently, the hair back from his temples. . . .

It was late in the afternoon when David, having drifted first from a profound slumber to a delicious semi-consciousness, and then into a drowsiness so comfortable and satisfying that he had no wish to stir and break it, opened his eyes. The sun had gone down behind the Vermont hills, and the quiet place where he lay was full of lengthening shadows; but, across the limpid river, the mountains in New Hampshire were turning from blue-green to rose-color in its reflected light—slopes and mounds and peaks transfigured with its fiery glory. Through the stillness, a church bell was ringing for an early evening service; somewhere, very far away, a whip-poor-will was singing . . .

Without moving his body, he looked up at Jacqueline. She had taken off her smock, after he had fallen asleep, and folded it into a pillow to tuck under his aching shoulders, which, miraculously, no longer ached; but her neck and arms, left bare by her sheer cambric underwaist, were partly veiled by the cloud of bronze-colored hair which she had let down and thrown about them, to shield

68

his smarting eyes—which, miraculously, no longer smarted—from the light. She was still unaware that he had wakened, and was gazing straight ahead of her at the rosy hills; she was very pale, and there were violet circles under her eyes; he realized, for the first time, with a pang of contrition, that she too, had probably not slept the night before, that she, too, had passed through a new and bewildering experience; her face seemed to have lost something of its fresh childishness; but there was something in its place—an exaltation—a consecration even—passing far beyond the hot ecstacy of the night before, and yet, containing and embracing that also. For a long time he lay, immeasurably rested and refreshed, immeasurably comforted and strengthened, watching her silently; and, as he watched, he knew that there was no need of speech between them, no need of doubts of himself or of fears for her; knew too, that she had taken him out upon that "boundless sea" of bounty of a woman's love, revealing to him the new heaven and the new earth which contained treasures that he had never glimpsed before, and which were now his for the taking.

"Désirée," he said at last softly.

She bent over him, her tired face brightened with tenderness, her arms tightening about him.

"You feel better now," she said happily, "you're all right again—"

David drew a long breath. "Yes," he said slowly, "I'm all right again. I'm going to stay all right—the rest of my life—for you."

CHAPTER VIII

DAVID BURNS HIS BRIDGES

HAMSTEAD went to bed early. Evening chores were not over until nearly eight, morning chores began between five and six. It was therefore necessary to retire soon after the former were finished, in order to refresh oneself for the latter, and insomnia was not one of the complaints which the village doctor was called in to treat very often. By half-past nine, practically all lights were out, and after some event of unusual hilarity, like the annual church supper or a reception to a new minister, when later hours necessarily prevailed, the next night was pretty sure to see the maple-bordered street shrouded in darkness sooner still. But on the balmy June night, following the one on which he had seen his eldest son graduate from the High School, Hiram Noble was still lying awake when the village clock struck twelve, wide-eyed and rigid with excitement, not daring to give way to his longing to toss about for fear of rousing his sleeping spouse on the other side of the feather bed.

The boy had done so darned well. Hiram said it over and over to himself, and his pride increased each time he said it. There wasn't another fellow who could hold a candle to him in looks, in the first place, as he stood up to take his diploma, with that black head of his thrown back, dressed in new ready-made blue serge—bought, of course, for the occasion in Wallacetown—and stiff, snowy linen. And that crimson tie he wore—someway it hadn't looked like a Wallacetown product, but then, where else could David have got it?—wasn't any brighter than his glowing cheeks. Then that valedictory speech— how did a boy nineteen years old—not quite that, come to think of it—have sense enough to know all those things, let alone brains enough to write 'em down on paper? Most valedictories were kind of flowery and wandering, but this was straight stuff. And on top of all this, to have him win the Manning prize, bestowed yearly by Miss Manning, Hamstead's one wealthy and aristocratic spinster!—well, it was almost too much glory—

"The boy's done darned well," muttered Hiram again, and grinned in the darkness.

Mr. Huntington and Jacqueline had attended the exercises, and Hamstead, which affected to scoff at the Big House, preened itself with satisfaction. Sheldon, going to the old gentleman with the farm accounts, as was his custom the middle of every month, had lingered a moment after gathering up the scattered sheets.

"Very satisfactory indeed, Sheldon. You ask me to take more personal interest in the farm, but really there's no need, while I have a man like you."

"I'm glad them's your feelin's, Mr. Huntington. But I'm afraid we shan't make quite so good a showin' after David leaves."

"David?" asked Mr. Huntington vaguely.

"Yes. He came here as a chore-boy, you know, it'll be five years ago, come August—to sleep in the barn, and

do what odd jobs he could after school-hours and durin'
vacations. His father's the postmaster. Now he's goin' to
graduate from High School in about a week, and he aims
to go to college in the fall. I don't know whether he'll
stay the summer or not, but I'd like real well to keep
him until after hayin', no matter what I had to pay him.
He does the work of any other two men I kin get, and
keeps his mouth shut about it. There ain't no yap about
overtime, or this or that bein' some one else's job—no,
sir, not from him."

"It seems a pity," remarked Mr. Huntington, "that so
valuable a workman should have mistaken ideas of his
calling, and desire to educate himself above his station.
College for chore-boys! What are we coming to? Perhaps
a word from me—"

Sheldon shook his head, coughing to hide a smile. "I
wouldn't try to argue with David if I wuz you," he said.
"He's been plannin' this thing out—his 'career,' he calls
it—ever since he was a little shaver without a quarter to
his name. Now he's got twelve hundred dollars in the
Wallacetown Bank. He ain't thinkin' nothin' 'bout his
'station,' except the station where he's goin' to take the
train away from here to go and learn to be a doctor. But
I tell you what, Mr. Huntington, if you and Miss Jacqueline could feel to go to the exercises when he graduates,
I think 'twould be a real proper thing."

Mr. Huntington had always felt the relation of country squire to tenant in England to be extremely pictur-
esque. There seemed to be few opportunities for him to
play such a rôle in Hamstead, but though a High School
Graduation was hardly the same sort of an occasion as a
May-pole festival or a barn-dance, it would serve the

purpose. He graciously signified to Sheldon, as he waved his hand with a suggestion of dismissal, that he would attend. And that night he informed Jacqueline of the fact.

"My dear," he said at dinner, "have you ever noticed a boy about the place named David Noble?"

Jacqueline was buttering a cracker. It seemed to be a fairly absorbing process.

"Why, yes," she said at length, "I met him down by the river years ago, when we first came here, and brought him to you myself. Don't you remember? You turned him out in short order, but later Sheldon hired him after all, and now he thinks the sun rises and sets on David's head. He's the paragon of hired men. Why?"

"I recall the incident, now that you speak of it. Perhaps I was a little hasty, but I've always been so afraid . . . Well, it seems the boy has done very creditably at the High School, and is to graduate there shortly. Sheldon thinks, in view of his long and faithful service, it might be well for us to attend the exercises."

"I think so myself," said Jacqueline.

So, as has been said already, they went, Jacqueline in a pink, crisp, frilly dress, the like of which Hamstead had never seen before, with little satin slippers and silk stockings to match. In larger places, like Wallacetown, the "Graduation Ball" was a separate and very grand event, but Hamstead, where dancing was still more or less frowned upon, contented itself at that time with a "promenade," after "speaking was over." And David, coming straight down from the platform, walked across the floor before any of the rest of his class had stopped whispering and giggling behind the curtain, to the place where she sat beside her grandfather.

"Will you lead the march with me, Miss Huntington?"
he asked.

All this, of course, Hiram Noble had seen, and the
whole of Hamstead beside. Saw, too, that Mr. Huntington—his mind revelling in mental pictures of the squire's
daughter dancing with the handsome young tenant—
smiled his approval, and that Jacqueline, instead of
merely nodding her assent, according to the village custom, swept David a low courtesy, and slipped her arm
through his; and after the "promenade" was over, she
came, at her own request, and was introduced to the
Noble family, from Hiram down to Susie—who was
pretty sleepy by this time, and alternately nodding and
staring—and stood chatting with them, "just like folks"
for some minutes. Then when the music began for the
next number, taking David's arm again, she went back
to her grandfather's side, and David held up a wonderful
shimmering velvet cloak, lined with white satin, and
wrapped it around her, and went out of the hall to help
them both into the waiting carriage—and came back,
looking as unconcerned as if graduating exercises, and
rich, lovely girls to promenade with were everyday occurrences in life.

And what Hiram and all the rest of the village had
seen, Lizzie Noble had inevitably seen also. But not once,
on the drive home from the Town Hall, did she open her
closely pressed lips, or even glance down at Susie, sleeping serenely in her lap, wrapped in an old shawl. She
sat staring straight ahead of her into the fragrant, misty
June night, as unseeing as she was silent. And having
descended unaided from the carryall, telling the boys to
"go help their father put up the horse," she lifted the key

from its hiding place under the door-mat—where every-body in Hamstead always hid their keys—entered the dark house, fumbled for the matches on the table in the front entry—those were kept in a small china lamb—lighted a lamp, and, without waking Susie, undressed her and put her to bed. When Hiram came in from the barn his wife was standing in front of the small pine bureau in their bedroom, unfastening the cameo brooch that had been her mother's. Her back was towards him. But, through the dim light he could see in the cracked and blurred little mirror that her hands were trembling.

"Why, Lizzie," he said, "you're shiverin'—this hot night! Hev you took cold?"

"No, I ain't took cold," she replied tartly, sticking the brooch in the red bead pincushion vindictively, and removing her only other ornament, a hair-bracelet that had been her grandmother's.

"Are—are you mad at somethin'?"

"No, I ain't mad—and I ain't one to stand an' spend the night in idle talkin' neither, when I got to be up an' stirrin' at four in the mornin'."

She unbuttoned the black silk dress in which, twenty years before, she had been married, turned it carefully inside out, and hung it in the shallow closet. Then, gaunt and unbeautiful in her coarse cotton undergarments, she faced him.

"But even if I ain't, I know a promisin' boy when I see one," she said with a note of fierce pride in her voice that Hiram had never heard there before, "an' when sech a boy's my own son, I guess I kin take some satisfaction in him, same as any one kin."

"Why, Lizzie!" gasped Hiram.

75

"An' I know a lady when I see one, even if I ain't one myself," she continued in the same voice, "an' if that pretty-spoken, nice-mannered little Huntin'ton girl ain't one, for all her mother was a lost creature an' her father was a drunkard, I miss my guess, that's all. There's somethin' back of her good-looks that's worth a heap more'n her handsome hair an' pink cheeks. I could tell the minute I saw her step out in the promenade, before she come an' spoke to us. And after I'd heard her talk I was dead sartin' of it."

"Everyone likes the girl, an' that's a fact, Lizzie," agreed Hiram, "but I don't see what that's got to do with David."

"You don't, eh?" snapped his wife. She flung the straight, scanty locks she had been braiding back over her shoulder, and sank on her knees beside the bed. "I thank Thee, Lord," she said distinctly, "for all Thy mercies. For—a son like David. For—that pretty, pretty, little critter that kin give him all the things his mother's ben too druv, an' too ignorant, an' too sharp-tongued to give him—if she only will. Oh, Lord, please make her feel to give them to him! For Jesus' sake. And bless them both. Amen."

As she rose and slipped into bed, Hiram saw that her rough, thin, cheeks were wet. He longed, dumbly and miserably, to comfort her. But this would have been difficult for him to do at any time, and in the light of her recent emotion—for he had never seen her display emotion before—it was impossible. He was infinitely relieved when her regular and not over-quiet breathing assured him that she was asleep. After a few moments he dismissed the recent scene without much trouble from his

76

mind, allowing it to revert to the pleasing spectacle of his firstborn, with Miss Huntington's velvet cloak on his arm, escorting her from the hall.

The sequel to this Hiram did not yet know. However, if he had, no amount of terror inspired by the fear of waking Mrs. Noble, and the consequences if he did, would have kept him from tossing about. When David, all festivities over, reached his little room something after midnight, he was startled to find Jacqueline, still in her crisp, frilly, pink dress, curled up on his bed, half-asleep. She sprang up with an expression of joyous welcome, and threw her arms around his neck.

"Oh, David," she cried, "it was splendid! Your speech was great! I don't wonder you got the prize—and the tie I gave you is so becoming! And wasn't it wonderful to march together? I could hardly wait for you to get home to talk it over with you."

He put his arms around her and kissed her, more tenderly than passionately, and drew her down beside him. Since the little straight chair by the desk was the only one in the room, they were forced to sit on the bed if they were to be side by side.

"Look here," he said gently, "all this has got to stop."

"All what?"

"Coming here to see me; and letting me make love to you; and kissing back when I kiss you."

"You mean—you don't love me any more?"

"I love you a great deal too much to let you get into trouble; I've got an awfully guilty conscience."

"If you were half French, like me, you'd have less conscience and more intuition."

"Well," he said smiling, "I guess that's true—and your

intuitions have sure suited me all right so far! But it looks to me as if they were all the more reason why I'll have to have conscience enough for both of us."

"What have you done so very dreadful?"

"Stolen," said David grimly.

"For heaven's sake! What?"

"You," he answered briefly.

Jacqueline burst out laughing and shook him. "You miserable wretch!" she exclaimed, "I thought from your manner it must be the Chinese porcelains, at the very least."

"I wish you wouldn't joke. It doesn't look much like a joke to me. You know we haven't any right to see each other like this."

"But we've been doing it for almost five years, and you haven't minded."

"We weren't doing it just like this, were we?" he asked, suiting his action to his words, "I should say the situation had changed a good deal, since the night we went to Wallacetown. It makes all the difference in the world if you know in your own mind that what you are doing is all right—as it was before—or all wrong—"

"*Wrong!*"

"Not in itself, darling, but under these circumstances— as it is now. Besides, we were lucky never to get caught, except by Sheldon, but if we had been, when you were eleven, and I was fourteen, we'd have been scolded, and told to keep away from each other, and that would have been all there was to it. But if we're caught now—do you think I want to make a scandal—out of you—for the servants?"

"David! We're engaged!"

78

"We haven't any right to be engaged."

"Because we're too young, you mean?"

"Because you're a lady, and I'm your servant."

She put her hand over his mouth, trembling, "No, no, no," she cried. "You shan't talk like that—I can't bear it."

He took the hand away, kissed it, and held it fast. "It's true," he said, almost roughly, "and you know it. And until it isn't— Listen," he broke off, abruptly. "I'm going away—immediately. I ought to anyway, if you want me to go to Harvard, instead of to the University of Vermont. I ought to go to Cambridge, and take the entrance examinations. I probably can't pass them all with the preparation I've had, and if I can't, I ought to stay there all summer, working off conditions, so that I can start college with a clean slate in the fall. But before I leave, I'm going up to the Big House to tell your grandfather how things stand between us. I'm not going to put up this miserable sham another minute!"

She tried to break away from him, panting with grief and anger.

"I think you must be stark, raving crazy! Do you know what will happen then? I'll be clapped into a convent in disgrace, and you'll be discharged."

"I can't be discharged if I discharge myself first, can I? And you won't be disgraced—I'll say this was all my fault, of course."

"But it isn't."

"Well," David smiled again, "don't get so terribly angry, darling. It's really about half-and-half, and that's the way it ought to be. But I think myself a convent would be a pretty good place for you—no knowing where those 'intuitions' of yours may lead you, without a little restraint—straight off to Cyril Wainwright, for all I know! Of course he's going to try to make them, and I won't be there to prevent!"

"It would serve you right, because you *weren't* there to prevent. You ought to think of staying around to take care of me."

"Lots of fellows," said David, more truthfully than grammatically, "spend their time hanging around a girl to take care of her, when she needs to be protected from them more than she does from any one else. Cyril won't hurt you—he's a perfect lady. But the other thing will be our case exactly, if you won't listen to reason."

"What do you call reason?" sobbed Jacqueline.

"Well—doing this out in the open, or not at all—and of course I know that means not doing it at all, at present. But when we're old enough—I'll come back—"

"I won't be here."

"Probably not. But I'll find you. If a fellow really wants to see a girl, he'll do it, if she hides in the desert of Sahara, or on top of the Himalaya Mountains. Five years from now you'll be old enough to marry whom you choose, no matter what your grandfather says; and I'll be fit to have you, by then. But neither of those things is so now."

"You'll find me," she flared. "And I'll be married to some one else! And it will serve you right."

For a moment the boy hesitated. How could he tell this sweet, loving, willful, hurt, innocent thing that he was fighting not only her but himself? That if he had not been . . . the little, quiet, dark room seemed suddenly to close around him . . . he got to his feet, almost hurriedly, pulling her with him.

"No, I shan't," he said, "not if the road to Wallacetown meant as much to you as it did to me. And if it didn't . . . I don't want you now—or then—or ever— Did it?"

They clung to each other, both too shaken to speak, a minute—two—five—possibly longer. Then he lifted her to the window-sill.

"Good night, darling," he whispered, "and good-bye —unless you'll meet me in your grandfather's library to-morrow night, and we'll tell him together . . ."

All of this, of course, Hiram did not know. Nevertheless, the village clock struck one, and still he lay, perspiring and quivering, and staring into the darkness.

There was a slight noise beneath his window. Bristling, he raised himself on his elbow.

"Dad," whispered David's voice outside.

Hiram crept cautiously out of bed and across the room. The vogue of pajamas had not reached Hamstead. He confronted his son in his abbreviated night-shirt.

"Don't wake your ma," he breathed, "what the heck's the trouble?"

The boy laughed softly. "Nothing," he said, "Come out to the kitchen and let me in. I'll be quiet—but I want to speak to you."

Hiram pulled on his trousers, and taking his shoes in his hand, tip-toed from his chamber, closing the door behind him an inch at a time. Then he lighted a lamp, and sped to the kitchen door. David stepped inside. He had on the blue serge suit in which he had graduated the night before, the same snowy linen, and strange crimson tie, and he carried a cheap new suit-case, a battered old

81

carpet bag, and an armful of books tied together with a halter.

"Do you think," he asked calmly, "that you can drive me to Wallacetown in time to catch the two-thirty express?"

"Where for?" gasped Hiram.

"For Boston."

"Land of Goshen, David! What's come over you?"

"Mr. Huntington. I've just been into his house for the second time, and got kicked out for the second time. The first time I wanted a job—and I got it after all, without his help! This time I want his grand-daughter—and I'll get her, too, when I'm the greatest doctor in New England—as I'm going to be—and take her to live in a place that will make the Big House look like thirty cents!"

Hiram stared at his son as if he thought he had suddenly gone mad. David, having delivered himself of his modest purpose, seized his father by the shoulder.

"Come on out to the barn and harness," he cried. "We've got to hustle to make that train. I'll tell you all about it—on—on the road to Wallacetown!" he ended, with the excited, exultant laugh of eternal youth starting out to seek its fortune.

Part Two

CHAPTER I

JACQUELINE'S BIRTHDAY

ON an unseasonably chilly afternoon in May, almost five years later, three persons were sitting before the cheerful fire in the drawing-room of a house in London, drinking tea, smoking cigarettes, and talking. They were apparently all excellent friends, and enjoying themselves to the fullest measure.

The man who sat nearest the fire was about twenty-seven years old, very fair, very slender, and noticeably well-dressed. Everything about him was eminently correct, from his faultless tie, to his perfectly manicured nails. His voice was that of an American, with a carefully cultivated English accent. The warmth of the fire seemed welcome to him, and indeed it is doubtful whether so super-civilized a being could have been comfortable without one.

The second man was at least ten years older, shorter, stouter, and also faultlessly dressed. He spoke English, indeed, instead of American, but with the decided accent of a foreigner. The fire apparently held few charms for him, but taking his cigarette from his mouth, he leaned over the table, and poured a generous contribution of cognac into the cup his hostess had just handed him.

She was a girl, who at first glance, seemed to be about twenty-five years old, so self-possessed, so perfectly poised, and so splendidly developed did she appear; but closer inspection revealed that she was considerably younger, revealed also the rather singular combination of extreme sophistication of manner with an unusually clear and direct gaze from a pair of deep hazel eyes, and an almost childlike outline of chin and throat. There was something about her as baffling as it was fascinating, a fleeting impression—almost instantly dispelled, to be sure —of very deep feeling—was it joy or sorrow, or a capacity for both?—suppressed beneath a mask of levity because it did not dare to show itself, of some sort of faith so betrayed that it would be slow to trust again—or was all that mere imagination, and was she merely a beautiful "society girl" of unusual brilliance and charm? She was dressed in a very low-cut tea-gown of white Liberty satin, long and very scant, and her knees were crossed, revealing plainly that she wore little beneath, but a generous length of white silk stocking, and white satin slippers with big rhinestone buckles. Great masses of golden brown hair, obviously all her own, were piled high on her head in a simple regal fashion, fastened with a great comb set in diamonds, and a single string of enormous pearls hung almost to her waist.

"Tell us something amusing," said the younger man, flicking an almost imperceptible ash from his knee. "She's not so amusing as usual to-day, really, is she Gustav?"

"That I should hardly say," replied the other, bowing as gracefully as his cigarette, his cup of tea, and his avoirdupois would allow, "She is more still—more *en repos*, shall we say? But then she is never dependable, two days the same. In that doubtless lies much of her fascination for us poor victims." He might almost have been discussing a china vase or a handsome animal. "What says your immortal Shakespeare, 'Age cannot wither'—here she has reached another birthday, very old!—'nor custom stale'—has she not been our constant custom this long time?—'the infinite variety of her charm.'"

"Oh, not Cleopatra, please, Gustav," cried the girl, leaning forward and throwing her cigarette into the fire —"she was always playing to the gallery, and roping in some man with theatrical effects! Think of the rug she rolled herself up in, and the painted galley! She didn't dare to be simple! And that asp story—I haven't any use for a woman who can't stick things out, no matter how bad they are. I'm not especially disturbed at her morals, but I think her tastes were dreadfully middle-class. I'm afraid I'm *not* very good company—but I'm pretty tired; partly because the season's been so awfully crowded, I suppose—what would Queen Victoria have said to the pace her son leads us?"

"Mon dieu, Désirée! Blame you the poor king because you ride miles and miles in the Row, go out to luncheon, go to a picture exhibition, to a dinner, to a ball, and then walk home at four in the morning, two miles, with Freddy Lambert!"

"Jealous, Gustav?" she asked lazily, half shutting her eyes. "I never can bear to get into a close motor when I've been dancing all night—and dawn is really a lovely time for a walk! And Freddy is such a comfortable person! It wasn't yesterday that tired me especially—that was like lots of other days, no fuller—and I often take

85

those early morning walks—is this the first one of which you've happened to hear? Sometimes with Freddy, sometimes with other people. The exhausting thing happened after I got home. When I reached my room I found a note from my first love on my dressing table."

Both men burst out laughing. "You are amusing, after all," said Cyril. "Who is he?"

"His name is David Noble. He used to be a stable-boy on my grandfather's estate in Hamstead, Vermont—you know what a perfectly barren time I had there for several years, while I was growing up, until grandfather finally made up his mind to venture out into the wicked world again. This fellow was very attractive, and I'm afraid I flirted with him—when I was between fifteen and sixteen years old. He had more conscience than common-sense, so one day he went to grandfather, and insisted that we were engaged—it wasn't proper, in his category to have a little *affaire de coeur*, unless the road to the altar was in plain sight. Of course he got discharged for his pains, and I got clapped into a convent—I've never felt especially grateful to him for his candor! What he is now, I haven't the least idea—the letter was on Claridge's paper."

"By Jove," exclaimed Cyril with an expression of real interest, "I remember that fellow! He came to Harvard when I was a senior, and was so extraordinary that he was conspicuous among four thousand men. He was very striking-looking, as you say, and strong as an ox—he played a fine game of football, made the freshman team right away. It was the only thing he did play—no one ever saw him drink or gamble or dance or go to the theater. It was reported that he turned up in Cambridge

86

in the June before college opened, and drove an ice-cart all summer, while he was working off his condition, living in the cheapest kind of a lodging house,—oh, respectable enough—he committed no human pleasing follies! In the fall he got a job as choreman for several of the professors—looking after their furnaces, you know, and that sort of thing—and lived with one of them, working free for his board and lodging. He haunted free lectures and museums and libraries and even churches when there was unusually good music, and I don't believe he missed a single free demonstration of surgery at any hospital within ten miles of Boston! How he managed to crowd in so many things no one could imagine and, as he didn't try to make any friends, no one found out."

"How thrilling!" said Jacqueline, evidently without a single spark of interest.

"Isn't it? I ran across him one day on Tremont Street, looking in a jeweler's window, at a really marvellous display of rings. He was such a queer devil that I wanted to hear what he would say, and I asked him if he was thinking of buying one. He turned and stared at me a minute as if I had committed an impertinence, and then he said, 'No, none of them is handsome enough for my purpose,' and walked off. Towards spring, he slipped on one of the icy walks he took care of, and hurt himself quite badly. He was run down—no other human being could have stood his pace half so long—and got ether pneumonia when his leg was set—but even that turned into a piece of luck. The doctor that was called in to look after him—Ross, a great friend of Professor Hildreth's and an awfully big bug, don't you know—took a tremendous shine to him, and asked him home for the summer.

His wife was dead and he'd just lost his only child—a boy about Noble's age—under very tragic circumstances. It looked to everyone like a tremendous chance—but I never heard definitely what happened after that—you know I came abroad as soon as I graduated. I wonder what he did next—did his letter give you any clue?"

"It said very little—ran something like this—'Dear Jacqueline, as tomorrow is your twenty-first birthday, I shall come to see you sometime during the afternoon. I am very busy, so I can't tell at what time I shall be free, but if you are not in when I get there, I will wait. Faithfully yours, David Noble.' That's the first syllable I've heard from him in five years."

"I say, what perfectly colossal effrontery!"

"It suddenly came over me," Jacqueline went on, fingering her pearls, "that he had insisted at the time of that volcanic eruption in my grandfather's library, that when I was twenty-one, legally of age, that is, he would appear again. He has. From what Cyril tells me, I imagine he has been fairly successful already along certain lines; from what I know of him, I imagine he expects to be very successful—along others. And I expect to have the most interesting experience of my life paying him back for his self-confidence."

She laughed, a laugh far too worldly-wise and weary for a girl twenty-one years old.

"If it weren't for giving him his deserts," she said, "I believe I would marry him—just to get out of this rotten life, and away from all the rest of you!"

The portières parted. A footman stood in the doorway.

"Dr. Noble, if you please, miss," he said.

The two men sprang to their feet; the girl cast a mocking glance back at them, and advanced with outstretched hands.

Her laugh died as quickly as it had risen. A perfectly dressed man, so tall that he seemed fairly to tower in the great room, his black head flung back, his dark eyes full on the girl's face, came forward silently, bowed to her companions, and stood waiting for her to speak.

It was no more the shamefaced boy whom Jacqueline had kissed on the road to Wallacetown than she was the fresh-faced, heartbroken little girl who had clung to him, weeping because he was forcing her to say good-bye.

CHAPTER II

THE STABLE BOY

JACQUELINE recovered herself quickly, "How do you do?" she said coolly, without holding out her hand again. "This is a very great surprise, and of course a delightful one. I think you know Mr. Wainwright? May I introduce my friend the Duke of Saxburg? Gustav, this is Mr. Noble, of Hamstead, Vermont. Let me offer you some tea."

David bowed slightly a second time. "I think the duke and I met once in Paris last summer," he said; and turning from the Austrian, who stared a moment, and then colored violently, muttering a few words unintelligibly, but in visible surprise, "Thank you, yes—clear, please—no sugar—no lemon—no cognac."

"And a cigarette?" she went on, as he sat down on the great sofa beside her, "we have all been smoking, but we got so interested in your note—I have been telling Cyril and Gustav about it—and your probable arrival in its wake, that we seem to have stopped. Have you been long in London?"

"About two weeks. There is a clinical congress here, as possibly you did not know. It meets in various capitals from year to year. Last summer it was in Paris, and next year, I believe, to be in New York. Will you try one of mine?" he added, taking a cigarette case of engraved gold from his pocket, and offering it first to Jacqueline and then to the two men, "They're fair, I think."

"But surely you are not a doctor yet?" She was extremely conscious of the grave eyes of the man beside her as she leaned forward for Gustav to light the cigarette between her red lips.

"I was fortunate enough to get my degree at Harvard in three years, and we get our title after two in the medical school; that of course would not admit me to the congress, however, if it had not been for the kindness of Doctor Ross, with whom I am traveling, and who was good enough to do a little wire-pulling for me."

"In—er—just what capacity are you with him? Cyril has been telling us something of your very interesting career during your first year at college, but was obliged to stop short at his own graduation, leaving you in the doctor's hands, more or less disabled, but planning, as he understood it, to be his chauffeur that summer."

"I am grateful," said David, "to Mr. Wainwright for abbreviating the story I had to tell you—I feared it might be tediously long! With one year already accounted for, I shall be able to be less tiresome. Yes, I went there first as a chauffeur—do you remember how crazy I was for an 'otter*mo*bile' when I was a boy? I still do all our driving, but his kindness took me out of the rank of chore-boy sooner than I could have hoped without it. My second year in college I was able to have a room in one of the less expensive dormitories, and to do tutoring instead of minding furnaces; and by the third—my last year—I had time to begin to make some friends, and enough money saved up after my second summer with the doctor to feel I wouldn't be 'sponging' if I did. The fellows—and their families—were all awfully kind—and so much less critical of the verdure of the Vermont hills, which I knew covered me pretty completely, than I expected! Dr. Ross insisted on my going to him for good and all as soon as I graduated. It's a little hard to answer your very natural question 'in what capacity?'—I'm not his chauffeur any more—that is, I think he would hardly allow you to call me that, though I shouldn't mind in the least! He's planning to call on you and Mr. Huntington very shortly himself, if you'll allow him, so perhaps he can give you a more satisfactory explanation than I can. He wanted to adopt me legally—funny, isn't it?—but my own father wouldn't part with his ugly duckling. I'm to be his assistant later on—and that, of course, means succeeding to his entire practice in time—a long time off, I hope! Meanwhile he indulges me most shamefully—aren't you ready for another cigarette, Jacqueline? You've let that go out. Allow me to light it for you this time—? I hope I haven't bored you? Ever know a fellow named Bobby Hutchinson—just between us in college—Mr. Wainwright? He'd have told that same story so that you would have been shedding tears of amusement and sympathy and interest—he says I'll never be any kind of a doctor, because I don't know how to talk. He ought to know—he's getting to be a very successful one himself. I think I've heard him and his sister Nancy speak of you. . . ."

Jacqueline glanced at Cyril. He was flushing no less painfully than Gustav had done a few minutes earlier. He rose, however, with dignity.

"I believe both brother and sister are noted for their wit," he said icily, "in our society we should call it vulgarity. Are you planning," he said pointedly, taking Jacqueline's hand and bending over it, "to get a little rest before your party tonight? I fear you are greatly overtired."

"I'm saving the first dance for you," she said gaily, "and I haven't half thanked you for your wonderful flowers—and all the wonderful birthday wishes that went with them—I'll surely answer your note very soon."

"And mine, Désirée?" the Austrian also bent over her hand, but looked at her lips.

"Yes, and yours, Auf Wiedersehn." She turned to David. "I'm having a ball tonight," she said, "in honor of my birthday. It would give me great pleasure—"

"I am sorry," he said, "I have already made other plans. But I will see you again before I leave London. May I not," he added, "take either of you gentlemen somewhere? I have my motor at the door."

All three went out together talking. Jacqueline bit her lip, walked to the fire, and kicked a half-burnt log viciously. It fell apart, blazing again. A footman came into the room, and took up the tongs.

"Dr. Noble has sent me for his cigarette case, miss," he said, when the log was in place again. "He thinks he must have dropped it. Will I disturb you if I look for it, miss?"

"Will you ask Dr. Noble," said Jacqueline slowly, "whether he will not come back and search for it himself?" and as David reëntered, and the footman withdrew, she put out her hand again.

"Won't you shake hands with me?" she asked. "And won't you let me tell you—that I wish to welcome you very warmly, and that I am filled with admiration and surprise."

"And I," he said quietly, "am filled with disappointment, and grief—and shame."

CHAPTER III

JACQUELINE'S SIDE

"CAN'T we sit down?" he asked, as the girl gave an exclamation of amazed anger, "and really talk? You know I never did like shams, and I see by your tastes that your 'intuitions' have been playing you false, just as I feared they would."

"My tastes?" she flared.

"Yes—in friends—and little customs like cognac for afternoon tea, and dresses—like this. We doctors believe a great deal in heredity and environment, you know, and are always quarreling as to which is the most powerful. I should say that in your case, they were pretty well matched."

Jacqueline sprang to her feet, and reached for the old-fashioned pull-bell that hung by the door. David was too quick for her.

"Don't have me put out quite yet," he said more gently, "I'll go directly, anyway, if you really want me to —I shouldn't have said that. You were fairly insulting yourself, you know, when I first came in—and I was so surprised that I am still a little stunned. You see, I've been hoping and waiting and working for five years to be worthy to come to the most loyal friend, the truest lover, the fairest girl God ever made. And when I thought I could, without too much presumption, do so, I find—she doesn't exist any longer. What happened, Désirée? I think I have a right to ask on—on account of the road to Wallacetown. You seem to me, in spite of all this splendor, so tired, and so bitter, and so lonely."

"Don't," she said quickly, "I don't want to talk to you. It's hardly fair—after all these years—to remind me of a silly episode in which I played a very foolish part."

"Is that the way it looks to you? It hasn't been an episode to me—it's been a lodestar to decent living, and high ambition, and success. It's seemed to me, all along, that the part you played would have been that of a guardian angel, if it hadn't been so divinely flesh and blood as well! You were a spirit and a savior, but a sweetheart, too —don't you believe me, my dear?"

"No," she said slowly, "I don't. If that is the way you felt, why did you leave me to face everything alone? Don't you realize, that in all those years, you never once tried to see *me*? It was always I that sought *you* out! Even the—the road to Wallacetown wasn't an accident! I went out that night because Sheldon had told me that you were in danger, and I wanted to help, if I could! I lied to you about the reason for my being there, just as I'd lied, or acted a lie, to other people, over and over again, in order to be with you. And that last night when I went to your room and you turned me out—oh, you were right to do it, of course! There wasn't a moment, ever, when you weren't a truer gentleman than any I've known since—but think, when my grandfather trapped me, of the part I had to admit I'd played. Boldness— 'shamelessness,' he called it—for the sake of—a servant!

And a servant who—I had to admit it—had never made the slightest advances to me! At whose head I'd flung myself! Who must therefore hold me so cheap that—that—"

"That he had probably proved how cheaply he did hold you?" asked David with a strange quietness.

"Yes—just that. He accused me of having done things —of having let you do things—which up to that moment I'd been only vaguely conscious that—that any one did. Young girls—sheltered young girls, I mean, like me—have certain intuitions—and—and theories of course—they're not fools—but everything ugly is so—blessedly hazy in their minds! I was so stunned—so horribly stunned and terrified when he made his hideous charges that—"

"That he saw how mistaken he'd been. Yes. He would do that." David's mind was traveling back to the lovely, impetuous child sitting beside him on the narrow bed in his dark little room. "He couldn't very well help it, if he was in his senses."

"But not until he'd taught me, when I was far too young and unprepared—truths I couldn't forget again. Awful truths about human nature—oh, why do they have to be true? I've never got away from the horror of the fact that they are!"

"No," said David.

"And then," she went on, "I was put into a convent. And the Sisters were told not to give me any liberty at all—a girl sixteen years old, with no outlet for her over-flowing vitality! I—'needed to be watched.' If I'd been a boy, I'd have gone—straight to the devil, of course. But I only—didn't sleep. For nights and nights I lay awake, because my mind, which they couldn't confine, was so much more active than my body! And when I lay awake I cried for you—very quietly of course, so no one would hear me—a sort of strangling sobbing—missed you till I ached all over—longed to see you for the tiniest minute, hungered for your touch! And I never had a letter or even a message—not a single word to tell me that you still cared—if you ever had cared, really! So of course I came to believe that my grandfather was right. That though you hadn't held me quite as cheaply as he had thought at first, still—. I think I suffered as much as I possibly could—as much as any one possibly could—and then I grew very hard. I'm hard still. I suppose I always shall be."

So far she had looked at him steadily. Now she turned away, her lips quivering.

"It had all been as mystical and beautiful and holy to me as—as the Eucharist," she said in a hushed voice. "And to you it had been merely—"

"No, it hadn't," interrupted David fiercely, "it hadn't— *it hadn't!* Oh, you poor little girl!"

The sincerity of the startled grief in his voice was unmistakable. Before she could prevent it, he had seized both her hands, and pressed them against his heart with a sort of rough breathlessness that was at the same time infinitely tender.

"And I never thought of all this before," he said in a voice which showed plainly that the thought, now that it had come, was utterly unendurable. "It—it was a sacrament to me too. It was because I wanted to keep it so that—I did what I did. That little room had been a sanctuary—and it wouldn't have been, any longer, if I had let you stay! I knew I couldn't stand it—the way things were

98

going. And you were so little and sweet, and innocent, that you couldn't understand—and of course I couldn't tell you! But I hoped—I thought—you'd trust me even if you didn't understand. I thought you knew I loved you— that you couldn't help knowing that—though you couldn't guess how much. If you couldn't believe this before— won't you believe it now?"

She drew her hands away, quite gently and without haste, her self-possession, apparently, strangely restored by the fact that he had been shaken out of his.

"Yes," she said, sitting down on the sofa again, "I be-lieve you now. I—I can't very well help doing that. There's something about you that's—very convincing. But if you haven't thought of my side, isn't it largely because you've been thinking of yourself—your side of it—all the time? Isn't that what you always do, unless you're very much moved, just for a moment, as you are now? Isn't it a question of *your* viewpoint—*your* happi-ness—*your* success always? How much have you ever helped your family—gone home to see your mother, had long talks with your father, tried to see that those three brothers and that little sister of yours didn't have to face the odds that you have?— Oh, you've succeeded, wonder-fully! But you couldn't have done it if you'd loved any human being as much as you love your career! And now you've come here, expecting me to fall into your mouth like a ripe cherry, and be a suitable ornament, in time, to your very successful establishment! I'm not too blind to see what would happen if I did, even if you are! I should probably fall in love with you over again, if I'd let myself, and then you'd fail me again, worse than you did before! And that would affect you very little indeed—and it

99

might affect me a good deal. You'd pursue your career—unhampered. But it might be rather difficult for me to find something that I would care to pursue!"

David, entirely calm again, was lighting a cigarette. The vivid color from the flame of the match flashed across his face for a moment, flared, flickered, and went out, leaving it in the shadow.

"Your opinion of human nature seems to be almost unnecessarily pessimistic," he said coolly. "What you so cheerfully predict might happen, of course, but it seems to me extremely doubtful."

The girl had expected as hot a denial to her statement as the one which he had made five minutes earlier. She made no effort to control her rising anger.

"Don't forget what brought about my present opinion of human nature in the first place," she said, "or forget that since then I've had nothing to raise it—only one thing after another to lower it. Since I left the convent I've had three years 'in society'—on both sides of the Atlantic. Do you realize what that means—to a girl like me? It means that almost every man who meets me tries to marry me, for one thing—that I'm flattered and courted and cajoled and —desired, and that all that is called—'love'! It means also that I'm watched, night and day, by women who are jealous of me—and there are many such; by men whom I haven't favored—and there are still more of those—who are hoping I'll make some kind of a little slip, that I'll soil my satin skirts just enough so that they can shriek to the Heavens that they're dirty! They haven't been able to yet, but I have to be eternally on my guard that they shan't be—and hating and despising them through it all! But dresses like this one—which you don't need to tell me isn't modest, or even decent—and friends like those you found here—and I know what sort of men they are—and cognac and gambling and flirting and dancing—and—and all the rest of it—everything that makes up a modern belle's existence—are just second nature to me now! I was shocked—oh, far more shocked than you are—at first —but now I never even think of it—in fact, I couldn't live any other way! You're perfectly right—that girl you used to know doesn't exist any longer. She was careless—because she was so innocent that she could be. I am careful, because I am very, very worldly-wise. She gave her favors freely, because she loved so much. I give none, because I love no one at all. You are wasting your time to come here. Just before you came I promised those two men you found with me to let them know tonight which one I am going to marry."

"Everything you've told me," said David, "is true, perfectly true, except that. You are going to marry me."

"I am not," said Jacqueline hotly, "if for no better reason than that you wouldn't want me to if I told you the rest of my conversation with them."

"I am open to conviction," remarked David smiling.

"I told them—about our engagement. I pretended that I had almost forgotten—but that it was just a silly case of calf-love—a pastime for a bored girl—a . . ."

Not the slightest change came over his face, and he made no effort to interrupt her, but she stopped, horror-stricken at something hidden beneath his perfect self-control which she could divine and feel.

"Can't you understand why I did it?"

"No," he said slowly, "I can't. I believe it's the only thing you ever did in all your life that wasn't—splendid.

And you've just accused me of not realizing that—our love was a sacrament. If *you* realized it, how could you defile it so?"

"Because I had lost faith in the sacrament. Since I had nothing holy left, there was no profanation. An atheist can't blaspheme."

"I think I see," he answered; "I'll—I'll try. Perhaps it was my fault anyway, not yours, if all these years I seemed to be robbing you of your holy thing. I wasn't, though, really. I must convince you of that before we go any further. May I sit down beside you and show you something?"

The quiet question was almost a godsend. It caught Jacqueline back from the torrent of pent-up emotion, which, for the first time in years, had swept her off her feet. She steadied her voice, and spoke quietly and courteously.

"Why, yes," she said gently, "anything you like. And please—let's try to be friends, after all, can't we? I meant, when I found you were coming, to 'pay you back in your own coin'—to insult you and hurt you. I can't do that, no matter how hard I try; you are too invulnerable. I'd only hurt myself. I see that clearly now—what did you know about Gustav and Cyril that upset them so? Lots of people are clever—but *you're* powerful—as the rock of Gibraltar, and just as hard, I'm afraid! I don't think it will be safe for any woman to marry you until you are ready to give up your career to have her—and to do it then to serve, not possess her! But you're very wonderful, David. And now that I've told you my side—if I've made you see it—I'm proud, very proud, to have you here—"

"I see," he said, "that the girl I used to know does

exist, after all. I thought she did, if I could only find her. Look!"

He drew from his pocket a little package wrapped in soiled paper and tied with a frayed string.

"You never had a letter from me while you were at the convent," he said, "because I was afraid it would only hurt you, if you did—that your mail would be opened and scrutinized and reported upon. Wasn't that so?"

"Yes . . ."

"But I wrote to you—from the time I left you that night in your grandfather's library and started for Harvard. Regularly, every Sunday night, before I went to bed. We've been talking of sacraments—well, that was my Evensong. Of course the letters in themselves—weren't much. They just told you that I'd got a new job, or what marks I had in my courses, or how much money I'd put in the bank. Once in a while—not often, partly because it was so hard, at first, for me to express my feelings on paper—I'd never tried to do it before, you see—and partly because I didn't suppose it was necessary—I told you that I loved you. Then I used to date and seal and address the letters—and put them away. When there were enough of them to make a little package, I tied them up —like this. I brought one of the packages with me today, because I thought it might interest you—I didn't realize that I'd need it—to prove my case! Will you open it, please?"

Jacqueline's fingers trembled over the knot. David took out his pocket-knife and cut it. Half-a-dozen cheap envelopes, covered with a sprawling, boyish handwriting fell from the crackling paper. He picked one up, opened it, and handed the scribbled sheets to her.

"This one is dated in December, in my first year in college," he said, "suppose you read it aloud?" . . .

"Dear Jacqueline"—the letter ran—"it is awfully cold in my room because I have no fire and I am writing with my mittens on, so I suppose this will look worse than usual.

"We have been having some awful 'tests' called 'hour-exams.' I have passed them all, but nothing to brag about. Some of them I just skinned through. Most of the fellows learned more at school, before they came here, than I could in Hamstead. Lots of subjects we didn't take up at all. But I guess I can do better next year.

"Everyone seems to be getting ready to go home for Christmas. I have looked up the fare to Hamstead and it's $5.91. So I don't think I shall try to. I wish I could send you a nice Christmas present. Some day I will.

"I think about you a lot, especially how I went to sleep with my head in your lap. You were awfully good to me that day. I'll never forget it.

"Well, I guess I must close now, with love from David.

"P.S. If I could put kisses on paper I would cover this whole page with them instead of words."

He took the letter from her, folded it, and putting it back in its envelope again, opened another. Jacqueline stretched out her hand.

"No," she said unsteadily, "not—not now. I'd like to have them all—not just this one package—if you'll give them to me. But I'd rather read them when I'm alone."

"Then let me show you something else."

He took her hand, touching her for the first time, and laid it palm-upwards on her lap; and into it he dropped a ring, a ring more beautiful than the girl, surfeited as

104

she was with jewels, had ever seen. The stones were large, but it was the quality rather than the size of the gems that was so remarkable. Jacqueline knew that there was a fortune in the gold circle set with a ruby glowing between two diamonds, knew instantly the symbol as well as the value—the red heart of love burning to the white heat of passion. She rose, and taking it to the fire, whose dying coals gave the only light to the darkening room, turned it over slowly again and again. At length she spoke.

"This ring cost a great deal—not just money, though of course I know how valuable it is—but heat and cold and hunger, slights and deprivations of every sort. It explains why, though you started out with twelve hundred dollars, and made more money all the time, you drove an ice-cart, and slept in miserable lodgings, and took care of furnaces. It represents five years of sacrifice —and I thought you had been thinking only of yourself!"

"Since you put it that way—yes."

"Five years of sacrifice for some one who does not exist—'the most loyal friend, the bravest lover, the fairest girl God ever made!' A lady who kissed her stable boy, and—rightly—gloried in her kisses. And what have you found in her stead? A woman in whom 'heredity and environment are pretty evenly matched'—in other words, the frivolous daughter of a drunken reprobate and a ballet dancer!"

"From the bottom of my heart," he cried, "I ask you to forgive me those words!"

"And from the bottom of mine," she said, going to him quickly, and kneeling down beside him, "I know that they are true! And now, please, go away!"

She slipped the ring back into his hand, and as she did so, he felt tears falling on it.

"Jacqueline," he commanded, "Look at me—get off your knees! *Go away!* Why, I've just *come!*" Then as she burst into convulsive sobs and tried to break away from him, he lifted her in his arms, and held down the hands that strove to hide her face.

"Do you hate me," he asked, "because I didn't understand? Because I thought only of myself—remember I was suffering too! Because I didn't guess how much you'd have to face when I told your grandfather, and left you with him? In short, because I was an ignorant, egotistical boy, trying hard to be square?"

"No—no—you know I don't!"

"Then why do you tell me to go away?"

"Because I know how much you must despise me—if I can measure it by the way I despise myself!"

She tried once more to wrench herself free, but this time she might as well have struggled against the strength of the sea.

"And if I told you that I didn't despise you—that I love you with all my heart and soul, and that I know, in spite of everything you do and say, that you love me, the same way, and always have?"

"It wouldn't make any difference. Grandfather—"

"I saw him *first*, this time. He feels rather differently than he did before."

"There are a thousand other reasons then. We're as far apart as the two poles in our habits and tastes and ideals. I'd surprise—and shock and grieve you. You were jealous before—you'd be jealous—with much more reason—now. I couldn't satisfy you, no matter how hard I tried. And you would come first to me—but I would come second to your career. . . ."

David laughed, a low, happy, triumphant laugh. "Who's jealous now?" he whispered, "You're fighting, just because you've made up your mind not to yield. But you will. I asked you once if any one but me had kissed you, and hurt you dreadfully, because you thought I shouldn't need to ask. I don't this time. I know, that in spite of yourself, you've been waiting for me."

She felt the wonderful ring slip on her finger, and the hand that bore it raised to his lips. Then his arms closed around her once more. She knew that she was powerless against his strength, his will, his love, and a feeling of glory in her weakness swept over her. He was kissing her hair, her forehead, her throat. In another instant she thought, it would be her mouth. But there he stopped.

"I have taken the rest," he said, "won't you give me that—*Désirée?*"

CHAPTER IV

THE ENGAGEMENT

FOR five years every battle that David had fought, with himself and his surroundings, had resulted in victory—triumph spelled in capital letters. It was therefore not strange, that with the usual healthy egotism of youth, he had come to regard defeat as an impossibility. It was equally natural, that having had little time for amusement, and little inborn taste for dissipation, he should have scant understanding and less charity, for the frivolity of others. Persiflage puzzled and horseplay disgusted him—without being consciously a prig, he saw no reason why every one else should not be as serious of purpose, and as austere of life as he was himself.

His natural dignity of bearing and character, his self-confidence, or rather, egotism—the natural result of his success against heavy odds—made him appear much more thoroughly a man of the world than he really was. The only world he knew was a very small one, and as severe in judging other spheres which revolved differently from itself as it was satisfied with its own revolutions; and even in the world which he did know, he had taken time to make so few friends, and these were so relatively unimportant in his scheme of life, that his knowledge of human nature of any kind was extremely superficial. Jacqueline, who as a child, had been so refreshingly naïve, and who still seemed, at times, to have retained much of her naïveté, was, in truth, mondaine to her very heart, though that heart constantly overflowed with sympathy and understanding and affection; while David, who seemed—and believed himself to be—entirely master of this and any other possible situation, was ignorant of the very A-B-C of the society into which he had so confidently flung himself—a fact which would, unfortunately, have disturbed him very little if he had been wise enough to be aware of it.

His engagement to Jacqueline, announced instantly, on the night of her twenty-first birthday—for he had refused to consider "the sham" of keeping it a secret—seemed merely another step—an important one to be sure, but by no means warranting a change in schedule, or undue satisfaction at having reached an important capital on time—on his single-track railway. Did he not deserve her? Had he not worked and waited long and faithfully for her? Was he not in every way her equal, in many her superior?

But if the betrothal scene which was only a few hours past had not brought elation to David, it had brought an exquisite torture to Jacqueline. She had fallen under the spell of his presence, almost as soon as her fortress had been besieged, her surrender had been both complete and unconditional. For the vulgar insinuations, the criticism, the sneers at her choice, which she knew were bound to come, she cared not at all, knowing the sterling metal of which the man she had chosen was made; that he had chosen her, that he still wanted her, in spite of

109

everything, was a matter for thankful prayer; but that there was a moat between them, which would be difficult, if not impossible, to bridge over, unless the conqueror possessed greater engineering skill than she believed—she realized with a pang of something very like terror before she was fully awake the next morning; nevertheless, she rose at once, lest she should not be dressed in time for the visit which she expected would take place at the earliest possible moment. Her room was filled with flowers, her bed-side table piled high with notes of congratulation, messages and gifts arrived steadily all day; but it was four in the afternoon when David finally appeared. She expected explanations, apologies for his tardiness, the caresses and regrets of a lover no less disappointed than she herself at the delay. Instead, he seemed to have no idea that he had been remiss; gave her a glowing account of a hospital he had visited that forenoon; a sketch of the maturing plan for his trip to the Continent, now less than two weeks off, and which he apparently saw no reason for giving up; a humorous description of his experiences in a fashionable shop; then after a scant hour with her, rose to leave!

"You say you wish me to join you to a fancy dress ball this evening—such things aren't much in my line."

"I rather hoped you'd dine and dress here, and that we'd go together."

"I can't arrange that—Dr. Ross and I have already made engagements for the evening—but I'll join you about midnight, if you really insist."

"I don't insist—you must do as you prefer. But it is only fair to tell you that if you don't, considering that the engagement is already announced, it will probably provoke considerable comment."

"From persons whose opinion isn't worth having! Well, I'll come! But don't accept any further similar invitations if you can help it."

"I am going to Lady Thornington's place near Oxford on the fourteenth for the week-end. She has just sent me a message saying that she had written you asking you to come too. You made a most favorable impression on her last night, and that is a family and a house which I know you will enjoy."

"I liked her, too—I'll gladly go there. Good-bye, my dear, I'll see you later."

Five o'clock found her alone again. With a desperate resolve to shake off her depression, she ordered her horse, and was putting on her habit, when she was told that Mr. Wainwright was waiting to see her in the library; if she were disengaged, he wondered if she would receive him.

"Tell him I'm just starting for a ride, Hodges; but if he'll have a cup of tea with me first, you may serve it there at once."

"So that's how you settled it?" was his greeting as she entered the room.

"Won't you sit down? Yes—I'm sorry, Cyril—I mean I'm sorry things didn't come differently for you. I realize that I had led you to think that perhaps they would. You don't feel very badly?"

"I? Oh, no—it is of course the most trivial of disappointments. I especially wish to embrace the first opportunity of extending my congratulations to your fiancé."

"Cyril—if this is one of your sarcastic days, would you mind going home?"

111

"I should, very much. I did not expect the pleasure of tea alone with you, and I shall certainly not forego it—I think I see it coming now."

"David has only just left," said Jacqueline, handing him his cup.

"It isn't necessary to sound so apologetic—he's not dining with you then?"

"He had some previous engagement—a medical dinner, I believe."

"Of course the Continental trip is given up?"

"No, indeed, it's too great an opportunity."

"Then you're not to be married immediately?"

"No—that is—" the girl stopped suddenly, her face flooding with color, realizing that the question had not even been brought up. "Not at present," she ended, rather lamely.

"And Mr. Huntington?"

"Oh, grandfather's disappointed, of course; but he's more reconciled than I had dared to hope."

"He had some other choice, perhaps?"

"Cyril, you have no right—you know very well what he wished."

"Can't you prevail upon Dr. Noble at least to establish himself in London? I really fear that a separation from you might bring about serious results with Mr. Huntington, and he would hardly care to move again, now that he is so congenially placed. Besides, I hate to think of you going to waste in the provincialism of Boston, Mass. Of course you know that every one is saying that you are absolutely demented to throw yourself away like this?"

"If they knew the man I am going to marry as well as I do, they would not say so."

112

"As well? Pardon me—isn't it five years since you have seen Dr. Noble?"

Jacqueline rose. "I'm afraid you'll have to excuse me," she said rather coolly. "I don't like to keep Sophie Second waiting too long. Will you go and see grandfather for a few minutes?"

"I'm riding myself—I'd much rather come with you, if you don't mind—" Then, as she hesitated, "Surely, we haven't got to give up all our good times—isn't old lang syne to count for something—in this very brand new engagement?"

David, on reaching Claridge's was told that Dr. Ross had just gone out, leaving no message. He waited as long as possible for him, then, disturbed and puzzled, he went to the dinner without him; no word had been received from him there, either; finally, when David returned to the hotel to find their suite a second time deserted, he became genuinely alarmed, and when the door at last opened to admit the doctor, wreathed in smiles and apparently unaware that he ought to be the cause of either anxiety or censure, the boy flung down the wrap he was holding and greeted him with the angry anxiety that came from long waiting.

"I was just putting on my coat to go out and hunt for you! Where on earth have you been?"

"Where I should think you would have been—with your fiancée!"

"Good Lord! I knew you meant to call on her sometime soon; but did you forget all about the Savoy? They delayed the dinner nearly an hour for you, and we telephoned to every club in London, I believe."

113

Dr. Ross regarded his protégé blankly for a minute, then burst out laughing. "What a joke!" he exclaimed, "I did forget it completely."

"You don't seem to take it very seriously," said David stiffly. "You broke an engagement, you know."

"My dear boy, do calm down a little. Supposing I did? If I were a little younger, I should certainly try to break yours—I think that girl's the most glorious creature I ever saw in my life."

David unbent sufficiently to smile. "You like her then?" he said, with evident self-satisfaction.

"*Like her!* Why didn't you describe her to me a little, so I wouldn't be so completely dazzled! She was just coming up the steps after a ride, with a tall, fair fellow, when I got there, and there's nothing like exercise like that to show off gorgeous color, and nothing like a black habit to do justice to a perfect figure. The whole thing nearly knocked me over! She gave me a glance, and then she held out her hand, and said, 'I think this must be Dr. Ross.' It was one of the most charming and graceful things I ever saw done."

"A little unconventional, wasn't it? You might have been any one else in the world."

"Yes, but you see I wasn't. I fancy that girl's a good guesser. She turned to this blond squire with the air of a queen dismissing a subject, and remarked without much enthusiasm, 'I'll see you again tonight, I suppose—I'll try to save you a dance, but I won't promise—' and then she devoted herself exclusively to me."

Dr. Ross took a whiff at his cigar, and glanced at David, who was still pacing the floor of the tiny drawing-room.

"She took off her hat when she got inside," he went on, "and her hair—loosened by the wind, I suppose, tumbled down and fell all around her shoulders—I bet it's down to her knees! So then she went and fetched her grandfather to see me, while she was 'gone to get tidy.' He wasn't enthusiastic, but he was decent, and he asked me to stay to dinner. I wouldn't have missed it for a dozen Savoys. She was in pale yellow when she came down the next time—soft and sheer— You can go to medical dinners every day, but you meet a girl like that once in a lifetime—David, how soon are you going to be married?"

"Why—I hadn't thought. In about three years I suppose."

"Three years—what's to prevent your making it three weeks?"

"We'll be in Stockholm by that time, won't we?"

"You're not serious, are you?"

"Certainly—why not?"

Dr. Ross rose, and with some embarrassment, laid his hand on the boy's shoulder. "Look here," he said, in a voice so gentle that he tried to make it sound a little gruff, "you're not making that—ridiculous plan—on account of—lack of funds, are you? Of course you don't want to be the dependent husband of a rich wife—and I wouldn't for an instant hear of that haughty old scoundrel being given a chance to do more than provide Jacqueline with pocket money. But I've meant—ever since you first came to me, David—that the money my poor son inherited from his mother, which she asked he should have intact as his wedding gift—should be yours, when you married, my dear boy. It isn't a fortune for these days, but it's rather a substantial sum, just the same.

And ever since that girl came laughing up the steps I've been thinking—if you'd only bring her to live in my old house—how that laugh would sound to me, ringing through its emptiness, what it would mean to me, in time, to have a little child there again—I had some lonely years, David, before you came to me—"

David gripped his hand. "And I had some lonely ones, too, before you took me," he said gratefully, "but I can't do what you suggest. Even if it weren't accepting more than I am willing to—I don't feel a man can do first class work if he tries to combine school and matrimony. I've always felt a good deal of scorn for the fellows who married before they'd completed their course, and for the girls who let them. A few years more won't hurt either of us—and now I suppose I must go and dress for that damned ball—"

It was nearly midnight when he entered the ballroom, having spent the greater part of an hour between the front door and that particular apartment, so enormous was the crowd at the colossal and splendid house where the party was being held. The beautiful apartment was filled with dancers, and the sparkling light from hundreds of crystal chandeliers, the blaze of jewels, the magnificent costumes which seemed to shift before him with the brilliance and swiftness of a kaleidoscope, gave him an immediate and involuntary sense of exhilaration and intoxication. He felt as if he were witnessing the sudden blooming of a huge, exotic orchid. Then a feeling of disgust came over him for the extravagance, the ostentation and the lack of dignity before him, and he stood, eagerly looking through the dancing crowd, to see if he could distinguish Désirée, and bear her away from this

116

abnormal atmosphere to some more quiet spot where they could have a few minutes alone.

Two other men were standing by the door talking together, and, in spite of a skillful and complete disguise, David recognized the one nearest him as the Austrian Count, by his rotund figure and marked accent. The conversation, which he naturally could not help overhearing, at first proved uninteresting enough to him—a detailed account of the respective merits of several fragile, though shining, "stars" of the music-halls. After singing the praises of various beauties, with whom he stood on various degrees of intimacy, he changed his subject.

"Those are all very good for London," he said lightly, "but we haf them much, much better in Vienna—there, there is really some choice. And ven Miss Huntington is also in Vienna, vat vill you amuse yourselves with here?"

"But Miss Huntington isn't going to Vienna, you fool! She's going back to America with this young doctor who's suddenly turned up out of thin air. All London is talking of nothing else. What did you say this fellow was in the beginning—a blacksmith?"

"Mein Gott! You do not suppose she really intends to marry him? Désirée is *grande coquette*—he is a blind, nothing more,—a tool to increase the infatuation of others by yet more uncertainty. But he will not long be a rival— a man who was with her but one hour yesterday—as I have it from Wainwright direct—does know the meaning of a *grande passion*. After his little call she went to ride with our cherub Cyril, and this evening did she come here with Freddy in his electric brougham."

"Good for her—she has the right idea! As long as she's so impartial, no one can get jealous, and I notice her

117

swains—if she goes about alone with 'em—are all that
harmless variety like Freddy and Cyril. Doesn't go much
with you, does she, old sport?"

The count grimaced. "I console myself with the
thought that no beautiful woman becomes *amoureuse*
of the men she trusts too much," he said cynically. "She
promised to unmask early, and I have in vain been trying
to discover her. Rest assured, it will be a sight worth
going far to find."

Seething with rage, and knowing that if he stayed
where he was another moment, he should certainly do
some violent injury to the Austrian, David pushed past
the two men, through the crowd, and made his way
towards the conservatory. It was dimly lighted, the air
was heavy with the scent of flowers, and in the middle
stood a great pool of water, its calm surface unbroken
by a fountain, reflecting the beauty of the luxuriant
growth all around it. He sat down on a marble bench
near it, leaning his head on his hands, and gazing into
its quiet depths, and again a feeling of being entranced
and bewitched overcame him. Decidedly, no such houses,
and no such parties, existed in Boston. And Jacqueline
must be rescued from this atmosphere—would it perhaps
not, after all, be better to follow Dr. Ross's advice? But
he regretted the necessity—two or three years later would
be so much better, from every standpoint. He was actually impatient with her for making him feel, by her choice
of living like this, that he ought to take her away—

A low laugh came from the further corner of the great
room—to his angry imagination it seemed to fairly ruffle
the placid water by which he had found an instant's seclusion and peace. He sprang to his feet and went rapidly

in the direction from which it had come. A circle of masked men stood about a seated girl, masked and wrapped in a great cloak.

"Oh, well," she was saying, "it's only a few minutes now, anyway, and if you wish a private view, so to speak, before we go into supper—*me voilà, messieurs!*"

She rose as she spoke, and David, forcing his way forward, stood before her. Apparently Gustav's suggestion of the evening before had not fallen on deaf ears, for she was dressed as Cleopatra. A wide band of dull gold bound her hair, completely covering her forehead; a wider band of the same metal encircled her waist, and there were pendant earrings, studded with gems, in her ears, and a golden fan hung by a jeweled chain from her girdle. Her flesh-colored gauze skirt was diaphanous; her slim white ankles were bare; her silver sandals glittered. She had clasped her bare arms behind her head, and stood looking at them all through lazy half-shut eyes. As she caught sight of another masked figure, she took a slow step forward and held out her hand.

"Welcome!" she said slowly, "Cleopatra is holding court tonight for all her friends alike. These gentlemen are about to cast lots as to which shall take her out to supper. Will you draw?"

He nodded without answering. The man nearest him was tearing up a slip of paper into narrow strips. He straightened them in his hand.

"The longest wins," he said, and turned to each man in succession. The longest slip fell to David.

Still without speaking he bowed, and offering her his arm, walked towards the ball room with her. At the entrance to the conservatory he paused.

119

"If you will excuse me for a minute," he said very quietly, taking off his mask as he spoke, "I will go back and get the cloak that you dropped. Then I may feel that you are sufficiently clothed not to mind taking you home."

"*David!* I felt it might be you! Do you mean to say you—don't like my dress? I've been so admired—having such a good time—"

"Do you refuse to come home with me?"

"Of course not—I'd like nothing better—but don't look at me like that!"

"I'm trying not to look at you at all."

He held back the curtains, and she went down the stairs in front of him, slowly, her white shoulders gleaming. They were in her carriage before he spoke to her again.

"Are men simply so many shuttlecocks to you?" he asked then, almost roughly. "A call from me, a ride with Cyril, 'Freddy' whoever he may be, as an escort to the ball! Then undecided where to cast your favors next, I find you in the most immodest dress I ever saw on any woman in my life, letting a crowd of mountebanks draw lots for you."

"Oh, my dear, I'm sorry! I never thought of any of it in that light at all—I told you we would be bound to look at things differently. But I waited indoors all day for you, and you wouldn't take me tonight yourself. Tomorrow I'll spend every instant with you—if you'll come to me—and wear a collar up to my ears, and drink cocoa."

"It isn't funny—I heard that vile Austrian talking about you—"

120

"Gustav? Remember he's dreadfully disappointed—he felt so sure—"

"Then you must have given him more encouragement than I should have believed possible. Is there no limit to your indiscretion?"

"You have no right to speak to me like that. Would you wish me to judge you so harshly—or so hastily?"

"You'll never need to," he said; but something in his voice warned him that he had gone too far. He leaned over and put his arm around her. She made no effort to withdraw, but did not return his caress. The joy had gone out of the evening for her, and when they reached the house, she pleaded fatigue, and asked him to leave her. He obeyed, feeling injured—was she to do whatever she pleased, and resent his criticisms? He too, went home, feeling that the day had been a failure; and neither of them thought, though it was to wring David's heart many times afterward, of the dusty moonlit road between Wallacetown and Hamstead; the slender, clear-eyed girl, riding a lame horse; the stable-boy stumbling beside her; the broken confession, "I've been drinking, Jacqueline," and the quiet answer. "I knew that all the time, David"; the gentle judge who did not condemn, but kissed away the guilt.

CHAPTER V

DAVID's plans for greeting Jacqueline with dignified coolness when he next met her, were unpleasantly upset by
a note which was handed him late the following afternoon telling him that she had been in bed with a severe
headache all day, and that though slightly better, would
be unable to see him that evening, in case he were thinking of calling upon her. If she were sufficiently improved
to undertake the trip the next day she and her grandfather were planning to motor down to Oxford to spend
ten days there quietly at the Inn, before she went to Lady
Thornington's, as she realized that she was entirely un-
equal to keeping her engagements in town. If David and
Dr. Ross would like to go with them or join them there
later, they would be delighted. If not, she would see him
Saturday week at tea-time at "Boxwood."

"Excellent idea," said Dr. Ross when David handed him
the note, which was quite guiltless of anything of a private or personal nature. "I'm a little worried about that
girl. She strikes me as an unusually healthy, normal creature, who's lived on her nerves lately more than is good
for her, and has used up her natural reserves by perpetually overtaxing them. I shouldn't be at all surprised to

hear of a reaction in the form of a serious nervous break-down before long. But of course I'm a surgeon, not a nerve-specialist, so I may be mistaken. If I were you, I should coddle her up a good deal, and see what it would do for her—it would be worth a trial, anyway, wouldn't it? Of course we'll motor down with them?"

The next few days were extremely happy ones. David had never been to Oxford before, but Jacqueline knew it well. She surprised him constantly by the scope, as well as the lack of pedantry, of both her intelligence and her information. They wandered about the beautiful, gray old city, with her as guide, through courts and churches and colleges, sitting wrapped in the soft English sunshine in the ancient green garden of St. John, and under the trees on the Broad Walk of Christ Church; they punted down the river, and had tea at Iffley. She seemed neither sulky nor resentful, but she was so quiet—almost apathetic—that David was frightened. Much has been said—and truthfully—about the inconsistency of woman, but no one has yet done justice to the incon-sistency of man. Confronted with the terror of seeing Désirée slip through his fingers, literally as well as fig-uratively, he forgot entirely that any such thing as a fancy-dress ball had ever taken place. He enveloped her with anxiety and tenderness, and just as a hurt child is reassured by his mother's caresses, and smiles through his tears, Jacqueline gradually laughed and talked again. She loved Oxford, loved showing it to David, loved the river and the old mill at Iffley, loved being quiet and alone with him and the two elderly men; she looked, in her broad hats and white dresses, sixteen years old again. When they reached the top of Magdalen Tower one morning when they had been there about a week, and sat down to rest for a few minutes, looking down on the city and the verdant country around it, she put her cheek against his shoulder, touching him of her own accord for the first time since they had parted years before.

"I wish we could stay on here," she whispered shyly, "like this."

He threw his arm around her, and bent to kiss her. He had been so afraid of startling her back into her defensive shell of passivity, that he had hardly dared embrace her; even now, he ventured only to brush her forehead; she lifted her head, and her soft lips met his. Involuntarily he drew her closer.

"Like this?" he asked, "or—just you and I?" Then, as she did not answer, he said, "Désirée—I don't think we should be married for a long time—are you willing to wait for me?"

"To the end of my life—"

"But in spite of knowing that, I may not be able to hold out much longer—you're very sweet, my darling! If I should ask you—"

Jacqueline smiled. "There are always churches on every corner—especially in Oxford," she said. And raised her face again.

Perfect as such moments seemed to David, he felt, before their holiday was over, that it was only when he and Jacqueline maintained a strictly impersonal basis as the groundwork for their conversations that such perfection was attained. Jacqueline, indeed, found no fault with anything, and seemed only too content to rest and drift. She was both too tactful and too weary to raise minor points of difference between them, unless David forced an issue. But David, far more analytical, was confronted at every turn with small irritations and trifling details to which most men are blind during their courtship and betrothal, and see in large print after their marriage. The more he saw of Jacqueline's habits, tastes and occupations, the less he liked them. She met his thrift with extravagance, his energy with indolence, his seriousness with levity. He rose at six, to find that she never appeared until ten—unless she were going to early church —a reason which was the last to appeal to him. She took a lady's maid as completely a matter of course as she did a traveling bag. She had never in her life, she confessed, drawn her own bath or picked up her own clothes, and no amount of argument could convince her that there was any earthly reason why she should. She loved to lie for hours among the cushions of a sofa or boat, her hands clasped above her head, her eyes half-shut. When she could be persuaded to go to walk, she sauntered when David wished to stride. He lectured her perpetually on her shortcomings but made no headway. She replied with an amused and good-natured raillery, and continued to do as she pleased.

On one of their rambles into the country they came to a charming and secluded cottage, almost concealed behind a high-hedged garden. There are, of course, thousands of such cottages in rural England; but it was the first one which David, whose traveling had largely been confined to cities, had ever closely noticed. He waxed enthusiastic over it. If they could find or build one like that, somewhere within motoring distance of the Harvard Medical School, perhaps—

"Way off in a lonely place without any neighbors?"

"Why yes. That's my idea of a real home. It's so safe from intrusion. One can live so simply and sincerely."

"You mean I could live there so simply and sincerely while you spend most of your time doing interesting things in the city."

David stiffened. It was the first time she had argued with him.

"You could be busy about the house and garden in the daytime."

"I don't know *how* to be busy about a house and garden."

"You can *learn,* can't you? And of course I'd get home for a late dinner. I could have a laboratory there and do research work evenings and Sundays. If I could live in a place like that I could get married without interfering with—"

"That *career?* Well, it all sounds to me very much like the story on the epitaph on the old tombstone, 'Here lies Mary Anne, resting on Abraham's bosom.'"

"Well?" said David impatiently. He never remembered frivolous stories and did not see the point.

"You know some one came along and wrote underneath it, 'Very nice for Mary Anne, but rather hard on Abraham.' I simply won't be Abraham."

She said it all lightly and happily, but David refused to smile. He continued to look back at the sheltered cottage.

"I want to do things *with you* after we're married," persisted Jacqueline.

"What kind of things?"

"Why, the kind of things we're doing this week—traveling, and going for walks and boating, and—and to parties, too, of course; and I want to keep lots and lots of time free just for *loving*."

David disengaged his hand. "I like to work," he said briefly, "I am going to, too. I'd never get anywhere if I lived that way."

"Get anywhere?"

"In my profession. I'd stagnate. I intend to be one of the big men in America ten years from now."

"Whatever else goes by the side?"

"Of course. That's the only possible way to succeed."

Jacqueline pressed her lips together. Then she bent over the grassy edge of the road and began picking violets without answering.

"We might try it," went on David at length.

"Try what?"

"Why, getting married."

The girl burst out laughing. "Mercy, David, how immoral you are! I never should have suspected you of such a suggestion! It all goes to prove that you can't tell by the looks of a frog how far he'll jump, doesn't it? I thought that was what you wanted all the time. I—"

"*Jacqueline!*" cried David, almost roughly, "How can you be so irreverent and indelicate?"

"Why, you started it! You said—"

"You know perfectly well I meant that we might *try a little house* like that and see how we liked it!"

"But suppose you liked it and I didn't?"

"Well, naturally the husband's convenience has to be considered first, doesn't it?"

"Yes, but he ought not to consider his wife as one form of it. I simply refuse to be a convenience to anybody. I want to be—"

127

"What?"

"*Grande amoureuse.*"

Again David stiffened. "Do you know what that phrase really means?"

The gaiety died out of the girl's face. She sat down on the bank and looked away from him.

"I didn't mean to hurt your feelings," he said after a pause during which she neither answered him nor looked at him.

"I wonder what you'd say if you *did* mean to hurt them?" she asked, raising a flushed and troubled face. "I'm afraid it would be something that we'd—that we'd never get over. And I'm so dreadfully afraid that sometime—before very long, perhaps—you are going to say it! And I couldn't bear it—I couldn't! I care so much—so much more than—"

She was trembling from head to foot. David was frightened. He had always held the comfortable theory that women's emotions are never, in love affairs, as violent as men's—or as deep.

"My dear girl—"

"You knew what I meant—just as well as I knew what *you* meant about the little house. Why should it be wrong to be a 'great lover'—unless you *want* to see wrong in it? Don't you ever forget about my—my mother? And even if you can't, why do you feel that she was so—dreadfully bad? She loved my father dearly, even if— And she gave pleasure to hundreds of people— If it were wrong for her to do that, why wasn't it wrong for them to go and see her—but you don't feel that! And she was generous and kind-hearted and brave—and so was my father, too! I am

128

not ashamed of my parents, or—or my love for you! If you are—"

"Jacqueline!" interrupted David hotly.

"Well, you seem to be. I'd—I'd rather go home alone, if you don't mind. I wish you would leave me."

There seemed to be nothing else for him to do. He reasoned—or tried in vain to reason—with her for a few minutes, and then strode off down the road alone.

He did not see her again until dinner time. The two older men were inevitably conscious of strained relations, and both, without knowing the cause of the trouble, sided mentally with Jacqueline. Mr. Huntington was glacially polite, and David, who was now quite equal to meeting him on his own ground when it came to icy courtesy, froze perceptibly. Instead of shivering in this chilly atmosphere, Dr. Ross became more and more genial, the girl more and more flippant. If her fiancé were not enjoying himself, she herself was apparently unaware of it, or at least saw no reason why he should not be. And later in the evening, when she had gone to bed, the elder doctor tried again to remonstrate with his protégé:

"David—don't you ever play?"

"What do you mean, play?"

"On general principles. More especially, with Jacqueline."

"We're not children."

"No, but she's dreadfully tired and overwrought—almost ill. She needs to relax. You hurt her all the time, and the only way she knows how to cover it up is by assuming a gaiety she is very far from feeling. Nothing could be worse for her. If she could only be natural—as she must have been as a girl—it would be her salvation. I meant to suggest something like this to you before we came down when I told you to coddle her."

"I believe she has you bewitched," said David coldly, "like every other man she knows—except me. I see her the way she really is."

"No, my boy, you don't—that's just the trouble."

"There isn't any trouble, said David, still more coldly, "and there won't be, if I have my way."

"But you aren't always going to have your way."

"Yes, I am," said David, setting his teeth, "I always have so far, haven't I? She'll see things differently before we start for the Continent."

"You may, too," said Dr. Ross under his breath, as, without further remonstrance, he left the room.

CHAPTER VI

LADY THORNINGTON'S HOUSE PARTY

BUT in spite of the drifting clouds over what both of them knew should have been a shining sky, David and Jacqueline were both extremely sorry to leave Oxford. They ignored the quarrel by the road-side, as if by mutual consent, and though they met with a little strangeness the next morning, this gradually wore off as the day advanced, and before it was over, the man, at least, had almost forgotten it, much the easiest course for a lover somewhat ashamed of himself to pursue. Their last evening was exceptionally happy. They punted down the river, drew up their boat on the grassy slope, and sat for a long time hand in hand, talking very little. The sound of a distant clock, striking eleven, brought them to the reluctant realization that they had been there far longer than they realized, and that they must start back to the city. As they went down the bank, Jacqueline made a suggestion, almost shyly.

"Why don't we take your motor and go off for the day tomorrow? Pauline and the luggage will go in another to 'Boxwood' anyway, and grandfather can take Dr. Ross back to London in ours. We didn't agree to reach 'Boxwood' until tea-time, and it wouldn't matter, even if we were late for that."

"Where do you want to go?"

"Anywhere—with you."

"I might never take you to 'Boxwood' at all, once we got started off," he said, with a humorous catch in his voice that was very rare.

"I shouldn't care much."

The abandon of her voice made him instantly serious. "Don't," he said gravely, "you mustn't say such things, even to me. But I like your plan—a long country ride, and lunch at some little inn, and a cathedral or two along the way, I suppose? It sounds good to me, too, dear."

So they had their day in the country together, and it proved to be the happiest one they had passed since their reunion. They went to Worcester for their lunch, then back to "Boxwood" through Coventry, Stratford and Warwick. It was all new territory to David, full of unguessed beauties and undiscovered delights; and again he was surprised, as he had been in Oxford, at Jacqueline's glowing and intimate knowledge of English history and poetry and at the power and charm with which she revealed them to him. Worcester porcelain—the river Avon—The Great Duke—Lady Godiva—what had he known of all these before? And what man had ever had so lovely a teacher? There was nothing in this heavenly little journey to antagonize or displease him—nothing to separate them and so much to draw them closer together. Not since the day when he had wakened from his long sleep on the Vermont hills, and lain, drinking in the glory of the rosy mountains and the still greater glory in Jacqueline's face, had David's heart been so filled to overflowing with tenderness and thanksgiving. And Jacqueline, sensing this, opened hers to him as an expanding flower turns toward the sun. Late in the afternoon, when they had almost reached their destination, David stopped the motor by the roadside near a tiny grove with a brook running through it.

"I'd like to go in there and sit down for a few minutes. There's a fence, of course, and a sign 'No Trespassing' in the usual hospitable English way," he said, laughing into her eyes, "but we can climb the fence in any case, and pay the fine if we get caught. I feel as if it would be worth it to get my hands off this wheel for a few minutes."

"Where were you thinking of putting them when you took them off the wheel?" Jacqueline asked demurely.

"I'll show you—"

But the embrace in which he silently folded her when they were hidden from the highway by the sheltering trees showed her far more than this alone—

They reached "Boxwood" barely in time to dress for dinner. A few minutes later, Jacqueline's maid tapped at David's door and handed him a note and a tiny package.

"Dearest," the letter ran, "I'm rather rushed, as Lady Thornington has been in my room raving about you ever since I got here. You're to take her out to dinner tonight. I find Freddy and Cyril and Gustav are all here—now please don't get excited! There are three charming girls as well, and they probably won't notice me at all. But I thought it wiser to break it to you at once. I'm to be quite at the opposite end of the table from you, worse luck, but I promise to be good, even if you're not there to keep your eagle eye upon me. Do wear these little things I'm sending you. Désirée."

"These little things" proved to be a set of beautiful

133

pearl studs, and David, smiling happily to himself, unfastened his plain gold ones, and put the new ones in their stead.

"She *is* a dear," he said to himself, "just as generous as ever, and just as shy at being caught at it—nothing would have induced her to hand them to me herself. It's been wonderful having those days in Oxford with her and I'm glad we've come here, too! I like Lady Thornington and her husband—they're so wholesome and jolly—and this is certainly the finest old house I ever saw in my life."

Lady Thornington met him with a smile as he entered the drawing-room. "Jacqueline isn't down yet," she said. "I delayed her, I'm afraid. You're going to take me in to dinner, if you don't mind too much. I'm selfish enough to want you to, and besides, Freddy wrote me a note asking for her more than a month ago—before we even knew of your existence!" she finished laughing. "Are you going to take Désirée away from us immediately? I do hope not!"

"I need not tell you that I should like to take her at once. But circumstances don't seem to be exactly propitious—I haven't finished my education yet, you see. I haven't decided yet what is best to do."

"But what does Jacqueline think?" Lady Thornington's voice expressed her surprise that the decision should rest entirely with him.

"Oh, she'll do as I wish, of course."

"I hadn't realized that she was so tractable—we haven't considered docility her strongest point! But she's wonderful—of course, you know that you have made a great many enemies?"

"I hope that I have made one friend?"

134

"You have, indeed—oh, there she is now!"

Jacqueline smiled and nodded, but went past them without stopping, straight to a girl who was sitting alone by the great fire.

"That's like her," said Lady Thornington warmly, "Rose Grey, my husband's niece, is only seventeen, and painfully shy. This is her first week-end, she doesn't know any of the men, and regards them much as she would howling hyenas, anyway. Jacqueline knows it, and will do everything she can to smooth the poor child's path. She thinks a match between Rose and Freddy would be quite perfect, and though I never should have thought of it myself, I can see that it *would* be the best thing on earth for them both—they're such splendid, wholesome children! Of course, Freddy's thinking of no one but Jacqueline just now, but that's just a healthy phase—it'll pass all right—and Rose adores Jacqueline herself—just look at the grateful expression in her eyes!"

Rose was, indeed, gazing at the older girl with mute adoration. She was a pretty little thing, with mild blue eyes, straight brown hair, and peach-blossom cheeks, short and rather plump, and dressed in the simplest of white muslins, obviously home-made. Jacqueline, her slender elegance sharply contrasted against Rose's dowdiness, stood with her arm about her, talking as if oblivious of the other's dumb embarrassment.

"It's a rather charming picture, isn't it?" said Lady Thornington. "Look at her pulling Rose's hair looser over her temples—and she's hanging some kind of a chain around her neck—the child's been so keen for a little ornament—I ought to have thought of giving her one myself—she's poor as a church mouse—and hasn't a par-

135

ticle of intuitive taste! Now Jacqueline's bringing her over to you, because she knows you'll be nice to her— but it's too late, for dinner seems to be served."

The table was a long one, and David could catch glimpses of Jacqueline only from time to time. At first she seemed very quiet, eating little, and drinking nothing at all, he noticed, as he drained his own glass of excellent champagne. It was unlike her to be so still— was she, he wondered, overtaxing her strength to come at all? Possibly Dr. Ross was right, and her recent head-ache of more import than he had realized. Or was it merely the delicate violet dress she wore that made her look so pale? As the dinner wore on, however, her face regained its animation, and he could hear the peals of laughter which followed some of her sallies. He tried to catch her eye as she left the dining-room, but she was looking straight ahead, talking to Lady Thornington, and when he reached the drawing-room, after an hour over wine and cigars that seemed to him interminably dull, she was already playing bridge and he was called to take his place at another table. He was extremely fond of the game, however, and quickly became absorbed in it; so when the evening was half over, he was surprised to have her come and stand beside his chair as he was playing with considerable skill a particularly difficult no-trump hand. She waited silently until he was through, and applauded his triumph with the others; she had not, it appeared, come to stay, but the question she asked nonplussed him.

"Have you any extra money about you, David? I've played abominably all the evening, and lost all I brought down stairs. It's such a journey to my room, I thought you might lend me a little."

"Are we playing for money?" he asked, looking across at his partner in astonishment.

"What did you think it was for—love?" mocked the girl. "And thanks to your playing, we ought to get enough tonight for me to buy a new frock with my half. Let's see—five tricks—four aces divided—*and* the rubber—that gives us three hundred and fifty altogether."

David handed Jacqueline his purse without speaking, and took up his cards again. She waited a minute, evidently expecting him to say something, then flushing at the quizzical expression of Cyril, who was at the same table, she moved away. When his own game was finished, David, after silently pocketing twenty-five pounds as his share in the evening's booty, went in search of her, fully determined to deliver his opinion on the subject of gambling in private houses, and to ask her if she ever bought her dresses with the earnings of her bridge partners. But Lady Thornington met him with a laugh.

"Your bird has flown to her nest," she said. "She was pretty tired, I'm afraid—I think she seems rather fagged. She left a good-night for you with me."

And with such rather cold comfort, he was obliged to go to bed, far from contented.

"She seemed to have rather original ideas about the way engaged persons usually say good night," he remarked to himself grimly. "And she's been gambling all the evening—I never should have dreamed that Lady Thornington was the sort that would countenance such a thing in her house. I must get hold of Jacqueline and thrash several things out with her the first thing in the morning."

Again, his plans were upset, and this time their reversal caused him no contrition, but acute displeasure. Miss Huntington, he was informed when he got down to breakfast and inquired for her, had gone to mass with the Count of Saxburg.

He waited for her in the garden. She came at last, alone, her face shining with a sort of inner peace, her white dress golden in the sunshine. She sat down beside him on the bench where he had settled himself, and slipped her hand through his, then sat looking in silence for some moments over the peaceful English landscape.

"Isn't it wonderful?" she said at length softly—"Sunday morning in May—and church—and country—and you—I'm so happy."

"I'm glad you're happy. *I* should be more happy if you had spent last evening differently, or gone to church with some other companion. Promise me not to degrade yourself by playing for money again, unless you do it unwittingly, as I did last night."

She raised a pair of troubled eyes to his, and hesitated before she spoke.

"I'll avoid it whenever I can, since you feel that way about it," she said, "I can't give a definite promise."

"Why not?"

"It might be necessary for me to break it, and I have never broken a promise in my life."

"I cannot see how such a necessity could arise."

"None of the friends with whom I am constantly thrown feel as you do—indeed, I do not myself. I might spoil an evening's pleasure for a number of people, by refusing to fill out at a table and make the right number. When I marry you, and go to Boston, I shall of course conform to your wishes, and the customs of the society in which I shall be thrown as your wife. But as long as I stay in my grandfather's house, the situation is entirely different."

"Do you consider that it also requires you to accept the conspicuous attentions of other men?"

She flushed painfully, and bit her lip. "To a certain extent it does. You are going to leave me very shortly, for an indefinite time. I can hardly arrange my life as if I were widowed instead of betrothed. But I certainly shall break no conventions—as I understand them, and I am too fond of you to care at all 'for the attentions of other men' and have always been. It is a little puzzling to me to understand why you have found this so hard to believe. The walk this morning was not pre-arranged. Gustav happens to be the only other Catholic here, and it was natural that he should join me when we were both going to church. I am sorry that you feel it is necessary for me to explain—or excuse—what I do."

"Good Lord, Jacqueline, you always contrive to twist everything I say until you put me in the wrong—if you wouldn't do these things it wouldn't be necessary to apologize or explain, would it? I suppose that you can contend that Wainwright is an old family friend and Freddy Lambert just a pleasant, harmless boy, but nothing you can say will reconcile me to Saxburg—I must ask you very definitely to have nothing further to do with him—and if you choose to disregard my wishes, I'm afraid I shan't be very patient with either apologies or explanations. Besides, you know what a cross it has always been to me that you are a Catholic. Isn't there some way of getting around that before we're married? It would be tremendously awkward in Boston. Further South, some of the good old families are Romanists, but in New England—"

She stared at him in bewilderment for a moment, then spoke with a hurt obstinacy which astonished as much as it displeased him.

"There are a few things no one should venture to speak against, David," she said, "and you don't seem to have learned that yet. One is a woman's mother—another her friends—another her religion. I thought you understood clearly that in all mixed marriages, the Catholic retains his or her own faith, and the—the children, if there are any, are baptised and brought up in the Church. Matrimony isn't sufficiently important in your eyes to interfere with a career. I'm willing to follow your wishes absolutely in that regard—we'll be married today, or ten years from now, exactly as you prefer; but neither is it vital enough in mine—though I believe I honor it more than you do, for remember I regard it as a sacrament, and you do not—for me to dream of permitting it to supplant my religion, and I'd enter a nunnery before I'd marry you on any other terms than those I have just mentioned!"

She left him abruptly. Again, he had taken all the joy out of her day; and again David, secretly knowing that he was in the wrong, was all the more angry and resentful on that account. At lunch time Lady Thornington told him that Jacqueline had gone to her room, and did not feel able to leave it. She expressed, moreover, the same fear in regard to the girl's health that Dr. Ross had done, but this time David hardened his heart. "I believe she's using those 'headaches' as a means to make me give in," he said over and over again to himself. "She's wound every man she knows around her little finger for so long that she thinks she can go right on doing it with me. I'll show her she's mistaken." When a singularly empty afternoon had dragged itself almost out, however, he relented to the extent of writing her a stiff little note, saying he was sorry she was under the weather again— the unwholesome excitement and late hours of the night before had of course been the worst possible thing for her, except possibly going to church fasting—and asking if he could see her for a few minutes. He understood she had a private sitting room. The maid who took this affectionate missive brought back the verbal reply that Miss Huntington was better, but was still unable to receive him.

He glanced at the clock. It was not quite seven—plenty of time for a good visit with her before dressing for an eight o'clock dinner—a quiet, intimate visit before an open fire. If he could only win back again that spirit of glad surrender, of complete yielding which she had shown on the afternoon of her birthday! What time could be more propitious? To be sure, she had asked him not to come, but that was just injured pride. She was better. He had every right. Without hesitation he mounted the stair, and walked rapidly down the long corridor.

Outside the door of Jacqueline's sitting room, he stopped short, growing cold all over. From within he could hear the hurried accent of a man talking rapidly in German, then Jacqueline's reply, hesitating—almost pleading—in the same language. He was a fair scholar, but they were speaking too softly and too rapidly for him to catch the words. Without knocking, he opened the door and walked in. Standing in front of the fire was Gustav von Saxburg, and Désirée was in his arms.

The Austrian, swearing under his breath, loosened the

141

girl, who fell back with a little cry, her face as white as paper; as she gripped the chair in front of her to keep from falling, the great jewels of her ring, seemed to flash in David's face with a consuming fire.

"Is it then American custom to enter a lady's room without knocking?" stammered von Saxburg. "Désirée is my braut—my fiancée—not yours—I have her promise!"

"Gustav—for your honor's sake—if you have any—"

"Do not interrupt—this is one matter between men, is it not, Mr. Noble?"

"Give me your ring," said David between his teeth, looking straight past the Austrian at Jacqueline.

"No—not yet—no—"

"Give it to me! If you don't, I shall take it!"

She slipped it off, and handed it to him without another word. Little things obtrude themselves in moments of great emotion. He noticed how loose it was, how white her hands were—and had he thought he was cold? Well, this thing burnt him like a living flame—he threw it into the burning coals. Still his hands seemed to be scorched—

"Perhaps you'll let me have a few words with Miss Huntington alone," he added, courteously, "I cannot congratulate you upon having won her promise, for I fear that carries very little weight—but I've not the slightest wish to dispute it with you." Then, as the Austrian did not move, he continued slowly, "Please do not let us disagree over this trifling matter—I desire to speak to her privately for a moment, and I pass for a very strong man, and am at least ten years younger than you." He held open the door with studied politeness, and Gustav von Saxburg walked out. Turning again to Jacqueline, he found her head thrown back, and her eyes, like blazing coals of fire in her white face from which every trace of gentleness had gone, fixed steadily on his.

"The other night," he said, "I heard this man comparing you with the *première danseuse* of a music-hall. I see that he had reason for his classification. You do not, of course object to sharing his affections with such worthy rivals. A count is a count, and a stable-boy is a stable-boy."

"When he does not become something much worse."

"I understand many things now that were not clear to me before—among others, why it was 'impossible' for you to receive me this afternoon. I only regret that you did not make my own position clear to me a little sooner."

"The regret is quite mutual."

"I shall go back to London tonight on urgent business, and will send a statement to the newspapers saying that the marriage arranged between Jacqueline Désirée Huntington and David Noble is indefinitely postponed."

A maid entered the room with a tea-tray. David turned to her with his hand on the door-knob.

"Your mistress has fainted," he said coldly, as she gave a terrified cry, and looked from him to the girl lying on the couch. "But you need not be in the least alarmed. It is not serious."

143

Part Three

CHAPTER I

IN WHICH AN UGLY STORY INTERRUPTS DAVID NOBLE'S CAREER

THE opening of the Edgar L. Ross Memorial Hospital was an event in the medical world—one might add, without exaggeration, perhaps, in the social world and the philanthropic world—not only of Boston and New England, but of the entire country. Splendidly situated in the Fenway, with grounds and approaches—those details so often sadly neglected in American architecture, to the unspeakable detriment of many a fine edifice—as carefully planned and executed as the great white marble building itself, it rose strong and dignified and enduring, with the promise of healing and efficiency written large upon it from slate roof to cement basement, from end of Right Wing, planned entirely for the convenience of the stork, to end of Left, given over to general surgery, in every rounded corner and thresholdless entrance, from the great sun parlor in the rear to the private suites above it, where anxious relatives and friends of patients could find quarters vying in luxury with those of Boston's newest and costliest hotel. Money, time, skill, knowledge, *heart*—all these had gone into its making. And ready to welcome the sufferers brought to its doors, were maids and matrons and nurses, housekeepers and cooks, orderlies and pages and porters; there were, moreover, doctors, of course. And in the *Boston Transcript* and the *New York Times* and the *Chicago Daily News,* and even in less exclusive journals; in the circulars mailed broadcast from Maine to California, as well as in the engraved cards of invitation sent to a more fortunate few for the dedication, who might read that the Surgeon-in-Chief was Dr. David Noble, formerly of Hamstead, Vermont, assistant—and many thought, adopted son—of Dr. Herbert Ross, who had given the hospital in memory of his only son.

The appointment of any man to so important a post would naturally have aroused some criticism as well as some approval; and the choice of David Noble aroused a good deal. He was still very young—the youngest man, "every one" said, that "any one" could remember had been given such a position. There were many, also, who found this a favorable opportunity to remark that *of course* he would never have obtained it if Dr. Ross had not been so biased in his favor; the boy—he was hardly more than that—was really an obsession with him; and when a man spends money like water on a hospital like this one, *of course,* his whims have got to be considered. The fact that Dr. Ross was himself on the staff, and might be expected to take the more critical cases where his maturer judgment would be essential, was in a way, reassuring, however. It was also felt on the Back Bay—and more or less openly expressed—that "one of our own doctors" would have been more suitable for an institution of this standing. Who had ever heard of Hamstead, Vermont, or of a family named Noble? If one of "the younger men" were to have the position what was the matter with—Bobby Hutchinson, for instance?

Bobby Hutchinson himself, whom this opinion promptly reached, of course, sat on it so hard that there was not much left of it. He was a plain, slouchy young giant, with prematurely grey hair, and a crooked smile, and an imperturbable habit of cheerfulness. He was not impressed; indeed, he was not even flattered.

"Who in Hell started that fool idea," he drawled. "The undertaking establishments and the mourning apparel shops would benefit more by that arrangement than the Edgar L. I'd run up more business for 'em in a week than they could handle in a month. I'm not a surgeon, or a specialist, or a—what you call 'em—diagno—I never can get the whole of that word. I'm a general practitioner—obsolete as hoop skirts and stove-pipe hats. I wouldn't swap that distinction to go and be diag—etc., to the Queen of Sheba. It suits me exactly. Who's kicking up all this fool row about Dave and me, anyway? He's strong as steel—can operate thirty-six hours out of every twenty-four if necessary, while I have to keep laying off for smokes and drinks and things. Besides, he's got more skill in his little finger than I have in all four feet—more than any doctor I know of has, for that matter, unless it's that old Frenchman, Norchais, over in Paris, and we've only heard about him. What do they *want* for a surgeon-in-chief, anyway? As far as I can make out from all this twaddle the main requirement is that he should have been born on Beacon Street, and about seventy years ago! If he measures up to the expectations in that regard, it apparently doesn't matter whether he knows a stethoscope from an incubator baby!"

No less a person than Dr. Ross himself had gone to confer with Bobby—people had a way of conferring with Bobby. He laughed, which was also usual when any one talked long with that individual.

"I notice all your patients seem to get well," he grinned, "so I'm afraid the trades you mention haven't profited by you much yet. And—your patients love you, Bobby."

Bobby pulled away at his pipe. He was sitting on the small of his back in an enormous morris-chair, clad in a pair of trousers which his choreman would certainly have refused as a gift, and a norfolk jacket which all his friends averred he had owned when he entered college and worn steadily ever since.

"Don't they love David?" he drawled at length, looking at Dr. Ross lazily through half-shut eyes.

"No." There was a short silence which Bobby gave no sign of intending to break. "As you are very well aware," added the older man.

"Oh, yes," said Bobby, "I know. But sick people—women especially, are such awful fools. They'd rather be ignorantly murdered by some one who really feels sorry for them and speaks to 'em kindly, than saved by a living miracle of dexterity and daring who regards 'em in the same light as he does his motor—thrilling machinery, that's all. But just the same, in spite of their stupid taste, what you want at the head of your hospital is the mechanician, and not the murderer."

"He does slip up on his after-care—"

"Simply because he isn't interested. Now I cut folks up if I don't see any way out of it, but what I really enjoy is watchin' 'em get well. It is just the other way 'round with Dave. The *human* side doesn't touch him at all. He's pretty selfish, you know, come right down to hard tacks. That's why he's got along so well. 'He travels the fastest who travels alone,' as my friend Kipling says. Bromidic, but true. He's fond of you and me, but I don't know as he would be, if we got in his way; as it is, we've helped him. He didn't care much—for his mother, for instance, did he?"

"No, I'm afraid not. She was a shrewish, ignorant, unlovely woman, who made his life miserable as a boy. He is hardly to blame for that."

"Well, maybe not. But I don't believe he's especially keen on women anyway. You've seen my sister, Nancy, haven't you, and her friend Helena Castle that's with us so much?"

Dr. Ross smiled. "I'm glad to say I have. They're certainly a sight for sore eyes, and I'm not surprised at the reports that masculine Boston from sixteen to sixty has capitulated to either or both. I suppose you infer that David has never shown the slightest interest in either of them?"

"Exactly. There—isn't any one else by chance, is there?"

"No," answered Dr. Ross rather sharply.

"I didn't mean to be prying. Abnormally ascetic, that's what I should call him. His sort always carves in cold blood. Even your hopeless roué, who tries to ruin almost every woman he meets, is often kinder to 'em than the sort that's never been interested in 'em at all—that is, *they think* he's kinder. Not that I'm suggesting a Don Juan for the Edgar L.—as I said before, Dave's just the man for the job—don't know any one who can touch him. Let 'em talk—they're always talking about something. But just the same . . ."

"Well, Bobby—"

"Dave's never made a single mistake yet, as far as I know," said Bobby slowly, "and if he only could—make a huge one—medically or otherwise, or both together—and have to go through a perfect hell of grief and contrition and despair and shame—well, then you'd see him come out—if he could come out at all—the greatest physician of his generation. Just now, he's only a clever mechanician, as I said before. And when you get right down to hard tacks, that's why there's some opposition to him. All these other considerations wouldn't count a continental, though the people who're making the row don't really sense it."

He rose to escort his guest to the door. "I feel I've been darn fresh, talking to you like this," he said. "Are you feeling first rate, yourself, sir? It's been quite a chore putting this thing through, and making the success of it that you've done. Couldn't you get a little rest now that it's all over but the shouting?"

"I'm going to—as soon as we're really in running order. I've been trying to persuade David to go to Hamstead to see his family—he's really neglected them shamefully—and when he does—"

"I hope you won't wait till then. The Edgar L. is all the family he'll be interested in for months."

"I'm afraid you're right. Well, we'll see."

But when Dr. Ross finally started on his much-needed rest, a few months later, it was for a much longer one than Bobby had sought to make him take. He had, indeed, given his whole strength to the erection of the

149

hospital; and not very long after it was finished, he died, suddenly and peacefully, leaving David stunned by the first real grief he had known in his life, and—incidentally —the sole and unquestioned possessor of his benefactor's enormous practice and substantial fortune. And Bobby, who saw a good deal of him in those days, finally spoke his mind, freely and frankly and without drawling, which was indeed, a rare thing for him.

"If you don't go off and loosen up," he said, "the Edgar L. 'll have to have a new surgeon-in-chief, and there'll be a sign, 'For sale or to let' in the bay-window of your house. You'll be taking your ease in a pretty little padded cell out at Waverly, or under a neat tombstone marked 'Sacred to the memory of' in the Hamstead graveyard. Now's the time to go and see your family, on your two feet or in your new Napier—excuse me, Mercedes—didn't know you'd have even a motor with a lady's name— instead of in a long mahogany box with a pretty wreath on top. After you've drunk deep of the rural delights of Vermont—I understand there is nothing else to drink deep of up there—why don't you run over to Paris, and play around with Norchais for a couple of months? Combine business and pleasure—take the French lady with you—"

"*What* French lady?"

"Why, Mercedes, of course! What are you so touchy about?"

David, after losing some valuable time in reluctant facing of facts, acted on Bobby's advice. He was, as he was very well aware, almost at the end of his long tether, before the death of Dr. Ross had added grief to fatigue, and set his much abused nerves quivering. The suggestion of Paris was extremely good. And his conscience had been reminding him for some time that he ought to go to Hamstead. He entrusted the Edgar L. to the tender mercies of his very able assistant, and turned his footsteps, or rather, the headlights of his Mercedes, in the direction of Vermont.

But a week in Hamstead proved more than his patience could stand. The little village, which had once seemed such a metropolis to him, proved stagnant to the last degree. His father had waited with impatient pride to show him the many local improvements which had taken place since he was last at home. The streets and most of the houses were electrically lighted, there was a town water system, bathrooms and telephones abounded where ten years before they had been almost unknown; the public library was no longer a tiny shanty which had once been a blacksmith's shop, but a neat little brick building donated by Miss Manning in memory of her father. The church had been "done over" and there was a new Masonic Hall where dances, no longer taboo, were frequently held. David beheld these marks of progress with an indifferent condescension which left his father puzzled and hurt. He was not even interested in news of a more personal character—that Jack Weston, for instance, was "going from bad to worse," and was "not himself" a large part of the time, and that Austin Gray, on the contrary, had not only "pulled himself together" but was rapidly becoming the "rising man" of the community, and had married a very lovely and lovable girl, who was as rich as she was beautiful, and had endeared herself to all the village; or that Hiram himself, whose sincere and unquestioning, if somewhat austere faith David had always considered as "countrified" as his habit of drinking tea from his saucer or appearing in public without a collar, had now become a Deacon in the First Congregational Church—a mark of respect seldom shown to a man coming from "out back," and a crowning glory in his simple mind, compared to which his long term as postmaster was as nothing.

To greater and more important changes, the spiritual and mental development which sprang from these more material changes, David was entirely blind. Narrowmindedness and prejudice were on the wane. The minister, instead of being the chilly and forbidding person of his boyhood was a "good sort" who mingled freely with his flock, in their pleasures as well as their griefs, and in their week-day as well as their Sunday life; there was a Men's Club which held weekly meetings in the vestry, where the discussion of Village Improvements and town politics were no longer excluded; the average farmer's wife, instead of toiling from sunrise to dark, her only diversions going to church and the discussion of the births, deaths and marriages—and other more or less private affairs—of her immediate circle of acquaintance, went, thanks to "modern improvements," to Wallacetown in her own Ford to do her shopping and attend the "movies," and to the gatherings of The Grange on alternate Saturday nights; she played cards and danced whenever she felt like it, unwearied by her own home tasks and uncensured by her neighbors. But all this David neither saw nor wished to see. He had, in his estimation, "outgrown" Hamstead, and he did not care who knew it—in fact, he rather hoped every one realized it as well as he did. A chance errand to Wallacetown filled him with disgust at the place. It was before the days of state roads, and the highways, deep with dust or mud, as the case might be, were "impossible" for motoring to his mind. Never having made any friendships, he had none to renew, and his family was prosperous, and really did not need him. Sam, already successfully started on a legal career, had gone West. The younger boys had completed courses at the State Agriculture College, and had bought the old Daniels farm, which they were running together. Harry, the elder of the two, had married, and was the proud father of a boy three months old. David vaccinated the child, and told his mother not to eat pickles, a piece of advice which she calmly disregarded; and as both she and the baby were bouncing specimens of humanity, he did not feel that any arguments he might advance in favor of her changing her way of living would have much force. Mrs. Noble was dead, and Mr. Noble, still occupied and contented with his position as postmaster, had gone to live with his sons, taking Susie with him. She was growing up a wild little thing, untrained and undisciplined, and alone among them, stood in no awe of David. Though she seemed to him entirely uninformed on all important points, she was quick and shrewd, and had already nearly completed her course at the Hamstead High School. David was horrified at her boldness and ignorance, and exasperated by her sharp tongue; she reminded him painfully of their mother. And yet he was forced to admit that there were great possibilities in the girl, and she was the only person who interested him in the least in the complacent household. She was handsome, in a sharp, ungentle way; generous and impulsive and capable; her untrained mind was keen. Reluctantly he faced the fact that he "ought to do something for her." Finally, feeling that he had made a great sacrifice, he offered to take her abroad with him, and place her in school in Paris, where he could see her well established while he was studying with Norchais. The following summer, he would see that she traveled under proper chaperonage; and at the end of that time, she could decide whether she would prefer to continue her education in Europe, or return to America and prepare for college at some good school near Boston. He was appalled by her ingratitude when she flatly refused to consider his proposition for one moment.

"I like it here with Pa and Hattie and the boys," she added decidedly. "I'd rather mind the baby than go to Paris. Besides, I'm nearly sixteen, and there'll be a lot going on here this winter. I guess I'll have a better time where I'm acquainted, than over in that heathen foreign country where I couldn't understand a word any one said to me, for if you think *you'd* be any company to me, you flatter yourself! I think you was born with a poker down your back, and an icicle in each eye, and alum in your mouth—and for all I know, you'd etherize me the first good chance you got, and quarter me, just for the fun of seein' whether you could sew it together again so it wouldn't show!"

In the end it was Hiram who won a reluctant consent from her. Unbiased by the fact that the two sons who had remained at home were the prop and mainstay of his declining years, while the two who had gone out into the world looked down on him and, indeed, almost ignored him, his proud affection overflowed for Susie when her "chance" came, just as it had done first for David and later for Sam. If none of his boys occupied quite the same place in his heart that his eldest had, his only daughter was dearer to him still. And Susie, sharply divining, in spite of her youth, the unselfish desire for her own good that lay behind his awkward arguments that "she had better go along with Dave, like a nice girl" capitulated after one final outburst.

"Well, I'll go—but it's not because I care a whoop about having 'a chance,' it's because you're so dead set on it, though I don't see why you should be. Do you want me to be mean and selfish and stuck-up the way Dave is? Do you want me to despise my family and home the way he does? Hear him talk about Hamstead, you'd think it was a regular hole in the ground. I think it's awful to feel that way about the place you was raised in, especially if it's a *lovely* place, like Hamstead is. He hasn't been near Mr. Sheldon since he got here, and Sheldon just counted the days to seeing him after he knew Dave was coming. I just hope he gets his come-uppance, that's all, some day, and that I can have a share in it!"

"Susie! Don't you lay out to bite the hand that's goin' to feed you!"

"Hoo! It isn't Dave's hand! It's Dr. Ross's money! Much Dave will miss what he spends on me! If he would, you can bet your life he wouldn't spend it!"

"You'd oughter be grateful to Dave, 'stead of slanderin' of him."

"I ain't a-slanderin' of him. I'm tellin' the truth! I'll be grateful to *him* when I see him bein' grateful to some one himself! To you and—and—Ma!"

"David an' your Ma never got on."

"Huh! Well, that was some Ma's fault, maybe, but it

155

was more his. He was too stupid to see that the reason Ma was cross was because she was so tired, workin' her fingers to the bone for us all! Gettin' up at four in the mornin' and hustlin' around till ten or eleven at night don't make a woman feel real *perky*, I guess! Washin', and ironin', and cookin' an' cleanin' an' scrubbin' for seven people year in an' year out an' gardenin' and preservin' too, in the hot summer time, an' helpin' in the post-office so's you could go trout-fishin' in the spring an' deer-huntin' in the fall! An' I've hear Sam and Harry tell, though I can't remember it myself, of course, that when we wuz babies, she useter put us to sleep on a haycock, an' help you pitch on hay out in the fields, an' pitch it off in the barn to save a hired man's wages when they wuz highest, in hayin' time! An' after the Men's Club got started, you wuz free to go to that any evenin' you wanted, while she worked an' worked an' worked! I guess 'twas Ma gave us our real 'chance' if you come to think of it right! We wuz always better fed'n any family in town, without much to feed us *on*, neither! And the house wuz just poisin neat, always, an' I had tattin' on my underclothes when all the other girls wore plain, an'—"

"Why Susie, I never knew you thought of all them things!"

"Well, I *did* think of 'em, an' I think of 'em still! I wuz ten years old when she died, and I guess I've noticed the difference sence! I ain't sayin' that Hattie ain't pleasant an' good to me—she is—but you can't make the best sister-in-law in the world come up to a sure 'nough mother, even if she is cross!—I didn't care if she was

cross! She had *grit!* An' that's more'n lots of awful pleasant wimmen hev got!"

"I ain't forgotten, neither," the girl went on after a
minute, during which Hiram, conscious of a tightening
in the throat, found himself unable to answer her, "that
when she wuz real sick, along at the last, she hankered
an' pined fer Dave to come home, and she got me to write
—she never said a word to the rest of you—that she warn't
feelin' first rate, an' that if it wouldn't interfere with his
'career' she'd like to hev him come home an' pass Sunday.
And he wrote back that he hoped she'd feel better soon,
but that it warn't convenient for him to leave Boston just
then. 'Convenient!' An' her a'dyin'!"

"Susie! he didn't know that!"

"Wall, I hope he didn't! But you ain't sure of it, are
you?"

"He couldn't 'a realized—"

"Huh! I'd like to *make* him realize some things! When
his letter come, she lay so still for a spell, I thought
mebby she'd gone already. And at last she sez, 'I kinder
wanted to hev a talk with Dave. But then, it don't
matter.' Nothin' 'mattered' to her except doin' every
livin' thing she could for us! An' after that she never
talked much to any one!"

Susie snuffled, and wiping her eyes and her nose with
the back of her hand, rose, and picked up her hat, which
was lying on the floor near her.

"Where you goin'?" asked her father, glad of a chance
to change the subject.

"I'm goin' to see the minister. An' Miss Sims; an' Mrs.
Elliott. I presume they'll hev considerable to say when
they hear I'm goin' to Europe with Dave, an' I guess I

might as well let 'em hear it from me first, an' hear it *straight,* before they start passin' remarks around."

"Susie, you do beat all," said Hiram helplessly.

"Well, I'd like to beat *Dave* for gittin' me inter this pickle," she replied, slamming the door behind her.

David, feeling complacent at the turn things had taken, next faced the unconsidered difficulty that Susie had no more proper equipment in the way of clothing than she had in the way of manners, and that though she must be made to pass without the latter until she could acquire them, she certainly must be supplied with the former. Hattie, with kindly haste, was running the sewing-machine early and late to supply the deficiencies in her little sister-in-law's wardrobe, and David looked aghast at the garments which he vaguely knew to be "all wrong," which, one by one as they were finished, she spread out on the bed in the "spare chamber" for his inspection.

"I've made her four of each," said Hattie with pride, waving her hand in the direction of certain articles of intimate apparel, made of heavy, substantial cotton, trimmed with durable Hamburg edging, which David instinctively knew would give a clumsy and shapeless appearance to whatever was put on outside them. "With what she has already mended up good, she can keep real clean with that many, and change more'n once a week if she should want to. I think that figured challis dress'll be real pretty for her best, don't you? I'm goin' to knit her a pair of mittens to wear with that crocheted toque on the steamer, and she's got six shirt-waists, countin' the blue taffeta, to go with her new wool skirt. I think she'll appear real nice. Susie'd be pretty if she didn't look so much as if she was cut out with a pair of scissors. If she hefts up a little, and gets more notion of being pleasant, it would help out considerable."

In desperation, David wrote to Bobby. And Bobby, by return mail, sent back the following answer from his mother's summer place at Manchester-by-the-Sea.

"Dear Dave: How did you happen to have such a brilliant idea? It's the best thing I've heard in a long time. Mother says to bring the kid here for as long as you want. I'm taking a few days off myself, and Nancy is home, and Helena is visiting her, and I bet between them they can lick her into shape in no time. I'll have a good time with her myself. You don't think she would do for me, later on, do you?

Yours,
Bob."

David was much relieved by this epistle, and favorably impressed by the jest at the end of it. Why not, he thought, looking at her as she stood out in the yard taking her leave of a bashful boy who had been one of her classmates, the wind whipping her faded cotton skirts about her lithe, boyish figure, her heavy braids of black hair lying over her breast, her red cheeks glowing like peonies. The girl might well grow up a beauty as well as a wit. Why shouldn't she make a brilliant marriage? Though he had supposed, vaguely—not having given the matter much thought—that Bobby was "interested" in Helena Castle.

It was early afternoon when the Mercedes with its two passengers came to a stop under the Hutchinson's porte-côchère; and Susie, mute with defiance and shyness and dread, found herself enveloped in a welcome such as she had not dreamed of. These people weren't "stuck-

159

up" like David at all! Why, they were just as simple as—as anything—

"I lived in the country myself when I was a little girl," Helena said that first afternoon, as they sat on the broad veranda which faced the sea, drinking lemonade, "and I remember how terrified I was when I came home from boarding-school with Nancy for the first time to visit. They don't do things a bit our way, do they, Susie? But really—after you get to know them of course—they're very nice."

"I always liked girls from the country better than any other kind, myself," drawled Bobby, at which they all laughed, and though Susie didn't know what they were laughing at, it made her feel very comfortable. "I have a nice plan—I think Helena and Susie and I will go off for a picnic tonight instead of staying here for dinner." And off they accordingly went. Then Helena kept the little girl in her own room that night, and brought her down to breakfast the next morning with her beautiful, straight black hair arranged as it should have been, and dressed in a white frock which she had filched from her own wardrobe, and hastily "fixed"—for Helena was wonderfully clever with her needle. That day, and for several days afterward, Susie went to Boston with Helena, and big boxes filled with all sorts of wonderful things—dresses and hats and coats and shoes and linen—began to arrive at the Hutchinson's house for her. Moreover, Bobby had a way of meeting them and taking them to lunch at big hotels, and to matinées afterwards. In a week, David hardly knew his sister; she had blossomed with unbelievable celerity into almost unbelievable attractiveness; she was happy, she was unembarrassed, she was "catching on" to everything. He motored all day long and every day along the North Shore, rejoiced in the excellent roads, and vowing he would never go near Vermont again.

The night before Susie and David were to sail was damp and chilly, and soon after dinner the five young people betook themselves to Bobby's den, a great half-timbered room with a huge fireplace, built apart from the main wing of the house. It was cold enough for a fire, and they piled it high with drift-wood and settled themselves comfortably about it—Susie stretched at full-length on the sofa, with her head in Helena's lap; Nancy in a big chair beside her brother; and David, a little apart from the others, absorbed in the enticements of an automobile catalogue. He was paying but scant attention to the others, when Susie broke the comfortable stillness into which they had lapsed with one of her sudden outbursts.

"Do you know what I wish?" she said abruptly, throwing her arms around Helena, "I wish I was a big man—as big as Dr. Hutchinson—and do you know what I'd do? I'd marry you!"

"What an original idea," drawled Bobby, "I am sure no one else ever thought of such a thing!"

"Well, then," went on Susie, as Helena only laughed a little and did not answer, "I wish besides that I could stay here with you and not go to Europe with David at all—just look at him, sitting over there alone! He looks so pleased at something, he must be dissecting a bug!"

"But I'm not going to stay here myself, you know," protested Helena, "I teach at a girl's college, where I hope you'll come some day yourself."

"Will you be there then?"

"I don't know, Susie."

Helena disengaged herself gently, rose from the sofa, and walked over to the fire. David, glancing up for the first time from his catalogue, saw Bobby looking at her intently, and then get up, and say something to her, which he could not hear, for it was almost whispered. But the girl's face, which seldom lost its expression of wistfulness, brightened almost unbelievably. Her eyes were full of tears, but she was smiling.

"That's like you," she said in a low voice, "bless you, Bobby." Then after a moment, "Come Susie, it's time for you to go to bed; and as I'm rather tired, I think I'll go too."

"So will I," said Nancy yawning, "Good night, Dr. Noble."

She kissed her brother, and left the room quickly, as she did everything. Susie, who was doing her best to imitate these wonderful creatures in all respects, walked over to David and put down her face, though she would never have dreamed of doing such a thing at home. He kissed her absent-mindedly, his eyes on the fair-haired girl in the black dress standing beside his friend. She had held out both hands to him, and he was holding them, looking down at her with an expression of wonderful tenderness and yearning; then they, too, kissed each other and Helena left the room, her arm over Susie's shoulder.

David laid down his catalogue and came towards the fire.

"I did not know that Miss Castle was engaged to you," he said slowly. "We must have been terribly in the way!"

Bobby knocked the ashes from his pipe, whistled through it, and settled himself in his chair again before he replied.

162

"She is not," he said at last. "In fact, she is so far from it as to be engaged to another man. I'm surprised you haven't heard the story—I thought of course you knew! Helena's mother made her promise when she was a little girl that she would never marry a man whose family did not approve of the match—her own life had been ruined because she did that very thing. Helena always had more beaus than you could shake a stick at—why, she was grown up at Susie's age—Susie's a great kid, but she's *just* a kid, that's all—I never saw anything so refreshingly immature!— Well, to go back to Helena—when she was eighteen Roger Lorrance came here to visit at the same time that she did. They fell in love at first sight. Roger's family refused to receive her, because of some silly old scandal a generation old, and not long after that, Mrs. Castle died, after extracting Helena's promise a second time. She was left almost penniless. The engagement still stands, for they are hoping that in time circumstances will alter sufficiently to permit them to marry, and still keep to the very letter and spirit of the promise. I believe myself they won't have much longer to wait. Roger's been in California for years, trying to earn a living wage —the last thing in the world he was trained for—and Helena's been as brave as a little Trojan, and teaching herself ever since she got through college. I think public opinion will be too strong for the Lorrances to contend against indefinitely. All Helena's friends—and they're legion—have done what they could for her—but of course it's pitifully little in a case like this!"

"And what," said David, "does her fiancé think of your intimacy?"

Bobby Hutchinson looked at him with surprised un-

163

concern, for a moment, and then answered, drawling more than ever.

"That's not a very pretty question, the way you ask it," he said at length, "thank the Lord Roger's not that kind of a fool—and I'm not that kind of a blackguard. He's my best friend, and she—well, bless her, she loves him with all her heart and soul."

"And kisses you good night?"

"Occasionally she honors me to that extent; a few years ago I couldn't have—stood it—but now—

"Your attitude of mind makes me think of a story I heard at a dinner in Vienna last summer," he went on after a minute. "It was a private dinner, and after the women had left the room the conversation turned on love-affairs. Delicate little way Europeans have of talking about such things, haven't they?"

"Very," said David, picking up the catalogue again.

"Well, they discussed the usual conquests of the usual kind, and then one of the men said he could tell a much better story than any of them—that he had once succeeded in winning a wager that he could break up a perfectly regular engagement of marriage between a girl whom he and several other men had been trying hard to get, and who had suddenly announced her engagement to an old sweetheart of her girlhood whom she hadn't seen for years, and who turned up without warning on the already crowded scene. They had naturally all been much annoyed.

"Everybody—except myself and one Englishman who was there—laughed, and asked for the story. He was only too eager to tell it. It seems that the girl in question, an American beauty living in London, and the fiancé—an

164

American, too, I am sorry to say, for he seems to have been a pretty poor sort—were all at a house-party with a number of others at a big place near Oxford when the wager was made. He'd about given up hope of accomplishing anything, for the girl was perfectly crazy about her beau, as we'd say here—one of those cases of a woman who never cares for but one man, apparently, and loves him to distraction, no matter how badly he treats her, and turns down a dozen better men, because she's either blind to his defects, or doesn't care whether he has 'em or not. This American certainly had plenty. He was a *parvenu* who'd been successful along his own particular line—the Austrian didn't state what that was—and took it for granted that he could be along every line. His opinions and tastes were to be the final word on everything and he was puritanical and jealous and dictatorial and a general ass. Every one else could see plainly enough that the girl was throwing herself away, but he seemed to feel that the favors were all on his side. Well, at last the Austrian's chance came. The girl got sick. She'd been near a nervous breakdown for some time, and her considerate fiancé had caused it really to arrive. She had a queer heredity, of which she was almost morbidly conscious, and her life as a great beauty and a great heiress in English 'smart society,' was just the sort to develop the characteristics she feared she might have inherited, and was trying hard to fight against—and yet longing to give in to. Interesting thing, heredity. Now in this case—"

"What did the Austrian do?" The interruption came sharply. "I'm more interested in the story itself than in your theories about it."

"All right. Usually you like a little friendly argument. Well, he happened to be passing her door when he heard her giving her maid a message—apparently in answer to a note—saying she couldn't see her beau, and at the same time telling the maid to go and get her tea. He jumped at the conclusion that the American would as usual, disregard her wishes, and decided to arrive on the scene first. He knew perfectly well how that would be interpreted— the American hated him, and thought the girl liked him —he would think she had sent him word not to come because she had another visitor. It doesn't seem credible, does it? I know if—if Roger found a *dozen* men with Helena, he'd never give it a thought—he'd *know*—I supposed any man—any decent-minded man—would, until I heard this story. Though from your question to-night, it seems that—"

"Go on with your story, will you?"

"Why, I *am,* as fast as I can—glad to have such an appreciative audience. The Austrian knocked, and the girl said, 'Come in'—thought of course it was her hostess. She had a private sitting-room, and was lying on a couch in front of the fire. She jumped up and told him, of course, to clear out. But he grabbed her, and poured out his undying love—his dirty lust, I ought to say—he timed it pretty well. She tried at first to interrupt him and break away, then kept quite still, thinking that would end it sooner—and just then the American walked in without knocking. He didn't even ask for an explanation. Of course he ordered his rival out of the room but the resourceful fellow listened at the key hole. Then he—the fiancé—spoke to her as if she'd been a—well, a common street-walker, and left her in a dead faint on the floor.

Then he departed for London, and the fact that the engagement was broken was announced in the next morning's papers. The Austrian of course won his wager—it was for a thousand pounds, which came in handy, he said, to pay up debts he'd contracted over a *première danseuse* at the Gaiety. He didn't get the girl, though, after all, which he seemed to think was rather strange. She vanished completely soon after—he didn't know what *had* become of her. That was several years ago—I wonder, sometimes, which of those two men was the worst. Of course she vanished—of course she's never looked at—at *a male thing* again without utter fear and loathing. I've wondered, hundreds of times since, knowing she was sick to begin with, if she lost her reason—or only died—or what—and I've hoped—that sometime she could make the man she loved suffer—the way he made her suffer. I've wondered a hundred times, too, of course, who she *was*—good Lord, David, what ails you?"

For David had risen, and was staggering towards him, his eyes blazing in his gray face.

"Nothing," he was saying between lips so twisted with torture that he could hardly form the words, "I was the man, that's all—oh, my God, what shall I do?"

CHAPTER II

Good-by, Susie, dear; I'll see you again Sunday."

"That's ever and ever so far off."

"Only three days—and I'll bring you something pretty when I come."

"I'd rather stay with you than have anything pretty. It'll be awful without you, David."

"I expect to be rather lonely myself; but it's the best thing for you, honey."

"Oh, David," wailed the child, her arms around his neck, "you're ever and ever so much nicer than you used to be! I do love you a whole lot, and I'm sorry I ever said I didn't. I'll try to learn a whole lot, and grow up to be exactly like Miss Castle; and I do hope you'll find—Her."

David left the prim little French drawing-room, and went out into the bright street, his eyes full of unwelcome tears. It was hard to part from Susie; but it was harder still to face the lonesomeness and bitterness of defeat that lay before him. For nearly three months he had hunted for Jacqueline, and he was no nearer finding her now than on the morning when he and Susie sailed for Europe, and he told her what he had done and what he hoped to do, because, in his misery, he longed to tell

168

some one, who, upon hearing him, would, perhaps, flay him less mercilessly than Bobby Hutchinson had done— the man whose own tragedy he had never guessed, and who was spending the best years of his life in the service of a woman from whom he neither expected nor sought any reward. Would he, he wondered, ever forget the utter scorn and scathing contempt with which Bobby had stung him, after he had traced the story of the lady and the stable-boy from the day when he met her by the river to the one on which he left her lying on the couch of her room in Lady Thornington's house?

"To think," flung out Bobby with biting sarcasm, "that for more than ten years I've considered you the cleverest man I ever met—you miserable fool! You thought she 'might deceive you because she had deceived her grand-father'—the two cases are synonymous, aren't they? A poor, lonely, loving little girl outwitting a stupid old snob in order to be with her only playmate—and later on, her sweetheart, and a grown woman vulgarly tricking the man she promised to marry! The very fact that you could compare them for a minute shows the calibre of your mind! You 'loved her so much that it made you half-crazy with jealousy'? How dare you flatter yourself that you ever loved her—really loved her—for one single second? Because, after watching her with indifference for years, you suddenly itched to get your hands on her when you saw her in a white dressing-gown in the moon-light? That isn't love, you blithering idiot—that's ele-mental desire, that we all have to face sometimes, no matter how many pretty names you call it, or how much you gloss over the bald fact. Because you went to Wal-lacetown and made a fool of yourself when she didn't tumble straight into your arms? That wasn't love, it was stupid weakness, and would have been something a darn sight worse, if she hadn't been strong and good enough for both of you—as she would have been this time, too, if you had given her a chance. Because you sent her away from you to cry her eyes out, simply because you knew you didn't have any self-control? Oh, it may have been *right* if you can define right and wrong as easily as black and white squares on a checker board— but it was clumsy and cruel just the same. Because you went without luxury for a few years to buy her a ring? You did that to prove to yourself—and to her—what a wonder you were—to gratify your own pride in achievement. Because it peeved you to see her smoke cigarettes and to drink cocktails and play cards for money and wear dresses which weren't like those you'd been used to seeing in Cambridge, Mass.? You've got lots of talent distinguishing between the essential and the unessential, haven't you? Because you've kept *so straight?* Well, how often have you wanted—desperately wanted—to be anything else? If there is anything I loathe it's the Pharisee who goes about thanking God he's not like other men when he hasn't the slightest *wish* to be like other men! I bet she's suffered 'keeping straight' a thousand times more than you have, but neither she nor any other woman gets any credit for it, nor even a girl constituted as she must be. *Désirée Huntington!* Why, I remember meeting her more than once, when she came to Boston as a girl! I suppose that tow-headed simp, Cyril Wainwright, who was after her even then, though she couldn't have been much older than Susie, was one of the lordly suitors who made that devilish wager! She rode horseback a lot, and

170

danced like a—well, like something we'd never seen here before. She had a figure that you couldn't miss in a hundred—no normal man could keep his eyes off it—and a great mop of wavy, bronze-colored hair and hazel eyes that looked straight at you from a face that was beautiful, and sincere, and lovely—"

"For God's sake, stop!"

"I won't stop! And in addition to that face and that figure, she had three or four millions in her own name, and a temperament—of course—all gold and fire! Do you suppose *she* hasn't been tempted? Why, she's the kind of woman that knocks men silly, they want her so—and they will take every known means to get her, too. I would have myself, if it hadn't been for—if I hadn't, that's all. And you had a chance—no, a certainty—of marrying her! Help you to find her? I won't help you to a damned thing—and neither will any one else who guesses half this precious story. I almost wish I need never see you again as long as I live!"

But two days later, when David, having left Susie at the Hutchinson's and hastily returned to Hamstead to see if Sheldon could give him any information, returned with a white face that seemed to have suddenly grown ten years older, Bobby met him with a sympathy and understanding that were like balm to his wounded spirit.

"Could he tell you anything?"

"I don't know whether he could or not; anyway, he wouldn't. I didn't go near him when I was home before and he lays that—and some other things—up against me. He bought the farm that goes with the estate himself several years ago, and pays the taxes on the Big House for the use of its orchards and gardens; he says he hasn't

171

heard from Jacqueline since this arrangement was completed, though he's written her a number of times—in fact, some of his letters have come back to him unclaimed. I told him I wanted to find her because I thought the world of her when we were kids. 'She thought the world of you, you mean,' he said. I believe what you say is true. No one will be willing—"

"Now, look here, Dave—"

Bobby took hold of him, and swung him into the house, where cooling drinks and wafer-thin sandwiches awaited them on a silver tray. "Of course Sheldon doesn't know where she is—what do you think he is—a clairvoyant? And of course I want to help you. I *was* pretty mad the other night, and I guess I said more than I meant to. But I know you loved her all right. You did your level best to be square as well as straight, and to make yourself worthy of her before you claimed her—all of which is more than nine fellows out of ten in your place, and with no knowledge or experience to steer you right could have done. And you're a genius—there's absolutely no doubt of that, and it can't have helped going to your head a little. You did slip up pretty badly in England, but—haven't you suffered any for it? I mean, even before you heard me talk the other night?"

"*Suffered!* What do you think I am? Of course I suffered. But I never doubted that I was right, not for a minute. She wrote me once almost immediately, but I tore the letter in two, and sent it back to her unopened. I—"

"Well, you certainly were a general ass and then some, about that time, as I said before (drink some of this stuff, why don't you, it's good), but of course you'll find her

172

in time. Only don't go about it as if you were trying to track her down—"

"What do you think I am going to do? Use bloodhounds?"

"Well, I thought you might use detectives, and I bet she'd regard them much in the same light. Let her feel, when she next sees you, that you've been seeking, not claiming—just trying for the chance to lay an offering of repentance and—and love at her feet. Don't—don't assume anything. I shouldn't wonder—she cared a lot for you, and I sized her up as the kind that—well, I don't know. Remember, she's been dreadfully hurt—that's why she's hiding. Be gentle first, and last—and all the time—it's a mistake to believe that all women need to be bullied into marriage . . ."

"*Marriage!* Surely you don't for a minute imagine—"

"I'm not imagining anything—personal. I'm only telling you, on general principles. So far you've been honest enough—that's all right, as far as it goes. Keep on being honest. And you've meant to be just—that's plain enough in the light of the fact that you're so darn cut up now that you find you haven't been. But don't be so damned stupid—and crude—and hasty. Wait—and wait—and wait some more—"

A flash of red went by the window; there was a ringing laugh outside.

"Susie," said Bobby with a grin. "She's really a great kid—I'm glad she's going with you. I intend to wait for her to grow up, if she ever does—"

"But I thought—"

"Well, stop thinking. You're so stewed you're in no shape to think. You never had a sensible thought yet

173

about a girl as far as I can make out . . . Do you suppose I'm going to spend all my life hanging my heart on a weeping willow tree? Not much! I'm going to get Susie to take it down and play tunes on it for me . . . The Edgar L. wants you to call up at once, by the way—I almost forgot to tell you. I believe they hope you can be persuaded to postpone your sailing for a week, and come back for that long—it seems some rather ticklish cases have come in—"

"Well, why didn't you tell them for me to go to Hell—and save me the trouble? You know perfectly well I'm off at four a. m.—I've sent in my resignation, anyway—they'll get it on the morning mail."

"You crazy loon, what next? Why—"

"I can't be hampered with the hospital now that I've got a real job, can I? It may be years before I can get back—Thornton ought to have my place, anyway—I've known that all along. Those old tabbies were right—I'm not fitted for it. I'm going—" Suddenly an old phrase of his floated back to his mind— "I'm going," he said, smiling for the first time in days, "to the top of the Himalaya Mountains, and the middle of the Sahara desert!"

Susie, leaning over the rail at the stern of the great liner, watching the foam, was intensely interested.

"She was the loveliest lady that ever lived," said David, finishing his story, "and she loved me— Heaven knows why. I've told you what I did—now I've got to find her again."

"Do you think she'll marry you?" asked Susie. "I wouldn't. But then, I don't want to marry any one—ever."

"*Marry* me? I think if she'll let me stay in her presence long enough to ask her forgiveness on my knees she'll condescend too much."

174

"Well," said Susie sensibly, "I think you did act pretty mean; but I guess she was some to blame herself. I don't feel as if she was a saint and you was a leper, same as Bobby seems to, from what you said. She was a high-flyer, and you was a pill, but I guess folks are apt to be like that when they're courtin'. I know before Harry was sure of Hattie, he was moonin' around like a sick calf most of the time, and he'd leave the chores for Leon to do all alone, and go and lean over the graveyard fence, and hang around just hopin' she'd pass by, and one night when she went buggy-ridin' with Bert Silver, 'stead of him, he acted like he'd sat down on the stove by mistake, he flew around so. He was an awful trial to live with, I know that—he was stupid and hasty, same as Bobby calls you, only he didn't show it the same way. You'd have thought to see him then that he'd wait on her by inches, all his life, if she'd only have him, but now when they haven't been married but a year, he lets her get her own water for washin' and drag that great heavy baby around —and if he takes her anywhere he acts as if it was a great favor to her, and put him out terrible. That's why I'm not aimin' to have any love-affairs myself—I've seen how they work out too many times before this.

"Why shouldn't you find Jacqueline?" she went on, as David turned his head away with a slight cough, and without answering. "Probably she'll be the first person we see when we get to London, all married to some elegant English earl, with three or four little earls and earlesses of her own." Then noticing that this picture did not seem to appeal vitally to her brother, "You talk as if the earth had swallowed her, and you had got to dig."

"No, Susie," he explained patiently, "but it's years since I lost track of her, and of course none of her friends will tell me where she is."

"She may be living right along in the same house."

But she was not, though they went immediately to London in the slight hope that this might be the case. The house was occupied by some brand-new people from Milwaukee, who were anxious to shine in society, and who were willing to admit any one who called.

"Yes, we bought the house from Lauder and Lauder," said Mrs. Beering volubly. "Of course you know Mr. Huntington died four years ago. Yes, I saw his grand-daughter once—she came to get a few little things after we moved in. We bought the house furnished, and paid for it that way, but of course we wasn't going to split hairs over a trifle like that, when all she wanted was some no-count little keepsakes. I've kept expectin' to hear that she was married to some Duke or something, she was so downright handsome, as one may say. Was you ever any acquainted with her? Well, she seemed like a real sweet girl to me that day she was here. No, I don't believe she's in London, for we keep agoin' all the time to all the swell places, and I've never set eyes on her since then. I read the society papers, too, of course, and I don't see her name mentioned. No trouble at all, Dr. Noble. Delighted to see you any time you'll drop in, I'm sure, and I'd be real pleased to have you come to dinner some night next week—I haven't a free evening before then."

David next directed his footsteps to the office of Lauder and Lauder, Real Estate Brokers; they also received him cordially, but the warmth of their greeting cooled when he stated his errand—he had looked good for a country manor, to say the least. However, they told him that Miss Huntington had placed the property in their hands to be sold, and they had not seen or heard of her since the time of that transaction, when she was stopping with her friend, Lady Thornington; they thought it probable that she managed all her property herself, but if she did have legal advisers, they were not known to Lauder and Lauder. Couldn't they interest Dr. Noble in a beautiful abbey that had just come on the market?

But David was half outside the door already. Lady Thornington! She had been kindly disposed to him—surely, if he went to her and made a clean breast of things, she could not help being convinced of his sincerity! He looked up the address of her town house, and hurriedly betook himself to it; but the footman who ushered him into the drawing-room came back after a moment with the chilling announcement that Lady Thornington could not receive him, either then, or at any other time.

If it had not been for Susie, who trudged patiently beside him as he went from place to place, he sometimes felt that his courage would have failed him completely; but she insisted on taking a hopeful and practical view of the situation, and cheered him in spite of himself.

"Wasn't she half French? Why don't you try France?"

"Why don't I hunt for a needle in a hay-stack? I don't know what her mother's maiden name was, even, or where she came from."

"Well, this whole thing is hunting for a needle in a hay-stack—but if the needle's *there*, you're bound to find it sooner or later. She went to a school at a Convent in

Paris, didn't she? Maybe the nuns may know where she is —probably they keep track of their old scholars, especially if they're rich and good-lookin'—send 'em Christmas and Easter cards, and ask them in to Donation Days. And you said she always had her clothes made there—her dressmaker must know where she had things sent to, and a good many other things about her, besides— I'm sure Miss Sims, at home, don't miss much."

David had to admit that all this was good advice; and Susie followed it up with some that was still better.

"You'd think of some of these things yourself if you'd do something else for a change; your head's so dead beat because you try to work it all the time that it don't work at all. Why don't we have a cute little flat in Paris and a motor? Why don't you take a course with the French doctor—Norchais, was that his name?—like you planned to in the beginning, and get some kind of a teacher for me so that I won't be so green when I start in school that I'll *sprout*. You don't take any notice of what I do—I'd still be pickin' my teeth and chewing gum if it wasn't for Bobby. You've met some folks in Paris, times when you've been there before, haven't you? Why don't you look 'em up, instead of tryin' to play lone hand? You want a list of dressmakers, and a list of convents and a list of schools, and you want to take things easier for a spell, or you'll have us both all tuckered out."

"Susie, you'll be a treasure to some man some day."

"Well, that ain't my plan—I'd a sight rather have some man a treasure to *me*. But I'm tryin' to knock a little common sense into you just now."

To Paris they accordingly went, where they established themselves comfortably and pleasantly, and began

178

to study, David with Norchais and Susie with a wizened little old tutor; to ride about in the new Mercedes that David bought, and to present themselves to his former acquaintances. And in due time, the establishment of Paquin and Worth and Doucet, and other very great personages in the dressmaking world were interviewed—but interviewed in vain. Ah, yes, was the almost invariable answer, they well remembered the young lady of whom monsieur spoke; they had formerly made her many gowns; but it was now more than four years since the orders had entirely ceased.

"That is the more strange," he was told at the last of the famous houses which he visited, "as at one time we received a letter from Mademoiselle Huntington saying that she was fiancée, and that though she was not to be married immediately, we were to begin at once to collect the most beautiful fabrics that we could find. We found a white and silver brocade, from Venice, monsieur, that was of a marvel, for the bridal robe, and other things— but almost immediately came another letter, saying that, after all she would require nothing. And since then we have not heard from her. Does not monsieur desire to order for mademoiselle something very charming, very discreet?"

"Oh, David, do!"

"I thought you had no feminine foibles?"

"I don't know what you mean; but I like clothes—oh, yes, that one!"

He bought her the frock in question, and ordered another; as they went down the carpeted steps together, she squeezed his hand.

"It's a shame that you should be buying dresses for me

instead of for her," she whispered. "Say, wouldn't she have looked sweet in that white brocade?" Then, noticing how bleak and drawn his face looked, "Let's start right in at the convents now."

After a long search, they found the one which Jacqueline had attended; the Mother Superior received them; and there was something in the cool and gentle aloofness of her manner that made David believe instantly that she knew the whole story. His heart gave a great bound of hope.

"Jacqueline Désirée is not here now," she said quietly, "but it is true that she lived with us as a child, yes, and that she was called then 'the convent's sunbeam'; and always, for a long time, she returned to us at least once a year—for retreat during Lent, or for her birthday, or for some feast of which she was especially fond; and when her grandfather died, she made us a long visit— she was very weak at the time, for she had had a long illness."

"And you know where she is!" David cried. The Mother Superior touched a bell. A sister entered.

"Pray take mademoiselle into the garden," the even voice went on, "it is necessary for me to speak to monsieur privately." And, when they were alone, "Will monsieur not be seated?"

He sat down, and waited for her to speak again. "Monsieur is not of our Church?"

"No."

"Nevertheless, there are times when men of all faith, or of none at all, know that confession is good for the soul."

David met her look squarely. "I see," he said slowly,

"you—you don't trust me. You think, if you tell me where she is, I'll hurt her again. But I won't. I don't ask to see her for more than five minutes. I only want to tell her—"

"Suppose you tell me what is in your heart to tell her, my son."

To the best of his ability, he did so; but he was laboring with deep emotion which he was trying to conceal; and he was speaking in a foreign language of which he had only uncertain command.

"Did you never think," she asked at length, "that the religious life might prove a refuge to Désirée?"

"You mean—that she might become a Sister?"

"In truth I have heard her say so more than once. Do you not know enough of human nature, my son, to realize that *la grande amoureuse* and *la réligieuse* are own sisters, and sometimes actually the same person? History furnishes you with many an example. Désirée was deeply attached to her faith—"

David bowed his head. "I know it," he said huskily, "but I—I never thought of *this*. Why, that means—" All that it actually did mean came over him with rushing force.

"It does not mean that you would not be allowed to see her for five minutes, if that is actually all that you desire—but it is true that she is not here. She does not write to me often—suddenly, some day, she comes. When next she comes—"

"I beg of you," was all David could say.

And then October came, and Susie had to go to school, leaving him to wait alone for the five minutes in which he was to see Jacqueline.

He motored a great deal; the country about Paris was

181

still very beautiful, the roads perfect, and he found a thrill and excitement in driving the Mercedes, which the true lover of machinery, no less than the true lover of horses, often experiences. It kept him from thinking.

One Saturday afternoon he chanced to pass through a small village more than thirty miles from Paris just as the bells were ringing for vespers; he sometimes went to services now, aimlessly and faithlessly, but deriving a certain amount of comfort from them all the same, and he was moved to do so on this particular afternoon. The little church was bare and cold, with a few tawdry decorations; the curé was old and rheumatic, and the congregation consisted of a handful of peasants, in rough woolen garments and wooden shoes, and two or three women shabbily dressed in black belonging to the small *bourgeoisie*. David dropped a gold-piece in the alms box as he passed out.

"Somehow I like that place," he said to himself as he got into his motor again. "It was clean and well-aired, and there were fresh flowers on the altar—it seemed different, someway, from most of them." He remembered, suddenly, that he had a dinner engagement, and switched, immediately, into high gear, in spite of the cobblestones of the little square. There was a crossing in a turn to the left before he reached the highroad for Paris; and, as he approached it, he saw one of the black-gowned women who had just left the church start to pass over to the other side of the street. She had plenty of time to reach the other side. He was still several rods away. But when she was about half-way over, she glanced casually in the direction of the motor, then stopped short, uttering a little cry. David flung himself

182

on the brake, but it was too late—the machine slid over her, and jerked itself to a standstill three yards further on.

David sprang back and bent over her. It was almost dark, but he could see a bright flow of blood gushing through the veil which hung from the small hat she wore, and which completely covered her face. As he pushed it away, the filmy black thing seemed to wind itself about his arm, impeding him. He shook himself free of it, shuddering, and looked into the woman's still face.

It was Désirée.

CHAPTER III

ALL his life David was to remember—and marvel in re-membering—that his first sensation was a marvellous rush of thanksgiving and joy—the knowledge of persever-ance and love rewarded, of fear and despair overcome. *He had found Désirée.* Then, the next instant, came an-other bounding certainty—*she was not a nun;* and he saw, in one dazzling, throbbing moment, that the most colossal lie he had ever told—even though, when he told it, he had believed it to be the truth—was that it made no difference to him whether she was or not, that he only expected to see her for five minutes, just long enough to beg his forgiveness. As a man's whole life is said to be pictured before him when he is drowning, every word that the Mother Superior had spoken came back to him, so vividly that he seemed actually to hear her voice, and he realized for the first time that she had not really said— she had asked him a question, had given him no hope, had allowed him to believe—but she had only been test-ing him, trying to see whether this time—oh, *this time* he would prove to her—he gathered Désirée to him with a little cry of triumph. And the horrible, murderous fact *how* he had found her burst upon him.

The door of the nearest cottage stood half open. He pushed his way through it, his burden in his arms. A white-capped peasant woman sat knitting before the peaceful hearth-stone of a raftered kitchen. There were copper kettles glowing in the fire light, the fragrance of *pot-au-feu* filled the room. She started up with sudden alarm.

"Monsieur desires—" she began; then seeing what he carried, she cried aloud. Her knitting fell, the steel needle clicking against the stone floor. "There has been an accident!" And coming nearer, she cried again, "Holy Virgin! It is my Désirée!"

"It is *my* Désirée," said David, stupidly, in English; he stared at the little elderly peasant, bewildered, forgetting again. Then he remembered and spoke in French— "She's been run over by a motor—where shall I take her?"

"Where but to her own room? Follow me, monsieur, and may the Saints preserve us!"

As he mounted the tiny, dark, narrow stairway, it seemed as if he understood only in waves, like a man recovering from an anesthetic—he had found her, she was not a nun, nothing should ever take him away from her again—she was hurt, dying perhaps, he himself had done this unspeakable thing. If he did not think quickly, act quickly—

"Oh, my God, help me!" It was the first conscious prayer he had ever made. And, as he laid her on her narrow bed, and felt her dead weight slipping from his arms, suddenly, as if by a miracle, his mind cleared. He wrenched off a pillow-slip, and began tearing it into narrow strips, speaking rapidly.

"I'm a doctor. I know what to do. Help me all you can.

It's going to be all right. And later, I'll explain. Now every minute we waste may mean this lady's life. Bring me some cold water—have you any ice in the house? Well, would any of your neighbors have any? Find some one to send for your village doctor, *quick!* Tell him to bring morphia, ether or chloroform, too, if he has it, but surely morphia—do you get the word? And—all the instruments he has—*hurry—*"

He made a make-shift tourniquet, wound the linen strips about the girl's head as he spoke, and bent to listen to her heart. The little peasant, he saw instantly, after her first natural outburst of terror, was not going to be hysterical, and the water she fetched him was cold and clean.

"Marthe, *ma bonne,* runs for *monsieur le médécin,*" she said firmly, "and if ice there is in Fleursy, that also will be here, in a quarter of an hour. *Et alors—*"

"Fill all your kettles, and place them on the fire—we must have hot water as well as cold. Is there a telephone in the village, and do you know how to use it?"

"*Mais, oui, monsieur—*"

Holding his left hand against Jacqueline's temple, he scribbled with his right on a scrap of paper.

"Can you read that?"

She lighted the tallow candle on the little bedside table, and scanned it, slowly, painfully. But in the end her face lighted.

"To Monsieur le médécin Norchais, 17 rue T—Paris. If out, leave the message. 'Come instantly to village of Fleursy, house opposite church, bring instruments for major operation, ether, and a nurse. Life or death. David Noble.' Shall I wait for the doctor and ice before I telephone?"

"Wait for nothing."

"*Parfaitement, monsieur—*" but she had not reached the stairs before she called back, softly, "Marthe enters with the ice, monsieur."

The little maid, tears rolling from her round black eyes over her rough red cheeks, handed him the bowl silently.

"You'll have to break that up—use a poker—anything—and bring it back—then go and watch the hot water—" His own swiftness found a rival in these untaught women who flew to serve him; almost instantly the broken ice was thrust into his hands. He saw soon, that the red stain was spreading less rapidly, that it was not spreading at all, that it was drying a little—he reached for a towel from the little washstand, tore that up too, felt the tourniquet once more, wound the new bandage firmly over the first one. He asked for scissors, began to cut away her clothing, searching for further injuries. The right arm was broken—shattered—so were four of the right ribs—there was, of course, internal damage, too, though how much he could not instantly determine. If she regained consciousness before he could procure morphia, her suffering would be terrible. But when he raised his head after making his examination, a small, shabby man stood beside him, extending a hypodermic needle. David seized it without a word, and drove it into the uninjured arm.

"I have no ether, monsieur, and only a little chloroform—"

"Enough to keep her insensible until we set that arm?"

"*Que monsieur regarde—*"

David looked, set his teeth, and threw off his coat.

187

"Of course there isn't—to play safe, but I think we had better risk it—it's a nasty break, and I think we better get it fixed—there'll be harder things to do later, without being bothered with that—you have more morphia?"

But when it was all over, and the little room silent and tidy again, and Jacqueline had been clad in a soft fresh night-dress, and her bronze-colored hair gathered in two great plaits, she still lay, white and serene, with no sign of returning life. David pulled up a chair beside the bed, and sat down, his fingers on her wrist. And after he had watched the younger man, who had apparently quite forgotten him, for a long time, the shabby village doctor spoke with hesitating admiration.

"I will return when you need me, but there is nothing I can do here now—I but obtrude my clumsy presence on your genius, monsieur. With your permission, I will go downstairs, and try to comfort Mère Thérèse—the poor woman has made no sound, but her heart must be breaking for her granddaughter."

"Her granddaughter!"

"But yes, monsieur, our beautiful Désirée is the granddaughter of the good Thérèse. Her mother, *hélas!* was a lovely, wild, little creature, who ran away from home when she was very young, and danced upon the stage in Paris. I have heard that she was ravishing, with the frail charm of a fragile flower. She married a young man who became infatuated with her there, but both died when Désirée was but an infant, and she was brought up far from here by her grandfather—her father's father, a haughty American of great wealth, who never recognized the existence of her mother's family. We had almost forgotten the sad story in Fleursy, and we were

188

glad to forget it, for it had brought shame as well as sorrow to Thérèse—"

"Then Désirée came here herself!" David spoke the words with a kind of excited joy, as one who has suddenly seen a shaft of light in utter darkness. "Wasn't it so, monsieur, four or five years ago, after a dangerous illness and the loss of her grandfather, seeking her mother's family, asking you all to welcome her—"

"Is monsieur then a magician as well as a genius? It was even so. She thought of taking the veil—indeed, she wished to do so, for it was plain she had been through a great sorrow, which had left her crushed and bleeding, though she was so fair and young and rich. In those first days she kept much to herself, thinking, praying—but there was so much to be done here, such misery and want! She was quick to see it, to forget her own grief. No angel from Heaven could have done for us more than she has done. If monsieur could but look from the window, he would see the crowd that has gathered, waiting for tidings! May I say that she is safe, that she will be restored to them through your skill and the goodness of God?"

"Tell them what you think best. And go, by all means— to the grandmother. When I need you—"

"Parfaitement, monsieur."

David bent over the bed again, listening for the girl's heart-beats; there was no change. He glanced at his watch—eight o'clock! Three hours since—Norchais must have been out, and in that case there was no telling when he would arrive. There was nothing to do but wait. He looked about the room, dimly lighted by two great tallow candles. It was plain, even to the point of bareness. There were in it a narrow bed, a chest of drawers, a wash-stand, two straight-backed chairs, a small bed-side table. The walls were white-washed, the floor unpainted, and without rugs. Over the bed hung a crucifix of ebony and ivory. Had Jacqueline actually been a nun, her cell could hardly have been more austere.

Through the open window—the only one in the room—he could hear the eager voices of the people outside, below it, the curses of men, the crying of little children.

"Where is the devil that has murdered her? Let us burn the car! What does monsieur the doctor say? Come, to the church to light candles to the Virgin for her recovery! Will the Holy Father have her canonized if she dies? Monsieur the curé is praying for her. I will spend my five sous to buy her flowers—"

Half-past eight—would Norchais never come? David tore fresh bandages, though they were not needed, and laid them in neat piles by the bed-side table; picked up the pile of clothes, which, overlooked, were lying on the floor in a heap in the corner where he had flung them, and folded them carefully over a chair—a plain black dress, with bands of sheer white linen at the neck and sleeves, the simplest of undergarments. As he laid them down, something fell from among the folds to the ground. It was a tiny gold cross on a fine gold chain.

Nothing to do but wait. He could hear the crowd still surging outside, and from downstairs the sobbing of Mère Thérèse and the bonne, their fine self-control broken at last. He called softly and the little woman came and stood beside him. And stumblingly, as he had told the Mother Superior, he told her his story. But this woman understood him better.

"My granddaughter has indeed spoken of you," she said, simply, when he had finished, "but she has told me no evil of you—only that as a child, she loved you dearly, that later you were betrothed. Of the Austrian Count she had also told me—something. But these matters concern you and her, and not me, and it was plainly the will of God that the chance should be given you to speak of them together, else you would not have found her; and since you have done so, we must not question the way in which it has come about."

She laid her quivering hand on his shoulder. "Monsieur—"

"You'll tell the doctor and the curé as much of this as they ought to know—they're wondering of course, and probably resentful. And—you mustn't call me 'monsieur' —I come of very plain people, *petits fermiers*—"

She understood the feeling that prompted everything he said. The hand on his shoulder quivered still more.

"David," she said softly, *"mon fils—"*

He snatched it in his own, and kissed it, his hot tears falling unashamed upon it. And then she left him again.

Nothing to do but wait—for the doctor who did not come, and the signs of life which did not show themselves. To wait, while he thought of the Jacqueline that used to be, the fresh-faced child who came to him, singing, through the moonlit garden and kissed him on the road to Wallacetown; of the radiant beauty surrounded by luxury and frivolity, with her loveliness and her elegance, and her marvellous charm; of the Jacqueline that might have been—the wife in the glory of her passionate surrender, the mother with her final crown of womanhood; and then of the Jacqueline he had found—the

191

recluse of a poor village, the gentle, ascetic divinity—but ever and always—the giver. And in those hours the remnants of selfishness and self-righteousness, of vain-glory and uncharitableness that still lay on David's soul fell from it, as a dark mantle, freed from a woman's white shoulders, falls to the ground, leaving the fair soft flesh bare beneath it. What, he asked himself, in the slow torture that was beginning to burn away the bitter misery of the last three months—what had *he ever given?* He had *taken*—snatched—squeezed dry. He had crashed ahead, blindly, on his single-track railway, triumphantly sweeping aside all obstacles, had reached the great city which was his terminal, and lo! the city was barren and empty, and not worth the reaching. What were the successes of years, the thousand miracles of skill he had performed worth to him now if he could not save this one girl's life and set her in a throne in his empty city, so that it might no longer be empty, and fall down and worship her? He fell on his knees now, and buried his face in the coverlet of the bed.

Suddenly, without warning, David felt a slight movement beneath the sheet. He sprang to his feet.

Jacqueline was looking around her with wide, quiet eyes, as a child, waking, looks for its mother; as they turned on the man beside her, they lighted, slowly, as if they had found what they sought. A little fluttering sigh came through her white lips, and then she smiled—the smile of the singing girl coming through the garden.

"Hello, David," she said.

CHAPTER IV

KEEPING

"WHAT happened?" she asked, a little confusedly, after a moment, as he did not answer, "I was crossing the street, coming from church—and then I saw you, driving a motor—it startled me, and I stopped—did I get run over?" Then, as David nodded, still dumbly, "I'm not in great pain—am I much hurt?"

"You have had a good deal of morphia—I want to save you all the suffering I can; but I must not give you any more at present, for I am sure you are internally injured, and I'll need your help to locate the extent and position of the trouble. Your right arm was broken; but I have set that—the village doctor had a little chloroform."

He had always sneered at the doctors who "coddled their patients by lying to them." Had it been sometimes as hard for them to tell the truth as it was for him to speak those few sentences—he knew that he would never sneer again—

"Your head was cut, too. Does it ache much?"

"No—not badly. Don't give me anything more—if you need my help—everything seems a—a little hazy still."

"Yes, but that's all right; you're more comfortable that way."

"You'll take care of me? You won't go away—"

"Never, until you send me," he said, "but I've telephoned Norchais, of Paris—or, rather, your grandmother did it for me—he must have gone out on a case, or he'd have been here hours ago! I had of course—nothing with me, and your own doctor has not much, either; Norchais will be able to do much more for you than I can. And I'm going to cable to Boston for a nurse—of course Norchais will bring one, but I want one of our own women from the Edgar L.—the best in all the world—for you. She can get here in a week."

"Do you think there may—have to be an operation?"

"Yes, if what I fear has happened."

"At once?"

"Yes, tonight—"

"You'll—you'll do it?"

He turned away from the entreaty in her eyes. "I think Norchais is more skilful," he said gently, "But it shall be just as you say, of course."

She seemed, for a few minutes, to have sunk back into the merciful stupor into which the morphia had naturally sent her; but presently she stirred again, and held out her left hand.

"I wrote to you," she said, "but the letter came back, still sealed, and torn across—I never—could try again—"

"Yes, I know."

"David, I wasn't—I didn't—"

"I know—I've known for three months—I've been hunting for you ever since—"

"Without a single clue to guide you, giving up everything that you were doing . . . then you must have forgiven me!"

194

The torture was growing unbearable—surely, the robe that Nessus had worn held no such white heat as this! It seemed to David as if there must be some way in which he could tear it off, as if he must fling himself at Désirée's feet, and cry out with repentance and love and passion, in the hope that, as on the road to Wallacetown, he would be shriven and healed. But this time, he knew, the sin was too great; even if, in her infinite mercy, she could forgive him, he could not ask it; and passion had long since passed from the life of this gentle saint. He took the hand that she extended very reverently and quietly.

"Jacqueline," he said, "I did you the greatest wrong that a man could possibly do a woman. I never can atone for it. Some day, when you are well again, we'll speak of it—but you're very ill now—it isn't good for you to talk, or even to try to think. I am a doctor, and you are my patient; we must try to forget, for now, that we were ever anything else."

"Is there any chance that I may not get well?"

David dropped her hand and walked over to the window. The crowd outside was smaller now, because many had gone to the church to pray; but there were still many there. There was no sign of Norchais. The wind was blowing, and there was not a cloud in the sky.

"Don't feel so about it. I don't. I only asked because, if there is, I want to talk about my money—there's such a lot of it, and the people here are wretchedly poor. You have no idea what their existence used to be. I've been able to help them a little, and they mustn't lose anything, if I have to leave them. You could send some one for the attorney, couldn't you?"

"I think he's outside now. I can hear a woman addressing a hungry-looking little man as 'monsieur l'avocat'—"

"Please ask him to come up."

When he had done this, and the little man, snuffling with grief, stood beside her, David was amazed at the brevity and clarity of Jacqueline's directions. There was no mawkish sentimentality, there were no vague desires or half-formed, impracticable plans. So much was to go to the Church, so much to the school, besides two yearly prizes to be given to the graduating pupils of highest rank, that they might be able to continue their studies further; a sum to be used for general charities at the discretion of the curé; a fund from which five hundred francs should be given to every girl of the village upon her marriage—

"Every girl of good character?" said monsieur l'avocat, writing.

"Every girl," reiterated Jacqueline, "and a hundred francs for every baby born; fifty thousand for grand'mère and all the rest of it—"

She turned towards David; he read her intention instantly.

"I'm rich now myself, Jacqueline," he said quietly, "almost as rich as you are. I don't need it any more."

"But you'd know what to do with it better than I can direct—now. Is there a hospital in Hamstead?"

"No."

"Couldn't you have one built—and other things like that?"

"Yes, if you are quite sure it is what you wish done."

"All the rest of my property then," she went on, "real

196

and personal, I leave to David Noble, to be used at his discretion. That's all, I think. Please ask two persons not specified in the will to come in and witness it."

When the little room was quiet again, she lay for a few minutes with closed eyes, and David knew that she was not only exhausted, but suffering again, as the effects of the morphia wore away; but she shook her head at his offer to give her more.

"I think I can show you now where the worst pain is—right here."

He made his examination quickly, asking several brief questions. Did it hurt when he pressed it? Was it dull or sharp? Was it worse here—or here? It was very soon over.

"Is your general health good? You are very thin."

"I'm perfectly healthy. I had a bad nervous break-down when—several years ago. Since then I haven't had a moment's sickness worth mentioning."

"What does 'worth mentioning' mean?"

"I don't sleep."

The words were simple enough. He guessed at what lay behind them.

"That's all, dear lady. Now you must let me put you to sleep, so that you can save your strength."

"All right. Good luck, David!"

She seemed to be almost unconscious, when she reached for his hand again.

"Do you remember," she said drowsily, "that you said once you'd find me if I was on the top of the Himalaya Mountains, or in the middle of the Sahara desert?"

"Yes, Jacqueline."

She laughed, softly. "Apparently you meant it! And do you remember what *I* said once—"

"Well, dear?"

"That it wouldn't be safe for any woman to marry you until you were ready to give up your career to have her, and do it then to serve her, and not to possess her—"

Did he remember! Could he ever forget the magnificent, firelit room, the beautiful girl dressed in white satin sitting on the crimson sofa, the sweet, wilful self-consenting rebellion that came before the exquisite surrender—

"David—it would be safe now, wouldn't it?"

"I don't understand," he said stupidly.

"If I am dying—perhaps—I have a right to any of the sacraments which I desire—"

"You wish to confess, to receive communion?"

"That first, of course, and then—"

He had no way of telling just how far she was aware of what she was saying and doing. He put his face closer to hers to catch the whispered words.

"I told you, too, once, that marriage was a sacrament, didn't I?"

"Oh, my dear!" he said, brokenly. Then he pulled himself together. "Darling, you don't know what you are saying. You can't—mean—"

"But I *do*. I do know, I do mean. David, won't you marry me—that is, if you still—"

"Oh, my dear!" he said again, and stopped for a moment, powerless to go on. "When I found I'd failed you *once*," he managed at last to say, "I insisted that I still had a right to—even though I'd left you where your grandfather could insult you and torture you. And just what you predicted happened— I failed you a second time—and that time it was *I* who insulted and tortured

198

you. Don't think I'm such a fool—such a wicked and pre-suming—"

She stretched out her hand. "It seems—to be getting dark—I can't see you, David," she said like a pleading child, "please hold on to me—" And when he had taken her hand, she whispered, "But I never said you'd fail me a third time. And you *wouldn't*— Would you?"

"Oh, my God, *no!*" he cried, feeling that his very soul was crumbling within him.

But before he could gather her into his arms, he saw that she was again unconscious.

·   ·   ·   ·   ·   ·   ·

It was after midnight when Norchais reached Fleursy, accompanied by a gray-clad nun, who looked, with her pallid face and her great crucifix, like the very messenger of Death—Norchais, already weary from a tedious vigil which had ended disastrously, and angered at his pupil's unreasonable presumption in calling him to an unknown woman in a poverty-stricken village—Norchais, who listened with scant attention as David, hurriedly sorting instruments, told him the main facts of the accident.

"Deaths as the result of motoring increase in number every day," he said, smothering a yawn. "I didn't know what instruments to bring—'major operation' isn't espe-cially definite, you know—but if your diagnosis is correct there's not one chance in a thousand that you can save the girl, anyway—and you can't see to operate by the light of two tallow candles!"

David was rolling up his sleeves. He turned on the other doctor with a ferocity that was as primitive as that of a cave-man, fighting for his mate.

199

"This is the thousandth chance," he said, savagely, "I'm going to do it, and do it well—and I would if I hadn't anything but a pair of shears and a piece of twine to do it with, too. Go down and get the acetylene lights off your motor, and then scrub up and get ready to help me, and be damned quick about it. Now I'm all ready. Take the ether cone, *ma soeur*."

"There must be something—" the great doctor was murmuring with startled excitement, as he returned with the flaring lights in his hands—he held them high over the bed, and broke into an exclamation of amazement. "*Ma foi*, David Noble!" he cried, "That's no village girl—it's Jacqueline Huntington, the great American heiress. I saw her once years ago, and I have never forgotten—"

But David did not answer him. He had begun to work.

CHAPTER V

THE BATTLE

THE leaves in the forest of Fleursy turned from golden to bronze, and fell, quivering, to the dull earth; October, with its crisp coolness and mellow sunshine passed; November dragged its dark length through, and December came with its frozen roads, and its futile flurries of snow. And still Jacqueline lay, very white and quiet, on the narrow bed under the crucifix of ebony and ivory, while David fought for her life with the gray shadow of death that hovered over her, and which over and over again seemed about to bear her away in its tenuous, powerful arms.

It took ten days for the nurse whom he trusted to reach Fleursy from Boston, and during that time he did not have his clothes off, did not go further from Jacqueline's room than the kitchen, and seldom as far as that. The constitution which, as Bobby had humorously put it, enabled him to "operate thirty-six hours out of the twenty-four, if necessary," stood him in good stead now. He ate his meals in gulps, he slept, when he slept at all, for an hour at a time on a couch just outside her door. Like most doctors, he had seldom watched a patient coming out of anesthetics longer than was necessary to assure himself that "everything was normal"—an expression which causes physicians untold satisfaction, nurses untold responsibility, and sick persons untold suffering. There was no question of the "normal" this time. Jacqueline, as sometimes, though fortunately rarely, happens, was almost completely paralyzed by the ether. She could not get rid of it in the "normal" way, she could not swallow or speak or move. David had seen this difficulty arise but once before, in the case of an Italian woman at the North End, in Boston, with whose lividness he had felt nothing but impatience. Why couldn't she drink tepid water, and succumb to nausea, and tell all her life's secrets, and shiver and cry, and then drift off into her "ether sleep"? He recalled the hysterical, noisy, rebellious grief of the Italian woman's husband, the ironical calmness with which he had met it . . . And now here was Jacqueline, lying motionless, the perspiration dropping in great beads from her white forehead, her hair, her night-gown, her sheets, as wet with it as if she had been plunged into a bath, her great eyes fixed on him, asking him, dumbly, why he did not help her . . . Like most doctors, also, he had seldom watched beside a patient through the night; that was a task relegated to a night nurse, while he went peacefully home to bed. He wondered now, how he had ever done it. Morphia did not make Jacqueline sleepy. She grew drowsy, suffered less acutely for a short time, and then lay staring wide awake again; this, too, was an "abnormality" seldom encountered, "a nuisance" when it had been. He felt he would willingly have been cut in tiny pieces if he could first see her drift off into a painless, dreamless slumber. One night—one hideous, panting, agonized, writhing life-time, that seemed alive with horror and might—revealed more to him about suffering—the way it must be endured, the way it must, if possible, be conquered—than months of complacent practice had done. Ten of them, coming one after the other, without respite, made him marvel that he had ever thought he knew anything about bodily pain and mental anguish. One, slightly less dreadful than those that had gone before it, buoyed him into exultant hope. The following one was worse, far worse, than any that had gone before it. He thought of deserts—of mirage —and knew now why travelers killed themselves.

Bobby, David had often told him, "pampered his patients"; they were all "medically babied."

"The clean cut of a surgeon's knife is just like any other clean cut," he had said, impatiently many times, "Why should it be regarded as something so different? It's exactly the same. If you slashed your arm with a saber— provided it was sterile—you wouldn't expect to be under par indefinitely, would you? I have my patients out mowing their lawns before yours are sitting up in an easy chair drinking cool drinks."

"I know you do," drawled Bobby comfortably, "also, six months later, when mine are beginning to mow lawns and have got my modest bill all paid, yours are seeking refuge in expensive sanatoriums. Nerves all shot to pieces, no one can imagine why, 'the operation was so wonderfully successful!' You don't stop to think that they've also got to recover from whatever made that nice clean cut necessary—a trouble hidden, or patiently borne for years, sometimes; from pain, which you underestimate, and which is a bigger factor than you seem to know—it isn't over when it's over, to be rather Irish, but entirely truthful; from shock; from ether; oh, I know some people tell you they 'like to take ether.' One woman who told me that—"

"Well?" Bobby's stories were usually worth listening to.

"She came to me for a major operation which had been made necessary by the stupidity of a former doctor; came all alone, two hundred miles,—she lived in the country— because she 'really preferred to.' She was 'used to being sick'—that was true all right—'didn't mind it a bit; a hospital was a colossal joke.' She was the most magnificent liar I ever saw. There was a husband somewhere in the dim distance; he couldn't stand the smell of ether, so she 'hated to bother him.' Well, I'm glad to say it bothered him a little when she died. Oh, yes, the operation was successful— I'm not such an awful bungler as you like to pretend—but she'd bluffed too much, and stood too much, before it, and there was no one to stand by and help her stand and bluff after it was over. I did what I could, but what she needed was some one to love her, love her good and plenty—oh, hell!"

That was what—between incoherent, formless prayers —David kept saying to himself now: he had of course, made a "perfectly clean cut," there was "nothing to recover from." He dwelt on the words with scathing sarcasm of his own former theories. There were five years to reckon with, five years which had not been spent "normally," followed by a fearful shock and great suffering. Jacqueline, he suspected, had observed the fasts of her church more conscientiously than she had done its feasts, even if the abrupt change from luxurious living to coarse peasant fare had not inevitably wrought havoc. She was thin to the point of emaciation. Moreover, her taste for beauty and pleasure, her emotions, her senses, had not died the natural death that comes from peaceful middle age; they had been torn up by the roots with her own hands, trampled on with her own feet. She had lain awake for nights, weeping until exhaustion overcame her, throbbing for something she was denied—suffering until the power to throb had left her altogether. "*Nuits blanches*"—"white nights"—David had heard the phrase, had thought it rather expressive—now he knew for the first time what it really meant.

Soeur Célestine he instinctively distrusted. Nuns, he thought, probably essayed to cure their patients by rosaries rather than routine. He watched her constantly, expecting to find that she had neglected to take a temperature or failed to scrub a hand. He frowned when she rose or moved about, as if waiting for her shoes to squeak. If she had "only been one of our own women!" Gradually he realized—and the realization was one of the few bright spots in his existence just then—that he had misjudged and underrated her. She prayed indeed—the little room was filled with the purity and sincerity of her prayers— but while she prayed, she watched and she worked. She had no "two hours off for rest and recreation" every afternoon, she did not state that "she could not do Miss Huntington justice unless she had at least seven hours sleep every night"; she did not relate lengthy tales of the "very wealthy family of her last patient," who had been so "extremely considerate." Her work of healing was not a means of making money to her; it was a dedication. There were many great and noble characters among "our own nurses," and the one whom he so eagerly awaited was one of them; but there were many others who were neither—as there are in every profession—to whom he had not hesitated to entrust his patients, whom he had even engaged a second time. There was the one who woke a sufferer from insomnia to give him a sleeping-powder, that other who lost a hypodermic needle in a bed and "thought it didn't much matter"; the one that gave a child with a temperature of 104° roast goose for dinner, and the other who blistered a young girl's back with the hot water-bag from shoulder to hip before she came out of ether. These occurrences had once seemed to him to have rather a humorous side. Now the greatness of his carelessness began to assume such magnitude in his eyes he wondered how any one he had ever taken care of had come through alive. Pulling himself together, he knew how silly and morbid that was—he had done good work, skilful work, yes, *great* work, only there had been so much he had not understood before. Did he understand enough now? With everything else that he had to fight, he found that he had to contend with that sinister thing called Fear, which he had never met before—Fear that he himself might not be "normal"—sane, calm, alert, watchful; fear that no matter how "normal" he was it would not prove enough to keep Jacqueline; fear that he ought not to want to keep her, if she were to suffer like this. And then Fear, of course, began calling her sisters, Failure and Defeat. David thought more than once, that they were actually on the threshold. He rose, towering, and slammed the door in their faces. After that, Fear left of her own accord.

He did not have to fight alone, either. For with him

was Norchais, indifferent no longer, and coming daily to see the patient whom his pupil never left. There were Soeur Célestine and after the first ten days, Miss Houston, who taught each other much; there were Marthe and Mère Thérèse downstairs, who cooked and washed and swept, and went to sleep at a neighbor's that the nurses might have their beds. And finally there were monsieur le curé and monsieur l'avocat, backed by the entire village. Old men and women came with tears in their eyes to ask what they might be permitted to do for *notre Désiré*. Children brought pitiful little presents of vegetables and flowers, as votive offerings are brought to a beloved shrine; there came also the Marquis de Fleursy, who lived, with his widowed mother, in a château some three miles from the village, and who, before Jacqueline came, had paid his tenantry but scant attention. He brought with him Hamburg grapes and truffles, which Mère Thérèse and Marthe enjoyed extremely, and gardenias, which adorned the church altar. On the occasion of his third visit, he insisted on seeing the doctor in charge; David, somewhat reluctantly, left Jacqueline's room long enough to go down and see him, though this was after those first awful days were past. He could not help finding something very engaging and attractive about the young nobleman, who treated him with a Gallic courtesy and charm that were very pleasant.

"Tell Mademoiselle Huntington," he said, gathering up his reins to depart, "that she is not to feel concerned; there will be plenty of coal and warm clothing in the village, just as usual, and a tree at the château for the children at Christmas time. My mother has charged me to ask you if you would not bring her to us, as soon as you feel it would be safe to move her. We could perhaps make her more comfortable? And for you, monsieur, when you are able to leave her to enter Paris again—may I not have the honor of mentioning your name as a guest —or, if you are to remain indefinitely—as a member—of my club, or show you some other trifling attention?"

David watched the smart trap out of sight, and then walked thoughtfully up the stone stairs again. It was not hard to guess, from the short interview that had just taken place, that Jacqueline might, had she so chosen, have become Marquise de Fleursy. He wondered that the idea had not appealed to her—she could have remained among the people she loved, and continued to be their ministering angel, and yet she could have been surrounded by the comfort, the culture, and the love that were her due. But as he bent over her again, she seemed so frail a thing that the thought of her in connection with any earthly joys seemed futile, and the hope for her recovery, which had been definitely taking shape the last twenty-four hours, faded away altogether.

"Tell me where you suffer most," he said gently.

"I don't suffer at all—that is, worth mentioning."

That was one great trouble. Jacqueline, docile and uncomplaining though she always was, helped neither them nor herself; she alone could not be made to fight. She did not seem to care whether she lived or died.

He repeated the message of the Marquis. She smiled.

"He is so kind," she said, "tell him so for me, the next time he comes." Her voice implied the natural courtesy of a gentlewoman, nothing more. Clearly there had never been any question of the Marquis.

"Are you wondering about him and me now?" she

asked suddenly. David knew there was no intentional unkindness in the words; nevertheless, they stung him to the quick.

"Oh, my dear!" he exclaimed. Then, after a moment's pause, he said, trying not to show how hurt he was, "Not in the sense you mean. Can't you believe that stupid and base as I was to ever 'wonder' as far as you were concerned, I have had a sufficiently terrible lesson to teach even a man as bad as I was to be better? But I couldn't help thinking—he is so attractive, so obviously devoted to you, and it would have been—ideal—as far as you are concerned, it seems to me—"

She shivered.

"Has love—become abhorrent to you, Jacqueline?"

"Yes—that kind. It isn't love at all—it's selfishness and greed. There have been dozens of men who—wanted me —but I doubt if one of them—loved me."

"I know. But men are not all alike. This one does love you, he would have been unselfish and self-sacrificing—"

"Perhaps. But don't you see, if you lose your faith in one person, you lose it in *everybody*. I wanted to get away entirely from the kind of life I'd been leading—I couldn't bear it—not because I felt it was wrong in itself, but because its—customs and usages had—antagonized you, had come between us. Fleursy and its poverty—and this bare little house—and my peasant grandmother— were—"

"Yes, dear, I know."

"And after the way, Gustav and Cyril—whom I thought were my *friends—in love with me*—treated me (he wondered how she could help saying 'after the way that you treated me') I didn't want to—to think of that sort of

209

feeling again—in connection with anybody. I was—just aflame with feeling—*for you*—and I didn't want to feel—*at all* if it was going to bring me to . . . I wanted to *rest*. And, after I got a little rested, I wanted to *work*—to get so tired, physically, that I couldn't think or feel either. I—oh, David, don't say this isn't 'normal'—"

"I'm not going to—I hate that word, anyway. It may not have been normal, but it was perfectly natural—"

He was sitting on the edge of her bed, stroking her hair. She gave a little sigh, and turned her head, resting her cheek on his hand. He saw that she was tired, reproached himself bitterly for having let her talk so long. But after a few minutes he was stupefied to see that she had fallen asleep—into the quiet, peaceful, natural slumber that he had been praying for so long. Hour after hour went by, it grew dark. Miss Houston herself was resting. Soeur Célestine came in softly with Jacqueline's supper tray, saw what had happened, and stole silently back to the kitchen to tell Mère Thérèse. When she came back, David had slipped to the floor, his head resting beside Jacqueline's on the pillow, his hand on hers. He, too, was sound asleep.

The nun fell on her knees with a prayer of thanksgiving. The morning sun was streaming in at the little window before any of them stirred.

Up to that time, Jacqueline had accepted David's constant presence as unquestioningly as she had that of her grandmother. She had not been encouraged to talk, and she had been too ill to wish to. But the following day she began to question him, and her first query was characteristic.

"You don't know what it meant to talk to you that way

yesterday—and to have you *understand*," she began, "I've led such a *silent* life these last years. I feel almost—almost—"

"Yes, dear?"

"As if a stone had been rolled away from a sepulchre—"

"I felt that way, too, when I saw that you *wanted* to talk to me—and that you'd fallen asleep. Jacqueline, you are going to get well."

"Because you've made me! But I've been terribly selfish. I'm taking up all your time. I don't see when you've slept or eaten, even. I've never wanted you that you haven't been here, quite close beside me. It's wrong of me to monopolize you like this. What were you doing when you found me?"

"Hunting for you."

"No, no, I mean for a serious occupation."

"Lord, I thought that was plenty serious enough!"

"David, you know what I mean—" She was almost laughing.

"Well, I was taking some lectures with Norchais in Paris; and I have a little sister in school there who needs considerable looking after."

"Susie! That cunning youngster who went to sleep with her thumb in her mouth at your graduation? Why, how old is she?"

"She's almost sixteen; but she seems more like twelve. When you get strong enough I'm going to fetch her out to see you—you'll get a lot of fun out of her. She's an awful savage—but there's something splendid about her just the same."

"Family traits? I remember you when you were that age! Does she look like you?"

David laughed. "I believe she does," he said, as if he were pleased that this was the case.

"Well, you've been neglecting her terribly. You must go and see her tomorrow."

"I shan't go one step."

"David! Just as stubborn as ever?" They were both laughing now.

"Rather more so. Anyway, I'm not going to Paris until you're well enough to sit up at the window and wave good-bye to me out of it."

"Well—you might go out around the village a little, at least, and come in and report to me how things are going. I'm pining for news. Or walk over to the château and see the Marquis—you know he wants you to, ever so much, and I'd like to feel that you two were friends." She paused a moment, then, with no less gaiety, but with an abrupt change of subject, she said, "Do you know what attractive ties you wear? They've made me reflect, someway, that I'm rather a fright. If you won't go into Paris yourself, will you let me send Miss Houston some day? I want a lot of *pretty* nightdresses, and some négligées—if I've got to sit up and wave to you out of a window—and violet water and scented talcum and—"

David left the room feeling as if he could weep for joy. That afternoon he told Norchais, when the latter came, that he thought the fight was over.

"No, it isn't," said the older doctor sharply. "I've seen these flashes of spirit before in persons with her temperament, and they're often followed by complete exhaustion, or worse, because there's no physical strength back of them. She has about as much vitality as an Easter lily. You've put up a wonderful battle—one that would be

212

enough, in itself, to make you famous if all the facts were known—don't lose it now from over-confidence."

David began to comply with Jacqueline's request, and to leave her for a little while each day, finding, to his amazement, a surprising number of things to interest him in the little village. He and Mère Thérèse were already deeply attached to each other. He loved to loiter about the copper-hung kitchen, so different from the one in the little cottage "out back" from Hamstead, where he had grown up. While he praised her housekeeping, he told her about that one, showed her how his mother used to make doughnuts, initiated her into other mysteries of New England cookery. He made friends rapidly with all the neighbors, he who had never had half-a-dozen real friends in his life! They were enchanted to find that "Monsieur David" could milk a cow and feed a pig, and harness a horse—that he could actually give practical and valuable suggestions as to the best way to doing all these things. The village children tagged at his heels. He brought them into the house with him, and sitting by the hearthstone with two or three on his lap, and several more around him, told them stories about America which made their round eyes bulge, stuffed them with sweet chocolate sent out from Paris, sent them away, laughing, with their pockets full of coppers. He went sometimes to talk over Materia Medica with monsieur le médécin in his dusty little office, lent him, more than once, a helping hand when sickness arose. Once a week, at least, he went to smoke a pipe with monsieur l'avocat or monsieur le curé, sometimes they all had a game of cards together. He found that he liked all these men, that they all liked him. At last he walked over to the château. The Marquis welcomed him as if he had been a visiting prince. They found that they were almost exactly the same age, that they had been to many of the same places, that they had quantities of tastes in common. David was persuaded to stay to dinner. Madame la Marquise was more formal than her son, but she was handsome and gracious. She, too, urged him to come again. It was wonderful to find so much kindliness in the world. David suddenly knew that he had never been so happy in his life.

With his happiness, however, came much self-questioning, the reversal of many other theories besides those which Jacqueline's illness had overturned. He had always thought of the French as a frivolous people, with no knowledge of sanitation, and lamentably bad morals. He found them natural and gay, courteous and splendid. What *was* frivolity, after all? Was it not often a wonderful "bluff" to cover trouble? Was cleanliness something deeper than daily baths and perfect drinking water? Had he confused morality with chastity—or still greater mistake—with marriage? What were, after all, the qualities that counted most in the sight of *le bon Dieu?* He found he was going more and more often to services, that prayer came to him as naturally as breath. He would, probably, never be able to accept all the dogmas of the church that Jacqueline loved, or to be blind to some of its errors. Nevertheless, it towered before him, a bulwark of strength to millions of souls through countless ages.

For the first time, too, the severe sincerity of the doctrine of his own Puritan forefathers revealed itself to him in its austere and dignified beauty. He saw, in his spiritual awakening, hundreds of little white churches with

214

slender spires pointing to the sky, scattered through the valleys and hills of New England, as the tabernacles of courage and righteousness. He understood his father's simple belief, and a great longing to see him and tell him so swept over him. There was no longer any question of his being able to accept and revere the spirit of faith in whatever form he might find it.

Meanwhile, as far as Jacqueline was concerned, he feared that Norchais had been right. She grew no stronger, though her arm was out of splints, and the "clean cut" of David's knife was long since healed and all that remained of the ugly gash on her temple was a little triangular scar that her nurses covered with her soft hair. And at last Miss Houston, the practical, spoke her mind to him, as he was starting in to Paris to see Susie for the first time.

"If you want to know my opinion, Dr. Noble," she said, though, as a matter of fact, he had not told her that he did, "I don't think Miss Huntington will ever get well if she goes on this way, though there's not a thing organically the matter with her now, of course. She needs to get away from this cold, uncomfortable house and this raw disagreeable climate—the idea of trying to live without plumbing or steam heat, or *anything* civilized, especially when it's way down below freezing, and the sun doesn't shine from one week's end to another! And she needs more playing and less praying, some companions of her own age, and some pretty clothes, and a competent maid, and not a trained nurse or a nun to wait on her. I'm going back to Boston next week. I advise you to send Miss Huntington to Nice."

"With whom?"

"Oh, there are plenty of competent companions; and she can go through quite comfortably on a *wagon-lit.*"

David pondered the question carefully as he motored into Paris. He found Susie overjoyed to see him. She was looking remarkably well, too, in a simple dress of red smocked silk; it was astonishing to see how much her English had improved and how rapidly she was blossoming out. She sat on his lap, ruffling his hair as he talked to her, telling her something of what had happened in the three months since he had seen her.

"Well, you did get your come-uppance, all right, didn't you?" she said, but quite tenderly, "I didn't half realize, from your notes—though you were a perfect *saint* to write me so often—I don't see how you ever managed to! Well, I must say I think you've pulled off a pretty neat job, and if I had my way, I'd take a megaphone and brag about you in the Place de la Concorde, I'm so proud of you. What are you going to do next?"

"Just now I'm going out to do some shopping—want to come with me? You haven't had any Christmas present yet, for one thing—I thought you might like to help me choose it. By the way, I hope your holidays weren't too doleful?"

"Doleful? Hoo! Didn't I tell you the Graingers,"—mentioning friends of his—"asked me to their house for the entire time? By the way, they know the Marquis de Fleursy—he came in several times while I was there. He's terribly impressed with you. He was nice to me too. He—"

"I wonder if she's going to make a specialty of other girls' cast-off beaus?" David smiled to himself.

"But mercy, the French have got chaperons on the brain, haven't they? I'd never heard of such a thing before—I guess they don't grow good—I mean, well—in Hamstead. The soil wouldn't be favorable to 'em. But they certainly flourish in Paris. I thought when I first heard of 'em, they were something to eat—chaperon—sounds like it might be a kind of fancy pudding, doesn't it?"

David laughed aloud. "The Marquis told me he had met you. He's a good sort. I don't think you need to worry about a chaperon as far as he's concerned."

"I'm not worrying about 'em as far as any one's concerned. It's every one else that worries the breath half out of themselves. Well, speaking of Christmas presents, I want a little pearl heart. Are you going to get something for Jacqueline, too?"

"If we can find anything good enough." He recalled with some bitterness, that he had had no gift for her on Christmas day. Two servants from the Château had staggered in under the enormous basket of roses that the Marquis had sent, and even Norchais had appeared with a very stiff, round bouquet with a punched paper frill about it. He might have ordered something from Paris, but he wanted to choose it for himself. He had tried to explain, and had been suddenly tongue-tied, and awkward. He wondered if she had understood.

But it was impossible to do much wondering with Susie in tow. She was enchanted to be out with him again, and dragged him jubilantly from shop to shop. She needed, it appeared, pounds and pounds of candy for herself and all her intimate friends at school. She saw a pretty hat in a brilliant window, and insisted on going in and ordering that—a great floppy red thing, trimmed with poppies, which became her exceedingly. She stood over him with sage advice while he ordered shirts and gloves and collars to replenish his own depleted stock. At last she led him to Cartier's to buy the pearl heart, and finally to Columbin's for tea. It was not until they were saying good-bye that she spoke again of Jacqueline.

"No, I didn't forget it, but this was your day, honey. Besides, I didn't see what I wanted for her."

"Well, you're a bang-up brother, anyway, if you do slip up as a beau. Do come again—*soon*."

It was nearly eight o'clock when he reached Fleursy again. Jacqueline's room was unlighted, Miss Houston downstairs eating her supper. Soeur Célestine rose silently and went out as he entered. Jacqueline did not speak, and he went nearer to see if she were sleeping. Inadvertently, in the dark, his hand touched her cheek. It was wet with tears.

He had never known her to cry; it was strangely unlike her. The fact was the more appalling.

"Oh," he exclaimed, putting his arm around her in quick alarm, "what is the matter? I knew I ought not to go off and leave you!"

"Yes, you ought. I—didn't mean you to find me this way. But I got so lonesome and Miss Houston has been talking to me and—"

"Well, I'll talk to *her!*" said David under his breath. Then, aloud, "Have you had any supper?"

"I didn't want any."

"Well, I haven't had any either, and I've bought all kinds of things out from Paris with me—squabs, and champagne, and *petits fours* and flowers—let's have a party!" He called Soeur Célestine back and gave her hurried and merry instructions. Then while they waited for the little feast to come, he lighted the candles, propped Jacqueline up on her pillows, fetched her a pink bed-jacket, arranged violets and roses on her bed-side table. A little color came into her cheeks. Before they had finished it had deepened, she had caught his mood, was laughing with him about Susie and the "chaperon" pudding. When Soeur Célestine came for their tray, he closed the door after her as she went out.

"Are you too tired to talk over some things with me?" he asked quietly.

"No. What?"

"I've been waiting for a long time to ask you—how much you remember—about the night I found you."

"Why, everything."

"Are you sure? I thought then you were more or less— rather more *than* less—under the influence of morphia. Since I have seen how little it affects you, I've been wondering."

He paused, his heart beating like a trip-hammer. Jacqueline did not help him.

"Would you mind telling me all that happened from the time you opened your eyes and said, 'Hello, David!' until you went under ether four hours later?"

"You thought I didn't *know!* So that's why you've never spoken of it!"

"Please, dear—I've got to be sure!"

Speaking still more quietly than he had done, she began to go over the events of the night. She seemed to remember, with perfect distinctness, everything that had passed between them. She had asked him if he had for-

219

given her, he had answered—she had asked whether there was a chance that she might get well, he had said—she had made a will, had allowed him to examine her, had had more morphia—

"Yes?" David found the monosyllable almost impossible to articulate.

"I asked for the Sacraments. I asked you to—marry me, if you still cared. You spoke to grand'mère and the curé and the doctor and monsieur l'avocat. He drew up a contract, performed a civil ceremony—then the curé *really* married us. I told you where my mother's wedding ring was, in my chest of drawers. Afterwards you asked me to let you put it back until I was better. We both knew I probably never would be better—you called me darling, you kissed me once—David, you are not *sorry?*"

She slid from the bed, and walked, trembling all over, to where he stood, with arms folded, looking out of the window. He caught her up.

"Jacqueline, what are you doing?" He carried her back to the bed, covered her with hands that were shaking no less than hers, tried, unsteadily, to laugh and made a failure of it, "You mustn't start walking off like that when you haven't had your feet to the ground in months . . . *Sorry!* But you see, I thought, we all thought—you might not realize what you were doing—"

"And if I hadn't?"

"Oh, my dear! Of course, we'd never have told you! Don't you think I know that I forfeited all my right to—to even think of you, five years ago? And the others are true as steel, no one else has guessed anything except, of course, that they know we knew each other before—"

"But I *did* know. I wanted—"

"You did then. What about now?"

There was a long silence. David set his teeth and locked his hands behind him.

"Because," he went on at last, "of course a marriage like that is all right—solid as the rock of Gibraltar—there's not a court on earth that would question it, unless—"

"Unless—"

"Unless you *wanted* it questioned. But if you do, you ought to know—I ought to tell you—that done the way it was—when you were partly unconscious, could claim that you were anyway—and never—and only—nominal—would be the easiest thing on earth to annul."

The word was out at last. He bowed his head and waited. At last Jacqueline spoke to him. "I thought of course, I was dying, or I wouldn't have asked," she whispered, "but just the same I—I don't want it—annulled—unless—you do. I didn't know it could be—I've been worrying for fear you—that's what I was crying for when you came in. You see, it's so long, and you never mentioned it and—but if you've been satisfied and—and happy so far—if you think you can go on being satisfied and—happy . . . You've given up your home and your friends and your profession and tied yourself to a girl who may be an invalid for years, who isn't giving you anything in return—"

"You don't seem to realize," he broke in, "that it's an hourly miracle to me that you don't hate me so that you can't bear the sight of me!"

He groped his way over to the little chest, half blinded by emotion, and opened the top drawer, rummaging among the soft, scented things there until he found the tiny gold band that he sought.

221

"You're sure?" he asked again, dropping on his knees. When he spoke again, his voice was entirely cheerful and steady and matter-of-fact.

"We're going to tell everybody now," he said, "they must have been doing an awful lot of wondering, mustn't they? Though they didn't suspect a secret wedding, it must have been plain as the nose on your face that we weren't a common or garden variety of patient and doctor. Tomorrow morning I'm going in to fetch Susie, and stop at the château and pick up the Marquis, and bring 'em both here to see you, and we'll have a good laugh all around. And you can try fancy stunts walking around the room, and as soon as you can wobble around as well as a year-old kid, you and I and a good maid are going to Nice. Miss Houston's perfectly right. That's where you ought to be for the present, though the idea doesn't seem to appeal to you. We'll have a good time, see if we don't! I'm not always so solemn and stupid as I've been these last three months, but you certainly did have me scared stiff, for a while! But you're coming out as fine as silk now—invalid for life, nothing! In the spring we can go to Italy—I never have, and I'd like to, a lot, and when it's really warm, we'll come back here, if this is where you're happiest. Do you suppose monsieur le médécin would take me for a partner? I'd have the time of my life practising in Fleursy!"

He smoothed the upper sheet over the blankets, tucked them in tightly, bent over and kissed her cheek.

"I'm going to call Soeur Célestine now to 'fix you up,'" he said, "and go forth and spread the news. Good night, sweetheart."

Four hours later, before starting to bed himself, he went in again, fearing that she might be wakeful; but she was sleeping quietly, lying on her side, her soft hair tumbled over the pillow, her left arm thrown out over the counterpane. Her wedding ring gleamed in the light of the little night lamp that he carried. He stood looking at her for a few minutes, his heart overflowing with ineffable thanksgiving and tenderness. Then he closed the door gently behind him and left her.

CHAPTER VI

THE TRUCE

THE following day, after Susie and the Marquis had been brought to see Jacqueline, and the "good laugh all around" had taken place, David announced his intention of taking his sister back to the boarding school, and then setting out for Nice on the night train without returning to Fleursy.

"And as soon as I find a place fit for you to live in, and get it fixed up according to my views of what is suitable for you at present, Miss Houston can bring you down; I'll have a maid—two or three of 'em—waiting for you there. Wouldn't you rather have a villa, in the suburbs, than go to a hotel? Of course, you would! Well, I'll write you every day how I am getting along with my house hunting, and you can write me every day how far you can walk without trying any sudden spurts, of course, and we both ought to find the mails fairly interesting!"

He left her, gaily, without having seen her alone for a single minute. Susie, after they had dropped the Marquis at the château, took him to task.

"You *are* the biggest fool I ever saw in my life," she said scathingly, "Jacqueline looked good enough to eat alive—she's ever, ever so much prettier than I had any idea she'd be—and you kissed her as if she was a kid with a dirty face whose nose needed wiping—what a way to say good-bye to a bride! Why, Harry—"

"Do you want me to act as if I'd sat down on a stove? Jacqueline doesn't want to be treated like—like a regular bride. She's been too unhappy, and she's been too sick. I don't want to—upset her—I want to *do* things for her."

"Oh, glory!" ejaculated Susie. "I never heard that it upset a girl to have a feller she'd been crazy over for more'n ten years who had just got around to marry her act a little affectionate! First you thought you weren't good enough for her, and you stewed around for five years over that; and then you thought she wasn't good enough for you, and you more than stewed for five years over *that*. And then you went right up in the air, and made up your mind that you was a regular Judas Iscariot and she was a sort of holy Saint Agnes, and—no, I'm not either sacrilegious, I've got some sense. Talk about sitting on stoves! Harry wasn't half so unsettled as you are. He never worried a mite about being worthy or unworthy, and neither did Hattie. They quarreled some, and always have, but in the main they take considerable comfort out of life together. They kept company for quite a spell, and Hattie had him on edge part of the time whether he would get her, but down deep he liked her a sight better for it than he would have if she'd acted like she wanted to snap him right up for fear she'd never get another chance. And by and by they got married, and every one was pleased about it, and they went to Niagara Falls on their wedding trip. Then they came home, and settled down, and after a while they had a baby. That's the way most every one in Hamstead does."

"Well, it isn't always as simple as that," said David, choking with laughter.

"No, I should judge it wasn't, from some of the books I read at the Graingers' during Christmas vacation. Such goings on! Miss Sims, our dressmaker, could never keep up with 'em, and even ma, in the post-office like she was, most of the time, would have had hard work. I don't wonder chaperons got thought of—not that I can see they make much *difference!* Looks to me as if when anyone *makes up their mind* to cut up, they do it, chaperons or no chaperons—"

"Well, when you have a love affair, try to strike a happy medium—"

"Hoo! I'm not figuring on getting married at all— I've told you so more'n a dozen times! The Marquis is real nice, isn't he? He said he thought likely his mother would be in to see me some day—"

David left her and took his train, feeling as if he had had a cold shower and a good rub-down after a sleepless night. True to his word, he wrote to Jacqueline every day during the next fortnight, reporting the progress of his "house hunting." He had found a furnished villa which he thought would do, so he had hired it for four months—they could keep it longer if they liked, but he thought by that time it would be too hot to stay in Nice. It overlooked the sea, it had a big garden, there was an upstairs balcony off the room that was going to be hers— she could sit there a lot, or even sleep there if she wanted to. The plumbing didn't suit him, but he was having it fixed, it would be all right soon. He had engaged two men, one for outside, one for inside, a cook, and a personal maid, named Jeanne, who seemed a very good sort indeed, for her—he thought they ought to be able to do the work, but if they couldn't, it would be easy to get more. He was awfully stupid about buying linen and such things, but they'd go shopping together and get more as soon as she felt like it—he'd laid in enough to start with. He was delighted to hear she was getting along so fast—he had felt quite sure she would—would she please climb into her clothes, just to see how they felt, and take them off again in fifteen minutes? She was to kiss Mère Thérèse—and any one else she thought would like it—for him, and he was, as ever, David.

It was mid-January when Jacqueline joined him. He met her at the station with a motor ambulance, and promptly relieved Miss Houston of her charge, telling her with a grin to go and try her luck at Monte Carlo before she started away, and almost wringing her hand off as he said good-bye and thanked her for all she had done. Nevertheless, he did not seem especially broken-hearted at her departure—in fact, Jacqueline thought she had never seen him in such good spirits. When they reached the villa, he picked her up and carried her over the stairs as easily as if she had been a baby and dropped her on the middle of a great mahogany bed covered with snowy, embroidered linen and a rose-colored down puff, and stood over her, laughing a little anxiously.

"Do you like it?" he asked her, flushing like a schoolboy.

"*Like it!* Oh, David, what a perfect room!"

It was, indeed—soft rugs were scattered over a bare, polished floor, long windows, draped with snowy, frilly curtains under pink silk ones, were flung wide open, looking out to the sea; a rose-colored couch stood beside them. On the hearth a bright fire was burning, in spite of the mildness of the day; the dressing table was covered with silver brushes and boxes and cut-glass bottles filled with toilet water. On the bed-side table were a shaded reading-lamp, and two or three uncut crisp magazines. And everywhere were flowers—roses and lilies and violets in bowls and tall slim vases.

"Like it!" she said again, "*Oh, David!*"

"Well, in a day or two I'll show you the rest of the house. I think you can walk, if I put my arm around you, but if you can't, I can carry you, though you are a little fatter already—good for you! Now I'll send Jeanne to help you undress, and when you are ready, sing out—I'm coming in to have tea with you."

She was, as he had known she inevitably must be, completely exhausted, and something besides tea, though she did not see it, went into the dainty china cup which he handed her a few minutes later. She did not realize, either, when the pretty tea-service had been removed by the capable Jeanne, and he sat down beside her, that his fingers were feeling her wrist, anxiously, all the time that he seemed to be nonchalantly holding her hand. She only knew that he looked boyish and eager and altogether adorable, with his white teeth gleaming and his black head thrown back, and his slim, long, graceful body stretched out in a big willow chair, while he talked to her . . . And then she seemed to be getting drowsy . . . and then, suddenly, she opened her eyes again—and mid-morning sunshine was flooding the room, and Jeanne was moving noiselessly about bringing in more flowers.

The first few days were very quiet. She walked as far

as the glistening bathroom, reveled in the deep tub of water into which Jeanne had emptied fragrant salts; then in the afternoon, to the couch by the window, had her tea there, stepped out on the balcony, a cloak thrown over her négligée, to see the early stars come out in the dark blue sky over the dark blue sea—and then came more long, dreamless nights, more peaceful wakings to another day. But after the first week she explored the whole house. The villa was cheerful and airy and sunny, but it was simple and unpretentious. David had bought such extra furnishings as he thought would make it more comfortable and attractive, but he had spent no great amount of money. Downstairs there were two living-rooms, opening into each other, with a loggia facing the sea leading from them, a little dining-room, and the kitchen quarters. Upstairs, opening from Jacqueline's room, was a tiny one where Jeanne was installed, the bath-room, and a little alcove which David had fitted up as a chapel. Beyond, another good-sized chamber, which he said they "would fill with Susie during her Easter vacation," and his own, of which Jacqueline made fun, saying it looked exactly like the one he had had years ago in the big barn—a big desk with a clutter of books and papers, a narrow iron bed with a honey-comb spread, a chest of drawers, one straight-backed chair. He laughed.

"My bed-rooms always look like that," he said, "the one I had in college did, too. It's no matter where I am— some people's do, haven't you noticed it? But the rest of the house is nice, isn't it?"

"Nice? Oh, *David!*" He loved, in those days, to hear her say, "Oh, David,"— "How did you happen to think of the chapel?"

"I tried to think of everything that would be likely to please you—is there anything—"

There was nothing, she said, that he hadn't thought of, that he didn't keep thinking of. Sometimes he left her, and went into Nice on further shopping excursions, began to bring her home little personal gifts—a box of candy, a new book, a bit of lace; and finding that these trifles seemed to be received with an enthusiasm quite out of proportion to their value, he ventured on more costly presents—a carved fan, a pendant of semi-precious stones, and finally appeared with a big box, from which he shook free of tissue paper, a crisp, pink, frilly dress.

"I saw it in a window, and it looked to me so much like the one that you wore at my graduation that I went in and bought it. Do you think it is pretty—do you suppose it will fit? Do try it on, and come down to dinner in it if it does—and after dinner I'm going to take you out for a little ride—oh, yes, you are, plenty well enough—and there's such a moon—you can't half see it from the loggia—and it's warm as—as—"

He took her for rides—a little longer one each day—he read aloud, he played the piano with stumbling untaught fingers—in fact, there was hardly a minute all day that he was not doing something for her, and yet, as she grew stronger, David felt that in spite of his constant devotion, she needed more people about her, a wider outlook, the gayer atmosphere that some of her old friends could give her. His feelings were therefore those of the startled gratitude that usually comes with an unexpected answer to prayer, when one day, as he was coming out of a jewelry shop in Nice, he saw Freddy Lambert looking in the window. Freddy hailed him cordially, and shook him by the hand.

"Who'd ever have thought of seeing you here!" he exclaimed, "though of course, every one gravitates to Nice sooner or later. You didn't know, did you, that Rose Gray and I were married about two years ago—we're stopping at the Grand. And now you and Jacqueline, after all—I'm darned glad—always felt that someway things *ought* to come right even if that fuss wasn't explained—" he checked himself, blushing. "Excuse me—I'm always putting my foot in it. How is she?"

"Thank you; she's getting better—but she's been very ill—"

"I didn't know—I'm no end sorry! Would it be prying into things too much if I asked—how it all came about— your getting married, I mean? None of us had heard a word from her since her grandfather's death, and then as suddenly as bombs, came little notes from a place called Fleursy, saying she had married you—they weren't much more communicative than regular announcements would have been. Shall we walk along a little way together?"

"We have a villa not far out—won't you come back to tea with me? Jacqueline would be so glad to see you, and she can tell you what there is to tell—there really isn't much—"

But Jacqueline, though courteously surprised and cordial, did not show the overwhelming delight at the sight of her old friend that David had expected. She was glad that he and Rose had married, it was a happy coincidence that they should all have come to Nice at the same time. How soon would he bring Rose to see her? How nice that there was a little Freddy—she adored babies, the baby must come to call, too. Would he have lemon, or cream, and how many lumps of sugar? Her account of her own marriage nonplussed David.

"What is there so extraordinary about it? You've heard, by this time, I suppose, what the trouble was in the beginning? No? Well, I'll tell you some other time, then, if you want to hear, but what does it matter? Don't you and Rose ever quarrel? Of course you do! But David and I made up, like everybody else, and I wasn't well, and there didn't seem to be any reason why we should wait any longer—I've been living with my French grandmother—my mother's mother, you know—for several years, so we were married at her house, yes, very quietly. I suppose I might have written more details, to Lady Thornington, anyway, but I've been rather apathetic, and besides, I've felt perhaps she hadn't been quite fair to David. But I'll write her—now. David's been studying with Norchais in Paris, so we were quite near each other, you see. David, I think Freddy would eat another cake."

David drove Freddy back to town, finished his errands, and drove back somewhat thoughtfully. On his return he found Jacqueline still on the loggia, engaged in fastening a bunch of white violets on the lace of her dress with a bar-pin he had recently given her.

"You magnificent liar!" he exclaimed, kissing her cheek, and putting his arm around her, "Do you expect to go to heaven after all that?"

"Why not?" she laughed back, "Anyway, it was all perfectly true—as far as it went."

"Oh, yes, as far as it went—and it went a darned short

distance! Where did you get those flowers? More callers?"

"Yes, you'd never guess—this is a day of surprises, and mine is worth two of yours—Bobby Hutchinson came while you were gone—"

David gave a whoop of joy.

"*Bobby!* Where on earth did he drop from?"

"Paris—he had been to see Susie. She told the principal of the boarding-school that he was her uncle, and Bobby said he didn't contradict her—can't you just hear him? He said they had the time of their life together!"

"For a young lady who doesn't ever intend to get married, Susie is making quite rapid progress," said Susie's brother, dryly. "But how does he happen to be on this side of the Atlantic at all?"

"He said he felt he needed a vacation, and decided that he might as well come to see us as to go anywhere."

"Rather better, I should say. I hope you didn't tell any fancy fibs to him? It really wouldn't be worth the trouble!"

"So I should judge. He said your letters had been few, far between and brief, which was one reason he wanted to look you up—but just the same I felt as if he 'knew all the facts, in ten scenes and seven acts,' as a musical comedy I used to enjoy put it. Besides, I didn't have much chance to speak, anyway—he did most of the talking himself—doesn't he always? I hadn't seen him since he was nineteen or twenty, but he seemed to me exactly the same as he did then—shrewd and witty, and oh, so kind. He—he had a good deal to say about you."

"Any very dark disclosures?"

"On the contrary. I knew you were wonderful, of

233

course, but not *how wonderful. Oh, David!* Why didn't you tell me about the Edgar L.—and all the rest of it?"

"Look here, what stuff has Bobby been putting into your head? He's got you worrying, making you think I want to go back"—and seeing the brimming tears in her eyes, he went on savagely, "I'll fix him, if he interferes with my star patient! What do you think I care about that stuffy old hospital? I wouldn't mind if I never saw it again. I'm having the first good loaf I ever had in my life, and if you knew what that meant you'd realize that it seems pretty satisfactory to me to lie on a loggia and bask in the sun instead of messing 'round an operating room all day and half the night."

"They need you back; they *want* you—"

"Well, they can go on wanting—do 'em good. They weren't so darned enthusiastic about me a year or so ago. Just wait until I get my hands on Bobby."

"I've asked him to come to dinner tomorrow night."

So Bobby came, and, in spite of David's threats, was made very welcome by both of them, and they sat on the loggia, talking of pleasant, unimportant things, until Jacqueline's early bed time. But when she had left them, and the two men were alone again, Bobby slid down a few inches further in his chair, and began, in his usual lazy drawl.

"Well, you're a wonder, and then some. She's as graphic an advertisement to your genius as the picture of a Mellin's Food baby."

"You upset her yesterday—"

"Shucks! I set her thinking, a little, about several things. Who's pampering patients now? It's time you came back. She's getting well so fast, she ought to be—

mowing lawns, too. You are not going to keep up this in-valid-doctor rôle forever, are you?"

"No—we seem to have rather passed that already."

"Or this breezy, friendly, elder brother, distant-cousin, attitude?"

David got up, with something between a sob and a laugh. "Don't, Bobby," he said a little uncertainly, "Don't —you're uncanny. You guess too darned much."

"I guess you're having pretty rough sledding just now. As long as your passion was overcome with your *compassion*, so to speak—"

"You've told me once that I didn't have either in my make-up—"

"I've told you a number of lies, in a good cause, first and last. Of course, you've got 'em both, and of course you've had a hell of a time between 'em, and gritted your teeth, and said to the former, 'avaunt, clear out, git,' and you deserve a gold medal and a crown of glory, and all the rest of the usual heroic paraphernalia for having done it. But I'm hanged if I see why now you shouldn't be rewarded according to your merits."

"I'm rewarded far beyond my merits—"

"You're not—your merits are greater'n you give 'em credit for being. And Lord! Don't you think I can see how you feel? I've—I've felt that way myself, you know."

"I know," said David huskily, "but you see, I feel be-sides that—I forfeited my—reward five years ago. I've no right to claim it now, or even to ask for it—just because a turn of chance has happened to put it in my reach."

"Well, you did forfeit it then—but you sure have re-deemed it since. I'll add another perfectly truthful state-ment to the ones I made that eventful day when we discussed this matter before—you may be hasty and crude and stupid, et cetera, et cetera, et cetera, but at that there isn't one woman in a thousand that gets a man that's fit to black your shoes, and Jacqueline knows it, and always has! When I told you to wait—and wait—and wait—" he added, speaking more lightly, as David still did not turn around, "I didn't mean until you were both in your grave! But you may know best. I'm certainly not going to risk trying to upset your apple cart, after you've driven it with pretty steady hand and clear eye through all kinds of heavy traffic. What I really came here for wasn't to meddle. It was to pour out a few griefs myself . . . Helena and Roger are married at last."

David turned quickly. "Say, Bobby—"

"Yes, I knew I could count on you to feel that way about it. I didn't think I was going to be such a fool over it—but I found I wanted to get away for a while. She's awfully happy—gone to live on a flower ranch in California—they'll have bread and butter, and perhaps a little more than that, but I doubt it. I told Susie—she was greatly interested—you know she took a tremendous shine to Helena."

"Would you mind telling me what she said? Susie's comments on love-affairs are apt to be entertaining. Perhaps she regaled you with Harry and Hattie—"

"Oh, yes. But she said I was cut out for a bachelor, same as she was for an old maid."

"Just about the same, I should think."

"And—and several other things. If you can get her down here for her Easter vacation, she and I are going to paint the town as red—as her cheeks. Gosh, but she's a healthy looking kid! . . . By the way, I see you've got one of those new cars with all sorts of fancy attachments —were these included in the original price or did you pay extra for them?"

"No, everything included, and the lights work finely; but the best part of it is—" David was off. For the next half-hour automobiles, undisputed, held the stage.

"I've got to go home," exclaimed Bobby, as they both started, almost guiltily, when the clock struck midnight, for medicine had succeeded motors as a topic of conversation. "Won't you and Jacqueline come in to dine with me tomorrow night, and go to the opera with me?"

"She hasn't been anywhere yet except to church—"

Bobby threw up his hands— "Haven't you *asked* her?"

David laughed. "All right, *you're right!* We'll come."

So the first little dinner was followed by another, and then another, and still more. Freddy and Rose joined the circle, other friends and acquaintances were discovered in the vicinity, or just far enough off to make motoring to find them in the new car a delight. Susie telegraphed that measles had broken out in school, and that such pupils as possessed parents who were willing, might go home until the quarantine was over, and appeared, in charge of an exhausted "chaperon" as soon as the return telegram saying that her relatives, including her "uncle" would be delighted to see her. There had been two young French officers on the train. They were most kind about helping her practice her French and buying fruit and chocolate at railway stations, and explaining military tactics—explanations which they would be glad to continue and enlarge upon at some future date, as they were to be in Nice for a fortnight, if Jacqueline would ask them to call.

237

"Didn't you ask them?"

"Oh, yes, but these foreigners are so queer. Now none of the fellows at home ever dreamed of waiting for Hattie to ask them over. What *are* you all roaring at?"

The villa began to be invaded for dinner, for tea, even —by Bobby—before breakfast if he felt like it. The Mercedes vanished more than once before David knew it was gone; and when David informed Susie that she was too young to dream of going to the Mi-Carême Ball, he found he had insurrection on his hands. Jacqueline not only upheld her sister-in-law, she announced her intention of going, too.

"Just for a few dances—wouldn't you like it, David?"

"Who with?" asked David, more expressively than grammatically.

"Well, say three out of twelve with me."

He grunted, smiling in spite of himself. "The prospect seems to hold some compensations. Are you just teasing for the kid, or do you really want to go yourself?"

"Of course I want to go. Don't you think it would be fun to dance together?"

The days of négligées had long since passed. Great boxes filled with pretty dresses had been coming out from Nice steadily during these last few weeks, and Jacqueline had on one of the prettiest of them now—a crisp, embroidered pale blue linen with a round neck and elbow sleeves, that fitted her like a glove. She was standing by a wicker table, her arms lifted, arranging long sprays of pink blossoms in a clear green glass vase. She turned from her task, drying her damp fingers on her handkerchief. "We might try one together now, just to see. Play something for us, Susie." She placed her hand on his

238

shoulder, then drew back. "David, how white you are! What's the matter—are you ill?"

"Oh, *no!* You're ready?"

He had known that she would dance beautifully. Still, he had not been prepared for such absolute perfection of rhythm and unity—it seemed, as they moved, hardly possible that they were two persons. Involuntarily, as Susie stopped playing, he pulled Jacqueline closer to him, instead of releasing her.

"I want more," he whispered.

"Why, of course! I told you it would be fun—perhaps you would like four at the ball, instead of three? Go on, Susie—"

There was, after that, no question about the ball, except that he exacted a promise from her that she would leave Susie in Rose's charge at midnight, and come home then, and that she would stay in bed all the next day if she were tired. If she were not, they could go to others, after that. Susie, thereafter, did her own dictating. She spent, without a murmur of disapproval from her brother, a thousand francs on a dress of scarlet tulle to wear to it, which was quite evidently as fragile as it was exquisite. Jacqueline bought her a pearl necklace. Bobby, the two young officers, and several other swains whom she had by this time added to her collection, all sent her flowers. Jacqueline was delayed with her own dressing because she and Jeanne both gave so much attention to the child. At ten o'clock David found her, still in the sketchiest of toilets, sitting on Susie's bed superintending the finishing touches.

"Oh *David!*" she cried, as he entered, "how handsome you are—how becoming those clothes are!"

"Allow me to return the compliment—still—is that as far along as you are? Or were you intending to go to the ball that way? If not—" He took out his watch expressively.

"If you were Harry," interposed Susie, "you'd *know* how far along she was. He'd be hooking up Hattie's back long before this, while she squeezed in her waist at the sides with her fingers. She's grown fatter since the baby came, and she hasn't had any time to let things out. No wonder you can't keep track of Jacqueline, half way down the hall from her! If you and she and a baby all slept in one room that wasn't large enough to hold anything but a big bed and a little bureau, same as Harry and Hattie do—"

Jacqueline sprang up, regardless of scanty draperies, and threw her arm around Susie's neck, stopping her mouth with a kiss.

"You run along down to Bobby," she said a little breathlessly, "and don't tell him too many intimate Hamstead histories. I'm not very fat, you see, and with Jeanne here on purpose to help, it seems rather foolish to make David do up hooks, doesn't it? But if he will come to my room in twenty minutes—I promise not to be any longer than that—I'd like to have him tell me how he likes my dress before the rest of you see it. I only hope it'll be half so pretty and becoming as yours, my dear."

David paced up and down the little corridor, his heart pounding, the blood surging in his head. What had become of the self-control he was so sure of? Once he had sent Jacqueline away from him, because he knew that he was only an undisciplined boy, that she would not be safe with him because he had none. This time he had

240

ventured to keep her near him because he thought he had so much. Was he wrong, after all? Was it only the memory of that brief dance the other day, the prospect of longer ones this evening, that made him throb all over until he ached? Or was it Susie's thoughtless speech that sent insistent, white-hot questions through his brain—if he were like Harry—well, why *not?* What was there to prevent—nothing, nothing in God's world —except the tardy and repentant humility of his own estimate of himself, his worth, his deserving; the fear of shattering Jacqueline's new found faith, and confidence, and joy in life by any act—yes, even any word—that would seem to her still supersensitive and easily-startled senses ungentle or unchivalrous—the thought of the phrase she herself had used, "until you love her well enough to serve and not—"

The door opened, and Jeanne came out. *"Madame vous attend, monsieur,"* she said quietly, and went down the stairs with Jacqueline's cloak over her arm. David nodded, and passed her without speaking.

He had sent Jacqueline a bouquet of white orchids and lilies of the valley, and, as he entered the room, she was standing in front of her long mirror, lifting them from their tissue-paper wrappings. A robe of silver and white brocade fell in unbroken line from her shoulders to the ground; a scarf of white tulle, which she had thrown over her bare shoulders, had caught on a jeweled pin in her hair, and partially covered her head as well. David thought, suddenly, of the fabric of which the great dressmaker had told him, saw that the misty gauze enveloped her like a veil—

241

"Oh, you lovely thing!" he exclaimed, almost involuntarily, "Jacqueline—my dear—"

"Is it really all right?"

"*All right!*"

"I mean—you don't think it is—too low, or anything, do you?"

There was a little catch of wistfulness, almost of anxiety, in her voice.

He flushed. "No, darling, of course I don't. What ornaments are you going to wear?"

"All my jewelry of any value is in England. It does need something—beautiful, doesn't it? Rubies and diamonds, for instance."

There was no premeditation in the words. But as soon as she had spoken them she flushed too, and tried to catch them back. If she had hurt him, however, David gave no sign of it.

"You'll need your jewelry, now that you are going out so much again—I can easily run over to London and get it for you. But meanwhile—wait a minute."

He left her, hurriedly, and came back the next moment with a velvet box in his hand.

"I bought this for you some time ago," he said, hesitating a little, "the day I met Freddy, in fact. I have been waiting for the right time to ask you if you would wear it—and the time seems to have come." He handed her the box, gravely, and watched her, almost breathlessly while she opened it. Inside lay a necklace—a necklace of rubies and diamonds, worth a queen's ransom, sparkling and glittering and glowing on the soft satin. Instinctively Jacqueline saw what this represented, though David, perhaps, had hardly been conscious of it—the

242

sacrifice that the ring had meant multiplied a thousand times, not brought, as that had been, from a victor to a captive, but as a subject to a sovereign—almost as a worshipper to a sacred shrine. She came closer to him, trembling with emotion, half-blinded with tears.

"Aren't you going to put it on yourself?" she asked—"The way—you did the ring?"

CHAPTER VII

VICTORY

DAVID's room was dark, and groping his way to his desk, he lighted the reading lamp, and flung himself into the chair. It was one o'clock in the morning. Jacqueline, flushed and lovely and laughing, but true to her agreement, had left the ball promptly at twelve—"just like Cinderella" she had said, merrily, "only my glory is all *real*," and had come home with him and gone to bed, insisting she was "not the least bit tired"; Bobby had not yet brought Susie home, and from indications when David departed, he felt that it might be some time before he did. The house was silent, almost hushed . . .

The desk was littered with a collection hardly less miscellaneous than that which had lain on the one in Hamstead, many years before. David pushed aside a few letters, some receipted bills, and several medical journals and pamphlets, and opened a volume of many closely printed pages, with somewhat sinister illustrations, bearing on its back the forbidding title, "Aseptic Surgery as Applied to the Major Operations." He read for some time, at first with deep interest—for the book was a new one, which Bobby had just called to his attention, and written by one of the "big men"—and making notes as he read.

244

But after a time his attention wavered, and he tossed it aside to pick up something more suited to the hour and his mood. He took the first thing that came to his hand. It was a book of Jacqueline's which he had been reading aloud to her, and had carried into his room by mistake, and which opened of its own accord, at a page of verses. Something in the first two lines arrested his attention. Instead of laying the volume down again, he read them through.

"For lo! thy law is passed
That this my love should manifestly be:
To serve and honor thee.
And so I do; and my delight is full
Accepted as the servant of thy rule."

"Lady, since I first conceived
Thy pleasurable aspect in my heart,
My life has been apart
In shining brightness and the place of truth,
Which, till that time, good sooth,
Groped among shadows in a darkened place;
Where many hours and days
It hardly ever had remembered good.
But now my servitude
Is thine, and I am full of joy and rest—
A man from a wild beast
Thou madest me, since for thy love I lived."

He closed the book, and laid it from him, picking up another, and began to turn the leaves, with trembling, irresolute fingers; then, suddenly, it dropped, unheeded on the floor, and bowing his head on his hands, he wept like a little child.

. . . .

He was startled by a slight rustle, and looked up quickly.

Jacqueline was standing beside him. She had on a soft white dressing-gown that hung loose from the shoulders like the one she had worn so many years before. Her neck and arms were bare. Her hair, still damp about the temples from her bath, hung like a veil of bronze around her. A delicate perfume enveloped her in its fragrant mist.

"What is it?" he cried, mastering himself quickly— "You did get overtired—you're not sleeping— Oh, I'm so sorry!"

"No, no," she said, detaining him as he tried to rise, "I never felt better in my life. But history repeats itself. I felt just as I used to when I ran away and came to your little room in the barn—which as I've said before, wasn't very different from this—I couldn't seem to wait another minute to find out what you were doing, to talk to you—"

She bent over the desk and glanced at the titles of the books and papers, straightening out the chaos as she did so.

"Is this the way you spend your nights?" she asked, gravely. "I take up all your days—and you miss it as much as that?"

"Oh, no," he protested, "I don't miss it at all. Sometimes, when I don't feel sleepy, I read a little, that's all."

She did not answer at once, continuing to straighten the mass before her.

"All this makes me realize," she said at last, when order was completely restored, "that it is almost time we went home. We've had a lovely holiday, and we've given Susie one. But we must send her back to school pretty soon. Bobby's half-serious, and half-earnest, and still so badly hurt over Helena that I'm glad we've been able to help him over this hard place. But just the same, she's growing up so fast now—she's changed so almost unbelievably in

246

just a few months—that I think he ought to wait now until she's grown up a good deal *more* before he sees much of her again. And when she's back in Paris, we'll go to Italy in Mercedes—and then,—we must go home. I'm well— gloriously well—again. We're—just throwing part of the most beautiful time of our lives away if we keep on pretending I'm not."

"Home!" echoed David, stupidly. "You mean to Fleursy? Wait until you are a little stronger, dear—you *are* well, but you haven't much endurance yet, and you work so hard there."

"No," she said slowly, "I wasn't thinking of Fleursy. Of course, I want to go back there for a week or so, to make sure that everything is all right, and say good-bye to grand'mère—and I hope we'll always be able to go there often. But, when I said home, I meant Boston."

He sprang to his feet in spite of her this time. "What do you mean?" he asked, his voice shaking.

She dropped her eyes, and stood silent for a moment, then raised them to his face, and looked straight into his.

"David," she said softly, "Can you—look back at me— the way I'm looking at you—and tell me that you don't want to get back to work—to Boston, and the Edgar L.— and everything that stands—for your career?"

He hesitated, but the unwavering truthfulness of a lifetime was too strong for him.

"Yes," he said at last, "I can. I am done with the Edgar L.—and Boston—and all that they stood for in my career. I am done with the career itself—the career I meant to have. But—"

"Yes?" asked Jacqueline.

"For a while," he went on, hesitating, "I honestly didn't

care if I never went back to America at all. I was so thankful to find you, to be with you again, to know that you didn't hate me, that nothing else mattered. But I wasn't just ambitious in my work. I loved it, too. I suppose I shall always love it. The only difference that way is that I don't love it *best* any more. And I feel now, some way, as if I'd do better in it than I ever did before—as if I wouldn't be merely a 'clever mechanician' as Bobby called me—quite rightly. Because you've taught me so many things, these last months, my dear, that I didn't know before. About success."

"Yes."

"It's—it's service. There's no trade that isn't—a trust."

"Yes, David."

"It doesn't matter much where or how. I mean, for one person it's one kind, in one place. For another, it's another kind, in another place. I've known, of course, for a long time, that Dr. Ross was a 'successful' man, that he had a wonderful 'career.' That was perfectly obvious. Any one could see that. It's you that have taught me the things— that aren't so obvious, but that really matter more. For I didn't realize until I went to stay in Fleursy that my— mother—was a 'successful' woman—that she'd had a wonderful 'career' too. And it's—it's marvelous for a man who —hasn't loved his mother—who's felt that he'd missed something great and sweet and precious—to suddenly learn that she was—great."

"Yes," said Jacqueline, a third time.

"And now—I seem to have a lot of new power stored up—with all this new knowledge. Power—that ought to be *used*—not folded in a napkin like the talent in the Bible! But I don't want to use it in Boston. That, of

248

course, is where Bobby ought to use his—where he can be most successful because he can serve most there—and Bobby has served—is serving all the time! He calls himself a 'stupid bungler.' It's I that have been that always!"

"No, never—never stupid, never a bungler. Just—mistaken, sometimes, or a little blind."

"Well, perhaps I'm blind and mistaken now—I—I haven't as much self-confidence as I used to have. But the way I want to serve—the place I want to go . . . Oh, you wouldn't be willing! It wouldn't be fair to you!"

"But I *am* willing! *I* want to do what you want. I don't know where the place is, but that's where I'll be happiest. . . . *David!* Is it *Hamstead?*"

"What made you think so?" he asked, breathlessly.

"Because—because that's what I've been longing for, too! Only I supposed *you* wouldn't be willing! If I had died, you'd have built a hospital there—well, why shouldn't you build it if I'm *alive*—and let me help? And we'll make it everything that it *can* be made—not just what a 'clever mechanician' would have made the Edgar L., but what your genius—and my love—can do for your work—and our home . . .

"And," she went on, kindling, after a moment's pause, "It isn't just—just the hospital! I think we owe your father at least as much as we do my grandmother, don't you? That we must try hard, these next years, to make him think how truly we're his children, how much we love him. I want to see Sam and Leon, too, and Harry and Hattie and the baby." She stopped, laughing, at the memory of the anecdotes that the last names brought back to her. "I want to see Sheldon and old Miss Manning. I want to open the Big House, to keep it open always, to feel that we aren't just 'summer people' but that we really *belong,* and make other people feel it too! I want to see if we can *help* Hamstead—just as we helped Fleursy—to see how much we can do for it. And that isn't all! Think how much Hamstead can help—has helped us!

"Are there any places in the world," she continued, her voice trembling a little, "that produce finer men and women than those little villages in the Connecticut Valley? Why David—I'd rather have married a man that was born on a tiny farm 'out back'—than one who was born in a king's palace! I think there's something—the spirit of their ancestors, who settled the country, still surviving, or perhaps the country itself—that makes them what they are—that's made—that's made *you* what *you* are! We were both so wrong, so mistaken, when we were children, to underestimate it. Can't you shut your eyes now, and see the river and the mountains glowing in the sunshine, or white with snow, or shining under a harvest moon? Don't you want to go down the lane with the willows with me again? Don't you—want to go over the road to Wallace-town?"

She swayed toward him slightly. He caught her hand in his.

"Jacqueline," he said hoarsely, "don't—unless you really know what you're saying—can't you see— Oh, my darling, I have tried—just to serve—but I—I *want you*—"

"Do you know," she said, her eyes still holding his, "that in all these months that is the first time you've told me so? That you've never called me by my second name? That, until tonight, when you put my necklace on, you've never kissed me—really kissed me—since the night—you found me?"

"I beseech you—" he began, but she went on steadily. "Do you know, that you've never let me tell you, either, any of the things I've wanted to say? How freely I forgave you, long ago, if there should ever have been any question of forgiveness between us—everything that happened—five years ago? How well I see now—though it nearly killed me to lose you then—that we both had too much to learn to be happy together at that time? I think, now, we've—both learned it, don't you? You would have sacrificed your whole life to me, if I would have let you— and still you doubted whether I would pardon a trivial fault in return. You'd have gone on, forever, like this . . . I couldn't wait any longer, David—I had to come and tell you how much I love you!"

"Jacqueline," he cried, "you must stop! It's only your boundless generosity, your everlasting mercy, that makes you talk like this. If I had been crucified for what I did, it would have been far less than I deserved!"

"And haven't you," she asked, "been crucified—more than once? The night you learned from Bobby—that I was not to blame? The night you—found me? And—tonight? Oh, my darling, you've been wonderful—but I've pitied you so!

"Did you really think," she said, as he turned his head away from her, without answering, "that I was so supremely selfish, even if I had not loved you with all my heart and soul—as to accept all that you were willing to give—and give you nothing in return?" She waited a full minute before he stirred. Then he dropped on his knees before her, laying his hot face against her soft, cool dress, and covering her hands with kisses.

"You dear saint—"

"No, no—not *that*—"

"What then?"

"Get up and look at me, and you will know—"

"My darling—*Désirée*—"

"It's—it's more than—that—"

He took her in his arms, the full glory of what she was trying to make him say breaking on him like a flood of golden light. He pressed his lips against hers, drawing her closer still.

"My wife," he whispered; "is that it?"

But this time he did not need an answer.

THE END